HIS SURGEON UNDER THE SOUTHERN LIGHTS

ROBIN GIANNA

REUNITED IN THE SNOW

AMALIE BERLIN

Any resemblance is entirely coincidental.

This book is sold subject to the condition that it shall not, by way of trade or otherwise, be lent, resold, hired out or otherwise circulated without the prior consent of the publisher in any form of binding or cover other than that in which it is published and without a similar condition including this condition being imposed on the subsequent purchaser.

® and ™ are trademarks owned and used by the trademark owner and/or its licensee. Trademarks marked with ® are registered with the United Kingdom Patent Office and/or the Office for Harmonisation in the Internal Market and in other countries.

First Published in Great Britain 2019
by Mills & Boon, an imprint of HarperCollins*Publishers*
1 London Bridge Street, London, SE1 9GF

MILLS & BOON

CLACKMANNANSHIRE COUNCIL	
31513400400532	
Bertrams	27/09/2019
HIS	£5.99
ADU	AF

His Surgeon Under the Southern Lights © 2019 by Robin Gianakopoulos

Reunited in the Snow © 2019 by Amalie Berlin

ISBN: 978-0-263-26991-8

MIX
Paper from
responsible sources
FSC™ C007454

This book is produced from independently certified FSC™ paper
to ensure responsible forest management.
For more information visit www.harpercollins.co.uk/green.

Printed and bound in Spain
by CPI, Barcelona

After completing a degree in journalism, then working in advertising and raising her kids, **Robin Gianna** had what she calls her 'awakening'. She decided she wanted to write the romance novels she'd loved since her teens, and now enjoys pushing her characters towards their own happily-ever-afters. When she's not writing Robin fills her life with a happily messy kitchen, a needy garden, a wonderful husband, three great kids, a drooling bulldog and one grouchy Siamese cat.

Amalie Berlin lives with her family and her critters in Southern Ohio, and writes quirky and independent characters for Mills & Boon Medical Romance. She likes to buck expectations with unusual settings and situations, and believes humour can be used powerfully to illuminate the truth—especially when juxtaposed against intense emotions. Love is stronger and more satisfying when your partner can make you laugh through the times when you don't have the luxury of tears.

HIS SURGEON UNDER THE SOUTHERN LIGHTS

ROBIN GIANNA

MILLS & BOON

To Amalie Berlin—what a privilege to get to write book one of a duet with you. There's no one better in the world to brainstorm with, talk with and laugh with, and I've never drunk so much tea in my life. Let's do it again sometime. xoxo

Researching Antarctica has been a fascinating experience, and I'd like to note two resources I particularly enjoyed and appreciated. Thanks to both authors for such interesting and informative reads:

Lost Antarctica: Adventures in a Disappearing Land by James McClintock

Antarctica: A Year at the Bottom of the World by Jim Mastro

CHAPTER ONE

WITH THE SHIP pitching from side to side and up and down like a stomach-churning roller coaster, trying to get any sleep felt impossible. Normally Dr. Jordan Flynn could sleep anywhere, anytime, as long as she wore her eye mask, had earplugs stuffed into her ears and soothing sounds were coming from the white-noise machine by her side. This time, though, none of it helped one bit.

Maybe it was because the top bunk of her cabin seemed to threaten to toss her out of it with every swell of the ship as it crossed the infamous Drake Passage on their way to Antarctica. Or because the noise machine's nature sounds were completely drowned out by real ones—the shrieking wind that she suspected no earplugs were heavy-duty enough to truly muffle.

She rolled to her side and it seemed the ship rolled along with her. Some people might pay big money to go on a crazy ride like this one at an amusement park, but at that moment, she'd pay even bigger money to get off it, if she could.

She squeezed her eyes closed behind the mask, then laughed at herself a little. Early October might be closer to bringing all-day sunlight to Antarctica, but she knew the low glow coming from a small window above her head wasn't what was keeping her awake. Trying to somehow force her mind away from the uncomfortable rolling sensations, she tried to think about the plus side of the adventure she was embarking on. And working as a doctor at an Antarctic science station would definitely be an adventure.

Fletcher Station was brand-new, and despite her current discomfort, she was still thankful she'd been chosen to work there as a surgeon and general practitioner for six months. Not only work there, but be the very first person to set up the medical clinic and hospital and get it ready for the thousand or so crew members who'd be arriving in a week or so. Plus, they'd seemed to love the idea of having the marine biologists test her parents' diving invention while they were underwater gathering samples, which was equally exciting.

Right now, only about seventy-five people were crossing the Drake Passage on this ship, getting things set up just like she was. Chefs and others prepping the kitchen and food, engineers getting machinery and equipment ready, and other support staff of all kinds. And, of course, a few scientists, with more on the way. Because scientific explorations, studies and discovery were the whole reason Fletcher Station existed.

Jordan thought about her little flat in London, her steady surgery job and her predictable life, which was exactly what she'd wanted when she'd decided to set down roots for the first time ever. Living all over the world with her doctor parents had been a great way to grow up, but she wanted something different for her adult life, and was happy with her choices.

She'd had to think hard about taking on this six-month stint in Antarctica. Then had decided, why not?

One of these days, she expected that her roots would deepen and grow to include a husband and family, living in the same house together forever and ever. Until then, though, she'd enjoy this adventure, take care of patients and get further testing of her parents' diving invention, one that would hopefully solve the problem of barotrauma. Doing a trial on how well it worked in Antarctica's extremely cold water as compared to other places would be another strong step toward getting it on the market.

The boat tossed hard, and to focus on something besides the rough ride, she tried to visualize what the medical center would look like, and how much would be involved in getting the equipment set up. Then, inexplicably, that picture was interrupted by an absurdly handsome face floating in her mind's eye. A face that belonged to the man in the cabin next door.

She'd been trying to get her door unlocked, hanging on to the doorjamb with one hand so she could stay upright, when he'd rounded a corner and strode down the hallway toward the door next to hers. He'd paused, with the key in his hand, to send her a charming smile and ask if she needed help. She'd given him a quick smile back and a "No, thanks" before she finally got the door unlocked and opened. She'd stepped inside and bolted it, relieved to climb up on the bunk and not have to wonder if she'd fall down before she got there.

Making small talk with anyone while working to keep her balance and swallow down a slight queasiness hadn't seemed very appealing. But now, in the rolling darkness of her cabin, his tall, muscular body, dark skin and deep brown eyes seemed to float in front of her. Eyes that held humor and intelligence, and a hint of a twinkle that had drawn her in the second she'd looked at him. Had even sent her heart into a ridiculous and unwelcome flutter.

She frowned, wondering why in the world she was thinking about a guy she didn't know. The deepening pitch of the boat had her grabbing the metal rungs at the top of the bed and holding on. Good thing she wasn't prone to full-on seasickness, or she'd probably be crawling her way to the bathroom by now.

Maybe sleeping on the top bunk hadn't been the best idea. With the way the boat swayed, she'd been afraid that the equipment she'd brought would slide across the floor, or be dislodged from the top bed, so she'd secured it on the lower bunk. Probably, though, being higher made her feel the pitch of the boat more than she would otherwise. Just as she was pondering if maybe she should just try to sleep somewhere on the floor, the storm sent the boat into its deepest roll yet. First one direction, then the other, then back so suddenly and violently she was flung from the bunk.

Her brain took a second to compute that she was airborne at the same time an automatic shriek left her lips. When her body reached the other side of the tiny cabin, her head connected with the wall as she slammed into it before dropping hard onto the floor like a rag doll thrown by a toddler. "Ow! Damn it!"

Dazed, she lay there a moment. The bruises on her elbow and shoulder started to complain. Her head throbbed. Something warm slid onto her forehead, and she lifted a shaking hand, coming into contact with sticky blood. She shoved off her eye mask and felt around her hairline, confirming that her darned head was cut open. Carefully moving her fingers to figure out where exactly the blood was coming from, and to gauge how much was oozing, she determined it was a fairly small trickle. Must not be too bad a gash since scalps normally bled a lot, so nothing to stress over too much.

She drew a shaky breath before gingerly sitting up. Figuring out what first aid might be necessary and how to actually accomplish it wasn't going to be easy. Did she even have a mirror in here to try to look at it?

Three loud raps on her door had her turning to stare at the gray metal panel and blink. It also made her realize that one of her earplugs had fallen out, even though she was sure she'd have heard that banging through double sets of the foam things.

Breathing deeply through her nose again, she tried to compose herself and removed the other plug, too, shakily shoving it into her pocket.

"Hey! You okay? Let me in."

Great. She closed her eyes and slumped back against the cabin wall. She'd bet good money that was her sexy neighbor's voice. Last thing she wanted was to have him touching her head and making her feel all fluttery, which she had a bad feeling might happen again, considering she'd been thinking of him just moments ago. But of course that was ridiculous. Attractive? Yes. But so were a lot of other men on this ship. And all were men who traveled for their work, and that she didn't have interest in.

Jordan opened her mouth to say she was fine, but as the blood trickled on down to her eyebrow, she had to grudgingly face reality. It made a whole lot more sense to let him see what was going on with her head wound than her trying to figure out how to check it herself. In a dark cabin with no mirrors, while the seas threw the boat around like a toy.

"Okay." She tried to stand, but realized she felt surprisingly shaky, which wasn't helped by the pitching of the boat. She ended up crawling to the door, feeling a little foolish as she reached up to unlock the knob, then leaned back against the wall next to it. "Come in."

The door crept open only a few inches, which she realized was smart on his part. Easy to accidentally bash someone if you shoved it wide open without first figuring out where they were. She could see him scan the room, then quickly look down, his brows rising and his eyes deep with concern even in the low light of the room.

"Are you hurt?" He flipped on the light switch, then crouched down next to her, his hand on the doorjamb to keep himself steady as the boat rolled. "I heard a loud thud, then somebody—you—cry out. What happened?"

"Got thrown from my bunk. Banged up. My head is bleeding, but just a little. Will you take a look and see what's going on up there?"

Another violent roll had her sliding sideways several inches on her rear, and his arm shot out to grab hers. "Let's get you off this floor and onto the lower bunk, since it's the only thing screwed down to the floor."

"No room. I have a bunch of equipment and stuff secured on there."

"Now there's a good idea. Keep the equipment safer on the lower bunk than your body and head." A disgusted sound left his mouth. "Hang tight. I'll be right back."

She leaned her aching head back against the wall, hoping this wasn't a bad omen to start the trip. Then again, some of the craziest and worst stuff that had happened to her and her parents on their working treks around the world later made for some of the best stories and laughs.

At the sound of his feet coming up the hall, she turned to see him staggering into the cabin with an armload of bedding while the boat tipped deeply to one side again, and she couldn't seem to keep from sliding back the other direction. "I'm going to tuck you into this corner over here so you'll be still while I take a look."

"Little Jordan Horner sat in a corner eating her curds and whey," she muttered.

"You're getting your nursery rhymes mixed up. Not to mention that's a little weird." He picked her up in his arms like she weighed nothing and gently sat her in the corner, stuffing the bedding on both sides of her hips, instantly making her feel more secure. "You feel nauseated? Confused?"

"I'm pretty sure I don't have a concussion," she said, wincing as she lifted her fingers to touch the tender lump on her head. "And feeling nauseated would be a given, considering the way the ship's been rolling for the past who knows how many hours."

"True." He shot her that smile that made her feel a little weak in the knees. "I'm Ezekiel Edwards, by the way. Friends call me Zeke."

"Jordan Flynn."

"I know. Fletcher Station's doctor." He nodded. "I'm a marine biologist and climatologist. PhD. Also a trained medic, so you can trust me to take care of your head."

"How do you know I'm the station's doctor?"

"Saw your name on the roster. And okay, true confessions." That quick smile again. "Someone on this ship told me the doctor on board was drop-dead gorgeous, and as soon as I saw you in the hall earlier, I knew it had to be you."

"Is this your usual chitchat when you meet a woman?" She rolled her eyes, not even close to surprised about that, then regretted it when it made her head hurt worse.

He chuckled. "It's just nice to finally meet you." He pulled a flashlight from his pocket and kneeled in front of her, lifting her chin to look in her eyes.

"Honestly, I don't have a concussion."

"How do you know? Do you usually recite nursery rhymes just for the hell of it?"

"Actually, yes. It was something my parents taught me to do when I felt worried about something, or if I was hurt, to distract me." And right now, she seemed to need a distraction from his chiseled features and sexy lips and the manly way he smelled, way more than from her bruised body and the movement of the boat.

"Huh. That's a new one." He gave her a crooked smile as his thumb moved from her chin and slipped across her cheek before dropping away. "Lean your head down so I can see what's going on with your injury."

His mouth was so close to her face she could feel his warm breath on her skin as his fingers gently moved through her hair. Her heart beat a little faster, and she had a bad feeling it was from his nearness and not her injuries. If she lifted her head back up, her lips would be in the perfect position to come into contact with his and…and…

Not happening, she reminded herself, scowling at how stupid she was being. She didn't even know the man. Why was she feeling this serious attraction in the middle of a storm while she had a busted-open head? Maybe she had a concussion, after all. Or brain damage.

"It's not too bad," Zeke said as his fingers touched around the rest of her scalp, obviously looking for more lumps or cuts, his voice a deep rumble against her face. "I have some derma glue, which will fix it right up."

"I have some, too. In that blue box on the bed."

"Good. I need to get this washed first. Sit tight while I get some stuff."

Sitting in the corner with the boat moving side to side made her stomach decide to complain even more. Probably it had something to do with her bruises and bleeding, too, but either way, it was bad. Bad that she felt sick, and bad that it was looking like she just might vomit right in front of the world's sexiest man.

Her eyes popped open in horror at the thought. Wildly, she looked around to see if there was something, anything, within reach she could barf into before he got back. Relief filled her chest when she saw a metal trash can sliding a few inches across the floor as the boat rolled again, and she stretched over as far as she could, desperately wiggling her fingers to try to grab the rim. Before she could get her hand on it, Zeke came back into the room and she stared up at him, a full-blown panic starting to fill her chest over the situation.

"Um... Can you...go away...and...come back in a little bit?"

That smile she'd already fallen for slowly stretched his mouth until his teeth shone white against his dark skin. "Feeling seasick? In a storm like this, that's totally normal. Not to mention you're hurt, which also can make you queasy, as I'm sure you know. Here."

He set the stuff he was carrying on the floor and

put the trash can in her hands. She glared at him as her stomach roiled. Swallowing hard, she knew she couldn't control it much longer. "Can't you see I need some privacy? Go away, please!"

"Don't worry. I've seen plenty of sick people on this exact boat. No point in fighting it. You'll feel better, then I'll get your head fixed up."

"I don't—" Oh, Lord, she couldn't hold it back any longer, totally mortified as she got sick into the can.

He stroked her hair, rubbed her back, talking the whole time in a soothing voice. She wasn't sure what he said, and also wasn't sure if his sweetness endeared him to her even more or made her want to hit him for not leaving her alone like she'd asked. What a way to get to know a guy.

Except she didn't want to get to know him, right? Trying to think of this horror as a potentially positive thing, she gave up trying to hold it back and got sick all over again.

Finally, the awful feeling subsided. She went to wipe her mouth, avoiding looking at him, and he tucked a damp cloth into her hand along with a tin of mints. He disappeared with the trash can and she was torn between feeling beyond embarrassed he was having to play nurse, and grateful that he was getting rid of the mess. In minutes, he was back and reaching into the box he'd brought.

"You feeling up to me cleaning your head? I can wait if you're not ready."

"Ready." Or as ready as she was going to be, with his body so close and his hands touching her, her embarrassment warring with a quivery feeling that had nothing to do with being tossed around the boat or with feeling sick and being injured.

With a last swipe of the cloth across her mouth, she popped one of the mints. Feeling marginally better, and glad to have minty fresh breath instead of the prior awful taste in her mouth, she leaned her head against the wall to let him take care of the first aid she needed. Whatever he'd put on the gauze stung as he cleaned the wound. He obviously knew what he was doing, working slowly and gently, but she still couldn't help but wince.

"Hang in there. I know it hurts. Almost done with this part. Then I'll glue it."

"Why do you have derma glue?"

"Did you think I was lying when I said I'm a trained medic?"

"I…forgot. Did you become a medic first, then decide to get your PhDs in marine biology and whatever else you said? Or the other way around?" she asked, as much to distract herself as because she wanted to know.

"I grew up in a place where knowing first aid came in handy." That seemed like an odd answer, and just as she was going to ask him what he meant, he continued. "Now I spend a lot of time in potentially dangerous waters and up mountain ranges and glaciers, like here in Antarctica. Cuts on coral, and bites and stings from sea life, or falls and other injuries, happen sometimes despite good planning. You better know what to do to treat yourself, or the people with you."

She nodded, and he cursed in response. "Hold still. I'm about to put the glue on now to close it. The cut's barely an inch long, so won't take but a second. Don't. Move."

She steeled herself, but didn't need to because she

didn't feel a thing. "Thanks so much for everything. I... really appreciate it. Trying to clean it and glue it myself wouldn't have been easy."

"Hopefully, I won't need your assistance the same way, Dr. Flynn, but we never know, do we?" He gave her another knee-weakening smile before he stood, his legs wide to keep his balance. "Stay put for a minute. I'm going to move everything off the lower bunk and secure it somewhere else, so you can sleep there instead of the top bunk."

She opened her mouth to protest, because some of the equipment was delicate. If any of it got broken, it would take a long time for more to be sent on a future ship. Then she realized that he was right, and she trusted him to make sure everything would be kept safe. Must be the calm strength and confidence that simply oozed from the man.

She knew she'd sleep better, assuming she slept at all, if she was only a foot from the floor. And the last thing her banged-up body needed was another jolt out of that top bed. If that happened, she might not be able to get the clinic and hospital ready to go before the next ships arrived.

"Thank you. Again."

"You'll find we're all a team here. No need to thank me for anything."

In no time, he had everything off the bed and secured as well as possible, the covers pulled aside, then came back to her. She felt strangely comfortable tucked into her corner with all that bedding and wasn't sure she wanted to go back to that bunk. Except it was probably Zeke's own bedding wrapped around her. He doubtless needed it back, or neither one of them would get any sleep.

"Okay. Bed's ready."

His arms moved to slide beneath her legs and back, and her independent side kicked in, knowing she shouldn't let him carry her again.

"I'm… I can walk."

"I'm sure you can. But why would you, when you're probably shaky and the boat is still moving all over the place and I'm here?"

"Well… I admit my head is throbbing, and I don't much feel like staggering across the room right now."

"Appreciate a sensible woman."

He lifted her against his wide chest and held her close as he stepped to the bunk to lay her on it, then pulled the covers up to her chin. She had to smile even as she felt a little ridiculous. "You're making me feel like a little kid with a boo-boo."

"Want me to tell you a nursery rhyme?" He smiled down at her, and her heart beat a little harder as their gazes met and held.

Somehow, she shook herself out of the trance that Zeke Edwards seemed to put her in all too easily. "Not necessary, thanks. But can you do me one more favor?"

"What's that?"

"My eye mask is somewhere on the floor near the door."

"Eye mask?" He barked out a laugh. "Is it filled with cucumber essence to keep you bright and beautiful?"

"Funny. It's great for travel, so don't knock it until you've tried it. Makes me feel like I'm in a little cocoon, along with the foam earplugs I wear. Helps me sleep on long journeys or in strange places."

"Can I borrow yours to try?"

That grin and the humor in his eyes tugged her mouth into a reluctant return smile. "Yes, because I always have at least two with me on a trip. Just in case."

Another chuckle as he picked the eye mask up from the floor and brought it to her, carefully sliding it over the top of her head before adjusting it to cover her eyes.

"Sleep tight, Jordan Flynn."

"Good night, Zeke." Jordan lay there still and quiet until she heard the click of the door.

Well, damn.

Yeah, she just might be in trouble here, but no way was she falling for a guy like Ezekiel Edwards. She wasn't a fling kind of woman, and her next relationship would be with a steady man who wanted to share a perfect little house with a picket fence in a lovely neighborhood. Live in the same place for years and years, and have a few children who'd get to see their cousins and grandparents all the time. Grow up with the same friends their whole lives.

Antarctica was not the place she'd find her future husband who wanted the same things she did, only men like Zeke who traveled the world for their work just as her parents had.

She fished her single earplug from her pocket, having no idea where the other one had ended up, and stuffed it in her ear. Tried to eliminate thoughts of Zeke from her mind, without success. But it would be okay. Once at Fletcher Station they'd both be busy and she'd have no trouble steering clear of him, except in the most superficial, coworker way.

She was sure of it. And never mind that her body still tingled from his touch.

CHAPTER TWO

THE ROLLING OF the boat lasted all night and into the next morning, and when the storm finally subsided, Zeke drew a deep breath of relief. He had trouble sleeping no matter where he was, and figured that, between the deep, rocking waves and her poor, sore head, Jordan probably hadn't gotten much, either.

When Captain John Stewart announced over the loudspeaker that everyone was now allowed out of their cabins for lunch before they docked, Zeke couldn't wait to get some fresh air. Out in the hallway he paused, wondering if it would be too pushy to knock on Jordan's door to see how she was doing. He decided that, since she'd had a head injury, it was perfectly acceptable for him to check on her.

He rapped on the door. "Jordan? Zeke. Wondering how you're feeling."

"I'm fine." Her voice was muffled, but she sounded fine. Very fine, just like the rest of her. "Thanks again for your help last night."

"You're welcome." He stuck his hands in his pockets, wondering if she'd invite him in. Waited for the door to open so he could see her pretty face and deep blue eyes. When it didn't, he was surprised and annoyed at how disappointed he felt. Probably shouldn't be, though, since thinking of her just one cabin over, and how she'd felt in his arms, had been part of the reason he'd been awake half the night. "So, I guess I'll see you around."

"'Kay."

With that clear dismissal, he shook off the odd feeling and headed to the deck to breathe in the now-calmer wind and talk with people he knew. The main conversation was about last night and how it had been one of the worst Drake Passage storms they'd been through, which morphed into everyone trying to one-up each other with nightmare sea stories from their pasts.

Grinning at the good-natured arguments and obvious exaggerations, he decided to head to the bridge to find out how much longer they'd be until landfall.

"What's with the roll of this tub?" he asked John as he stepped through the door. "Two days ago, you said it looked like smooth sailing. Pretty sure last night didn't qualify."

John laughed, but kept his eyes on the gently rolling swells in front of them. "Sorry. It was one of those times when the weather changed in the blink of an eye. But we're at a steady twenty knots now, and I think it'll stay there until we get to shore."

"Says the man convinced it would be Lake Drake this whole trip, flat as a pancake." He thought about Jordan getting hurt flying out of her bunk and pondered telling John about it, since, as captain, he'd want to know. But he had a feeling Jordan wouldn't want a bunch of questions about it, and he'd look at her head when he had a chance. No need to have John check on her when Zeke could do it himself.

"Yeah, well, it takes a big man to admit that sometimes he's wrong," John said, "and I pride myself on being pretty big."

Zeke chuckled, knowing he was referring to his girth as much as anything. "How long until we get there?"

"About…" He peered at the dials, then the horizon. "Forty-five minutes."

"That soon? You told everyone they could come to the lounge for lunch, but there won't be time for that."

"We made better time than I expected. The plus side of the winds and currents we had last night. But we've got lunch all ready, so we're still going to hand it out to those who want it." John shrugged. "Just sandwiches, though. It was all the kitchen crew could put together with the weather we had, and I didn't know when it would clear up. So I told them to go ahead and make a sandwich lunch. Trying to eat bacon and eggs from a plate isn't easy when the ship's all over the place, as you know."

"Sandwich sounds good. Thanks. I'll grab one before I get all my equipment pulled together. Appreciate the ride, such as it was."

"Anytime." John grinned as they shook hands. "See you the other way in…what? Six months?"

"That's the plan, unless I have to leave earlier to make sure my next grant gets approved. See you then."

Zeke headed to the lounge to make sure he got one of the sandwiches, since he suddenly realized he was hungry, not having had much for dinner. An empty stomach in stormy seas wasn't a good thing, but neither was a full one, and he'd tried to find the right balance before he'd headed to bed.

Thinking of how he'd startled awake with a pounding heart when he'd heard Jordan slam against that wall, then cry out, had him wanting to check on her again. Except she'd made it clear she didn't want that, so he planned to do the next best thing, which was to be a considerate guy and grab a sandwich for her, too. After getting sick last night, and everything else, she was probably starving.

The moment he walked into the lounge, his gaze went straight to the tall, slender woman with shiny dark hair to her shoulders. She was standing next to the rows of wrapped sandwiches, and his heart did a strange little pit-a-pat to see her there.

Apparently, he'd been right. Jordan was indeed hungry.

He moved to stand next to her, leaning down. "I'm a fan of the Reubens, but the turkey with bacon is good, too."

"I thought about getting the veggie, but saw it has raw onions. Yuck."

The way she cutely screwed up her face in obvious distaste made him smile. "I'm with you. Raw onions on a sandwich is a solid *no* for me."

"Yes. A solid *no*." Her mouth relaxed into a wide grin, and he realized it was the first full smile he'd seen from her. He liked the way it made her deep blue eyes twinkle, and a dimple poke into one cheek. "Any idea when we'll be docking?"

"Captain Stewart said about forty-five minutes. Less than that now. So before we do, I want to take a look at your head. How's it feel?"

"Honestly? It hurts. Way more than last night. But that's to be expected of a gash and bruise like that."

"Let's go out on the deck so I can see it."

"It's fine."

"You just said it hurts."

"Like there's something you can do about that? Just needs time to heal, that's all."

"So, when you have a patient that refuses to let you follow up after their treatment, you nod and are perfectly okay with that? I just want to look at the glue job, and see if it seems to be holding well." He wasn't sure why he felt so frustrated at her stubbornness. She was a surgeon, after all, and knew all about wounds and derma glue, and if she wanted to deal with it herself, what was it to him?

Maybe because the sound of her hitting that wall in the middle of the night had woken him from the terrifying dreams he sometimes endured, and he still felt a little unsettled by all of it. Wasn't it normal to want to check on her now, to make sure she was really okay?

For long seconds, her gaze clashed with his, until she released an exaggerated sigh. "Okay, fine. But can we please find a place where not everyone on the ship is going to be coming up to us and asking what happened?"

So he'd been right that she wouldn't want John, or anyone else, making too big a deal of her injury, and what happened last night.

"I know a good spot."

He nearly reached for her hand, but was pretty sure she wouldn't appreciate the familiarity, even though they'd shared an unusual closeness last night. He stuck his fist into his coat pocket instead. Most people were at the bow of the ship to see Antarctica in the distance, so Zeke led the way to the back of the boat and around a corner where they'd be alone.

Wind whipped her soft hair into her face and she

reached back to gather it into a ponytail behind her head. He tried not to get distracted by the beautiful line of her jaw that he'd noticed in the low light of her cabin last night.

He drew in a breath and put his hands on either side of her head, tipping it slightly down. Moved her hair gently out of the way so he could see the wound. A raw, red line spanned the bruised lump that resembled a miniature purple eggplant just above her hairline. But the edges of the gash seemed firmly closed together, and it obviously hadn't bled during the night, so it seemed the glue had done its job.

"Looks like it hurts like hell. But the good news is the wound is still nicely closed, so unless you whack it again, it should heal just fine."

"I thought it felt secured, but couldn't be sure." She gave him a twisted smile that showed she knew her stubbornness a moment ago about her dealing with herself hadn't made a lot of sense. "Thanks again for patching me up."

Shocked by an urge to press a soft kiss to her head, he dropped his hands and stepped back. "I'm going to check with the captain, see when it would be okay to go below and start to gather my gear, which is going to take a while. If I see you, I'll give you the heads-up on how close we are so you can pull yours together, too."

"Thanks. Appreciate that."

An awkward silence fell between them, and he gave her what he hoped was a relaxed smile before moving to the bridge to get the information he needed from John. He wished he had eyes in the back of his head to see if she was watching him go. Because he sure as hell knew if she'd been the one walking off, his attention would have been riveted until she was out of sight.

Jordan Flynn was a beauty, no doubt about it. But he hadn't had any kind of real relationship since he'd broken it off with his last girlfriend after the worst week of his life, and didn't plan to go there ever again.

John gave him the go-ahead, and he went below to the cargo area to search for the boxes of dive equipment and everything else he needed. Being one of the first to get his gear on the shuttle meant it wouldn't have to follow him during the next round of supplies-toting when the shuttle got full, and he began stacking everything onto several carts.

A cardboard sign caught his eye as he moved his first cart to the huge exit doors so he'd be at the front of the pack. Large letters printed in orange noted the multiple boxes that held medical equipment for the clinic and hospital.

He hesitated. Should he help Jordan out by stacking it on some of the empty carts and getting it ready so her stuff would be on the first shuttles out, too? Being a newbie on these expeditions, she wouldn't know that it could be another full day before the medical gear got delivered to the station if it didn't go out on the first round.

He shook his head at himself. Being helpful when someone needed it was all well and good, but at what point did it border on being a busybody, or even a creep? No, his own stuff was plenty to deal with right now. The crew was there to help Jordan. If he ran into her while they were both still on the ship, he'd give her the heads-up about how things worked around here. Otherwise, he'd mind his own business, and concentrate on work, like he always did.

* * *

With the ship nearing shore, Jordan hurried to the bow with dozens of others wanting to admire the scenery before they disembarked, so excited to get her first glimpses of the place she'd be calling home for the next six months. She'd seen so many photographs of the shoreline, and the icebergs and sea creatures that could be sighted, and each one had seemed more incredible than the last. She nearly had to pinch herself that she was about to experience it for real.

Standing on the open deck with the cold wind on her face thankfully much less ferocious than the day before, Jordan grasped the handrail and wondered if Zeke Edwards was somewhere within the crowd, too. Though why she couldn't get her mind off the man, she had no idea. Whether she wanted to or not, though, she'd be lying to herself if she didn't admit she wished he was standing there next to her, talking to her in that beautiful bass voice and charming American accent of his about this amazing world she was about to enter.

She stared out at one of the incredible white mountains of ice in the water, one side gleaming with a blue so deeply iridescent it took her breath away. It seemed fairly close to the ship, but she suspected that was an illusion, that it was actually much farther away than it appeared. Other flat icebergs floated nearby with groups of seals lounging on them. She knew Antarctica was home to dozens of species, but had no idea what kind these were. Wouldn't it be helpful if a certain marine biologist with warm eyes and an all-too-appealing smile was there to educate her about some of the wildlife she was seeing?

"Pretty, isn't it?"

Her heart jolted, then sped up. As though she'd con-jured him with her thoughts, Zeke Edwards stood next to her, his face tipped down toward hers, his mouth re-laxed into a small smile. The cold air stung her lungs as she breathed in and smiled back, and suddenly the incredible images in front of her seemed even more staggeringly beautiful.

"Pretty? It's incredible."

"The icebergs are truly wonders. Some are so big, hundreds and even thousands of feet thick and miles wide, that they're given names and tracked. Captain Stewart is giving this one a wide berth because sonar doesn't show if there might be a lot of ice reaching horizontally under the water. Don't want to end up like the *Titanic*."

"An even bigger accident than my small one last night is not the way I want to go. Thrown into freez-ing water, fingers and toes quickly numbing from hy-pothermia. Then convulsions, mental disorientation, organ failure. Finally, death. I hope to get to see more of Antarctica before that would happen."

A laugh rumbled from his chest as his amused eyes met hers. "Showing off your medical knowledge, Dr. Flynn?"

"Always do, whenever the opportunity arises."

The way they were smiling at one another, taking her back to that intimate feeling last night, sent her heart into a silly pit-a-pat.

"Glad to hear that. Upping my education on all things medical is something I enjoy." A strand of her hair in-sisted on flying into her eyes, and his finger reached to tuck it back inside her hat. "Good news is I think you're safe from hypothermia at the moment. Ship has neoprene immersion suits on board, and lifeboats. We're close enough to shore that we'd make it before the death phase."

"Thank heavens I can stop worrying now." Again, that chuckle rumbled from his chest, warming hers. "I've lived in a lot of places around the world, but usually in hot locations. Freezing to death is something I hope to avoid."

"Why have you lived lots of places around the world?"

"My parents are both doctors who work for an international organization that took us all over. It was an interesting way to grow up, but I'm glad to be done with it. Never had the comfort of living in one place, having the same friends for years and being close to grandparents and extended family. So I'm happy to finally be putting down roots somewhere."

Oddly, he didn't respond after getting her answer, his expression strangely serious.

"So." The awkward silence had her wanting to fill it with more chitchat. "Do you travel a lot for your work?"

"Yes. Various places, but for a marine biologist and climatologist, Antarctica holds the most interesting discoveries. I've been here thirteen times."

"Thirteen times?" Wow, the man was nearly as rootless as her parents. "You come more than once a year?"

"Sometimes. What we're learning here about the climate changes in the world is invaluable."

"I'm embarrassed to admit I don't know exactly what a marine biologist does. Other than study the ocean."

"We study the ocean floor and gather samples. Collect data on how warming and acidification of the polar waters is affecting all kinds of life, from the smallest plankton to penguins."

"And climatology?"

"Interconnected, but that involves gathering ice cores aboveground, among other things. I usually focus on either land or sea on each trip. The goal is to gather enough data to make private companies and governments see that significant changes need to happen to slow down the warming of our planet."

The passion in his eyes was intense, and she wondered how he'd decided to do that kind of research. She opened her mouth to ask more questions when a young man came to stand behind her, and she turned to look at him.

"Excuse me, are you Dr. Flynn?"

"Yes."

"Captain Stewart told me to load your equipment onto transport carts. Help you get it off the ship and onto the shuttle. It's ready to go down in the cargo hold as soon as we land."

She'd hoped there might be a few crew members in the cargo space that would be able to help her pull all the bulky equipment together, but hadn't counted on it. To hear it was already loaded up was a big, but pleasant, surprise.

"Well, thank you. Should I meet you down there?"

"Yes, ma'am. I'll be at cargo door three."

The young man left and she turned back to Zeke. "Wow, that's a nice surprise. I wasn't sure how much help I'd have, and there's a lot of stuff to take. The amount of equipment and supplies they gave me to open up the medical center is crazy. I'll have to thank Captain Stewart for thinking about it."

"He'd appreciate that."

Something about the expression in his eyes and the way he rocked back on his heels with his hands in his pockets struck her as slightly odd, and suddenly she knew why.

"It was you, wasn't it? You're the one who asked him to help me!"

"No. I asked Captain Stewart to see who might be able to give you a hand."

"I don't want to be treated differently from other people just because I'm a woman. It's my job to—"

"Jordan. There are times to be independent, and times to let people help. And it has nothing to do with you being a woman." His dark eyes met hers. "I already told you how many times I've been down here. If you don't get your stuff off the boat on the first round, you'll be waiting for it for another day or two. And since you wouldn't know that, and you'll be wanting to get the clinic and hospital set up as soon as possible, I figured I'd grease the wheels a bit so you'll be ready in case of a medical emergency."

A confusing mix of frustration and gratitude filled her chest. She did need to get everything set up as soon as possible, both because she had to begin doing baseline physicals on everyone who'd arrived in this first round, and also in case there was an emergency, as he'd said. But it sure seemed like the man was a little controlling.

She drew a deep breath. "I appreciate that, and admit I'll be glad to have everything at the station. But I would have liked for you to have given me the heads-up so I could be the one asking the crew for help. As the station's doctor, people need to know I'm fully capable of dealing with whatever I have to deal with here."

"My apologies for not talking to you first." He reached out to shake her hand, and even through her glove she could swear she felt the warmth of his hand clear down to her toes. "Good luck with your clinic setup—that's going to be a big job. Don't let that independent streak of yours keep you from asking me or someone else for help, okay? See you around."

She held her now-empty hand in her other one and watched his long legs jog down the metal stairs of the boat, probably going below to the cargo area to get his own things ready.

What was it about the man that had her feeling all wound up? Slightly irritated and ridiculously attracted?

She blew out a breath. There was zero point in being attracted to him. He lived the kind of life she'd left behind. This trip was about caring for patients and testing her parents' device, right? When the time came that she wanted to become interested in a man, it was going to happen back home in London. Period.

CHAPTER THREE

Satisfied that all the scuba gear and other diving equipment had been scrutinized, confirmed to be in good working order and organized, Zeke moved on to get the new aquarium room built and everything installed that he and the other marine biologists would need for their samples. He'd never had to do this in Antarctica before. Usually, all the science stations had everything set up already, needing only some adjusting and tweaking.

But Fletcher Station was brand-new, and while starting from scratch would be a lot of work, it gave him a chance to create something better than what someone else had built. He got to work, and hours passed as he carefully set the rock work in place, then got the salt water prepared. Assembled the various hoses, filters and everything else the aquarium needed to support the marine life he'd be bringing here to study. He paused to stretch, pleased to be making good progress on this big job.

"Glad to see you're halfway done here, so you can't drag me into doing your work, and mine, too."

Zeke looked toward the door. Bob Shamansky, who

worked for the same Southern California university he did, stood there holding a cardboard box in his arms.

"I'm pretty sure it's usually the other way around," Zeke said. "You asking me to bring up who knows what from the seafloor for you to study instead of learning how to dive so you can do it yourself?"

"Why should I learn to dive when I have people like you to do it for me?" Bob grinned as he set the box on one of the long tables lining the outer wall. "Besides, you don't fool me. Diving is your favorite part of the job."

"One of my favorites, I admit. You don't know what you're missing."

"I'll stay in the lab and you macho types can go dive into dark ice-cold water—thanks, anyway."

"Hey, I read about your latest breakthrough with a medicine you created through halogens in seawater. Treats neurological disorders, doesn't it? Congratulations."

"Thanks. Happy about it. Took me about five years from creation through the clinical trials to finally get it approved. Your samples helped make it happen, so congrats to you, too."

Another reminder of why the work they all did here was so important, and Zeke's fatigue slipped away as he turned back to the aquarium tasks. "What's on your list of things for me to collect this time?"

"I'll tell you about it after we get set up. This study is something totally new, and I'm pretty pumped about it."

"Which I know means you're giving me some tough jobs." Zeke grinned. "You need help carrying anything in?"

"I've got a crew guy giving me a hand down in the

storage hangar, then he's going to help bring it here after the Ski-Doo training. Which I think I saw is in about an hour. Want to race?"

"We'd get in trouble with the station head for being a bad influence on the newbies."

"Well, dang it. Since we'll be at twenty-four hours of daylight in no time we won't be able to race in the dark, so he can't see us. Risking falling in a crevasse is such a thrill."

"Says the man who won't even go diving. You're all talk, Shamansky."

"True. I'm about as risk averse as they come." He clapped Zeke on the back. "Going to grab my cart and bring it up. See you at the training."

"You'll be easy to spot, if you still wear that blue top hat over a balaclava."

"I traded it in for an orange one this year. And something else, but you'll have to come to the practice to find out what it is."

Zeke shook his head and chuckled as Bob left the room, turning back to his work. Digging in the plastic containers he'd brought up here, he realized he didn't have some of the tubing and filters he needed. A lot of his gear was still in the storage hangar, but several of the boxes were crammed beneath his bed.

He glanced at his watch. Since his cabin was about halfway between here and where they'd be conducting the Ski-Doo practice, he might as well see if what he needed was there to save time on his way back. He made his way through a covered, aboveground bridge that connected this building to Pod B where he'd be bunking. He moved down a hallway past rows of doors until he found his small cabin. With one single bed, a small table he used as a desk and built-in closet for clothes, it was comfortable enough. Good thing, since he'd be calling this place home for the next six months.

Home. He tried not to think about the home where he'd grown up. That it didn't exist anymore, and neither did his parents. Or the other two people he'd loved and who'd raised him after his parents died. Home was San Diego now, or at least as much of a home as he ever wanted to have again.

But there was no point in going over all that again. He'd learned what he'd had to about himself from that horrible experience, and would never forget.

He rolled up the shade covering the small window so he could look out over the ice fields beyond. In the summer months of endless sun, the light-blocking shades were essential to a good night's sleep, which he had trouble achieving even when it was dark. The shades took his mind back to Jordan Flynn and her eye mask, and he had to smile, thinking about her spunk and her shiny hair and deep blue eyes the color of the Pacific.

He turned and grabbed the things he needed from one of the boxes, put on the standard-issue red snowsuit the station had given everyone, then headed for the Ski-Doo practice. Pointless that it was, he couldn't seem to help the sudden spring in his step, knowing he'd see Jordan there.

Jordan stood near the big snow machines, deciding they looked a lot like motorcycles, and if that was the case, she'd be okay riding one. Living in so many unusual situations and places, she was probably more experienced driving all kinds of vehicles than most people, and hopefully this wouldn't be anything particularly new or different.

With her peripheral vision, she noted a tall form approaching. Despite wearing the same red snowsuit as everyone else out there, she knew without even looking that it was Ezekiel Edwards, and frowned at the way her heart beat a little faster. Couldn't help feeling that, when his gaze met hers, a small smile on his lips, it all somehow seemed to warm the freezing air.

"Ready for the Ski-Doo instruction?" he asked. "Have you ridden one before?"

"Not exactly. Motorcycles and scooters and such, yes. I told you my life experiences have been mostly in hot places, except for England. I'm guessing they're a lot like a Jet Ski?"

"Except without waves to hit and maneuver over. Here, you just have to make sure you don't drive over a crevasse and disappear deep inside, or get too close to the edge of an ice shelf and have it crack off so you end up in frigid water. Experiencing that hypothermia and death you talked about."

"You're making that up."

"Why do you think they have practice? There's a lot involved in knowing the safest ways to get around the area, especially if you're going out in the field."

"Well, that makes me glad they're doing this, to train newbies like me."

"I'd offer you help, but I know how you react to that. Don't want you annoyed with me again." His eyes crinkled at the corners as his smile widened. "Good luck and have fun."

She watched him move toward one of the Ski-Doos, and found herself still watching him as he slung one long leg over the saddle, got settled, then let it roar. She shook herself from the trance he seemed to send her into every darned time she was around him. When she was instructed to mount the machine and drive, she was more than glad to have something else to focus on besides how handsome and appealing the man was.

Relieved that she managed to get the machine started without any problems, she set out across the snow. Motor scooters and cycles were always fun, and riding the Ski-Doo was even better. Cold air tingling her face as she zoomed across the white world in front of her, maneuvering around the orange cones, had her deciding she'd definitely use this as transportation into the field whenever possible.

She brought hers to a stop to give someone else their turn to learn how to drive it, and her attention immediately slid to Zeke as he went through the obstacle course.

His obvious confidence as he operated the machine showed he was an expert driver, which wasn't a surprise since he said he'd been to Antarctica thirteen times. An incredible number since the man couldn't be more than thirty-five or so. He must have taken these trips sometimes twice in one year, unless he'd started doing this as an undergrad, and even then, it was impressive.

He pulled up next to her, sending that appealing smile her way. "Ready for the next lesson?"

"Yes. This is really fun."

"Next part is less fun, and a lot trickier, but essential to know when you're away from the base."

Zeke's gaze moved past her, and when he started laughing, she turned to see a man wearing an orange top hat that looked like something out of *Alice in Won-*

derland, and a scarf with polar bears all over it wrapped around his neck.

"Good look for you, Bob!" Zeke called. "Though you know some of the newbies are going to expect to see polar bears here now."

The man responded with a laugh and a thumbs-up before Zeke turned back to Jordan with a grin. "Bob Shamansky. Works for the same university I do."

"That hat would be a good look on you, too," she said. In truth, she found that impossible to picture, since Zeke Edwards simply oozed masculine sex appeal and sophistication. "But everyone who comes down here to work has to know polar bears only live around the north pole."

"You'd be surprised." He dismounted the machine and picked up a nearby pair of skis, leaning them against the snow machine. "Bob's a chemical biologist who creates new medicines—you might be interested in talking to him about some of them, Dr. Flynn."

"Really? I know marine life here can be used to create them. That's so interesting."

"It is. Now for the tricky part of the lesson." He pulled some rope from one of the storage boxes on the side of the Ski-Doo and handed them to Chip Chambers, the station head who'd been instructing everyone, as the crew all crowded around.

"Okay, everyone," Chip said. "It's important to know that crevasses are everywhere out in the field. Those of us who've been here a lot learn to look for signs of them, but when they're covered with blowing snow it's a lot trickier."

"Then how do you know if they're there?" one man asked.

"You can't always know. Which is why we try to

have those less experienced travel into the field with someone who's done it a lot of times, and why we have strategies for when things go wrong." Chip held up the two ropes and began to tie them to the machine. "We attach these to the back, like so, set the throttle to a low speed and hold on as it travels, skiing behind it. If the machine heads into a crevasse, you have to release the ropes and just let it go."

"I'm not sure I know what you mean," another crew member said.

"I'll demonstrate." Chip sat sideways on the snow-mobile, put the skis on, then to Jordan's surprise, he actually got the machine moving with the ropes trailing behind in the snow. "There's a kill switch right here. If you fall while you're skiing behind it, hit the switch to stop the machine. Once it's moving, stand up and pick up the ropes, like so, then let the skis take you until you're trailing along behind it."

As Jordan and the others watched him stand and let the moving snow machine and attached ropes tug him along on the skis until he was slowly pulled forward, she had a feeling he made it look easy. One of the young men—a guy who'd told her he worked in the kitchen—volunteered to try it, and she was glad, because she didn't want to be the first one and possibly end up on her face.

"Okay," Chip said. "Skis on, throttle going, stand to pick up the ropes, then move to ski behind it. Ready?"

"Ready."

Doing exactly as he'd been shown, it looked like it was going to be an easy ride. Until he pushed the throttle a little too fast, which made him hurry and stumble trying to grab the ropes. Jordan gasped when he got tangled up and went down onto the hard ice, shrieking in obvious pain as he was dragged a short distance before he let go.

"Hell," Zeke said, sprinting after the machine as it kept on going. Jordan and the station head ran to see how the man might have hurt himself.

She knelt down beside the guy, who was clutching his upper arm and rolling back and forth on the snow. "Tell me what hurts," she said.

"My arm. Shoulder. Damn it, I think it's broken."

"Maybe not. We'll see. But we need to go inside. It's too cold out here to take off your snowsuit and everything. What's your name?"

"Pete. Pete Sanders."

"Think you can walk, Pete?"

"I… Yeah."

"Damn it. I'm sorry this happened," Chip said. "But Dr. Flynn will take good care of you, I know."

Two people who'd been participating in the snowmobile practice came over to assist as Jordan and Chip carefully helped the man to his feet. As they moved toward the station, Zeke jogged up next to them, barely out of breath.

"Looks like you're doing okay. Hang in there. I'll take over for you, Chip."

"Thanks. I'll check on you as soon as I'm done here, Pete."

Chip moved away and Zeke held Pete steady as his dark eyes moved to meet Jordan's. "What did he hurt?"

"About to find out. Arm or shoulder, based on what he said."

"Are we taking him to the clinic? Is it ready?"

"Is that a real question, Mr. Field Medic?" She

smiled. "It's not fully pulled together yet but ready to see patients. But you don't need to come."

"Might as well see if I can help, since you're alone there until the next boat arrives."

"Appreciate it." And she did. Much as she could handle whatever was going on alone if she had to, if something was broken or dislocated, having someone there to assist would be a big help, especially without a nurse.

"That was a pretty exciting maneuver there, Pete. Wish I'd gotten it on video," Zeke said as he kept a steadying hand behind Pete's back.

The man managed a weak laugh. "Yeah. I'm never going to hear the end of this."

"Being famous for crashing during the snowmobile practice is better than nobody knowing who you are, right? A good way to introduce yourself to the women at the base, who'll all feel sorry for you and ask how you're feeling."

"One way to look at it, I guess. Thanks for that."

"You're welcome."

Zeke grinned at Pete, and Jordan had to smile at the way he was taking Pete's mind off his pain, which she had no doubt had been his goal.

As they moved through the long building, he proved to be a big help even before they got to the clinic, since he knew where to find an elevator so they could avoid most of the stairs. A good thing, because she'd been a little worried that the patient might be feeling lightheaded and have trouble with that kind of exertion.

"Okay, let's get your coat and shirt off," she said once they'd gotten him seated on the exam table she'd thankfully just fitted with sheets and a blue paper cover. She and Zeke each carefully tugged at the wide sleeves of his coat and slipped it off, then unbuttoned his flannel shirt and did the same thing, exposing a fairly tight long-sleeved shirt beneath it.

"I hate to tell you this, but we're going to have to cut this shirt off. Trying to move your arm and shoulder enough to get it off over your head isn't a good idea. Okay?"

"Aw, man, I only have one duffel of clothes here to last me the year. But okay."

"I'll find scissors and get that done, Dr. Flynn," Zeke said. "And don't worry, Pete, we can always get more clothes sent here. It just takes some patience before it arrives." With quick, efficient movements, he had the shirt off in mere moments, which surprised Jordan. Trained medic or not, it wasn't what he did for a living, and she couldn't imagine he dealt with medical emergencies very often in his line of work.

Slowly, she moved her hands along Pete's arm, elbow and up to his shoulder, and when the man gasped and uttered a sharp cry, her eyes lifted to meet Zeke's.

"Dislocation, probably, don't you think?" Zeke said.

Just looking at it, she'd suspected the same thing, but her physical exam pretty much confirmed it, and she nodded. "Most likely. Which isn't fun, but better than a break. I'll get the portable X-ray to be sure. Is your arm numb or tingling, Pete? Can you move it?"

"Can hardly move it. And yeah, numb, and it hurts. A lot."

"How much pain, on a scale of one to ten, with ten being the worst?"

"I think an eight. Or nine." Pete grimaced.

"Okay. Be right back." She rolled the X-ray machine over to take the pictures, with Zeke coming up behind her to study the computer screen over her shoulder. He seemed big and unnerving, the scent of him in her nose and the sound of his soft breathing in her ear. Disgusted with herself, she shook off thinking about how close he was, the hyperawareness of him that seemed to happen every time he was near. She called on her training to study the images and think about her patient and nothing else.

"Definitely a dislocation, with just slight damage to your glenohumeral ligament. That's the ball and socket between your scapula and humerus—your shoulder bone and the top of your arm. See?" She pointed to the X-ray. "I'm going to do a reduction to pop it back into place again."

"Will that fix it?" Pete asked.

"It'll be tender for a while, and you'll need to wear a sling to protect it and help the ligaments heal. And yes, it'll fix it but you'll have to be careful not to injure it again. I'm going to give you a muscle relaxant, and an analgesic for the pain, so the reduction won't hurt too badly."

"How about I find those drugs for you?" Zeke asked.

"That would be great. Except they're still in a jumble in the box. I had them perfectly organized until that crazy earthquake while crossing the Drake Passage tossed them around, along with me. So you'll have to look for them."

Zeke's brown eyes met hers. The twinkle and warmth in them showed he was remembering everything about that night, too, and all of it made her belly feel a little funny as she smiled back.

"There was an earthquake? While we were on the ship?" Pete asked, his eyes wide.

"No, no." Jordan's face felt a little warm, realizing she was dangerously close to flirting with Zeke, which she absolutely did not want to do. Especially since she enjoyed it too much. "Just a joke between me and Dr. Edwards."

"Dr. Flynn seems to be accident-prone like you, Pete. Hopefully, not when she's reducing your shoulder, though."

"He's joking about that, too, Pete." She frowned at Zeke. Kidding around patients was good to a point, to help them relax, but not if the kidding made them worry that she didn't know what she was doing.

Thankfully, Pete didn't look horrified, chuckling instead. Jordan asked him for his personal information and filled out paperwork on the station's hospital computer. She continued making notes regarding her diagnosis, X-ray results and treatment plan, while Zeke brought the medications and water so Pete could take the pills, and was glad he'd come with her to help.

With the meds now having had enough time to take effect, she stood next to the patient and firmly grasped his arm and shoulder, preparing to do the necessary reduction to put it back in place. "Ready? This is going to hurt some."

Zeke reached to hold Pete's hand. "Hang on to me and squeeze. It'll help you get through it."

Pete nodded and pressed his lips together, and Jordan could tell he was gripping Zeke's hand so tightly it had to be uncomfortable. She concentrated on manipulating Pete's arm to reconnect it into his shoulder socket. After a long moment of maneuvering it around, she heard the satisfying *thunk* and felt it lock back into place. "There! That wasn't too bad, was it?" She stepped back to smile at her patient.

He huffed out a long breath. "Not gonna lie—it hurt. But it feels a lot better now."

"Good. Now I need to get you a sling, so sit still until we get your arm immobilized. I'll—"

"I grabbed one when I was back in the storage closet," Zeke interrupted, holding it up. "I'll put it on him."

He didn't even wait for her to respond, efficiently getting Pete's arm and shoulder set up in the sling. She opened her mouth to comment on the way it should be done, then closed it. Obviously, he knew exactly what to do. Obviously also liked being in charge, even when he wasn't. But she wasn't about to complain, because it had definitely been better for Pete, and for her, to have Zeke there with them, helping get the procedure done as efficiently as possible.

With nothing to do at that moment, she found herself distracted by Zeke's dark lashes fanning his cheeks as he concentrated on fastening the sling. At the focus in his brown eyes, interrupted with flashes of humor as he'd say something to Pete that made him laugh.

The man was too charming for his own good—or for hers—and eye candy, to boot. She didn't want any distractions from her work or her diving device trial, and wasn't about to get tempted by a guy who was not at all what she wanted for her future. Seductive brown eyes and a teasing, sexy smile didn't change that reality.

"Pete, I want you to come back the day after tomorrow so we can talk about how you're doing. Here's more of that pain reliever, with my instructions." She scribbled on a notepad, then handed it to him with the medication. "And sorry, but no snowmobile training, or anything else physical that uses your arm or shoulder, for at least two weeks. I suggest you rest for a while before you try to get back to work today."

"Will do. Thanks."

After another nod to Jordan and a shake of Zeke's hand, Pete was gone, leaving Jordan alone with Zeke. Their eyes met again, and the sizzle between them was disturbingly obvious. To cover her awareness of it, and of him, she turned to strip the blue paper from the exam table and tossed it in the trash. Before she moved to put away the equipment, she paused and gave him a deliberately impassive look, hoping to squelch the electric zing she could swear she physically felt crackling in the air around them.

"You...you have an excellent bedside manner," she managed to say, hoping to break the mesmerizing connection. "I'm impressed that you didn't even flinch when he squeezed your hand so tight I thought he might cut off your circulation."

"I've dealt with a lot of injuries in the field over the years. Offering a hand to someone in pain is the least I can do."

"I assume you'll be going back to the snowmobile practice?" she said.

"Nah. It'll be almost over by now, and there are other people to help the newbies if they need it."

He just stood there looking at her, his hands in his pockets, rocking back on his heels a little, and her silly heart sped up all over again at something in his expression she couldn't quite define, leaving her feeling breathless.

"Well, if you'll excuse me, I need to get to work. I

have to organize all the things that are still a mess before more crew members get here, because as soon as they get settled in, I'll be recruiting some of the scientists to try my parents' earplug design for equalizing pressure during dives. Then schedule some dive time with them."

His brows practically hit his hairline. "What? What do you mean?"

The shock on his face made her realize she should have told him about the earplugs before, since he'd be diving a lot for his work here. Why hadn't she, when that was a big part of the reason she'd come to Antarctica? The obvious truth hit her. Feeling this constant push/pull of attraction every time he was near, and not wanting to feel that way, had knocked all thoughts of recruiting him straight from her brain.

"My parents have designed a device they hope will eliminate, or greatly reduce, problems with barotrauma. I'm an experienced diver and I'll be testing it here, and asking for volunteers to be part of the trial." She licked her lips and made herself ask the question she knew would result in them spending a lot more time together if he agreed. "Do you… Are you interested in being part of the trial, and diving with me sometimes?"

CHAPTER FOUR

ZEKE STARED AT HER, stunned. If she'd told him she wasn't really a surgeon at all he wouldn't have been more surprised. "You're a diver?"

"Yes. It's my parents' hobby. Their passion, really, after medicine. I told you that both worked as doctors in international hospitals, and I grew up diving with them all over the world. My dad studied biomedical engineering before deciding on med school, and he's sort of an amateur inventor. My mother loves to do underwater photography, has even sold some photos to magazines. I tried to dabble in that, but don't seem to have her artist's eye for it."

It took him a moment to respond, still astounded that in all their conversations about his work she hadn't said a thing about being a diver herself. "What is this device they invented?"

"Earplugs that equalize underwater pressure on the ear canal, without the diver having to clear their ears manually. They've just begun testing it various places. When I got this chance to come work in Antarctica, we all thought it would be a great opportunity to see if there are any differences in the way they perform in extremely cold waters."

"And you need volunteers to wear them. But why would you be diving, too?"

"Obviously, working in the clinic and hospital, I'd only be able to come along on dives occasionally. But I want to do that to record divers' thoughts right away, take their vital signs when possible and…okay, I admit it." A small smile played on her lips as her beautiful eyes met his. "I can't wait to see what it's like under the ice. Excited and scared, both, to be honest."

"Scared? Why?"

"You know as well as anyone that it's got to be different diving beneath ice than in the Caribbean. Isn't it?"

"It is." And he suddenly knew that, more than anything, he wanted to be the one diving with Jordan for her first time here, making sure she felt safe. "I'd be happy to be part of your trial. The rest of the marine biologists will be coming on the next boat. How about I talk with them about your trial as soon as they get here? And you and I can plan on a dive as soon as we can make it happen."

"Sounds perfect. I should have known that you'd dive right in…ha-ha—" she sent him an adorable smile "—and take over to help make it happen. And you know what? I'm getting rid of that independent streak you've scolded me about to tell you I really appreciate it. Having you be part of the trial and talk with your colleagues about it is going to be hugely helpful."

The smile on her face and the way she was looking at him seemed to show she felt sincerely pleased, and his chest felt like it was expanding as he thought about how good it would feel to help her. About how it would feel to spend more time with her and dive with her. Then he forced himself to remember that he couldn't let himself get attached to Jordan, that he'd be there for her when it came to working and diving, but anything more was out of the question.

He couldn't deny that the attraction he felt for her seemed to grow every time he saw her. But how he felt didn't matter. She might not be interested in a relationship, anyway, but if she was, she deserved someone she could rely on in every way.

He definitely wasn't that man.

Zeke doubled down to get everything ready for when the rest of the crew arrived so he and Jordan could get diving as soon as possible. He and some of the station crew spent the entire day out on the ice shelf, using chain saws, drills and heating equipment to cut two dive holes about twelve meters apart. Having them finished left him feeling satisfied and excited about getting down there to see what they'd find this trip, and to see how Jordan felt about diving under the ice.

His prediction? She'd love it, and he was counting the hours until the next ship would arrive with the other scientists, so he could get busy with his grant work and go underwater with her.

With the dive holes ready, he finished the aquarium setup and tested it to make sure it was operating properly. He checked the filter systems he'd had up and running for the past twenty-four hours, then the water quality. Pleased that all systems were go, he knew the other marine biologists would be glad he'd come early to get this done. Once they were diving, they'd bring back algae, zooplankton and other marine life samples to test, study and, in some cases, tag and return to the sea.

He forced himself to do paperwork so he'd have it

behind him when everyone arrived. The ship should have left Chile an hour ago, which meant only two more days until he'd have dive partners as anxious as he was to get in the water.

Revision of his most recent academic paper, soon to be published in a science periodical, was the first priority. That study was complete, and an important piece of the complex data he'd be presenting to get his new grant application finished.

His current research project would take the full five months he'd be down here, but initial data had to be compiled in time for the first grant deadline, which was in just less than a month. For every grant available there were at least ten applicants, and getting the fieldwork done, the initial data compiled and the preliminary paper finished by early November would take hard work and a lot of hours.

Being one of the first to submit the application was critical. As a presenter at next year's international climate summit, he needed to have additional, irrefutable evidence of how the ozone hole above the Antarctic would continue to affect coastal cities and its inhabitants. Proving ways to reduce the amount of ice melt and disturbing water temperature rise, which was affecting the size and impact of hurricanes and typhoons, was what his life's work was all about.

He knew, firsthand, that people were dying because of it. Many more, if he failed.

Zeke drew in a deep breath. He'd get it done. Then he'd knock the socks off various nations' leaders and private enterprises interested in making corporate changes, and the global impact of all that would save lives around the world.

His grandfather's laughing face, his grandmother's sweet one, floated in his mind's eye, and with the ache and guilt came a familiar feeling of determination. He made a call to the vehicle coordinator to make sure they had a PistenBully or one of the six-wheel vans available to get to the ice shelf the day his colleagues showed up, so he could start pulling samples. Then he worked on more paperwork until his eyes were blurring.

"Might want to cancel your reservation for transportation," Bob Shamansky said as he strode into the room. "Looks like both of us are going to have to find more lab- and paperwork to do for a while."

"What? Why?"

"Just heard that John Stewart notified the base supervisor that he's keeping the tub docked in Chile because of the weather. Forty-knot storm on Drake Passage right now, and with the ship full, he doesn't want to risk it. Planning to wait a couple days and see if it calms down."

"Damn." Zeke pressed his palms to the table, trying to figure out how to get rolling on fieldwork without waiting another four or five days. "Maybe you can be my dive partner. Just to be ready to throw me a line if something happens."

"Pretty sure you need someone who can actually dive with you, in case you get the bends or a tear in your hose or whatever the hell can happen down there. Those things being why I don't participate in that particular activity."

"Yeah." Diving alone wasn't a great idea under normal circumstances, and here in Antarctica? Doing that would qualify as just plain stupid. "I'm going to see if anybody who's already here is a diver."

Except he already knew of one. Jordan Flynn. Would she be interested in diving with just him? Thinking about the excitement in her eyes when she'd spoken about it, he had a feeling the answer was a clear *yes*.

"Might be," Bob said. "Don't worry. If I know you, you'll get that grant money done come hell or high water." He clapped Zeke on the shoulder. "Time for first-round lunch. Why don't you go to the galley and ask around to see if there's a diver you don't know?"

"It's worth a try." Without much hope that he'd get lucky and find someone, he headed to the galley and, as expected, struck out. Feeling too restless to go back to his paperwork, he decided to see if Jordan was willing to dive with just him, and if she was, find out when she could take the time to do it. And it wasn't just an excuse to see her. He needed to get to work on gathering samples.

Though he couldn't lie to himself—the thought of seeing her did make his step feel a little lighter, whether he wanted it to or not.

He found her in the storage room of the clinic, sitting on the floor with her legs crossed. Bags of medicines and medical supplies were sorted in front of her, next to multiple zippered satchels, her head tipped forward, a waterfall of smooth hair covering her profile. He knew how soft it felt from when he'd glued her wound and now stood there a moment, wishing he had an excuse to skim his hand down all that dark silk.

He cleared his throat. "I wanted to talk with you, but looks like you're busy."

Her head lifted and her eyes met his, her fingers pushing her hair behind her ear as she smiled up at him.

"No, just getting travel bags ready. Which I'm sure you know all about."

"What are you packing?"

"Drugs, syringes and other equipment, labeling each bag. Catheter. Fluid. Trauma. Circulation. IV. The usual."

"The usual for Antarctica. I'm impressed that a hospital-based surgeon knows everything you might need down here for out in the field."

"Well, much as I like to impress people whenever possible, I can't lie. I was given a list when I was hired, before I even came down here." She held up a sheaf of papers with a cute self-deprecating smile on her face. "Want to take a look and see if anything's missing?"

He lowered himself to sit next to her and liked the way his shoulder felt pressed against hers as he leaned in to read it. "Looks pretty complete to me. You're ready to go if there's an accident or illness in the field, Dr. Flynn."

"Good. I was a little worried that I hadn't finished this yet, so I'm glad to get it done."

"I'm glad, too. Because I came to talk to you about your work schedule and diving."

She began to push to her feet, and he regretted no longer getting to sit so close to her, oddly comfortable considering how hard the floor was. He stood and held out his hand to finish helping her up, taking as long as possible to release her hand's warmth. She didn't seem in too big a hurry, either, looking up at him expectantly until she finally slid her hand from his.

"Do you have a dive scheduled with the new crew that I can come on?"

"Not exactly. Drake Passage is acting up again, and

nobody's getting here for a few days. I don't want to get behind on gathering the samples I need for my grant application so I'm wondering—are you willing to dive with me alone?"

"Well, let me think." She tapped her finger against her chin. "You've been diving in Antarctica during thirteen trips and I doubt if anyone coming can beat that. So, is that a real question?"

"Wasn't sure if you'd feel safer as part of a bigger group, since you haven't been under the ice before."

"I know I'll feel totally safe with you," she said. The eyes meeting his were serious and trusting, and a strange feeling filled his chest that she seemed to truly feel those ways about him.

"We won't wander too far from the hole, and stick close together. And whenever you're ready to go back up, just let me know and we'll finish right away."

"When can we go?"

"Does tomorrow afternoon work for you? Bob Shamansky said he'd come with us whenever I get a dive pulled together, and I know he won't be free until about three o'clock. He doesn't dive, but whenever we go out, we have at least one tender along to help with all the equipment and keep an eye out up above."

"An eye out? For what?"

"Marine mammals, among other things. Most are fun to see, like the penguins and the various seals, though you'll notice that some of the male seals glare at you if you get too close. Especially underwater, so give them a wide berth if you can."

"Sounds amazing."

"It is. Except there is one thing you have to steer

clear of—leopard seals. They're dangerous, and if we see any in the water we move on and keep our distance."

"Do they attack people?"

"Sometimes, and even follow divers occasionally, like the predators they are. They have sharklike teeth and are huge. Males are about a thousand pounds and females even bigger. A few years ago, an intern was badly mauled by one at a station south of here. Just one more reason why diving here isn't like diving other places."

"Being mauled by a leopard seal sounds about as appealing as hypothermia," Jordan said, and her captivating smile showed him why he'd felt so attracted to her that very first day on the ship when she'd joked about that. "Which do you think would be worse?"

"Probably a toss-up. And I don't want to experience either one to find out the answer." But experiencing diving with the smart and fascinating Jordan Flynn? That he couldn't wait to do. "Can you be ready tomorrow at three in the vehicle hangar? I'll have all the equipment we need for when you and Bob get there."

"I brought my dive clothes and equipment, but I'm not completely sure I won't need something more. Do you have extra gear required for this kind of water?"

"Is that a real question?" For some reason, he couldn't help but tease her. "Yes. And I'm sure you're also prepared. All you have to do is wear what you'd normally wear when it's twenty degrees below Fahrenheit."

"Pretty sure there's no 'normal' in that kind of water temperature. Except here." Amused blue eyes met his. "Are you willing to try the earplugs?"

"Looking forward to it." And he was, but not nearly as much as he looked forward to diving with her, and wished they could head out right then.

"I appreciate that. So—"

Voices from the lobby outside had them both turning their heads, and the deep stab of disappointment that he wouldn't get to banter with her alone anymore surprised him.

"Uh…" He drew in a breath, knowing he had to quell this desire for her, because there was no point. "I guess you have a patient you need to see?"

CHAPTER FIVE

JORDAN GLANCED OUT through the door at the people filing into the meeting room, wondering how in the world she could have forgotten she had a group coming in for first-aid instruction.

Except she knew how. Something about Ezekiel Edwards seemed to make her forget everything except how much she enjoyed talking with him, and laughing with him, and looking into his deep, dark eyes, and she felt herself falling every time. A hardworking man dedicated to his job and who liked to help people. A man whose smile made her feel annoyingly gooey inside whether she wanted to or not.

"Um…" She glanced at her watch. "I actually have first-aid instruction scheduled. For crew members coming…right now. The first ten for two hours, then another ten after that."

"Ah, the first-aid lessons. Need a hand?"

"Wow, you must be really bored." Or could it be that he didn't want to end their time together any more than she did? Which wasn't something she should want. But she did, anyway, fool that she apparently was.

"Not bored. I just know from experience that teaching newbies how to stitch, and place IVs, isn't easy."

"Are you offering your arm to let them place the IV? That would be entertaining to watch."

Amused brown eyes met hers as he laughed. "I'm not quite that much of a masochist. With this many people, I just know that having two instructors makes it go faster."

"I'm sure that's true." Jordan hadn't actually taught nonmedical people how to do the things on her list, but didn't want to confess that. It sounded like Zeke had, and she felt a pang of disappointment that it was probably the reason he'd offered, and not because he found being with her fascinating, the way she'd unfortunately been feeling about spending time with him.

But she wasn't too proud to learn something professionally from him, was she? Even if it was medical related? "We're going to start with first-aid basics, like treating shock, how to stop bleeding and such. Then go to the stitching and IV placement. Sure you don't want to be the human practice dummy?"

"Not that big a dummy."

That twinkle in his brown eyes and crooked, engaging grin were irresistible, and she couldn't help but laugh. Standing there next to him in what should have been a normal, casual interaction between colleagues felt strangely intimate instead. Like they'd known each other a long time, and shared a closeness she shouldn't feel after knowing him a matter of days. Though she supposed the time they had spent together had been unusual, with him patching her up and working at a science station that currently had a comparatively skeleton crew. Not to mention that she needed him to help her get underwater, and test her parents' device.

She couldn't seem to help that her breath felt a little

shallow and her heart was doing that annoying pit-a-pat thing. Her brain knew very well that he was not at all the kind of man she wanted in her life, but her body hadn't seemed to catch up with that fact.

She drew a deep breath and tried to shake it off so he wouldn't suspect her unwitting reaction to him. Though she feared he already knew.

"Don't worry, Zeke. I brought a phlebotomy and venipuncture practice arm, so your flesh and blood are safe."

"And speaking of flesh and blood, can I check on yours?"

She nodded and he stepped close again, his wide palm cupping the back of her head as his other hand gently moved aside her hair to look at her scalp wound. He smelled so good, his own mix of the outdoors and a faint whiff of soap and of *him*, and she found herself wanting to lean into him. To feel his big body pressing against hers, the memory of which seemed imprinted in her brain from when he'd carried her to her bunk.

"It's an even more impressive rainbow of colors, but the swelling is down. Looks like it's healing well."

"When I was a little girl I wanted to be a unicorn the worst way, so I guess I'll think of having a rainbow on my head as a positive."

He gave a soft laugh. "Maybe you'll find something equally colorful and fantastic when we dive."

"I can't wait to find out." The damned breathlessness wouldn't seem to go away, and she was glad to have the excuse of starting the first-aid class to put distance between them. "Thanks again for patching me up. Maybe during class I'll show everyone my head and we'll demonstrate closing and gluing a wound, too."

"Gluing takes more skill than stitching, when it comes to emergency field treatment, though some don't believe that." His voice was a warm rumble, and she wondered if he realized the hand behind her head had brought her to within an inch of his broad chest. *She* realized it the second he'd done it, because being so close had her heart beating fast and her hand lifting to press against his chest, barely resisting the urge to slide it up around his neck and close the small gap between them.

"I guess we'll stick with teaching stitching, then."

Their gazes met and held, his hot and alive. His strong jaw, covered with dark stubble, looked taut, and his wide shoulders blocked the view of the people coming into the lobby, creating the illusion that they were still alone. Suddenly wanting, more than anything, to rise up on her toes and kiss that tempting mouth of his, to wrap her arms around his neck, foggily trying to remind herself of all the reasons she shouldn't... But then he broke the mesmerizing connection. Dropped his hand from her head and stepped back.

His chest rose and fell. Noise from the other room got louder as more people arrived, talking and laughing, and still, neither of them moved. It felt like time had simply stopped as they stared at one another.

And then he turned away.

"Sounds like everyone's ready to learn the basics, Dr. Flynn."

She watched him walk out into the lobby, then managed to pull herself together to follow. Which was completely annoying, since she was the one teaching this class, and should have been the first in there, smiling and welcoming everyone. Time to get her act together and remember why she was here, which definitely wasn't to make goo-goo eyes at a man who made his living researching and traveling, and was not someone she wanted to get personally involved with.

She hurried into the meeting room and greeted the crew, hoping her expression was relaxed and professional. Half the group was already seated at the table, picking up and examining the medical items in front of them, while the rest were still standing and chatting.

Her hyperawareness of Zeke's tall form at the other end of the table was a distraction, but the interest the crew had in learning about the first-aid techniques made it easier to move her attention to teaching. Everyone there knew there might be times they were away from the station in the field and would need to know how to do basic emergency treatment, or an occasion when Jordan was in the field herself and someone would have to take over here at the Fletcher during an emergency. The two hours went by quickly, and the whole thing turned out to be fun, to Jordan's surprise.

A big part of what made it fun? Ezekiel Edwards. His joking had everyone laughing at the same time they were learning. The man was not only knowledgeable, he seemed to have that perfect balance of knowing how to teach while keeping everyone engaged.

Just like he'd been there when she'd needed her scalp repaired, he'd been here for this, too. A man you could count on whenever you needed to. Having him as a partner for this training made it much less stressful and a lot more enjoyable, and the next important step was to convince her body and not just her brain that they needed to keep it strictly professional.

"Last is stitching a wound," Jordan said to the group, holding up a needle and suture. "It's really just like sewing, except you need to stop the bleeding the way we've already discussed, then clean the wound as best you can before you close it."

"Remember this is a field technique, though, as there might be a better option if someone is injured here at the station," Zeke said, seated between two people who were riveted by his every word. "Either Dr. Flynn or I will have derma glue on hand, which often can be used in place of stitching for smaller wounds. Especially scalp injuries, should your head make contact with a wall, or something."

He sent her that teasing smile of his, and the secret little connection between the two of them about what had happened the first night they'd met made her belly feel all fluttery. Their eyes met, and she just couldn't help but smile back, everyone else in the room seeming to fade into the background except for him.

She drew a breath and managed to turn away and focus on the crew. Ezekiel Edwards might be beyond appealing, but he was not irresistible. She could dive with him, and work with him, and still keep her heart firmly to herself. Work colleagues and simple friendship would be the goal.

The six-wheel van lumbered across the ice shelf, and Zeke hoped like hell that the dive would go smoothly without any kind of hitch. Having only two divers and one tender wasn't the norm down here, but he'd done it before. So why did he feel this niggle of worry?

The answer was obvious. He wanted today's dive to be a special experience for Jordan.

He glanced across the seat at her and wondered if the hum between the two of them as they drove was palpable even to Bob, who sat in the back seat. Then Zeke wondered if maybe it was all one-sided and he was imagining the connection between them. A connection, if it was real, that he shouldn't encourage, anyway.

"I can't believe how incredible it is out here," Jordan said, turning to look at him. The awe on her face made him smile, though he'd known all along she was the kind of person who would appreciate this crazy southern world of intense blue sky; barren, snow-covered mountains and the slow ice melt over beautiful blue-green waters as much as he did.

"It is incredible. The way it changes from day to day, even hour to hour sometimes, is like nothing you've seen before." He worked to keep his voice even and not warm and intimate, the way he couldn't seem to help feeling toward her ever since they'd packed up in the hangar earlier. Since yesterday, working together in the clinic. Since the moment they'd met. "Wait until the hours-long sunsets. Crazy storms. And, if you're lucky, the aurora australis—though that might not happen during your trip here. Once it's twenty-four-hour daylight, in another week or so, it'll be too late, and I don't know how much solar activity there's been lately to make them visible."

"I so hope I get to see it. But even if that doesn't happen, just being here is so much more amazing than I ever dreamed."

He took in her shining, excited eyes and wide smile as she scanned the expanse of white in the clear air, the iceberg chunks floating far out in the water, the Adélie penguins waddling along in groups of over a hundred, and hoped she'd be just as pleased once they were actually diving.

"Was it you who placed all these flags along where we're driving?" she asked. "I assume they mark the route?"

"Yeah," Bob chimed in from the back seat. "Zeke and I spent a day getting the markers placed before he and a few burly engineer types came back to cut the dive holes. A couple trips ago, I learned how important it is, believe me."

"What happened?"

"We were at a small station with a group that got the holes placed, but didn't post flags. A nasty storm blew up and we couldn't see a thing. Barely made it back. I thought for sure we were goners, our bodies about to be buried under the snow before being eaten by a leopard seal."

"Bob is a little melodramatic, as you can tell. I always get the flags in first, so stop trying to scare her." Zeke sent a frown back to Bob, not wanting him to worry Jordan. It was true that getting lost in a blizzard was no joke, and preparation was critical.

Also true that no matter where you were, Antarctica or anywhere else, if you didn't plan for the worst-case scenario it could result in a tragedy you would never forget.

Zeke's chest tightened, and he battled back the familiar and unwelcome anxiety that would come from nowhere and that was beginning to well in his chest. Slow, calming breaths, in and out, usually pushed it away now, and he breathed and focused on the white road in front of him.

"How much farther to the dive hole?"

He turned to look at her, and seeing her beautiful face smiling and calm managed to help him relax, too.

"See that speck of red in the distance? That's a tent set on top of the closest hole we cut. As we get deeper into the summer we can usually do without the tent and leave it open. This early in the season, though, it helps protect us from cold wind and snow as we're getting in and out of the water."

"I admit it's amazing to me that you dive here at all."

"Are you feeling nervous about it?" He reached for her hand, wanting to show he was there for her. "You don't have to go in. With both you and Bob as tenders, I'd be fine, especially if I stay fairly close to the hole."

"No, I want to experience it. Test the earplugs. But I've heard people feel claustrophobic under the ice sometimes. A little worried about that, to be honest."

"I don't want you to worry." He tightened his hold on her hand, and when she twined her fingers with his, his chest felt that strange expansion thing again. Hopefully, her holding on to him meant that she trusted him. "It's not that common with experienced divers, which you are. But if it happens to you, just like in any other dive situation, it's important not to panic. We'll attach a rope to your weight belt, so if you get weirded out, you know you can always follow it back up."

"I won't need a rope."

"Do you always try to act so big and tough and over-confident?" His heart jerked, wondering if she was going to pay attention to everything he said, or feel a need to show her independent self. If she did, he'd end the dive early, period. "Most divers here use ropes every time they go out, especially during midsummer, when the phytoplankton bloom and the water's murky. It's easy to be exploring and getting samples and not realize how far you've gone until you can't figure out where, or what direction, the hole is. That's when people freak, and bad stuff can happen."

"I promised you I'd stay close to you, didn't I?"

"You did. And I want you to keep that promise."

"I promise I'll keep my promise."

She said the words in a light joking tone, and gifted him with a smile that stole his breath. He squeezed her hand before he had to let it go, stopping the vehicle next to the tent.

"Here we are. Ready?"

"Ready or not, here I come."

"I haven't been a tender on one of these trips for a while, Zeke, so you'll have to remind me what to do with the equipment," Bob said.

"Okay." Since the whole reason they were here was to dive and get work started, and they needed a tender to do that, Zeke shouldn't feel slightly resentful of Bob's presence. He couldn't seem to help that he did a little, anyway, wishing he and Jordan could enjoy being here together all alone, even though that made no sense at all. "I'll explain as we get it set up by the dive hole."

Zeke shoved open his door and went to the back of the van, with Jordan and Bob following. After getting everything inside the tent, he turned to Jordan to talk with her about what was necessary for cold-water diving, because it was crucially important she understood how different it was from whatever diving she'd done before.

"Getting the gear on right matters. First, the dry suit goes on over your long underwear, then a jumpsuit on top of that. So, let's get it on you before we go to the next step."

She took off her snowsuit, boots and thick pants,

folding and stacking them in a pile on the ice, and Zeke couldn't seem to keep from staring at her. He'd been on dozens and dozens of dives and never once had he thought of anything but work when everyone got their gear on, until today. That she could look so sexy in black long underwear that closely fitted her slender body had him imagining what she'd look like in scanty undies.

Or nothing at all.

Nearly groaning at the vision, he yanked his mind from where it had instantly gone, and held the dry suit open for her. "Step in, and I'll help you get it on."

"Remember I've dived many times in my life?" She reached for it instead of doing as he asked. "I know how to get on a wet suit."

"Except this is a dry suit, and they're even tighter so you stay well-insulated in the water. But suit yourself. Literally."

"I always do," she said with a grin.

He tried, again, to think only professional thoughts as he watched the way she shoved her feet into the tight legs, tugging them up her delectable body an inch at a time. Wiggling and wriggling. Huffing and puffing, until he and Bob both couldn't control laughing just a little at her struggles.

"Another reason I don't dive," Bob said. "Way too much work before you even get in the water!"

"Well, sometimes it takes a little work to have a lot of fun," she replied, sounding breathless from her exertion.

"Very true." Zeke worked to get his on, too, but since he had the technique down pat, he'd already fastened his closed while hers was still twisted around her hips. "At this rate, the sun will be setting by the time you're ready," he said, cocking his head at her. "You going to let me help you or not?"

"Fine." She threw up her arms, sounding exasperated. "But what happens on the ice stays on the ice, right? I don't want anyone knowing I couldn't do this on my own."

"It's our secret. And next time, you won't have as much trouble, I'm sure."

"While you finish, I'll get the last tanks from the van," Bob said before he disappeared from the tent.

Barely acknowledging Bob's words, Zeke looked down into amused blue eyes. He loved that Jordan could poke fun at herself, despite that independent streak of hers that didn't like asking for help with a dry suit she wasn't familiar with. He reached for where the suit was currently squeezing her hips, curled his fingers inside the rubber clinging to her body and tugged it upward, feeling her firm waist and ribs as he did. Her eyes lifted to his again, and his breath backed up in his lungs.

Being alone with her in this tent, touching her body and standing so close he could hear her breathing, was doing all kinds of things to him that he couldn't let happen. His gaze moved across the delicate shape of her face, her parted lips, her eyes staring up at him, and all he wanted to do was pull her into his arms and kiss her until neither of them could think.

He nearly did. He began to lower his face to hers, then gritted his teeth against the desire for her that pumped through his veins. He squeezed his eyes for a moment to block out how beautiful she was and the hot thoughts he had to control.

When he opened his eyes again, he focused on the dry suit as he tugged it up her body, making sure he didn't touch places he shouldn't touch, which wasn't easy. Finally, he got it high enough for her to stick her arms inside, and expelled a breath of relief that he'd survived it without doing something they'd both regret.

"That feel okay? Not crooked?"

"No, it's okay."

She sounded breathless, but probably from the exertion of getting the suit on, and not for the reasons he felt that way. He moved around to her back and took her soft hair into one hand to move it aside as he got the Velcro fastened around her neck. It felt like torture that he couldn't lean in a little closer to breathe in the scent of her skin. Press his mouth to her nape and taste it.

God, he needed to get out of this tent and into the water.

"There." He cleared his throat and stepped back. "You're in, but there's more."

She turned to face him, and something about her expression made him grit his teeth all over again, wanting more than anything to reach for her and kiss her and to hell with any consequences.

"The face masks. I've never worn one before."

"Yeah. They have that special perfume smell called eau de rubber. You'll like it."

Her laughter helped ease the uncomfortable closeness he kept feeling for her, standing alone and so close inside this tent, and he breathed a little easier.

"Eau de rubber sounds like it might become my new favorite," she said, and he didn't think he was imagining that she looked a little relieved to be back to their joking.

"I think this is everything, but you need to double-check, Zeke," Bob said, coming back inside.

"Looks like it. Except for one thing. Where are the earplugs you want to test, Jordan?" he asked.

"Right here." She reached for a small bag inside a pocket of her folded snowsuit, and pulled out four small black things, handing him two. "I want you to put them in without me instructing you how. To see if you think they're user-friendly."

"Okay." Shaped a little like a music earbud, he easily settled it down into his ear canal. "There. I'd say definitely easy to put in. Looking forward to seeing how they work."

Her pleased smile in response to that seemed to sneak right inside his chest, warming him despite the chill in the tent. He turned away to grab the hoods, face masks and dry gloves, putting his on to show her how. Focusing on her midsection and getting the rest of the equipment on her didn't help dull the desire he couldn't seem to control, which seemed impossible, since she was covered head to toe with black rubber that obscured every inch of her skin except the little bit he could still see until she put her goggles on, and her lips.

"Weight belts next, then the buoyancy compensator vest, goggles, regulators and tanks."

His gaze met hers, gleaming blue from inside the black mask, and he nearly told her she was the only person he'd ever dived with that he wanted to kiss while literally covered head to toe in rubber.

He was in so much trouble here.

"Here's when I finally admit it." Her eyes were filled with rueful laughter. "I thought I'd researched most of what I needed to learn to dive here. But I sure didn't know I'd feel like a human tire, complete with inner tube and snow chains. Not sure I can even walk the five feet to the dive hole."

"Consider it weight and cardio training." He handed her the regulator and needed to make sure she knew how diving here was different from what she'd done before. "Remember that regulators are more prone to get stuck in this kind of cold, so pay attention to that. Don't get stressed about it, just replace it with your spare if it does. If your hands get cold, which they probably will, hold them above your head for a couple minutes. The warm air from inside your suit will rise into your fingers."

"Interesting. Okay."

"We're not going to stay in a long time for your first dive, so you can see what it's like. Are you ready?"

"Ready as I'll ever be."

"Bob will be at the other end of the rope up top, so if you get worried, you can follow it and tug hard if you want Bob to help pull you back to the hole."

"Want me to tie it?" Bob asked, holding it up.

"No, thanks. I'll tie it to one of the loops at the back of the suit." The slight prick of fear that something could go wrong and she'd suffer because of it stabbed at him, and he wanted to be the one to ensure the rope was tied correctly. It was a little obsessive, and he knew it, but he couldn't help but check three times to make sure the rope was attached to her good and tight.

"You want to go in first, or follow me?"

"I guess I'll go first."

"You sure?" Most divers new to Antarctica wanted to follow, but he shouldn't have been surprised. Jordan Flynn obviously was the kind of woman who refused to let herself be intimidated, or if she was, she dealt with it head-on.

"I'm sure."

He watched as she waddled to the dive hole, smiling at the way she stiffened her shoulders at the edge as she looked down into the water. Standing there and taking a long pause to mentally ready herself like most people? Not Jordan. Three seconds later, she plunged in and he followed.

CHAPTER SIX

THE MAGIC OF underwater Antarctica never failed to thrill Zeke, no matter how many times he'd dived here. Gathering samples could wait until he saw how Jordan adjusted to this dark and amazing world. His chest feeling a little tight, he watched her, wondering if it might bother her to be under the ice. She pointed at the hundreds of red and pink starfish strewn across the ocean floor, the sea urchins and coral and brightly colored fish, her eyes looking at him with obvious delight, and the tightness eased.

He reached for her hand, partly because he wanted to hold it, and partly because it calmed the slight tension he couldn't seem to help feeling as they swam together. He showed her more of the amazing marine life, from beautiful to strange to the algae and small creatures he collected for his work.

It struck him that he hadn't felt a need to clear his ears, and realized the earplugs must actually be doing what they'd been designed to do. Jordan would be happy to hear that, and he sent her a thumbs-up. She sent one back, though she couldn't have known why he'd done it, and they smiled at one another through the darkly shimmering water as they explored.

Wandering around like sightseers, enjoying her curiosity and pleasure, weren't the reasons they were down here, though, and he reluctantly released her hand to leave her on her own, but not far away. He tucked the samples he collected into the bag attached to his waist while trying to keep an eye on her as she swam around.

He smiled at her excited gesturing when several Weddell seals swam close, looking at them curiously. A hole in the ice fairly close by, not large enough for humans but big enough for seals to slide through, was doubtless where they'd entered the water, and he pointed to it. She nodded, her smile obvious even behind the regulator between her teeth.

A buoyant feeling lifted him, and it wasn't the water, it was Jordan. Had he ever enjoyed seeing someone dive for the first time here as much as he was enjoying her obvious delight? The pleasure of being with her in the magical waters of the Antarctic made him forget how long they'd been down there until he realized his fingers felt cold, and knew hers were probably even colder.

He pointed upward, and she nodded and followed him for the five or so minutes it took to swim back to the dive hole. Getting out of the water and onto the ice was the hardest part of diving, with the weight of all the equipment, and he shoved her rear end from below. Hopefully, she wouldn't think he was using the situation as an excuse to touch her. Or know how much he wanted to.

Her flippers thrashed a few times before she disappeared, then he followed, heaving himself up to sit on the side of the hole. He shoved his mask up to see her lying prone on her back, her mask shoved off and her regulator loose on the ice, a wide smile on her face even as she sucked in air.

"I'm guessing you liked it?"

"Oh, my God." She turned that beautiful blue gaze to him. "*Liked* isn't even close to the word. That was... unbelievable. So much more amazing than I'd ever dreamed. The colors! I thought it might be too dark to see much sea life but...wow! The creatures! The blue! The light! I'm...speechless."

"Not quite speechless." He chuckled, and that buoyant feeling filled his chest again, though he knew that was a little ridiculous. She'd come to Antarctica on her own, to work and dive, and she'd have done it without him. Still, he couldn't help but feel lucky that he'd been the one to introduce this special world to her.

"You're making me feel like I need to learn to dive, too," Bob said.

"You should. It's...it's..."

"Unbelievable? Amazing?"

"Yes. And a lot more."

"Go ahead and lay there for a minute and catch your breath, warm up a little," Zeke said. "Bob and I will help you with your gear after I get mine off."

Jordan sat up, and he lifted the heavy tanks from her shoulders as she shrugged them off into his hands. Bob carried them and some of the other gear to the back of the van, and Zeke grabbed a small towel to dry Jordan's hair and face.

"Helps you warm up faster if you're dry." Looking into her eyes, he wiped down all visible skin, then watched her squeeze her hair with the towel. It nearly had him forgetting they were just dive partners, not lovers. He barely stopped himself from leaning in for the kiss he'd wanted all day.

"Thanks for…warming me up. Got to admit, I was starting to feel a little numb."

He lifted his hand to slowly wipe another trickle of water from her cheek as they stared at one another, both wearing small smiles.

"Oh, I almost forgot. I need to take your vitals after wearing the ear devices. Do you feel like they worked?"

"You know, I do. Pressure pain isn't something that affects me very often, but I didn't have to clear my ears at all. I'll use them every time I dive, and see if it's any different next time. But go ahead and take my vitals."

"Should have done it the second you got out of the water, but I was thinking about…other things." She quickly turned to pull a stethoscope from her bag with an abrupt motion that made him wonder if the "other things" might have been exactly what he'd been thinking about since the second they'd come on this excursion.

She stared straight at his chest as she pressed the stethoscope against it, her brows lowered in concentration. "Your respiratory rate is slightly elevated, as is your heart rate, but that's to be expected."

"Yes, I would expect that to be the case."

Her expression told him she might have guessed from the tone of his voice exactly what he meant, which had nothing to do with diving and everything to do with her standing so close and touching him, but she apparently decided not to comment on it.

"I'll get your gear, too, Zeke," Bob said as he ducked back into the tent.

"Thanks. Appreciate it."

Bob's arrival forced Zeke to rip his gaze and his mind off Jordan's body as she peeled the wet suit off her torso and down to her waist. The thin underlayer of clothing slowly being exposed were molded to her gentle curves, and it struck him all over again.

Jordan Flynn's body was pretty much perfect.

Zeke turned away to gather more equipment, and his equilibrium, as Jordan finished getting her gear off and her regular clothes back on. He huffed out a sigh of relief, even as he wondered why the hell the sight of her wearing what were in essence long johns seemed incredibly tempting and beyond sexy.

The cold air on his face as he ducked out of the tent helped cool his thoughts, and he packed the tanks in the car, with Bob and Jordan showing up a minute later with more gear. With the last of it stowed, Zeke shut the back doors of the van and the three of them got into the vehicle and headed back to the station.

Jordan talked enthusiastically to Bob about the dive, enough that Zeke didn't feel a need to chime in. The chatter let him pay attention to the route across the ice, or at least as much as he could, considering his hyperawareness of Jordan sitting only a few feet away. He couldn't seem to keep from glancing over to look at her, even as he told himself not to.

Her smooth skin was pink from the cold. Her dark hair was in wavy disarray, and he wanted to run his fingers through it and mess it up even more. Thoughts of kissing her breathless as he held her face in his hands invaded his brain all over again, and if she'd taken his vital signs again right that minute, she'd have found his heart rate elevated and his respiratory rate high again just from thinking about her. Which was absurd, he knew, but he couldn't seem to control the insistent desire for her that had taken over all his common sense.

Somehow, those thoughts had to stop, but he had a bad feeling that the only solution was to stop spending time with her. Something he didn't want to do. Which was a quandary he wasn't sure how to fix.

Bob's satellite phone rang in his pocket and Zeke saw in the rearview mirror that the other man was frowning as he listened. Then he looked up at Jordan. "Okay. I'll tell her. We just left. We're about an hour away from Fletcher, right, Zeke?"

"About that. What's wrong?"

"Is someone injured?" Jordan asked.

"Sick. Not sure what's wrong, but he's out at one of the temporary field stations. Apparently felt bad the past two days, but now he's worse. The person with him says there's no way he's capable of traveling behind the Ski-Doo."

"Did they say what his symptoms are?"

"Confusion. Fatigue. Irregular heart rate." Bob leaned forward. "I guess the guy with him wanted to bring him to Fletcher's clinic as soon as he heard you were here and had it open, but the man who felt sick was sure he just had a bug. And now he can hardly walk."

Jordan grabbed her field bag from the storage closet, hoping she hadn't missed anything she needed. Good thing she'd finished putting it all together before she'd let herself be distracted and interrupted by a certain sexy marine biologist/climatologist.

The whole time they'd been together in the van, in the tent and even in the water that certain something had simmered between them, hot and alive, whether she wanted it to or not. Her brain kept trying to remind her that he was not the kind of man she wanted a relationship with, and that she wasn't a fling kind of woman, but it seemed the rest of her wasn't listening too well.

Professionally? It was good for them to spend time together. He'd needed to get diving, and she'd wanted to start the earplug trial, not to mention that diving here had been the most glorious experience of her life.

Was there any way for her to benefit from their professional relationship, diving and exploring Antarctica, without falling deeper under Ezekiel Edwards's spell?

She had no idea, which felt a little scary. And now, here they were again, with no choice but to be working together, and physically close, on this field expedition. She couldn't go alone to see the patient, and it made no sense to ask someone else to join her when Zeke was the only other person currently at the station who had any kind of medical experience. He also had significant field experience, driving the snow machines across areas that might easily have crevasses and other hazards. She had to admit that having him take the lead on this trek, instead of someone she didn't know, made her feel more comfortable, safer, when it came to venturing into the Antarctic wilderness.

"I brought my field kit, too, just to see if there's something in here we'd need in addition to your supplies," Zeke said as he strode into the clinic. "The crew attached a stretcher to the sled behind the Ski-Doo, so we have what we need if we have to bring him back."

She looked up and paused in shrugging on the backpack she'd stuffed full of supplies, unexpectedly riveted by the way he looked, dressed ruggedly for this trip. How could he seem somehow bigger, tougher, even sexier, than when she'd left him only half an hour ago? Apparently, she was becoming more idiotic by the minute when it came to Ezekiel Edwards.

She heaved in a breath. "Ready when you are."

"You have thick gloves and hat? A balaclava you can cover your mouth with? It's going to be a long, cold ride."

"It's all shoved in my pockets." Much as she wanted to see more of this amazing, white world, she couldn't claim to be excited about traveling out in the cold for over an hour. Though she'd better get used to it, since she was going to be working here for months.

"Let's get going, then. Your chariot awaits."

She turned away from the magnetic power of his smile. She led the way out of the clinic, conscious of him following close behind, both surprised and impressed, damn it, that he wasn't immediately telling her which hallways and stairways they needed to go down to get to the hangar. Her usual good sense of direction was finally kicking in, and in a short time they'd arrived to see the snow machines were all ready to go. Obviously, the crew all were aware that time could be critical when they had no idea how sick the patient might be.

She looked up at Zeke after he'd tied their packs to the machines and checked the stretcher ropes. "Can we ride them? Or do we have to do the skiing-behind thing?"

"Skiing behind, I'm sorry to say. Not as much fun for you, I know." He flashed that knee-weakening smile. "But since you didn't get to practice the technique, you can just stand behind it while I hit the throttle for you, instead of doing it solo. It'll be faster, and with less risk of our all-important doctor wiping out the way Pete did."

"Are you surprised that I'm not going to complain about that?"

"No, because you're a smart woman." He handed her the skis. "Put these on, then take the ropes in your hands. I've already got them tied tight. After you get going, I'll catch up and take the lead."

"Got it."

"I'll be keeping an eye out on the landscape, looking for cracks that could mean a crevasse. But like I said before, sometimes they're covered with blowing snow, and you're in one before you know it. If that happens, remember what to do?"

"Let the ropes go."

"Right. We never like to lose a Ski-Doo, but better than a lost life." His smile was long gone, his dark eyes serious as they met hers.

"Should we separate out the medical gear onto both the machines, so we still have enough to check on the patient in case that should happen?"

"Obviously, you're a natural for working on the ice, thinking about things like that." His grim expression lightened. "Losing a machine and equipment doesn't happen often, but I have my first-aid bag on my machine, in case we need it. Not as much as you have, but enough."

Zeke Edwards may be a scientist and medic, not a doctor, but his carefully thought-out plans for this trip, as well as their earlier dive, showed he knew exactly what he was doing no matter which career hat he was wearing. She'd learned a fair amount about medical preparedness from her parents' work in developing nations, but it was clear he had a lot more knowledge about emergency situations outside a controlled environment like a hospital than she did.

"Give me a thumbs-up when you've got the ropes in hand and are ready," he said as he stood to the side of her machine. "And if you ever feel worried about something, or just get tired and want to stop and take a break, give me a thumbs-down and I'll get it turned off."

"Thanks, but I think I'll be fine. I mean, it's pulling me so not much exertion on my part, right?"

"We might hit some snow that's frozen into waves, which will make for a bumpy ride. If we do, that's pretty damned tiring, so don't try to be all tough, as I've seen you like to be, Dr. Flynn." His dark gaze met hers, held, before he gently tapped her nose with his gloved finger, moved it down to stroke her cheek, then tugged her balaclava up to cover everything but her eyes. "Taking a short break isn't a weakness, it means we'll be ready to do the work we need to do when we get there."

She nodded and held her breath as he reached for the throttle, hoping she didn't fall flat on her face, and gave the thumbs-up. The machine roared to a start, then began to move—slowly enough that she felt totally in control, thank heavens, her skis sliding across the crystalline, brilliant white landscape.

She couldn't see behind her, but heard his machine start, too, and in a short time he was beside her. His mouth was hidden behind a balaclava, but the smile in his eyes as they met hers was clear, and she couldn't help but smile, too. What a wild feeling to be pulled along, crossing this spectacular frozen desert that looked like nothing else on Earth.

Zeke's Ski-Doo moved to the lead, and stayed there

for a long time. Jordan had no idea how long, but he'd been right—the machine doing all the work didn't mean it wasn't hard, but the beauty of the landscape made it easy to ignore any discomfort. She noticed that he kept looking behind to see if she was there, and knowing he was keeping an eye on her helped her feel confident that they'd get there in one piece.

Eventually, he slowed his speed to match hers and they rode side by side, with him turning to tilt his head at her, a questioning look in his eyes, every ten minutes or so. When she'd respond with a thumbs-up, he'd send her a fist pump, sometimes releasing his handlebars for an enthusiastic double pump that made her chuckle.

By the time they got to the field camp, which she was surprised to see was just two tents set up next to one another, Jordan's arms were stiff and tired. But the exhilarating ride had been worth every ache, and she was glad they'd made good time to see what was going on with their patient.

Zeke stopped his machine, then ran to stop hers, too. He pulled his balaclava down beneath his chin, revealing a wide smile. He moved in close, his thigh pressing against her leg as he leaned in to grasp her thickly gloved hands with his. "You did absolutely great. Feeling okay?"

"Good. Okay, my arms hurt a little and my legs feel slightly numb, but wow. I loved it! Just incredible."

"I fell in love with Antarctica the first time I came here, and still love it today. You're a woman after my own heart."

Her own heart gave a little jerk, then thumped harder at the expression on his face. Sincere and admiring, and the attraction that kept simmering between them, no matter how she felt about it, hung in the cold air. Something that felt alive and electric and oh-so-warm. Her gaze dropped to his lips, mere inches from hers. Would they feel cold against hers? Or had they stayed warm behind that cloth? Maybe sharing one little kiss with him wouldn't be a big deal...

"Thank God you're here!"

They both turned to the voice. A man with a thick beard emerged from one of the tents, a deeply worried expression on his face.

Time to forget about all that zing between her and Zeke that she still wasn't sure how to deal with, and get to work.

She dismounted the snow machine and held out her hand. "I'm Dr. Jordan Flynn. And this is Dr. Zeke Edwards, who's a marine biologist but also a field medic."

"Dave Crabtree. Really appreciate you coming out here."

"I assume the patient is in one of these tents?"

"Yes. He's been in a lot of pain, and having trouble moving his arms and legs. Then he got sick to his stomach, but kept saying he was sure it was just a bug that would pass. When he started acting confused earlier today and his legs seemed weaker than ever, I knew he needed to be seen by a doc, but also knew there was no way to get him to Fletcher's hospital without a stretcher here to pull him on."

"That's what we're here for." She turned to Zeke. "Let's get the supply bags, then check him out."

"I'll get them. You go on in."

Yet again, Zeke was proving what a great partner he was in these kinds of situations, fine with being her backup instead of wanting to see the patient at the same time she did to offer his opinions. She followed Dave, ducking into the tent behind him. There was barely enough room for the three of them, and it would be even more crowded once Zeke came in, but that couldn't be helped.

The patient lay inside a sleeping bag, his eyelids flickering open as she came to kneel next to him.

"I'm Dr. Flynn. What's your name?"

He didn't respond for a moment, which was alarming. Finally, he replied, "Jim Reynolds. Thanks…for coming."

"Tell me what's going on."

"My muscles feel…strange. Hurt. My arms and legs especially. Can hardly move them. Got sick to my stomach a couple times."

"When did you first start to feel this way?"

"Uh, I think…yesterday morning."

"Okay. I'm going to take your vital signs." She looked up at Zeke, who'd just come inside the tent but already had the field bags open and was handing her a stethoscope. "Can you find the oxygen saturation monitor?"

"Right here." Zeke clipped it to the patient's fingertip as Jordan listened to his lungs, then had Jim hold a thermometer under his tongue while she felt his pulse.

"Your heart rate is elevated." She frowned, because it was surprisingly fast. "Can you get me the blood pressure cuff, please?"

Zeke already had it in his hand and held it out to her. "Want me to put it around his arm and get the reading?"

"Yes, thanks. I'm going to check his pulse again." Maybe she'd gotten it wrong the first time, but no. Still far faster than it should be.

"Blood pressure is low," Zeke said, his eyes meeting hers, and she nodded.

"Let me see the thermometer now, Jim," she said, sliding it from beneath his tongue. Significantly febrile, and she held it up to show Zeke, then the results of the oxygen saturation, which was also elevated.

Their eyes met again. The combination of symptoms and test results weren't close to giving her a clinical diagnosis. She definitely needed to ask more questions to see if his answers would provide more clues.

"Tell me about your last few days here, Jim. You came by snow machine?"

"Yeah. Got here pretty early. Spent the afternoon climbing up to get some ice core samples until it got dark about ten."

"That was a damn tiring day," Dave added. "We both felt wiped out. Then the next day we took the machines to a high glacier farther out, and did some more climbing and core collection."

"So, a lot of exertion in a pretty short period of time. How long have you been in Antarctica?"

"Got here early this week."

"Probably on the same boat we did," Zeke murmured.

Sounded likely. She looked up at Zeke and nodded before turning back to the patient. "Tell me about your stomach pain. Are your bowels working? Does your urine seem normal?"

"Yeah." Jim's brows lowered as he seemed to think. "Actually, urine is really dark. Figured I'm a little dehydrated. Thought that might be why my stomach was hurting, too, but when I started throwing up, I realized it must be a bug. Been drinking water to get better hydrated and flush out whatever was making me sick."

"Have you been drinking alcohol, as well? More than normal?"

"Well, yeah. I have." His lips twisted. "Been hitting the bourbon to help me sleep. My back's been hurting like hell, and keeping me awake, and it's not easy to sleep in these tents, anyway."

"I see. I think I know what's probably going on, Jim." She looked up at Zeke again, a feeling of triumph filling her chest as the likely diagnosis now seemed clear. "Rhabdomyolysis. Extreme exertion compared to what he's used to doing at home. Dehydration. Excess alcohol contributing."

"Rhabdo?" Zeke raised his brows, then smiled and gave her a nodding salute. "That's one quick diagnosis, Doctor, but I bet you're absolutely right. I never would have figured that out."

"You might have, with more questions and testing."

"Nope. My field skills are good when it comes to injuries, heart attack and stroke—but rhabdo? That's out of my wheelhouse. Congratulations."

The warmth and admiration in his words put a little glow in her chest, which was ridiculous. As though she deserved credit for coming up with a diagnosis most any other doctor would have been able to figure out. But coming from Zeke, it seemed to mean something more than a simple compliment.

"So, now what?" Dave asked.

"We insert an IV line in to push fluids. Give him some analgesics to help with his pain, then get him to the hospital at Fletcher Station to continue with the fluids and keep him under observation for a couple days."

"Can't I just stay here with the IV in for a day or so?"

"Rhabdo is no joke, Jim. It's not something you can just let ride its course. Liver or kidney damage can occur if you're not carefully monitored."

"Here's the IV," Zeke said. "I'll get the bag of fluids ready to go."

Jordan shoved up Jim's sleeve, cleaned the skin and got the IV placed in his arm. Zeke attached the bag of fluid, placed the analgesic pills on Jim's tongue and tipped a water bottle into his mouth to help him swallow, then stood.

"Glad you figured out the rhabdo, and we have what we need to push fluids. But we do have a problem," Zeke said.

She looked up at him, surprised at how serious he looked. "What's that?"

"No way can we get him back to Fletcher tonight."

"What? Why not?"

"Sun sets tonight at ten p.m. and it's now nine. It's not safe to drive the Ski-Doos when it's dark, or even in very low light, because you can't keep an eye out for cracks. We'll have to stay here for the night, and take him back in the morning."

Jordan realized her mouth was hanging open as she stared at him, and forced it shut, her heart beating in her throat. "You mean, the four of us cram into these two tents?"

"No Antarctic explorer goes anywhere without a tent and sleeping bags, in case a storm moves in. Or it gets dark. Or some other emergency arises, like this, where we had to come right away even though it was getting late when we left."

"A tent? As in one?" Her voice came out in a little gasp.

"One tent. A tight squeeze for two people, I admit. But I'm sure you knew life could get tough sometimes working at the south pole." He stood and his grim expression showed he wasn't any happier about the situation than she was. "I guess this is one of those times, and we'll just have to deal with it."

CHAPTER SEVEN

WITH THE WIND kicking powdery gusts of snow into their faces, Zeke aimed the headlamp attached to his forehead at the tent, trying to get it set up as quickly as possible so Jordan could get out of the cold air. She hadn't uttered a word of complaint. But what he could see of her face beneath her balaclava, bandanna and hat as she helped him pound stakes into the ice showed her eyes were watering, and she kept slapping her mittens together to warm her hands.

The look of horror on her face when he'd told her they'd have to share this tent would have been almost comical, if he hadn't shared the same damn concern. The chemistry shimmering between them all day couldn't be denied. But he didn't do relationships, and it was pretty clear that she didn't want to go there, either.

The two of them being in extremely close quarters for the night was going to tax his already shaky self-control, and she probably knew that. But he couldn't and wouldn't make love with Jordan, even if she wanted to, because he wasn't the kind of man she deserved. Being close to someone, caring about someone, wasn't something he wanted in his life. Not ever.

He had to give her credit, though. Once the initial

shock had passed, she'd been completely calm and professional, immediately jumping in to help with their gear and set up the tent. Working together made the process go as fast as possible, even with the low visibility they had to deal with.

"That's about it," he said, tying down a corner. "Go ahead and get inside, so you can warm up. I just have a couple little things to finish."

"Not fair for you to be out here doing the work alone. What's left?"

He glanced at her pinched face, her nose and cheeks the color of a scarlet sea star, and had to admire the hell out of her. He'd worked with countless people during his many Antarctic expeditions, and plenty—both men and women—had been happy to duck out of cold wind when given the chance.

"I appreciate the offer. But—"

"Zeke!" She pointed behind him and her face lit with wonder. "Is that…? Oh, my gosh, that has to be the aurora australis!"

He turned and, sure enough, the night sky was lit with ribbons of green light, curling to meet luminous, salmon-pink waves, rising like a shimmering wall from the horizon to the stars. "Well, damn. You get to see it, after all, and that one's a beauty. You must have brought some serious good luck," he said, so glad she was getting to see this incredible phenomenon that everyone coming down here wanted to experience, but rarely did after September. "Last two times I came in the summer I didn't get to see it at all. Nothing like it, is there?"

"It's…unbelievable," she breathed, her expression rapt as she stared. "I hardly dared to hope I'd get to see it, since it's going to be twenty-four hours of sun in, what? Three or four days?"

"Something like that." He finished the last tent tie, then switched off his headlamp. The darkness fell around them as the green and pink ribbons undulated across the sky. He moved to stand behind her, resting his hands on her shoulders. "I always feel like the luckiest guy on Earth when this happens. It's like being in another universe, don't you think? Or acting in a movie with special effects, but this is real. Electrons, atoms and molecules colliding with the Earth's magnetic core. Wonders all around us, creating a spectacle like none other."

"The photos I've seen are beautiful, but this? Actually seeing it? More stunning than I could even imagine."

The heavenly display seemed to envelop them, wrap around them, making Zeke feel as though they were strangely cocooned together, alone in the universe, and he held her with her back close against his chest. His arms moved to circle her waist, trying to shield her from the biting wind as they watched the colors swirl across the sky, both of them silent for a long time.

Problem was, neither of them were as bundled as they needed to be, since they'd only planned to be out here as long as it took to set up the tent. As minutes passed, the raw, frigid air began to seep through his gloves and layers of clothes, and he knew she had to be feeling it, too.

It struck him that standing beneath this celestial wonder, sharing it with Jordan, was something he'd never forget. He hated for the moment to end, but knew staying out here any longer wasn't a good idea. Regret weighed in his chest, knowing he'd never experience anything like this again. He lowered his head and pressed his cheek to her temple, and even through the layers felt her warmth.

"I hate to say it, but probably we should go inside and warm up away from this wind. Our bodies will put off more heat than you'd think, and fill the tent space pretty well, but if we get too cold, it'll be hard to get comfortable again."

She turned in his arms, and the look of wonder and awe and joy on her face had him holding her a little tighter, feeling beyond blessed that they'd seen the wonder of the lights together. "I appreciate you staying out here with me. For keeping me as warm as you could, so I could soak in that incredible sight. It's something I'll never forget. Thank you."

"No thanks necessary." The words came out gruff, his throat a little tight that she would thank him for holding her close in the cold Antarctic air. God knew he'd done it both to keep her warm, and because folding her into his arms was something he'd wanted for days, and now had experienced for real. "I feel lucky every time I get to see it. And getting to share it with someone seeing the lights for the first time? That feels…good."

"The word *good* is not even close to what I'm feeling right now."

Something about the way she said it, combined with the way she was looking at him, sent his heart beating a little harder, his breath a little short. He couldn't help but let his gaze lower to her lips, pink from the cold, wanting to kiss her even more than he'd wanted to earlier, which seemed impossible. Then she leaned into him, grasped his shoulders in her hands, moved them to his cheeks. Tipped her face up to his and had a look in her eyes that told him she was thinking about that first night they met. How it had felt when he'd held her in his arms. All the times since that he hadn't been able to stop thinking about it, either.

She rose onto her toes, and with a soft groan, he took the invitation. Lowered his mouth to touch hers. Moved across the sweetness of her cold lips. Let his tongue slip inside her warm mouth, tasting and exploring, going deeper, and a gasp of obvious pleasure left her mouth and swirled into his.

"Zeke." She said it in a way that showed him she was feeling every bit as aroused as he was. He could feel the thin string of control he'd tried to maintain snap as he gave in to the desire filling his chest and stirring his body. He held her close, pulling her hard against him, wishing they weren't both wearing heavy snowsuits and gloves that restricted his ability to feel the curves and heat of her body. He kissed her until he lost all sense of time and place, thinking of nothing but how perfect she felt in his arms. How she tasted even better than he'd imagined, and how he wanted more. And more. And more.

A strong gust of wind blew across them, creating a snow devil that swirled up from the ground, spattering tiny shards of ice against the exposed skin of their faces, finally forcing them to pull apart. Breathing hard, they stared at one another until the snow had them squinting against it, and ducking their heads to protect themselves.

"Let's get inside," he said, grasping her arm and leading her to the small round opening in the tent, barely visible through the snow churning in the darkness. "Go in headfirst. I'll get the sleeping bags, then follow you."

He switched his headlamp back on, found the gear they needed to sleep comfortably for the night, then squeezed into the tent. "Here's a flashlight in case you need it," he said, handing it to her. "Your sleeping bag and an extra blanket."

"What about my other things?"

He looked up at her as he unrolled his sleeping bag onto the cold tent floor. "What do you need?"

"My eye mask and white-noise machine," she said with an impish smile.

"Well, damn. Why didn't I remember those for a wilderness roughing-it trip?" He loved her sense of humor, and had to laugh. Loved spending time with her, period. "Do you really use those all the time?"

"All the time. I told you I lived different places around the world as a kid, going wherever my parents worked. Believe me, those two things help you sleep no matter where you are."

"Your parents are doctors, you said. So why did they travel so much?"

"They work for an organization that sends medical teams to places lacking health care. It also responds when there are disasters like earthquakes and hurricanes."

"I…admire that. Those things are often a whole lot worse than anyone can tell from TV clips. The numbers they give about injured and killed don't tell the story. Every person affected is loved by someone." His throat closed at the memories, and since he didn't want her to see anything on his face that might make her ask questions, he busied himself getting some of the supplies set out, including a water jug.

"Drink some," he said, handing it to her. "You already know, Dr. Flynn, that in extreme cold, dehydration is a big issue." He watched her as she took a deep drink, her tongue licking a few drops from her lips. Memories of what they'd just shared outside tempted him to lean over and kiss her wet mouth all over again.

Maybe she saw a gleam in his eye, because she turned away, and he tried to think of that as a good thing, even though it didn't feel like it. She scooted down into her sleeping bag. Her gaze met his, and damn if all the humor had left her eyes, replaced by a serious look. "So, about the kissing. I admit it was incredibly special out under the lights and I… I really enjoyed it." She gave a small laugh. "A lot. Which I'm sure you noticed. I like you. I like spending time with you. But it's not a good idea."

"Getting to kiss you under the southern lights is about as good as anything will ever get in this world." Zeke reached to cup her face in his palm, and the way she pressed her cheek against it was at odds with what she'd just said. "But you're right. Anything more than friendship between us isn't a good idea."

"I have to admit I'm totally surprised you just said that. But I'm glad you're not mad at me."

"I'm not mad at you." He wasn't going to tell her why he felt that way, but wanted to know why she did. If it wasn't him, what was it? Had some guy hurt her?

He slid into his sleeping bag and looked at her, enjoying the intimate feeling of their faces being so close to one another, of being able to see the little dark flecks in her beautiful eyes. He wasn't sure what to do, or not to do. But talking seemed like a good first step.

"Since you don't dislike me, and I've agreed that our getting involved isn't something we want to do, tell me about you. Do you not do relationships?" If that was the case, she'd be more like him than he ever would have expected.

"It's not important," she said, staring up at the top of the tent. Her voice sounded a little forlorn, and he knew that talking about things from your past that still bothered you was always cathartic. Not that he ever did. He didn't like to go back in time and face failures and think about how things could have been different any more than he had to. But getting Jordan to confide whatever it was that was bothering her, then hopefully feel better about it, felt important.

He reached over and stroked her hair. Would have held her hand, except her head was the only part of her outside the sleeping bag. "I'm a good listener. And you can count on me to keep whatever you tell me just between us."

"Some of it's silly. I mean, it goes all the way back to being a little girl and how I felt when we'd go visit my grandparents and cousins maybe once every few years."

"Feelings are never silly," he said quietly. "We feel what we feel. So tell me about little-girl Jordan."

She sighed and turned her head to look at him again. "Part of me knows I had a special childhood. Living so many places and being exposed to so many cultures taught me a lot and shaped me in a way most kids don't get shaped, you know? But there was a huge negative that came with never having roots anywhere. No place I could really call home."

"I understand roots. They can be an important part of your life. Sometimes the most important part."

"I wouldn't know. So tell me about yours."

"We're talking about you." Touching her face again helped him shove down the familiar pain. "If you never experienced having a place to call home, what made you think you even wanted that?"

"I'd see my cousins, and how close they were, on those rare times we visited. Saw them playing with neighborhood friends, everybody knowing each other so well. I never felt like I fit in. I was the outsider, and wanted in so badly. After being there a couple weeks, I'd start to feel like I was getting there, maybe starting to be part of the family. Then we'd leave again."

"That would be hard for a kid." His own family had meant so much to him, and when he'd lost them, a part of who he was had gotten lost, too. "Did your parents know you felt that way?"

"I told them, and they tried to understand. When I was fourteen, they even offered to have me live with my grandparents for a year and experience the life I craved, but by then, my outsider status felt too entrenched, you know? I was… I hate to admit it, but I felt afraid that I'd never fit in and be stuck there and miserable, anyway. So I stayed with my parents and our gypsy lifestyle." She turned and gave him a half smile, obviously trying to lighten the mood. "Except we missed out on that whole gypsy-caravan thing—it was just us. And honestly, hearing myself talk, I sound ungrateful for all the good things my upbringing brought me."

Her eyes looked troubled, and the guilt he saw there tugged at his heart. "A person can appreciate things about their life and still wish it might have been different."

"I suppose. But anyway." Her voice brightened even more. "I went to medical school in the States, moved to England and fell in love with the place. I decided that was where I was going to put down the roots I never had. Have a good job, marry a nice man, live in a real house that belongs to us and have a small brood of kiddos. Like a normal person. Maybe that sounds boring to you, but it's what I want. It's what I've wanted forever."

"Doesn't sound boring." Again, he shoved down the memories of his own roots. His own family. "So, let me read between the lines. Wanting the whole husband-and-family-and-roots thing means a short-term affair with anyone who doesn't qualify as a potential mate isn't going to happen."

"You are remarkably astute."

Her smile was back, the real one that lit her face and made him smile, too, and he was glad that getting her to talk had turned out to be a good thing. He stroked her soft hair again, ran his fingertip down her cheek, because he needed to touch her. "I knew from the second I met you that you're a special woman. Adventurous, courageous, smart and damned beautiful on top of it all. You deserve everything you want in life. And you're right that I don't qualify. More than you know."

He leaned across the few inches between them and pressed his lips to her cheek. Slid them over her soft skin to give her lush mouth one last kiss, his heart squeezing that he couldn't be the kind of man she wanted. "Good night, Dr. Flynn. You should know that in the short time we've spent together, there are several things you've taught me. One just tonight."

"That I'm astonishingly conventional?"

"No." He swallowed, somehow forcing humor into

his voice that he suddenly wasn't feeling at all. "That I need to add eye masks to the emergency kits on the Ski-Doo. And invest in a battery-operated white-noise machine."

Her soft laughter sneaked into his chest and stayed there. It soothed the ache around his heart and warmed him until he fell asleep, the sound of her soft breathing in his ears better than any white-noise machine could ever be.

CHAPTER EIGHT

THE DRAKE PASSAGE had finally calmed and the boat would apparently be docking any second, which Jordan was glad about. She wanted to be busier, and she also wanted to get more divers to try the earplug device. Zeke had said he thought it worked, which was exciting, but she needed a lot of data, not just one man's opinion, from one dive.

Zeke. She didn't want to admit it to herself, but she missed seeing him. In the light of day, outside the intimate cocoon of that tent, she'd felt a little embarrassed at her confessions about her childhood longings that had formed what she'd decided she wanted for her adulthood.

But he'd been a wonderful listener, and his words in response had been supportive, not critical. Ever since they'd been back at the station, he hadn't come to sit next to her in the galley. Hadn't asked her to dive with him again. She hadn't even caught him watching her as she ate, the way she had the first few days she'd been there, just sending her a casual wave and a smile if they saw one another across the room.

She should be glad about that. The complication of a relationship with him here, when there could be no future for them after the expedition was over, wasn't worth it. The way she'd reacted to his kisses, to his smiles, to his touch, told her she could have fallen way too hard for the man, and for what? Six months of fun, followed by months of missing him? Or worse, meeting men at home and feeling like they just didn't measure up?

She huffed out a long breath. That would be terrible and she could absolutely see it happening. In so many ways, Zeke Edwards was larger than life, but he was *not* the "forever after" she wanted. He'd even told her as much. No, the future love of her life was waiting somewhere for her in London, and with any luck, she'd be meeting him in the not-too-distant future after she left Antarctica.

So why couldn't she get Ezekiel Edwards off her mind?

Practically every time she thought of the amazing aurora australis, memories of the seductive kiss they'd shared made her lips tingle and her mouth water. She'd thought of him during the next rounds of first-aid training, which he hadn't come to, even though last time he'd said he'd help again. She'd missed his teasing smile and amused eyes and the warmth he brought to every room the minute he walked in.

Fletcher Station was big enough that they rarely ran into each other, and yet she found herself looking for him wherever she went, hoping to see him. And that was just plain annoying. Ridiculous, when she'd been the one to tell him an ice affair was not on her list of things to do, and he'd fully agreed that he didn't want one, either. Thank heavens that, with so many new people arriving today, more work would provide the distraction she apparently needed.

She heaved a sigh and went to the hospital wing to check on Jim Reynolds, pleased to see how much better he looked than he had a few days ago in that tent when the rhabdomyolysis had left him temporarily paralyzed.

"How are you feeling? Good to see you've got some color back in your face," she said as she checked his pulse and listened to his lungs.

"I feel okay. Ready to go back to work."

"Your vital signs are all normal now, so I'm discharging you today. Which I'm sure you're glad about." She smiled. "But I want you to take it easy here at the station before you head into the field again. And when you do, don't try to climb and extract ice cores for hours on end. Be sure to pace yourself."

"I will, Dr. Flynn." He nodded. "Dave was just in here about ten minutes ago, and he said the next boat has already docked and everyone's on their way here. He's going to recruit more crew to come with us on our next trip to the mountains in a couple days, so we won't be working alone for nearly as many hours."

"Glad to hear that." She wrote out instructions for him, and made some notes into the computer. "I'll be back soon with your clothes, and medication that I want you to take for another week."

The distant ping of the satellite phone, which only worked a few hours a day, surprised her, and she hurried to the clinic office to answer it. Who could be calling? Her stomach tightened at the thought that it might be someone reporting another medical crisis to deal with in the field.

"Dr. Flynn."

"Hey, you! How's it going at the south pole for the amazing Jordan Flynn?"

The voice of her old med school roommate had her relaxing and smiling, and she realized she'd missed the kind of normal friends and normal conversations she took for granted at work back home. "Lia! How great to hear your voice. It's good down here. So beautiful, you almost can't believe it. It's been slow, work-wise, since the next boats were a few days late because of weather. But they're here now, so I'll be superbusy soon."

"I want pics when you can send some. Can't imagine you down there! Have you had a chance to test your parents' earplug thing yet?"

"I went on one dive, and tried them myself. And one other diver did, as well. Too small a sample, obviously, with uncertain results so far. I have to collect a lot more data, which I'll be getting soon now that more divers are here." She decided she wouldn't say anything about supersexy Zeke, because Lia would probably be shocked that she was attracted to someone here, and they weren't involved with each other, anyway. "Being underwater, seeing all the sea life, is mind-blowing."

"Diving down there sounds crazy to me, but you've always been an adventurer."

An adventurer. That had been true, from the way she'd grown up. But this probably would be her last adventure for a while. "Tell me about you. Are things… bad at home?"

"Yes. Worse than bad." Lia's voice turned angry, which was so unlike her. Jordan knew she must be facing a mess. "My father's still missing, but I know it's only because he doesn't want to be found. I have a private investigator on his tail, but so far no luck. No matter how much time and money it takes, I'm determined to find him. I didn't train to be a surgeon to stay here in my little Portuguese village and run it instead of working in medicine, just because he's abandoned everyone. But…anyway. I'll deal with it."

"I'm so sorry you're going through this." Poor Lia, having to step into her father's role at the family vineyard in Portugal. As if she hadn't had enough trouble and heartache after the big fire there, and her fiancé taking off and completely disappearing right before they were to get married. Everyone had seemed so happy, with all the plans for the wedding going so beautifully, and Jordan had been so pleased when Lia asked her to be her maid of honor. She never would have dreamed that Weston was apparently a huge jerk. "I know you probably couldn't get away, with all you have going on there, but if by chance you want a break from all that, there's a job posted for another doctor down here. If you're at all interested."

"Oh, I'd love to come work with you there, and see that place! I doubt I could make it happen, but it does sound interesting."

"I'll email you the link from the job board, so you can look at it. Meanwhile, I hope—"

Static suddenly filled the line, and after trying to reconnect with Lia for a few minutes, she gave up. The satellite phones here had a mind of their own, and having only short windows to talk with people, or receive TV news from the world, was something she'd soon learned that everyone accepted as part of life in Antarctica.

She set the phone back down on the desk and wondered if Zeke ever talked to people back home. Family, or coworkers. Or old girlfriends.

There the man was, back in her brain again, and she smacked herself on the head, only to wince because her bruise wasn't fully healed. How long would it be before she stopped thinking about him twenty times a day?

She heard the outer door open, and went to see who it was. A man walked into the clinic with a young woman by his side and held out his hand with a smile. "You must be Jordan Flynn. I'm Tony Bradshaw, the medical director, as you might have guessed. This is Megan Mackie, the nurse who's going to be working with us. Sorry to be late getting here. Weather was dicey even when we were finally able to cross, but we made it."

"A little wild when I crossed, too," Jordan said. The smile she sent the two of them faltered a little as she remembered that crazy first night in her cabin. Her split-open head. Being held in Zeke's arms. "Glad you're here now, though."

"Has it been hard working without help?"

"Only about seventy-five people came on the first boat with me, and once I got the medical center set up and the field bags done, I felt like I was looking for work, to be honest. Though getting baseline physicals has kept me fairly busy, and you probably remember I'm running a trial on earplugs designed to address barotrauma."

"I do remember that. I'll be interested to see how the trial turns out." He slowly ran his hand down his face and seemed to force another smile, and she wondered how tired the man might be after the long delay and the rough Drake Channel crossing they'd gone through.

She also had to wonder if he might have worked at

a different Antarctic station over the winter, since the man was about as pale as a human could be. But now wasn't the time to ask personal questions. They'd be working together for months, and there'd be plenty of time to learn about the other two medical staff working with her.

"I'm so excited to be working in Antarctica," Megan said. "Just the drive from the ferry was unbelievable."

"It's an amazing place, that's for sure." She opened her mouth to share the utterly magical experience of seeing the aurora australis but then didn't, because she realized she didn't want to talk about it, wanting to hold the memory close to her heart instead.

Sharing that moment with Zeke had made it more special, more intimate, more incredible than if she'd experienced it with anyone else. Enveloped by that dark night sky filled with stars and ribbons of light that had seemed to bind them together. A feeling of closeness that had her reaching up to kiss him without thought about whether she should or shouldn't, because it had just felt right.

"I heard there's a party tonight," Megan said enthusiastically. "So everyone can get acquainted. Are you going?"

A party? Jordan's feeling of melancholy suddenly faded as she wondered if Zeke would be there. "I hadn't heard. When is it?"

"They announced it on the boat. At the galley, wherever that is. Tonight at seven. Games and a band and stuff. Sounds fun."

"I'll stop by to meet some of the new crew. It'll be a good opportunity to find new divers to be part of my trial." And an opportunity to see Zeke Edwards's handsome face again. There might not be any point in her wanting to, but she did, anyway. Even if it was just from across the room.

It seemed impossible that the somewhat sterile-looking galley had been transformed into something resembling a cross between a disco and a casino. Colored lights moved across a dance floor, and country music blasted from huge speakers flanking the band. Jordan scanned the room for Zeke and, when she didn't see him, scolded herself for the disappointment she felt.

This party was a chance to make new friends, not moon over Zeke when they'd both agreed to cool the heat and stop with the kisses. She forced herself to look at the other tables for people to sit with, and saw a smiling Megan surrounded by young men. The male to female ratio at Fletcher Station was heavily skewed, and a pretty young woman was guaranteed to get a lot of attention.

Jordan smiled, glad the nurse was obviously getting along just fine. She wandered to a long table covered with finger foods, put some on a plate and settled into a chair at a small round table. She watched people laughing and dancing and decided that, when she was done eating, she'd get out of her work rut and get up there, too. Not wanting an affair with someone down here didn't mean she couldn't have other kinds of fun, right?

A guy asked if she wanted to dance. When she turned to answer, her heart jolted as she saw a tall, eye-catching man walk in the door. He was smiling and joking with Bob Shamansky and several other men, and suddenly she found it hard to swallow her food as her breath caught in her throat.

Really, Jordan? Back to this?

But scolding herself didn't stop her heart from beating harder and her stomach from getting that silly fluttery feeling. She said something to answer the man about dancing but had no clue how she'd responded, her focus entirely on Zeke.

So much for getting over her unwitting fascination with the man.

As though he knew exactly where she was, his head turned and their eyes met. The inexplicable electricity between them seemed to spark all the way across the room, raising the hair on her arms and leaving her breathless.

He moved toward her with a slow, steady gait, and her heart seemed to beat harder with every step. They just looked at one another, and it felt strange and thrilling and Jordan had no idea what to do about this thing between them that they'd agreed they didn't want, except to ask him to sit with her and maybe she'd figure it out.

"Would you—"

"Is this seat taken?"

A sexy smile slowly spread across his face and she laughed a little nervously. "No. Not taken. Would you like to sit down?"

"Thank you." He lowered his long body into the chair and scooted it right next to hers. "It's a little loud in here. But the music is good, don't you think?"

"I'm not normally a country music fan, but I do like this band. Especially the lyrics."

"The one about crying in your beer? Or the guy who chooses fishing over his girlfriend?"

"Hard to pick a favorite. Is there one about a scuba

diver who chooses zooplankton over a woman? Maybe you should write that one."

She'd meant it as a joke to cover her nervousness, but the eyes looking into hers weren't laughing. "Believe me, if I was a different kind of man, I'd want both. The zooplankton, and a beautiful woman who liked to dive for it with me."

She could feel her pulse fluttering in her throat. The man staring at her with what looked like longing in his gaze didn't seem to be the same man she'd shared a tent with. The man who'd agreed that anything between them was a bad idea. This man seemed to be eating her up whole with his eyes, and she found herself leaning close, all words drying up in her throat.

His big hand curled around her arm, slid down to grasp hers. "Want to dance?"

CHAPTER NINE

NOT SURE WHAT would happen if she tried to speak again, Jordan simply nodded, and they moved to the dance floor. He wrapped one arm around her waist and tucked her close against him, breasts to chest, their gazes fused, and her hand snaked up to the back of his neck before she'd even realized it. The music seemed to beat a primal rhythm through her body and the connection between them felt so intense it was like nothing she'd ever experienced in her life.

Neither spoke, and it almost felt like a dream. A different kind of dream than being underwater with him, but a fantasy nonetheless. Colored lights skimmed across his face, illuminating the dips and planes, his sensual lips, his dark eyes, and as they moved slowly together, his cheek pressed to her temple and it felt almost as though they were one, completely alone among all the other dancers in the room.

When the music stopped, it felt like they parted in slow motion, and she swayed forward, feeling bereft as they just looked at one another.

"You want a drink?" he asked, his voice rough.

"I… Yes, please. A glass of wine."

He nodded and went to the bar that had been set up

for the night. The line was fairly long, and Jordan figured she should sit down again, especially since her knees felt weak and wobbly. The band took a break, and someone turned on the television that was attached high on one of the galley's walls, which she now knew meant the satellite was working and they'd grab some news from the world outside Antarctica while they could.

Only half listening to the TV announcer, she tried to concentrate on the screen instead of a certain überhandsome marine biologist and her reaction to him and what, if anything, she was prepared to do about it. Maybe ruling out a fling with him had been an all-wrong decision, except he'd agreed it was wrong, hadn't he?

Except the man who'd held her in his arms tonight didn't seem to feel that way anymore, which was beyond confusing.

Deep in thought, she stared up at the television. Then the disturbing images caught her attention for real.

"Devastating flooding and wind speeds up to one hundred fifty miles an hour from the category five hurricane has destroyed countless homes in North and South Carolina, including many whose occupants had chosen not to evacuate. Uprooted trees and floodwaters have destroyed cars, bridges and roads, with some people taking refuge on their roofs. Helicopter crews have had to temporarily halt the rescue of survivors until the wind speeds have died down."

The images were horrible—homes blown away, cars floating down streets, boats smashed and awash on beaches and at marinas. She turned to look at Zeke, not even knowing why that was her first reaction to the terrible news. Maybe to see if he was watching the devastation. As a climatologist, hurricanes had to be part of his specialty, she knew, so he'd definitely want to know more about it.

Except his expression wasn't one of professional interest. He was standing now, staring at the screen, his hands fisted on a table. Maybe the lighting was creating an illusion, but it seemed his skin had turned a little gray, his eyes shadowed. His lips were pressed tightly together. He stood motionless as Bob Shamansky came to stand next to him, putting his hand on Zeke's shoulder and looking concerned as he spoke.

Zeke responded with a jerky nod, then, in a sudden movement, left the table to stride out the door with Bob watching him go.

Shocked that he'd left without a word to her, Jordan found herself walking over to Bob. She needed to know why Zeke had looked so upset, then had abruptly left without getting their drinks. Maybe he needed to record data about the storm for his work, but somehow she knew it was more than that.

"Bob. Is something wrong with Zeke? He seemed… upset."

Bob turned to her, his expression grim. "I'm not sure. But I'm guessing this kind of thing might bring back bad memories."

"Memories of what?"

"I know he grew up in New Orleans, and was visiting there when Hurricane Katrina hit. He's never said much, so I don't know how he might have been personally affected. Maybe he doesn't like to talk about it because the city was such a wreck afterward, with almost everyone displaced. Couldn't have felt good to have the place you grew up in destroyed like that."

So, hurricanes were personal to him, not just part of

what he did for a living, wanting to slow the impact of climate change. Warmer ocean waters meant stronger hurricanes and more devastation. More lives lost. Had Katrina been part of the reason he'd gone into marine biology and climatology?

When she'd shared her story in the tent, he'd talked about roots being important. Perhaps having his uprooted from that storm was a memory he didn't like to be reminded of.

Should she reach out to him, if he was upset? Be there for him, the way he'd been there for her when she'd hit her head? When she'd needed his help diving, and going into the field to see Jim Reynolds?

Maybe he wouldn't welcome her if she went to talk to him. Maybe he just wanted to be alone. In fact, he probably did, or he would have come back to tell her he had to leave, right?

She pictured the way his face had looked just now and decided that, no matter what, she wanted to be there for him, as his friend, if nothing else. Inhaling a deep breath, she left the party.

She kept going down the hallway, realizing she had no idea where to find him. The first places to look would be the marine biology lab, his office and the aquarium.

But he wasn't in any of those places. She asked the few people she ran into if they'd seen him, or knew where he was, but got shrugs and shaking heads in response.

Maybe he'd gone to his cabin, wanting to be alone. And if he did, would it be pushy of her to go there?

She didn't know. God, she just didn't know. But what kind of friend wouldn't check on him, and find out if he was okay? A bad friend, that's what. And she cared about him, whatever the status of their relationship. So she was going to knock on his door, and if he told her to go away, she would.

That decision had her straightening her shoulders and moving forward. Problem was, she had another hurdle to jump. She knew he lived in Pod B, but had no idea which cabin was his. It took her ten minutes to find a roster listing names and numbers, and every minute of it had her feeling more anxious, though she reminded herself she might be completely overreacting. There had been quite a few bad hurricanes since Katrina, hadn't there? So probably she was imagining that the look she'd seen on his face was one of anguish.

Finally armed with his cabin number, she stood in front of it with her heart beating in her throat. She drew a fortifying breath before she knocked on the door. No answer. She knocked again. Chewed on her lip. Wondered where in the world he could be, and if maybe not finding him was a sign that her mission was a little absurd. Just as she was about to turn away, the door opened.

She looked up at him, his face now wiped clean of all the emotion she thought she'd seen there earlier, and the different emotion that had been there when they'd danced. Her tongue stuck to the roof of her mouth, and suddenly she had no idea what to say.

"Jordan. Damn, I'm sorry. I…forgot about your drink. I remembered I had some urgent work to do, but I should have said goodbye."

"That's okay, I just…" She swallowed and forged on, even though this now felt like a really misguided idea. "Can I come in?"

He stared down at her for a long moment before he silently opened the door wide. She glanced around the room, briefly sidetracked from her worries as she saw the beautiful photography on the walls. Pictures of colorful starfish and urchins like those she'd seen with him when they'd been underwater together. Photos of unusual fish, and all kinds of coral, and a lot of other things she couldn't name.

"Did you take these pictures?"

"For my work." He nodded. "Photographic samples to supplement the physical ones is part of the research. Important to include in the reports when I apply for a new grant. Which is what I'm working on now. Got to get it done and turned in next week."

"My mother would be impressed. Yours are…beautiful."

Her gaze moved to a small table identical to the one in her cabin. For the first time, she saw that his laptop was open, with some kind of spreadsheet on the screen, and various papers were stacked on either side. Warmth filled her cheeks as she realized he was simply working, not moping or upset, and she had made a fool of herself coming there. Except she deserved to know why one minute he'd been holding her close, and the next he'd practically run from the room, didn't she?

No. He didn't want a relationship with her, and her stupid mooning over him probably had her reading things into their dance together that hadn't been there at all.

"I'm…so sorry I interrupted you. I'll leave you to it."

She turned to go, beyond anxious to get out of there before he found out why she'd chased after him, but his fingers wrapped around her arm and stopped her.

"Tell me why you're here," he asked quietly. "Is it because I left you? I'm sorry. Sometimes work makes me do strange things, but I hope I didn't hurt your feelings."

Maybe he *had* hurt her feelings, but that wasn't why she was there. She stared up into his brown eyes, and couldn't read them. "No. I was just being silly."

"Silly how?"

Lord, he wasn't going to make this easy for her. She wasn't about to tell him how mesmerized and confused she'd felt during their dance. But probably she should confess that she'd thought, looking at him as he saw the hurricane footage, that he was upset. That she'd been concerned about him. Maybe she had to embarrass herself that way because, otherwise, he'd think she'd decided to chase after him after one simple dance, which would be even more embarrassing.

"I was horrified by the hurricane footage. I looked at you to see if you were watching, and I thought maybe you seemed upset. And then you left. So I asked Bob, and he told me…" She stopped. Thinking about it now, it seemed ridiculous that she'd have been worried just because Zeke had been in a bad hurricane once in his life.

"Told you what?"

She drew a deep breath, and realized there was no going back. "That you grew up in New Orleans. That you were visiting when Hurricane Katrina hit. That must have been…stressful."

He turned to stare out the small window, his back to her. When he didn't answer, she didn't know whether she should respect his privacy, or press for answers about what he'd experienced. To see if he needed comfort.

Suddenly, she felt like the biggest fool in the world,

and couldn't wait to get out of there, away from whatever he must be thinking about her showing up at his cabin uninvited.

"Never mind. I'll just…go now."

He turned back, his expression grim. He closed the gap between them, took her hand and sat down on the single bed, tugging her to sit next to him, hip to hip.

"I might as well tell you. Which will prove to you that you have good instincts."

"What do you mean?"

"You knew from the minute we met that I wasn't someone you could ever count on."

"What do you mean?" she repeated. "I never said that. You *have* been a person I could count on. You fixed my head. Came diving with me even when you weren't sure you wanted to. Helped me with two different patients, not to mention that it would have been a struggle to find someone to go into the field with me to see Jim if you hadn't been around. You were there every time I needed you to be."

"That's different than what I'm talking about." He twined his fingers with hers and looked down at them. "It's true that I grew up in New Orleans. My parents died in a car accident when I was six, and my grandparents raised me there."

"Oh, Zeke. I'm so sorry."

"It was a long time ago, but even though I was so young, I still remember how strange it was to have them just…gone. How incredibly confusing and hard. The only thing that helped me get through it was my relationship with my grandparents. That comfort and stability when they took me in and gave me a home." He looked up at her, and her heart ached for him when she saw the deep sadness in his eyes. "I was going to college in San Diego, and went home to New Orleans for a few weeks, between semesters. To see my grandparents and friends. Dive in the Gulf of Mexico, like I always had growing up. It's what made me want to go into marine biology, and sent me to Southern California to go to school."

"And you were in New Orleans when the hurricane hit."

"Yes, at my grandparents' house. It was a category three hurricane when it made landfall, not normally the worst. But the winds weren't what caused the devastation. With the city sitting lower than sea level, when the levee broke, the gulf waters just poured in. The flooding was like nothing any of us ever imagined. The water just kept rising, until it was six feet up the walls of the house and still coming. My grandparents wanted to make a raft of some kind with the lumber they had stacked in their garage that we could use to float out of there."

Her fingers tightened on his. "Did you?"

He slowly shook his head. "I didn't think it was a good idea. My grandfather didn't know how to swim, and the best my grandmother could do was a dog paddle. A raft would have taken time to build, time I wasn't sure we had. And I was afraid if the water got fast, or we hit a tree or whatever while we were floating on that surging water, they'd get knocked off and maybe drown. I'm a strong swimmer, but I didn't feel confident I could save them both. Plus, I didn't even know where the water was running to, and wanted to figure that out while I came up with a plan."

She stayed silent, listening, her heart cracking, a

deep dread filling her stomach that this story might end with a tragedy.

A long minute went by before he continued. "I remembered where a rowboat had been tied to a fence, just a few blocks away. It wouldn't be easy to get there in the fast-moving flood, but I knew I could make it, and hoped like hell nobody else had used it. Figured that, on the way, I'd be able to study the different directions the water was flowing, then bring the boat back. Get them into it, which would be a lot safer than a rickety handmade raft, and easier to steer, too, because there were oars attached. So I told them to stay put on the second floor of the house. That I'd be right back."

"Oh, Zeke," she whispered. "What happened?"

"I was so glad to see that the boat was still there, and I rowed it back. It took a long time because the water was rising fast, scary fast, but I was sure that, with the boat, once I got there to pick them up, they'd be okay. The closer I got to the house, the more scared I felt, because I could see the water was way higher than when I'd first left. All the way up to the second floors of houses as I passed. I got there as fast as I could, rowing right up to the second-floor window and tying the boat to the drapes. Went through the window, and the water was up to my chest. I called and swam through the upstairs, but they weren't there."

"Oh, my God." She was afraid to ask where they'd gone, so she kept silent, dreading to hear the rest.

"I got back in the boat and went everywhere, calling for them. Picked up a few other people as I did, and took them to safety. Over the next few days, I kept looking for my grandparents. In the neighborhood, in shelters, followed miles of water and mud, everywhere I could think of. I thought they just didn't know how to reach me, you know? No cell phones. No power. I figured we'd eventually find each other."

"But you didn't." She didn't say it as a question. Because the answer was stark on his face.

"I looked for almost month. Wasn't going to go back to school until I'd found them. Then I finally did." His eyes lifted to hers. "They were in with the many unclaimed bodies in the morgue."

Tears thickened her throat and stung her eyes as she wrapped her arms around his body, but he stayed stiff within her embrace. "I'm so sorry. So very sorry. I can't even imagine what you went through."

"No, you can't. Because you're not a person who would have done what I did. You would have stayed with them, found a way out together. But what did I do? I left. I left them to die."

"Zeke." She leaned back, shocked that he would say such a thing, after his heroic efforts in the midst of a nightmare. "You did not leave them to die. You left them to get help. To find a way to get them out. You did the absolute best you could in a terrible situation."

"Obviously not true." He lifted his hands to cup her cheeks in his wide palms. "The reason I'll never have a relationship with a woman, the kind of relationship you're looking for, that you deserve, is because I didn't just lose my grandparents. I lost something inside myself. The minute I got back to San Diego, I broke it off with the girl I was dating, because I can't ever be close to someone again. I don't want to be."

"Zeke. The terrible trauma you went through isn't letting you see with clear vision. Your memories of that awful time are skewed. I know because, even in the short time I've known you, you've shown the kind of strength and character that anyone would admire. You didn't leave your grandparents to die. Do you think closing yourself off from ever being close to someone is something they'd want for you?"

"Doesn't matter. I can't feel things like that. Care about someone like that. Not anymore. Not ever again."

His eyes were shadowed with guilt and pain, and her heart squeezed hard in her chest for all he'd been through. Maybe there was nothing she could do to convince him that what she'd said was true. Perhaps all she could accomplish was to make him forget, for at least a short while, the torment he obviously still carried with him from that heartbreaking event.

She leaned forward, wrapped her arms around his neck and kissed him. Poured into that kiss the anguish she felt for him, the caring and compassion for all he'd endured, and yes, the deep attraction she'd felt from the first night they'd met.

CHAPTER TEN

THE SECOND HER mouth met his, she realized how much she'd missed kissing him. How foolish she'd been to resist this kind of intimacy with him, only letting herself now because she'd wanted, in some small way, to comfort him.

Except, for a long moment, Zeke didn't move as she held him in her arms. Didn't respond. Not pulling away, but not participating, either. She wondered if she'd been wrong to kiss him when he'd just shared such a tragedy with her, and a sliver of regret stabbed her heart. She began to ease back, a wisp of air now between their lips. Until she heard him groan just before his arms wrapped around her, smashed her body close to his, and he kissed her back.

But not with the kind of kiss he'd given her before. It wasn't the sweet, delicious kiss they'd shared beneath the southern lights. This was intense and unrestrained and felt a little desperate. As though the emotions wrung out of him through sharing the pain of his past were being channeled into the way his mouth moved on hers. Into a passion and desire that would make him forget. Make them both forget, all thoughts gone except for the undeniable chemistry that had crackled between them from the beginning.

His mouth stayed on hers, and stayed, and it felt like they were nearly fused together, her head light, her body hot. Long minutes passed until, through the sensual fog in her mind, she realized the kiss had slowly changed. Had moved from how it had started, a little wild and untamed, to a different kind of emotion. Something more tender. Something deeper. Something intangible that shook her heart in a way that felt both a little scary and special beyond belief.

"Jordan." His voice unsteady, his mouth left hers to slide down her throat, to the pulse wildly beating there. "I want you. I've wanted you from that first minute we met in your cabin. Do you have any idea how hard it was to stop myself kissing you that night?"

"I might. Because I felt that way, too."

His mouth moved to her ear, nibbling and licking his way back to her mouth for another kiss so heavenly it made her quiver. She felt her heart give an odd little skip, and realized it was from relief as well as pleasure. That she'd been able to help him move past the painful emotions he'd shared, that they could smile together again, felt like the most gratifying thing she'd ever done.

His mouth moved on hers, their tongues tangling as the kiss breathlessly deepened, and for the briefest moment, a question flitted through her brain. Why in the world had she been so hesitant to give in to this *thing* they shared, and the way he made her feel? At that moment, it absolutely felt meant to be that they'd make love together. That it had been inevitable all along.

With that thought, she decided it should be her who made the first to move in that direction. Unwrapping her arms from around his neck, she reached for the buttons on his shirt. She fumbled with them, distracted by all the heady kissing, and finally got it open, shoving it off his shoulders. He assisted with pulling his arms from the sleeves, and she took advantage of that to slide her fingers beneath the T-shirt he wore under it. To feel his warm skin and the rough hair on his stomach and the way his flesh quivered at her touch made her quiver uncontrollably, too.

The minute the flannel shirt was off, he stripped the next layer from his body, exposing dark skin and rippling muscles. Slowly, she ran her hands over everything she could reach, in near awe at his physical beauty.

"I guess all that diving and heavy equipment is a good workout," she managed. "Unless it's working with plankton in the aquarium that makes you so sexy."

"It's the plankton. Nothing sexier than plankton." He reached for the sweatshirt she wore and pulled it over her head, his eyes glinting as they roamed her torso, his fingertip reaching to slowly stroke across the lace along the top of her bra. "Tell me what makes *you* so sexy, Dr. Flynn."

"That I can laparoscopically remove a gallbladder with the precision of a diamond cutter?"

"Ah. I love it when a woman talks dirty to me."

That familiar teasing grin was back on his face, and she grinned back, only to gasp a second later when he leaned in to place his mouth over her breast, gently sucking on her nipple through her bra. The sensation was so wildly erotic she could hardly breathe, and she held his head against her and moaned.

With her brain capable of no thought other than the incredible way he was making her feel, she considered it a very good thing that he took the initiative to move the two of them around on the small bed. One second she was sitting up, and the next she was lying on her back, staring up into his handsome face before he kissed her. Warm hands roamed over her, slipping off her bra, removing her jeans and underwear, then his own. Then he sat up, looking down at her with a heated gleam in his eyes as he stroked his long fingers slowly across her bare skin, making her gasp and wriggle at how amazingly good that simple touch felt.

Late sunlight streamed through the window, skimming across every muscle on his gloriously naked body and highlighting the proof that he was every bit as aroused as she felt, and her heart stuttered at the image before her.

Wow. If anyone ever asked her if Ezekiel Edwards was a remarkable specimen of manhood, she'd tell them *that* would be a complete understatement.

"I never realized it until this minute, but… I'm very thankful for plankton."

He laughed, then leaned down to kiss her again, his mouth sliding across her cheek to nuzzle her neck, then slowly on down to her breast, teasing one at a time. She gasped, then gasped again when his fingers found her core, touching and caressing until she could hardly bear it. Little mewling sounds came from her mouth, but she didn't even care—all she wanted was more of the way he made her feel.

Her own fingers explored his body, loving touching him as he brought her such unbearable pleasure. His hard, defined muscles, his smooth shoulders, his tight buttocks. She reached to clasp him in her hand, and loved that she made him shudder and groan. Part of her wanted this moment to go on forever, but she wanted him inside her even more.

She wrapped her legs around his hips and he took that as the invitation she'd intended, briefly pausing to take a condom from the bedside drawer and roll it on. When they joined together, they began moving in a rhythm so perfect it was like nothing she'd ever experienced before. Like feeling fused together on that dance floor, but even more incredible. His dark eyes looked into hers with such intensity, such deep desire, and his name left her lips on a heavy sigh.

"Zeke."

"Jordan," he whispered back, his hands moving to cup her face before his mouth joined hers once more. He gave, and she gave, both of them taking the pleasure each offered the other in a connection that felt so deep it was nearly unbearable. When they finally shattered, her heart filled with something that felt so big, so special, so unnerving, she feared it might never go quite back to normal again.

Zeke's eyes flew open and he abruptly sat up, his heart racing and sweat pouring down his back. He sucked in deep breaths to get himself under control.

The nightmare had been more vivid than usual, and he fought down the panic attack, running his hands up and down his face and rocking back and forth. A small sound had him sitting dead still, and he dropped his hands and opened his eyes.

Jordan. Jordan was asleep, right next to him. Right there.

Memories of the night before seemed to calm the horrible, shaky feeling. Tamped down the panic. His breathing slowed, and got easier. His heart quietly settled into a normal rhythm.

Her long eyelashes fanned her cheeks as she slept, and Zeke looked down at her beautiful face, a peculiar mix of emotions in his chest. From the moment he'd met her, a part of him had wished for this to happen between them, even knowing it shouldn't. For them to get to know one another, spend time together.

Now that wish had come true, and he wasn't sure it was the best thing for Jordan. Thinking of what they'd shared last night, of their time diving together and working together, even just watching her sleep, brought a smile to his lips that started deep inside him, near the region of his heart. At the same time, a sharp stab to that same general area reminded him that he had nothing to offer her. That he could never give her that home and roots and happy-ever-after she wanted. Was it wrong for him to want to be with her, knowing all he lacked inside?

He didn't know. All he knew was that he didn't want to walk away. Not yet. She knew about his past. And since she did, that meant she also understood his limitations, right?

He heaved a sigh and shook off his worries, for now. Her eyelids flickered and opened. When she looked up at him, the smile that started in their blue depths before forming on her lips had him forgetting about anything but how beautiful she was. About how incredibly lucky he was that she'd decided to be with him. For now.

"Good morning," she said, reaching up to stroke her finger down his cheek.

"Good morning. I'm glad you seemed to sleep just fine without your eye mask and noise machine."

"I must have felt exceptionally tired and relaxed, for some reason."

"Me, too. For some reason."

He'd become such a sucker for the laughter in her eyes, and leaned over to kiss her again, wishing they had time to lie in bed together for longer. Much longer. To make love for hours. But that would have to wait.

Reluctantly, he dragged his mouth from hers. "Want to come diving with me this morning? I need to get a few more samples to add to my data before I send in the grant application. And you need more data for your parents' ear device. Otherwise—" he tugged at the sheet covering her delectable body and ran his fingers across her skin, loving the way she wriggled and laughed "—I'd beg you to stay here as long as possible."

"When are you going?"

"I booked the van for eight-fifteen, and a couple of the new marine biologists and a tender are coming with me." Since it was after seven now, that was way, way too soon. If he'd known they'd be lying in bed together this morning, he'd never have scheduled it so early. "I already asked them if they'd like to participate in your trial, and everyone was interested."

"I appreciate that so much. And diving sounds wonderful. But I'm afraid I can't go with you." Her lips puckered into a faux pout. "Dr. Bradshaw and the new nurse are traveling on the plane this morning to one of the other stations while the weather is good. He wants to evaluate how our new hospital and clinic compares to theirs, and see if we're ahead of the curve, or missing something."

Well, hell. Until she'd said she couldn't go, he hadn't even realized how much he wanted to dive with her again. Share her delight and see her amazement at all the Antarctic seas offered divers that they couldn't see anywhere else. "Will you look for a time in your schedule to go soon, and let me know when? Once I get the grant application finished and sent, I'll be diving most every day."

"I will. Believe me, I want to explore that incredible world again. With you."

The way she was looking at him made his heart beat harder, and he kissed her again, even as he knew he had to get going. Reluctantly, he broke the kiss and drew back. "It's a date. And when I wear the earplugs, you can check my vitals again. Though if you'd recorded them last night, my pulse and respiration would have been off-the-charts elevated."

"Mine, too." Her soft laughter sneaked into his chest and made him smile. "And that, Dr. Edwards, is a date I can't wait too long for."

That they couldn't share more than one quick kiss frustrated him beyond belief. But the crew would be waiting for him, and he had to go with them to collect the last samples he needed to finish the grant application. He pulled out clothes that would be warm enough for the excursion, letting himself watch Jordan as she got dressed. He admired her slim, athletic physique and her beautiful, smooth skin. Her round bottom and long legs.

Damn. It took all his willpower to keep from stripping off the clothes he'd just put on, to reach for her and kiss her and make love with her again, and to hell with the research.

He fought with his body's instantaneous reaction and

tried to focus. "Want to grab a quick breakfast, before we both go to work?"

"Do you think people will wonder if we spent the night together?"

"I have no idea." It hadn't occurred to him that she'd worry about that, but he could see how someone wanting the husband and kids and picket fence might not want anyone to know about a short affair. "Would that bother you?"

Her eyes met his, a slight frown between her brows. Then the frown cleared, and she wrapped her arms around his neck, looking up at him with a clear gaze and look of trust that was gratifying at the same time it sent that stab of worry into his chest all over again. "No. It wouldn't bother me. No more questioning if it's a good idea or not. I want to be with you while we're here together."

He couldn't think of a thing to say in return, and even if he had, the tightness in his throat at what she'd said might have made it hard to talk. So he kissed her instead, telling her without words how much it meant to him that she wanted to be with him as much as he wanted to be with her. That she understood the limitations of what he could offer.

He looked into her eyes and swallowed hard. "Ready to grab that breakfast?" he asked, his voice gruff from their kiss and the conversation.

"Ready."

The galley wasn't crowded yet, and they sat with the men he would be diving with. Jordan talked with them about the earplugs and gave a pack to each of them. The person who would be their tender on this trip, a guy named Lance, showed up to tell them the van was packed and ready to go, and they all stood.

"See you around, Dr. Flynn," he said, trying to keep his voice normal and professional.

"Hope your dive goes well, Dr. Edwards." Her eyes met his, briefly transmitting the warmth and intimate feelings he'd been trying to keep to himself, before she turned to walk toward the hallway leading to the hospital.

He watched her go, and blew out a breath. Was he making a mistake here, and would she get hurt because of it?

The men traveling with him began asking questions about the distance to the dive hole and what he'd collected so far as they stowed the last of their personal gear. They all piled into the van, Zeke sitting in front next to Lance, who was behind the wheel. The men in back began comparing notes about some other research project they'd done together, and Zeke found his mind drifting to Jordan.

She'd loved her first trip driving through this vast, icy landscape when they'd gone to the dive hole together, and her delight had made him feel like he was seeing it with new eyes, too. He thought about diving with her, and how special that had been. Thought about the night they'd just shared, and how it had been way beyond special.

That he couldn't get her out of his head, hadn't been able to for days, made him face an uncomfortable truth. He was falling hard for her, and it would not be good for her to fall the same way, considering everything. What the hell he could do to make sure that didn't happen, he had no clue.

A strange, moaning sound came from Lance, and the oddness of it shook Zeke out of his worrisome thoughts. He looked over to see Lance was holding his stomach, a deep grimace etched on his face.

"What's wrong?"

"I…don't know. My stomach hurt a little this morning, and I didn't feel like eating. But now it's a real sharp pain."

"Where is the pain?"

"Right…here." He held his hand over the lower right side of his abdomen, and grunted again. "Man. It was just kind of a dull ache in the middle of my stomach this morning, but it's a whole lot worse, and lower, now."

Zeke frowned. The symptoms he described didn't really tell him much, and he turned to the men in the backseat. "Can one of you grab my medical bag from behind you? It's tucked into the side slot of the van."

One of them leaned over the seat to look around, coming up with the bag. "This it?"

"Yes. Thanks." Zeke unzipped the bag, looking for his thermometer. "Stop the van for a minute, Lance. I want to check your temperature. If—"

Zeke and the other two were thrown forward as Lance jammed on the brakes, barely stopping the vehicle before he flung open his door. He leaned over, vomiting onto the ice, which was a new symptom Zeke needed to consider. Maybe it was a simple virus, but appendicitis was another possibility. Even if that was unlikely, Lance needed to be seen and have some tests run right away.

"Damn, I'm so sorry." Lance sat back up and wiped his mouth on his sleeve before looking over at Zeke, clutching at his stomach again.

"All right. No point in taking your temp now, or in trying to get this trip in, when you're feeling like this. We need to get you to the hospital so Dr. Flynn can check you out and see what's wrong."

"Hospital?" Lance looked shocked. "No, I probably have a bug or something. Don't you think?"

"Maybe. But your symptoms also could be from appendicitis, and waiting around to do something about that could result in a rupture. Believe me, you don't want that to happen." He'd seen it more than once, resulting in peritonitis, which was a serious infection. "We're switching seats, and going back to the station."

Once he was behind the wheel, he turned to talk to the men in back. "I won't be able to go with you today, but I think there's a good chance you can find a few others to join you. It's early enough that you can still get a mostly full day under the ice, if you do."

They nodded and looked at Lance, obviously understanding why they had to go back, which Zeke was glad about. There had been times when scientists he knew got so focused on the work they had to get done that, when something went wrong, they got frustrated and argued about the right course of action.

Things happened sometimes that couldn't be controlled. And that something was happening today. Which meant he would be one more day behind where he'd wanted to be to get his grant work finished and submitted.

He held in a deep sigh and hit the gas, wanting to get Lance to Jordan as soon as possible. He'd just have to work harder and smarter in less time. And he hoped that wouldn't mean he couldn't spend much time with Jordan until it was done.

CHAPTER ELEVEN

BEING IN THE hospital so early meant Jordan could get the paperwork finished that she'd set aside while working on the newest round of baseline physicals. With Tony and Megan gone for the day, she'd decided not to schedule too many appointments in a row, in case there was an emergency she had to deal with.

Which had proven to be a good decision, though she hadn't known at the time that it would have nothing to do with taking care of an emergency patient. Functioning even after drinking several cups of coffee was proving to be a little difficult, since she felt pretty exhausted after the night she'd spent with Zeke. Exhausted, but exhilarated.

If she'd known what a fantastic lover the man would be, she wouldn't have held him at arm's length, though even as the thought came, that niggle of worry she'd had from the beginning poked again. Ezekiel Edwards was head and shoulders above any man she'd been involved with before, both literally and figuratively. Would it be hard to fall in love with someone back in England, having known Zeke?

No. It would be okay. She loved adventuring beneath the water with him and out in the field here, but she also knew very well that he wasn't the man she'd spend her life with. So she was going to let herself enjoy being with him for the "now" and remember him fondly when it was over.

If only she could have gone diving with him today. Hopefully, there would be plenty of other days when they'd be under the ice together. Months of fun with him, exploring with him, making love with him.

Elation filled her chest and she tapped away at the computer with renewed energy. Living in Antarctica was going to be a whole lot more interesting than she'd ever dreamed it might be, in a way she hadn't imagined.

The clack of the hospital's swinging doors had her turning in surprise to see who might be coming in. Then was even more surprised when she saw Zeke. A man was with him, walking a little hunched over, his face pinched and drawn.

She hurried over. "Tell me what's wrong."

"Stomach hurts. A lot. Right here." The man pointed at his lower right abdomen.

"Lance was driving us to the site, planning to work as our tender," Zeke said. "Experiencing belly pain and vomiting. I haven't taken his temperature, but I knew there was a slight risk of it being appendicitis, and didn't want to wait for him to see you."

She looked up at Zeke, impressed yet again at his medical skills to even think of that. The symptoms were so vague most people would just assume he was sick with a virus. "All right. Lance, we'll start with a urine test, then I want to do an ultrasound and take a look at your appendix. Will you help him to the bathroom, Zeke? The sample bottles are in the cabinet above the sink. When you're done, I want you to take off your shirt and pants and put on a paper gown, open in the front. You can leave on your underwear."

"Okay."

"This way, Lance," Zeke said.

Her eyes met Zeke's as he gave her a quick nod and one of his trademark knee-weakening smiles. She got the ultrasound machine and gel ready, and when they returned, Zeke handed her the sample bottle.

"For you."

Something about the way he said it made her want to laugh. "Thank you. You're a peach."

"So, why did you want the urine sample?" Lance asked, pressing his hand to his stomach again as he nearly doubled over.

"To see if you might have a urinary tract infection." She held up the bottle and it looked clear, not cloudy, but she'd check it with a dipstick after the ultrasound, if that test wasn't conclusive. "I'm sorry you're in pain, but we're going to figure this out as quickly as we can. Please lie down on the exam table."

She rolled some ultrasound gel around Lance's belly, following with the wand. She studied the picture on the monitor as she slowly moved the wand across his skin, and saw that Zeke was staring at the images, as well, his brows lowered in concentration.

Sometimes ultrasound was inconclusive. But today, they were lucky. Zeke's eyes met hers, and she gave him a wide smile and nodding salute, because he deserved it.

"Dr. Edwards might not be a medical doctor, but he knows his stuff, Lance. You do have appendicitis, and figuring that out is the first big step. Next step? You're going to need an appendectomy."

"Ah, hell. You mean surgery?"

"I'm afraid so. We have to remove your appendix before it has a chance to rupture. But I'll do it laparoscopically, which means small incisions and less recovery time than traditional surgery."

"Dr. Flynn informed me earlier that she has the skilled precision of a diamond cutter when using a laparoscope. So you're in luck, Lance."

The amusement, and something else, in his eyes as they met hers had her nearly choking trying not to laugh, which wouldn't be very professional. Neither would letting her mind go to what they'd been doing when she'd said that…

She turned to the patient, getting her head back to her job. "I have done a lot of these procedures, so you don't need to worry. I'm going to give you antibiotics beforehand, then a general anesthetic to put you to sleep, so you won't feel a thing."

"How long will I have to be off work?"

"After a couple days of rest you'll be able to do light work. But no heavy lifting until you've had at least two weeks to heal." She looked up at Zeke, so glad that, with Megan gone, he was there with her. Doing this procedure alone would have been a lot more difficult, though she felt bad she had to lean on him yet again.

"I'm sorry to ask, but can you assist? I know you need to get diving, but having you here would be a huge help. Not very good timing for both Megan and Tony to be gone."

"I've never assisted with a surgery before, but I think I can figure it out."

"I know you can." She knew Zeke Edwards was smart and capable of pretty much anything he set his mind to. And it bothered her that, after what happened to his grandparents, he didn't seem to believe that about himself.

She gave Lance the antibiotic, administered the anesthesia, then got to work. Zeke proved to be an excellent assistant, not that she was surprised. With him responding to her every request, it all went smoothly, and when the surgery was over, she snapped off her gloves and lowered her mask to give him a big smile of thanks.

"You were awesome. Are you sure you don't want to add medical doctor to your list of advanced degrees?"

"I think two are enough." He returned her smile. "And I can confirm that 'diamond cutter' is a good way to describe your surgical skills, Dr. Flynn. Congratulations."

"Thanks. We make a good team."

"We do."

Their eyes met again. That crazy connection between them seemed to vibrate in the room, and the way he was looking at her, a little like she imagined a hungry leopard seal might look, made her feel breathless.

"Are you okay here alone now?" he asked. "I'll stay if you really need me, but I'd like to get to the dive site as soon as I can. I'm already behind on getting everything I need for the grant, so showing up late today is better than not at all."

"Go dive. With the surgery finished, I'm fine here alone." Somehow, despite the conversation being about work, her heart did that fluttering thing again, times ten. Because now she knew how beautiful he was beneath those clothes, how it felt to lie with him skin to skin, how it felt to make love with him.

He must have seen it in her eyes, since he closed the gap between them, drew her close and kissed her.

When they separated, the seriousness of his expression seemed at odds with his light words.

"Hold that thought, Dr. Flynn. Until tonight."

She lifted shaking fingertips to her lips as she watched him leave. She'd thought living in Antarctica meant nonstop cold? How wrong she'd been. Being around Zeke Edwards definitely made her feel very, very hot. And she had a feeling it would seem like a very long day until she got to be with him again.

Feeling a little like a giddy teenager was not the way to get her work done, and Jordan checked on Lance, pleased to see he was doing well after waking from the anesthesia. She gave him pain medication, then doubled down on the paperwork she had to finish. A couple of people came into the clinic to bring medical supplies that had arrived with the latest boat, and she absently pointed them to the supply closet.

Then did a double take. She stood to stare before they went into the room to stash the items they'd brought.

Was that…was that Weston MacIntyre? Lia's ex-boyfriend? Ex-fiancé? The guy who'd practically left her at the altar? The man who had completely disappeared from sight, not letting Lia or anyone else know where he'd gone?

Her heart beating double time, she crept to peek into the supply room. Sure enough, it was West who was taking boxes from the wheeled cart and stacking them on shelves.

Oh, my Lord. She practically ran back to hide behind the computer while her mind raced. Should she go talk to him? Let him know she'd seen him? Or should she let Lia know first?

Lia. Lia was her best friend, and after looking for West for who knew how long she deserved to know.

Jordan grabbed the satellite phone, having no idea if it would be working or not, and felt a little limp with relief when she got a dial tone. She shakily punched in Lia's number, and waited.

"Ophelia Monterrosa."

"Lia," she whispered, glancing up to make sure West wasn't coming her way. "It's Jordan. Are you sitting down?"

"What? Is something wrong?"

"I'm working in the hospital and clinic alone today. And who walks in but…are you ready? Weston Mac-Intyre."

"What?" Lia's voice rose to a squeak. "Are you kidding me? He's in Antarctica?"

"He's in Antarctica. Alive and well."

"Antarctica. *Antarctica.* No wonder I couldn't find him! The rat bastard!"

"I know a group just came here from another station last night. Since I haven't seen him in the galley or anywhere else, maybe he was there for the winter, then working in this new station for the summer. Or maybe not. Obviously, I have no idea what he's been up to. Want me to talk to him? Ask him anything?"

Lia was silent at the other end for a long moment before she answered. "No. No, I'm coming down there."

Jordan lifted the phone from her ear and stared. She was going to make the trek all the way to the south pole to confront the man who'd broken her heart?

"Are you sure? I thought you were dealing with difficult things at home."

"I am, but it can wait a short time. I'd actually been

thinking about that job opportunity you told me about. So I'm finding a way to get down there and do some work. I need to see him face-to-face. I've been looking for him for months, and I'm not waiting more months to make that happen, now that I know where he is."

"Wow, you amaze me. Always have, of course! Let me know when you might get here, okay?"

"I will. And please don't let him know you've seen him, if at all possible. I want it to be a surprise."

Her friend's hard voice was totally different from anything Jordan had heard come out of her mouth before, and she almost felt sorry for West, having to deal with a furious, betrayed Lia. Almost. But the man had hurt her badly, and deserved whatever Lia planned to throw at him.

"I'll steer clear from him if I can. And, Lia?"

"Yes?"

"Best of luck and safe travels. I can't believe I'm going to get to see you here in Antarctica, but I can't wait."

Held close in the warmth of Zeke's arms as they lay in his bed together had Jordan wishing that they could stay here together all morning and forget work and the outside world. Just as she had yesterday, and the day before that, and for every one of the seven glorious nights and mornings they'd spent together. The only thing making her feel better about leaving the pleasure of their naked bodies pressed to one another was her excitement about getting to dive with him.

"What time did you say you reserved the van to go out to the dive hole?" she asked.

"Not until after two." His warm palm stroked her

hair as he looked down at her. "But now that we have twenty-four-hour daylight down here, getting started late doesn't matter so much. I have work I've got to finish in the aquarium this morning, but we'll still be able to get in a decent day's dive."

Her pleasure-fogged brain finally registered that his usual relaxed or teasing expression wasn't there this morning, and she looked at him a little more carefully. There was a slight tenseness etched there, some distance, even, like his mind wasn't as focused on their naked bodies pressed together as hers was.

Her heart gave a little lurch, wondering what he might be thinking about, and if he was concerned about the two of them spending every night laughing and talking and making love. If maybe he felt uneasy about so much togetherness. That she might be starting to expect more than he wanted to give, since they both knew this couldn't be anything more than a short-term fling. Then the second the thought came, she wanted to thrash herself.

Was she becoming the kind of woman who got all needy and clingy? Wanting constant reassurance that things were still good between them?

No. Absolutely not. She might have a serious crush on the man, and have a hard time not thinking about him whenever she had a spare minute. But that was it. She'd gone into this knowing exactly what they could, and couldn't, have together. "You have a lot to do still, before your grant application is ready to go?"

"Yeah. Too much. Mostly the last of the lab work, then compiling the data. I got behind. But I'll get it done."

His chest lifted in a deep sigh, and she rested her

palm on his warm sternum, gently stroking his chest, hoping to ease the anxiety he was clearly feeling, and that she was suddenly feeling now, too. "If…spending time with me is why you're behind and feeling stressed about it, I'm sorry. And I'll stay out of the way until you're finished."

"Not why I'm behind. Or, at least, not the only reason. I admit that I would have gotten more work done if I hadn't had beautiful you as a distraction." He grasped her hand and held it to his chest, and she felt relieved that his lips had curved into a small smile. "But being with you is also a stress reliever. I'll be okay."

"About today, though. If you're going diving just for me, we don't have to. I'd rather you get your work done." Not going to the dive site would be disappointing, since she had the whole day off. But his not feeling stressed about finishing the research? A whole lot more important than her figuring out what to do with herself.

"I think it'll be okay." He dropped a kiss to her forehead, slid his warm lips to her temple. "Besides, we haven't been able to go diving together since that first time. We're way overdue. I want to share that underwater world with you again."

"Okay. But only if you're sure."

"I'm sure."

As if to prove that, he wrapped his arms around her and kissed her. Probably he'd intended it to be a short and sweet touch of their lips before they got up to get on with the day. For him to get to the aquarium as soon as possible. But as always seemed to happen between them, the kiss turned hotter, deeper. He rolled her onto his chest, his fingers tunneling in her hair, then moving to curl around her nape as he held her mouth against his. They both gasped, the kiss becoming frenzied, and she opened her eyes to see his lids lifting, too. His eyes nearly black, they shone with a desire that reflected exactly how she felt.

God, she wanted to somehow be even closer, and after helping him put on a condom she rose to straddle him. To take him in. They moved together, and the pleasure was nearly unbearable, and she wanted to feel all of him, his soft skin and hard muscle and rough hair, against her. Her hair spilled across his chest as she leaned forward, breast to chest, a deep groan exploding from his chest as he grasped her hips.

"Jordan. You're killing me here."

"Not ready for you to go. Not yet."

A rough laugh left his lips and she chuckled softly at the joke, too, before their mouths joined again. Except this kiss seemed to make her heart squeeze hard in her chest, and when they both climaxed, the truth struck her like a blow.

Not yet? Not ready for him to go?

The truth was, maybe she never would be. And that felt scary as hell.

CHAPTER TWELVE

ZEKE STOOD AT the lab tables set up next to the aquarium and worked on measuring and tagging the crabs he'd collected during his last dive, ticked at himself all over again.

Lying next to Jordan's delicious body, he hadn't wanted to move from that bed, even as he'd been thinking about how behind he was, and how he'd have to double his efforts to get the last of the research done and the data recorded and the paper finished on time. He'd told her he'd go on the dive with her, even though he damn well just didn't have time today.

Then he'd kissed her. Had meant for it to be a goodbye-for-now kiss, so he could get up and tackle the work he had to catch up on. But what happened? The second his mouth met hers, he was a goner. All worries from just a moment earlier vanished from his brain, and the only thing that seemed to matter was her. How good it felt to kiss her and touch her, and how he wanted more of all that. And when she rose above him, her eyes shining as she looked down, her soft hair skimming across his skin as she bent forward to kiss him again, his heart seemed to stutter, then nearly stop.

Somehow, in the span of just a few weeks, Jordan

had taken possession of his heart and soul in a way he'd never experienced before. And for several reasons, he knew this was serious cause for concern.

He put the crab into the aquarium box he'd be taking back to the water and snapped off his gloves. He ran his hands down his face and drew a deep breath before picking up a pencil to make some research notes, and for the first time in his life, his attention was only half on his work.

Having to face that he'd fallen hard for Jordan wasn't really the problem. The loss of his grandparents had taught him he could live through the most difficult times life could throw at him. When he and Jordan parted ways, he knew it would hurt like hell, something new for him when it came to the end of an ice affair. But he could handle it.

The problem was her, and any future sadness that would be his fault. The closeness they shared was real and intense, and he knew she felt that intangible connection every bit as acutely as he did. No matter how much she claimed to understand his limitations, and that what the two of them were experiencing now didn't fit into her future plans, he had a bad feeling it might hurt her, anyway.

He reached into the aquarium for another crab, his mind still only half on what he was doing, the other half on Jordan. He knew if he told her he felt worried about her being hurt, she'd tell him he was being an egotistical idiot and that she'd be fine. Maybe she would be. But how could he be sure?

He couldn't. And maybe that was just life. A part of life he had to accept. She wasn't trusting him to be there for her in a way he couldn't be, and he'd never put her in a position where he'd fail her that way.

The thought lifted his spirits a little, even as he shook his head at himself. Bottom line was, he didn't want their relationship to end until the expedition was over. Wanted to be with her as much as possible until then, and he was doing a damn good job convincing himself it would all be okay.

"How's it going in here?"

He turned at the sound of Jordan's upbeat voice, and just seeing her made him smile, despite all his confusion of just a moment ago.

"Making progress, but still way behind."

She came to stand next to him, peering into the aquarium. "This is so cool. Sometime, will you tell me more about the research you're doing? I'd love to know more about it."

"As soon as I have this grant-application monkey off my back, I'd be happy to."

"Thanks. So. Here's the plan for today." She planted her hands on his shoulders, surprising him with a steely look of determination. "I've been thinking. There's no reason for you to dive with me today, when you have all this work to do here. I'll just go with the other divers, so I can be there when they test the earbuds. Now that I've been under the water once, I have a better idea what it's like. You and I will dive another time. We've got months left here together, right?"

He looked into the serious deep blue of her eyes, struggling with what to do. He wanted to go with her. Wanted to spend time with her beneath the ice again. Also wanted make sure she was safe, even though that was probably absurd. She knew how to dive, and would be with other experienced divers. There wasn't anything he could do for her that they couldn't do, too, if something went wrong.

And he did have a hell of a lot of work left, and only a few days to finish it. He might have had trouble making it his number one priority with Jordan around, but the truth was, he had to make that happen for the rest of this week to make sure he got the application in on time.

"I really want to go." He put his hands on her hips and tugged her close. "But you're right. I should stay here and finish. After it's done, we'll dive. And do other things."

"Other things?" Her hands slid up around his neck and her face relaxed into the confident, amused, adorable Jordan he'd fallen for that very first night in her cabin.

"Things like finding sea butterflies and jellyfish. Things like finding the penguin rookeries. And... things."

A soft laugh left her lips before they touched his, warm and soft and sweet, and he was grateful she was the first to pull away because he wouldn't have been able to. Instead, he had a feeling he might have danced them over to the photography dark room, stripped them both naked and made love with her again, making her miss her dive and him late with his work, for certain.

"I look forward to all of those...things, Dr. Edwards." One more kiss, then she stepped back, the twinkle fading from her eyes. "Tonight, I think I'll hang out with a few of the people I've met the past couple weeks, then go to my own cabin. So you can get your work done."

He opened his mouth to protest, then closed it, glad one of them was thinking clearly. And maybe that meant he'd been wrong to be worried about her getting hurt and missing him when it was over.

Maybe the truth was, when that time came, he'd be the only one dealing with a seriously bruised heart.

As they drove along the marked road, Jordan talked with Bob and the two scientists who would be diving that day. Ronald Reardon and Maggie Schindler, both marine biologists, enjoyed talking about their work and their trips to Antarctica, and Jordan enjoyed listening, even as she wished Zeke was there to share some of his stories, too.

The van finally arrived at the dive site, and the sunlight on the ice and snow was nearly blinding. Jordan couldn't wait to get into the water to see how much the light would be filtering through. When she'd dived with Zeke that first time, it had been a fairly gray day, and still, the surprising brightness of the water, illuminating the seafloor and all its inhabitants, had amazed her.

As she pulled her gear from the van, she realized she'd been thinking of him that entire day. That it felt weirdly wrong to be here without him, as though, somehow, he and she and diving in that frigid ocean were unforgettably intertwined. But he needed to get his work done. When he did, the stress she'd noticed on his face this week would hopefully be gone, and they'd be able to enjoy more special times again that she knew she'd carry with her forever.

Her heart pinched, and the deep, cold breath she drew into her lungs made her chest hurt. Saying goodbye to him when the time came was not going to be easy.

Maybe he won't want to say goodbye.

The thought came without permission, and she fiercely battled it back. She'd gone into this thing with him knowing he never wanted any kind of committed relationship, and she wanted a completely different kind of life than the kind a traveling scientist could offer her. Stupid thoughts of a future were just that: stupid. And she wasn't stupid.

Determined to put those thoughts away for good, she hauled all her dive gear from the van and lugged them to the dive hole. It wasn't the same one she'd gone through with Zeke. This one was bigger, and didn't have a tent over it since the weather was getting warmer and the winds were generally calmer, though Zeke had told her that could change in an instant down here.

The four of them stood at the edge of the hole and finished getting ready. "Let me tie the rope onto your belt, Jordan," Bob said.

"Thanks. It feels so different to be out here in the open, instead of inside that little tent, like before. And this hole is huge! I thought Zeke said they'd cut the two the same size."

"He brought the crew out here with the chain saws to make it bigger a few days ago. Said it gets too crowded when more people are diving at the same time, and it's easy to make it big when you don't need a tent."

"That makes sense." She wriggled into the dry suit, and she couldn't seem to help that the memories came again. She and Zeke alone in the dive tent. Zeke helping her tug the suit up her body…

"Jordan, can you hand me my goggles? Sorry, but I dropped them on top of yours," Maggie said.

"Uh, sure." If she couldn't keep her mind on what needed to happen to get ready, she shouldn't even have come. "Here are the earplugs, too. And yours, Ronald. I really appreciate you both trying them."

"Interesting concept I'm happy to try," he said. He tucked them into his ears before pulling everything else over his head, then sat at the edge of the hole. "Here I go. Last one in is a rotten egg."

Maggie laughed and shook her head. "You always— *aahh!*"

Her shriek came just seconds before Ronald, Jordan and Bob screamed, too, as a leopard seal nearly as long as the van surged out of the water, rested its wide chest on the ice shelf and clamped its teeth on Ronald's leg, violently shaking him like a rag doll. The momentum sent Ronald's shoulders swinging into Jordan's legs and she fell with a crash onto the ice, knocking the wind from her lungs. With her heart pounding like a jackhammer in her throat, she tried to scramble backward like a crab, away from the monster, not getting enough traction on the slippery ice as terror gripped her. Staring into the creature's slit-like yellow eyes and sharklike teeth, she thought she might be looking at some giant prehistoric lizard come back to life in the Antarctic.

Bob acted first, grabbing one of the scuba tanks and slamming it onto the seal's back. Her breath coming in ragged gasps, Jordan took his lead and grabbed one, too, swinging it at the terrifying mouth that had such a grip on Ronald. The blow turned out to be little more than a glancing one, but combined with Bob's efforts, the seal let go, sliding halfway down into the water, its head still staring at them with what for all the world looked like a leering smile.

"My God." Bob stepped over Jordan as she rolled to her knees, and adrenaline poured through her veins as the three of them grabbed Ronald by the armpits and pulled the groaning man out of the water. No way were they safe with that creature so close and they kept going, dragging the poor man away to put some distance between them and the leopard seal still glaring at them, leaving a bloody trail across the ice.

"Leopard seals…" Maggie said, her voice a gasp. "They usually won't follow us this far out of the water. But to be safe we need to get to the van."

"And we need to hurry," Jordan managed to say, grimly noting the wide swath of red spreading on the snow. "He's bleeding badly. I need to get a tourniquet on the wounds, then get him back to the hospital as fast as possible so I can evaluate what has to happen."

She studied Ronald's face as the three of them awkwardly lifted him to carry him to the van, trying to determine if he was going into shock, expecting that he was. "Let's make room to lay him in the back, and elevate his feet. We'll worry about getting the equipment later."

"Agreed," Maggie said.

"I'll drive," Bob said as they got Ronald settled into the cargo space of the van as carefully as they could, with Jordan climbing in after him to work on his leg. "Maggie, you're in the backseat to help Jordan with whatever she needs."

"Hang in there, Ronald. You're going to be okay." Jordan said it with a confidence she didn't entirely feel. The gaping tears in his flesh weren't like anything she'd had to deal with before, but she called on all her surgical training to take care of him the best she could.

As though they'd done this before, the three of them worked in a strangely choreographed way, with Maggie helping to pull bandages and other supplies from the medical case in the van and Bob driving far faster than Jordan would have ever expected he'd be comfortable with on the icy road.

Jordan got a tourniquet on Ronald's thigh to slow the bleeding, and got to work applying pressure to the multiple gashes and wounds, with Maggie assisting. God, if only Zeke was there with her. Yes, she was a well-trained surgeon and doctor and knew her stuff, when it came to hospital medicine.

Saving someone from bleeding out, far from a medical facility? That was where Zeke was the expert.

She swallowed hard, and intently focused on trying to get the bleeding stopped. Zeke wasn't here, and it was up to her to save Ronald's life.

Elbow-deep in the aquarium as he worked to gather the samples he still needed for the database that would motivate those offering the grants for addition work, Zeke decided not to answer the in-station phone jangling on the lab desk ten feet away.

He barely glanced at it before turning back to his task. Probably an unimportant call to the aquarium lab or one of the scientists working there, and if it was more than that, they'd leave a message. Or come to the lab themselves to find whoever it was they were calling.

It wouldn't be Jordan, because she'd decided to spend time with new friends to give him work space, and he appreciated that she understood how important it was to get this done. If she needed him for something right away, she'd come to the lab herself, wouldn't she?

The phone rang again, and something about its insistence had him heaving a sigh and stripping off one of his gloves to pick it up.

"Ezekiel Edwards."

"Zeke. It's Maggie. We have an emergency."

"What emergency?" He straightened, alarm skittering through his veins. Maggie had gone on the dive this afternoon. The dive with Jordan.

"Ronald's been hurt. We've just now gotten back to Fletcher. Jordan and Bob are rushing him to the hospital, and I thought you might be able to help."

"What?" For a split second, he felt frozen in place as her words penetrated his brain. One second later, he'd yanked his other glove from his hand and was heading toward the hospital in a near run. "What happened?"

"A leopard seal bit him. Bad. I've never seen anything like it."

"Where were you and Bob when it happened?" He tried to suck in air. "And Jordan?"

"Right next to him. One second Ronald was sitting on the ice shelf, about to dive, and the next, the seal had lunged out of the water to grab him. Knocked Jordan over, too, but she's okay. Bob and Jordan grabbed scuba tanks and slammed them down onto the seal, and it finally let Ron go. But he's lost a lot of blood. I'm…scared."

His heart hammered in his chest. Poor Ron. God, he hoped he'd be okay. And Jordan had been right there next to him? Knocked down by the deadliest creature in these oceans? Knowing it could easily have been her the seal grabbed and nearly killed made it hard to breathe.

He burst through the hospital doors and saw Bob and Maggie both sitting in chairs, looking pale and worried.

"Maggie told me it's bad. I'm going in to see if Jordan could use a hand."

"That would be good. Megan is assisting her, but the tears in his leg…so many." He could see Bob working to sound calm. "It was unbelievable. Not sure I can ever tender for anyone again."

"What we do down here always carries risk. We just have to do what we can to reduce it."

Easy to say. To know and accept. But not when it came to someone who was diving for fun. Jordan probably never should have been there to begin with, since diving wasn't part of her work here, other than the trial, and other divers were participating in that, anyway. But when she did go? He hadn't gone with her, to make sure she stayed safe. Had opted to leave her on her own, and what did that make him?

The same man he'd always been. A man who hadn't been there when they'd needed him most.

The weight of that failure hung in his chest as he quickly scrubbed, then went into the small operating room. He stared at the blood spattering the floor, the gurney, the front of Jordan's gown and her gloved hands as she leaned in, stitching closed the ragged wounds on Ronald's leg. Megan stood by, assisting.

"Jordan." He could barely get her name out, and tried again. "I'm here to help." He recognized the irony of his words. Showing up to help when the worst was over didn't say much for him, did it?

"Zeke." She glanced up, and the relieved smile she sent him was one he knew he didn't deserve. "Why don't you work on the cuts at the back of his calf while I finish these on the front. It's been hard to control the bleeding, and the sooner the gashes are closed, the better."

Silently, they worked together until all the wounds were stitched and wrapped. Jordan checked Ronald's vitals and nodded. "Good. He's stable. I gave him antibiotics when he first came in, and we'll need to follow with another dose in a few hours. Here are the rest of the instructions, Megan, and I'll be back to check his vitals again in a little while, if you can keep an eye on him until then."

"Got it," Megan said.

Jordan moved to the small scrub room and he followed. Both of them took off their bloody gowns. The second hers was off she stepped to him, wrapping her arms around him and leaning her head against his chest. He held her close, and the adrenaline of getting the wounds closed as fast as possible seeped away, leaving him feeling shaken, both physically and emotionally.

"That was…so terrifying," Jordan said, her voice muffled in his chest. "I can't even describe it."

"What exactly happened?"

"Ron was sitting on the side of the dive hole, ready to go in, when the seal just burst from the water and grabbed him. For a horrifying second, I thought it was going to drag him underwater, but it just shook him, its teeth deep in his leg and ripping…"

He didn't know what to say. Leopard seals had hovered around threateningly before, and he'd always kept his distance. Never had he come close to one actually attacking him or someone else.

Iciness crept through his veins and he could barely breathe, picturing what Jordan described. Ron could have been dragged underwater. Or bitten on his torso. Or bled to death, and it was a damn good thing Jordan had been there to deal with his wounds, and probably saved his life.

Or it could have been her. Her leg and body. Her blood. Her nearly killed or actually killed.

Ronald had been lucky. She might not have been.

"Where were you?"

"Next to him. Getting ready to go in." She leaned back and looked up at him, a wobbly smile on her lips. "It's almost a blur, at the same time it's so vivid in my mind it's like watching a movie. Except I was in it."

He covered her hand with his, and that connection soothed, a tiny bit, the raw chaos burning in his chest at what happened, and what could have happened.

"I'm…sorry you went through this."

"I so wished you were there," she whispered. "When he was bleeding so badly and from so many wounds, I was really afraid I couldn't get it stopped. Knew that you being with me might make all the difference."

"But I wasn't there. Wasn't there for him. Or you. And you handled it fine on your own."

"We got lucky, I think." Maybe it was something in his tone, because she tipped her head and looked at him with a question in her eyes. "Is something wrong?"

"Yes. I'm what's wrong." He lifted his hand to her face and stroked his thumb across her cheek. Tried to imprint her beautiful face in his memory forever, as the reality of what happened today slammed into him all over again.

"What do you mean?"

"I wasn't there for Ron today. Not there for you," he said again. Everything inside him seemed to squeeze until it was hard to breathe. His heart was pounding, he started to sweat, and he worked to shove down the panic attack that threatened to overwhelm him. "I told you I can't be counted on to be there for anyone. Ever. And I wasn't."

"Zeke." Her brow creased in a perplexed frown. "You can't be everywhere, all the time. Things happen. Bad things. You did your best for your grandparents, and have to believe that. You would have done your best for Ronald, and for me, too, if you'd been there today."

"But I wasn't." He knew it was a dogged refrain, but she needed to hear him, damn it. "This is why I can't be close to anyone. Let anyone close to me. I can't be who you want, and who you deserve. You know that. And I hope you find that person. I truly do."

"Zeke—"

"Goodbye, Jordan." He let himself kiss her forehead, one last time. Stared into the beautiful blue of her eyes, a storm of emotion in his chest at the confusion and pain he saw there. But leaving now was for her own good. "You're going to have an awesome life, I know it. Take care."

Somehow, he forced himself to turn and go. To walk out the door and not look back, even as he finally admitted to himself that he loved her in a way he'd never loved a woman before.

It was a struggle to put one foot in front of the other, as though his feet were filled with lead, and he wondered if she could hear his heart cracking as the door closed behind him.

CHAPTER THIRTEEN

JORDAN SAT ON the floor of the supply room and refilled items in the field bags, which made her think about Zeke. Then she scoffed at herself. Who was she kidding? She'd thought of him way too much in the three weeks since he'd said goodbye, and wondered how long it would take for her to get over him. She knew that was pathetic, and even stupid, because their affair had always had an expiration date.

She just hadn't expected it to come so soon.

Ezekiel Edwards was a wonderful man in so many ways, and she knew that. It was so clear that he still felt tortured over the way his grandparents had died, and carrying that heavy load still deeply affected who he was today. A man who protected himself from pain by keeping an emotional distance. Refused to let himself get too close to anyone, and yet he felt responsible for everyone. She knew that had to be a difficult way to live, but he'd entrenched himself in that belief so deeply, and for so long, she had a feeling he'd stay there for the rest of his life.

For at least a week after he'd told her goodbye, she'd wanted to find him and rant. To tell him he needed to deal with his past and his guilt so he could move on with his life.

Let himself love someone. Let her love him.

Tears threatened and she heaved in a shuddery sigh. It wasn't until he'd walked out the door of the hospital that she finally admitted it to herself. She had fallen in love with him. And that love had turned on its head every conviction she'd been so certain about.

She loved him, and loved diving with him and being with him, but that was only part of why she loved this adventure in Antarctica. She loved sliding across the brilliant, frozen landscape on the Ski-Doo. Loved camping in a tent in the icy wilderness. Loved excursions to see the penguin rookeries and the wildlife. And all that love had made her see what her childhood longings had blinded her to.

A safe and steady life with a safe and steady husband and putting down roots in a safe and steady suburb surrounded by a white picket fence wasn't what she wanted at all. She'd loved the adventures she'd had as a kid with her parents. Exploring the world was a big part of who she was, and Zeke helped her see that's still who she was. How she wanted to live her life. How she wanted her future children to live their lives.

Problem was, Zeke didn't want to live it with her. He probably wouldn't admit it, but he was the one who wanted the safe and steady, at least when it came to his heart. He kept it inside a cage and refused to let it out and give it to her.

She thought about the stricken look on his face the last time she'd seen him. Thought about the pain he'd held in his heart for so long. Maybe she'd been wrong to not find him and rant, after all. Or at least try to talk

to him, to tell him how being with him had helped her
see what she really wanted for her life. Find out if he'd
let her help him see his own life in a different way than
he'd been allowing himself to see it.

Was that possible at all? Would he be willing to listen? Or was it just a foolish pipe dream?

"Jordan." Tony Bradshaw walked into the supply room
and interrupted her deep thoughts. "We have an injured patient in the field. Sounds like something you
can handle there, without bringing her back, but you'll
have to determine that when you get there. If you're
willing to go?"

"Of course." She stood, then her heart skipped as a
thought came to mind. "Um, who would go with me?"

"I asked the crew member you did surgery on.
Lance." The medical director smiled. "He's feeling good
now, and since he's grateful to you for diagnosing him,
he said he'd be happy to go."

It was actually Zeke who'd done the initial diagnosis, and her heart ached all over again, remembering
how well they'd worked together. "Glad to hear that. Is
he ready to go?"

"He's packing the snow machine now. Said to meet
him in the hangar."

"I'll grab my field bags and my coat and stuff, then
I'll be ready. I'll keep you posted."

"Thank you. See you when you get back."

She gathered the field bags and headed to the hangar as memories of Zeke and their field trip clogged her
throat. Kissing beneath the aurora australis. Intimately
sharing that tent.

That trip was when she'd first started to realize she

was falling in love with him, and still she'd told him all about how she'd wanted a safe and steady husband and that picket fence life, because she hadn't admitted to herself quite yet how she felt about him.

His beautiful dark eyes swam in front of her and she decided that, good outcome or bad, she'd be talking with Ezekiel Edwards as soon as she got back to Fletcher Station.

Zeke sat at the table in his cabin, holding the letter in his hand that should have him jumping with joy and celebrating.

The grant he'd worked so hard for had been officially offered to him. His goal of working to impact the negative consequences of climate change was ensured for another year. He waited for the feeling of joy to lift his chest, but it didn't come.

Of course, he knew why. Because he didn't have Jordan to celebrate with him.

The past weeks had been hell. Across the room in the galley, he'd often see her smiling face and shining hair and hear her laughter as she sat with new friends. Most of the time she ignored him, but on the rare occasions that their eyes met, she looked so serious, so sad, that he usually got up and left the room, hating that he was the reason she felt that way.

He'd never meant for it to happen. Somehow, though, he hadn't been able to keep his distance from her, never fully understanding why. He'd been powerless to resist the magnetic attraction he'd felt, even knowing she might get hurt.

Actually, he did understand why. He'd fallen in love

with her, and how the hell he'd let that happen, he had no clue.

Except he hadn't had a choice in the matter, had he? Jordan Flynn was the most special woman he'd ever met, and it was too damned bad he couldn't give her what she wanted and needed. That he wasn't worthy of the love he'd felt from her, a love that she'd given him without condition or words. It made everything inside him hurt, but she deserved a man who could give all of himself to her. A man who wasn't missing a part of himself that was gone forever.

A hard rap on his door had him swinging toward it in surprise. Surely it wouldn't be Jordan, weeks after they'd parted. His heart beating a little harder, he got up and opened the door to see it was Bob.

"What's up?"

"We have a search and rescue situation. I know that's something you excel at, and thought you'd want to be involved for a couple reasons."

Something he excelled at. Nobody but Jordan knew how little that was true.

"A couple reasons?" He grabbed his coat and followed Bob down the hallway to the hangar. "What do you mean?"

"A woman was injured at a nearby station that doesn't have medical care, and Jordan went with Lance to look at her. Except a sudden storm blew in and they never showed."

It felt like his heart completely stopped for a long moment before it began hammering against his ribs. "Jordan? Lost in a storm?"

"Apparently. The Ski-Doos are ready to go."

He ran the rest of the way to the hangar. Threw on

his coat, strapped the light to his forehead, shoved his feet into the skis and got going. Twenty-four-hour daylight didn't mean it was easy to see, not when the snow was coming down hard, and blowing nearly sideways in the wind. He and the others in the rescue team fanned out, and he squinted across the barren, icy landscape, praying he'd see her.

"Jordan! Lance! Where are you?"

Nothing. No answer. No sign. The thirty minutes since he'd started looking felt like hours, terror building in his chest that he wouldn't find her in time. In this kind of cold, hypothermia could happen fast, even with all the layers everyone wore outdoors. Being stranded meant little body heat being generated, and the thought of Jordan lying unconscious somewhere, dying a slow, frozen death, felt unbearable.

No. He would not let that happen to her. No matter what it took, he would find her and Lance.

Through the swirling snow, he thought he saw a patch of red. His heart pounded hard and his breath came fast as he punched the Ski-Doo into high gear. And then he saw it was Jordan, with Lance lying next to her. For real.

"Jordan!" He leaped off the Ski-Doo and slapped the throttle off before running to her, slipping on the ice before he dropped to his knees in front of her. Lance's eyes were open and he was conscious, but Jordan's eyelids were closed, her lashes covered with snow. He could see she was shivering, that her breathing was shallow, and his chest tightened. Classic signs of hypothermia. Then her eyes fluttered open to stare at him.

"Jordan." He quickly shot a flare into the sky, and lit another to get the attention of the other rescuers, placing it a few feet away before he reached for her hands. He pulled off her gloves to gently rub them, trying to get her circulation going. "Jordan, can you hear me?"

"What…took you so long?"

He nearly wept in relief. "Got here as soon as I could."

Her gaze moved to the flare, then back to him. "Zeke be nimble, Zeke be quick. Zeke jumped over the candlestick." The words were slurred, but damned if her blue, frozen lips didn't curve in a small smile. "See? Sometimes the nursery rhymes make…total sense."

God, how he loved this woman. Her bravery. Her spunk. Her attitude. He kept rubbing her hands and leaned close to press his cheek to her ice-cold one, trying to warm her that way, too. "Gonna get you on the sled now. We're getting you and Lance back."

He quickly checked on Lance again, who was thankfully still conscious. "Hang in there, Lance. I'll be right back. You're both going to be okay."

He lifted Jordan into his arms and prayed with everything in him that was true. As he wrapped her in a thick blanket and secured her onto the sled attached to the snow machine, he heard the roar of the other Ski-Doos as the team spotted the ground flare. He lifted his hand to give them a sign, then pointed at Lance. They pulled up next to Lance and jumped off their Ski-Doos and Zeke took off, knowing they'd get the man the help he needed.

Getting Jordan back as fast as possible was his priority now.

Zeke paced around the room outside the hospital, frustrated that Tony Bradshaw didn't want him by Jordan's side until he felt confident she was responding well to the warming IV and heated oxygen treatment.

"You're going to wear a hole in that brand-new floor," Bob said. "Try to relax."

"Relax? She nearly died out there!"

"But she didn't. Because you found her and saved her."

"I can't take credit. You're the one who came to tell me she was missing. And someone else could easily have found them." Though he was more grateful than he could possibly say that he'd been the lucky one. Finding her there, then seeing her open her eyes and manage a smile, to even recite one of her silly nursery rhymes while lost and nearly frozen, would always be the single most gratifying thing he'd ever experience.

"But they didn't. You did. So now what?"

"What do you mean, now what?"

"Are you going to stop being an idiot, tell the woman you love her and do whatever you can to keep her?"

"I...don't know what you're talking about."

"Jordan told me you broke it off with her, though didn't say why. Look, I know you must have been through something terrible in the past, and I'm really sorry." Bob stood and walked over to rest his hand on Zeke's shoulder. "But you can't let that pain rule your life."

"I don't let it rule my life. I just know that I don't have what a woman like Jordan deserves. I can't give her what she wants. That's why I ended it. I'm not enough for her."

"I guess you going into a snowstorm, finding her and saving her life doesn't count as enough? Loving her isn't enough?" He cocked his head. "Think about how ridiculous that sounds. Don't throw away your chance to be happy with Jordan. That chance might never come again. I know she's willing to take that chance, because she's bold and brave. Are you? Or are you a coward, protecting yourself, while you claim to be protecting her instead?"

He stood stone-still, absorbing Bob's words. Was he being a coward? Was what Bob had said a truth he hadn't let himself face? Was it time for him to look the old Zeke in the eye, and become the man he wanted to be, instead of the man he believed himself to be?

"Zeke, you can come see Jordan now, if you like," Tony said, coming into the room.

"Thanks." He turned to Bob. "And thanks to you, too."

"Anytime." Bob smiled. "Now, go. You've got some making up to do."

His heart bumped wildly in his chest as he stepped next to Jordan's bed, pulling the privacy curtain around it. Her solemn eyes met his. When he saw the discoloration of her skin from being in the cold for so long, his teeth clenched and he reached to cup her cheek in his hand, unlocking his jaw so he could speak.

"You've had a rough time of it."

"Are you talking about nearly freezing to death? Or being kicked out the door by the man I'm in love with?"

He had to smile, even as her words made his chest hurt. "Which was worse?"

"About even, I think."

"What do you think about me making both of them right?"

"How are you going to do that?"

"I found you on the snow, so that one's done. Now I

need to tell you I'm sorry. Sorry I hurt you, sorry I'm an idiot and sorry I didn't realize it sooner."

"What should you have realized sooner?"

"That I love you." He sat on the side of the bed and reached for her hands. "That I was being selfish by breaking it off between us, convincing myself I was doing it to protect you. That having you in my life is the best thing that ever happened to me, and when I thought you might die out there on the ice, I knew a part of me would die with you. But you didn't die. And I'm not going to let you go, ever again."

"Oh, Zeke," she whispered. "I love you, too. I never understood how you could possibly not believe in how strong and steady you are, because I know you're the kind of man who'll always be there in good times and bad. And I'll be there for you in good times and bad. If you'll let me be."

His throat closed at her words, and he had to try twice to speak. "Thank you for believing in me, and helping me believe in myself. I didn't want to let us start an affair because I was sure it wouldn't be fair to you."

"And now?"

"Now I hope our affair will happen on ice, snow, sand and surf. For the rest of our lives. If you'll say yes."

"Yes."

She reached for him, her eyes brimming with tears. He felt his threaten to do the same, and since he wasn't quite at the point where he'd want her to see that, he carefully pulled her into his arms and gently kissed her, but not for long because her poor lips were still bruised and tender from the frostbite she'd endured.

"I've been thinking about you wanting roots and that picket fence." He held her hands and knew she was worth any change he had to make in his life for her to be happy. "I'm going to ask my university to put me on the teaching schedule year-round now. I can still do marine biology research in California, and for the climatology—"

"No."

"No? What do you want, then? To move back to England? It might take some time for me to find a position there, but—"

"No, I want to find a job in Southern California where I can still travel with you to Antarctica, or wherever else your research takes you."

He stared at her, stunned. "What about those roots you never had? I'm not sure a few months a year in San Diego would qualify, especially if we have that brood of kids that's on your list of things you want in your life. And isn't the Antarctic too scary for you now?"

"Pshaw!" She waved her hand dismissively and grinned. "A near attack by a leopard seal and getting lost in a snowstorm could never dim how it feels to kiss you under the southern lights. Being with you down here has made me see that roots and a picket fence are way overrated. I grew up a gypsy, and I've finally come to see that it's in my blood, and how I want to live my life, after all. Including the brood of kids. If that's okay with you?"

Her words made him feel so overwhelmed he couldn't do anything but nod and hold her close against him for long minutes until he could trust himself to speak again.

"You know I have issues, right? I have panic attacks. Nightmares. But I know that I finally have to deal with all that, talk to a professional about it, because you've made me see I don't have to live that way anymore. Don't want to anymore. But do you want to wait to find out how I do before we decide on forever together? If so, I understand."

"I want to help you in that journey, like you've helped me in mine. I want us to take the rest of our journeys together."

Emotion welled in his chest. "I can't think of anything better. With a close second being kissing you under the southern lights."

"So when can we do that again?"

"Not until next winter. Unless you want to travel to the north pole for our next adventure together."

"Maybe a wedding under the aurora borealis?"

"Now you're talking." He kissed her again, and knew he was the luckiest man on Earth at either pole. "It's a date."

* * * * *

REUNITED
IN THE SNOW

AMALIE BERLIN

MILLS & BOON

To my Mamaw Mary, who reads more than any other person I ever met—because she's awesome—and who still reads all of my books. Except for the sexy parts. (I don't know if that's true but I want to believe it, so I do, no matter what anyone else says. La-la-la-la, I can't hear you!)

CHAPTER ONE

DR. LIA MONTERROSA had not inherited the seafaring, adventurous spirit of her Portuguese ancestors. But she talked a good game.

None of her traveling companions appeared to be any more sprightly than she was after the long, arduous journey. Each lugged modest amounts of luggage down the pristine, shiny corridors of the brand-new Antarctic research station where they'd just arrived, no spring in any thick-booted step. All of them were carrying what would see them through the long months of a dark Antarctic winter.

She'd heard various reasons for coming—once-in-a-lifetime experience, work they wanted to do and could best accomplish locked up for eight solid months with fifty strangers. For her, that was the upside of her trip—being surrounded by people who didn't know her, and therefore had no expectations about how she should behave. She didn't have to be the strongest person on the planet, and she didn't have to be the most docile, polite one, either.

But her ex-fiancé was who she'd come to find. To ask why he was her ex. What had happened during the four days she'd been gone, home in Portugal, that had made him decide he didn't love her anymore, didn't want to marry her? To ask why he'd been cold enough to also go missing while she was filing paperwork with the Polícia Judiciária to locate her missing father.

He hadn't left a message. Hadn't scribbled his farewell on a sticky note affixed to the bathroom mirror. He'd just stopped answering her calls, and three days before her wedding, when she'd had a moment free to go back to London and look for him, as well, she'd found his flat vacated, job vacated, mobile phone canceled. He'd left her with the beautiful ring they'd painstakingly designed together, and a hole in her chest so big a truck could pass through.

But she would see him today, the end of too many months of torture. If fate was with her, he'd provide answers. Closure, if that was a real thing that actually happened, and not just some psychobabble placebo. Closure, no closure—it didn't really matter. The end was coming. The final end. The official end that had been denied her when she'd come home to find him gone.

Right on cue, her stomach plummeted—a sensation she should've become immune to by now, but which still had the ability to wrench away brief control of her extremities. Her booted foot scuffed the floor, but she didn't fall—walking was a little easier to recover from than errant hand-twitches in surgery when a slight wrong move could end a life. Knowing what had ended *them* would help, even if it was just another case of her not being enough. No matter how much she wanted to, she couldn't fix whatever she'd done wrong if she didn't know what it was.

"Dr. Monterrosa, you're in Pod C," her guide said, jerking her from her thousandth thought-spiral of this trip, and gesturing to a nondescript door with a circular window at head height—the kind peppering the station, and which reminded her of doors on boats.

The group all stopped long enough for the woman to add, "With you lot arriving at the end of summer, you're getting stacked where there is an open cabin."

And she was the only one in C, which would practically become a ghost town in little more than a week when she could probably have her pick of rooms. After Jordan and Zeke left. After West…

Lia opened her mouth to ask the number, but her fatigue was starting to show. The guide answered before she even formed the first sluggish word.

"Last door on the left, end of the hall."

With a soft, tired grunt, Lia hoisted one of her two meager bags onto her shoulder and entered without another word. Through the door and into a much dimmer hallway, somewhere obviously designed for sleeping through the twenty-four-hour days of summer.

She had about three seconds to see it as the door swung closed and the bright light from the corridor dissipated, but all she really saw was beige. Walls. Low-static carpeting. White doors dotting both sides of the hall. Snow blind, she waited only long enough for general shapes to form in her vision, allowing her to navigate without bumping into walls or running over strangers in the hallway.

Dr. Weston MacIntyre would never know what had hit him. She had the upper hand, and she needed it. He'd expect her to come at him with guns blazing, and that method had its own appeal. It might help her hide the hole and all the raw-hamburger emotions lining the inside.

Jordan knew she was coming. Her best friend from medical school and almost maid of honor had been the one to call Lia the day West had shown up at Fletcher Station, the person she'd gone to for help shutting down a wedding when hope was finally lost, but she hadn't even known if he was alive. She'd had months to prepare herself for this confrontation, to script every word and every motion in her head, compose the best emasculating zingers and lists of all the ways she would never, and had never, missed him. But with the starting gun ready to sound, the idea of actually saying any of those things left her cold. Colder than the balmy ten below that she'd walked through from the bus to the station. No one who went halfway around the world to find another person could honestly say she hadn't missed him. Hadn't worried. But it felt better to pretend. Lies could comfort.

She made a sharp right bend in the hallway and kept walking. Halfway to the end, her vision had cleared enough to see a tall, broad man with a black knit hat and an equally black beard standing outside the last two doors, keys in hand, staring in her direction.

In another couple of meters, her stomach did that dropping thing again and this time when her limb control faltered, the only thing that saved her from further humiliation was the meager stability offered by the suitcase rolling beside her.

West.

It was West.

Her polished, ever-immaculate fiancé. Former fiancé. But far scruffier.

Her whole world slowed down, and the remaining length of the hallway grew longer than the thousands of kilometers she'd traveled to reach this hallway with this man.

Instead of a tirade, her mind filled with all the times she'd walked toward him. Right back to that first time they'd met in a London hospital, when a newly minted general surgeon had required an assist and been told to pull one of the not-busy neurosurgical fellows. Her. And the way he'd watched her approaching after having her paged, down the hallway to where he loitered at the nurses' station, his eyes broadcasting bold, open interest until he'd heard her name. How she'd pretended not to notice the looks, how she'd managed to ignore her own attraction for three whole days before she'd asked *him* out.

London Lia did those things. London Lia was fearless. At least on the outside. Because it was what everyone expected of her.

Lifting her chin, Lia held his gaze now, struggling to ignore the burst of other memories. All the church aisles they'd tried on looking for the perfect church for their wedding. When he'd looked at her with the promise of a long future dancing in his eyes, the future he delighted in planning and dreaming into existence with her.

Time sped back up. Her heart squeezed hard once, then began stomping a *chula* around her sternum, fast enough she'd have been silencing alarms on her fitness monitor if the battery hadn't died on the trip down. And her stomach, which had been lurching and freefalling for the duration of the trip, went hollow, and cold. Then the nausea hit.

He didn't speak or look away, just stared. There was an intensity in his gaze, but nothing loving. She'd call it a glare were it not for the pallor she could see when she got closer.

Was this it? The burning in her eyes said so. All happening before she'd even dropped off her luggage?

She wasn't ready.

What could she say? What had she even practiced? She was supposed to say something. She'd come all this way to say *things*. Learn things. Remove the weight of betrayal and loss that glittered on her left ring finger.

The ring that symbolized that future they'd planned weighted her finger and something like relief weighted her tongue. Relief. Regret. Betrayal.

If she'd slept at all on the way there, she would've been able to think. She'd be able to look away from his eyes, and her ears wouldn't be ringing in a way that made her worry about a stroke. She'd hear something other than her own loud, labored breathing in the dead space in her chest.

The Lia he knew would say the words. Slap him, maybe. Shake answers out of him. *Something.* But whoever she was now didn't have that in her.

As the seconds stretched out his shock turned to something else, something harder, and she gave up the mental scramble for words to wait him out, watching anger flare in his eyes, bitterness turn the mouth she'd lived to kiss into a slash amid the facial hair she'd never before seen him wear.

But he didn't say anything, either. No words from either of them. The only acknowledgment that she had any more meaning to him than a stranger came in the form of gritted teeth.

As if he had any right to be angry with *her*. She hadn't left *him* practically at the altar.

She opened her mouth, but before she'd even mustered a word, he stepped past her and silently stormed down the hallway, rigid and straight. Angry. So angry, with her.

He was nearly to the bend, with his rigid posture and determination to yet again get away from her. She'd gone around the world to find him, but in that moment, she had no energy left to chase.

She closed her eyes and breathed slowly out.

In her memories, it seemed she was always walking toward him—down hallways, church aisles, even on staircases in the hospital where they'd meet for a quick kiss between patients or rounds. She didn't have it in her to watch him walking away. That was the only kindness afforded her by the manner of his leaving—she hadn't even seen it coming, let alone had to watch him going.

God, she was so stupid.

There were other Antarctic research stations she could've gone to. A whole world where no one knew her and she could sort herself out without pressure, get ready for the new life waiting for her outside of medicine. This wasn't going to be productive enough to endure the pain that went with it.

Bending her head, she pinched her eyes harder shut, so the pressure swirled colors and shadow to light behind her eyelids, blocking out the mental replay of things she'd obviously never have again with him.

And none of this should surprise her. Of course he didn't want to talk to her. She was the personification of the past, and West had always avoided talking about the past. Only the future. And she was no longer part of his future. Or she was only part of his immediate future, for the next ten days, until he could escape.

He would talk to her. She'd figure out what to say to him, what she really wanted to say, not just what her broken heart wanted to shout. They'd be working together, seeing each other every day. He'd talk, or he'd *listen*. After she'd gotten some sleep, she'd conjure the words.

That was the one good thing about becoming Lia again. She'd been Ophelia while at home in Portugal, and that had taken time to adjust to, too. She'd remember how to be Lia. Lia, who always had opinions and wasn't afraid to share them. And maybe by the time she left Antarctica, she'd figure out who she really was, outside the judging eyes of people who had expectations of her.

Sleep would help. Being around her best friend again would help her remember Lia, the version of herself she preferred to the sober, sad child she'd been.

"Lia?"

She hadn't heard anyone approach, but the sound of her name in her best friend's voice pulled her eyes open again. Once again, she saw anger in the eyes of someone she loved, but this time, it wasn't directed at her.

"What did he say?" Jordan demanded, grabbing her in a quick, hard hug that grounded her enough to banish church aisles and promises of forever from cluttering up her ability to speak.

What had he said?

"Nothing," Lia muttered, making her arms contract, giving an underachieving hug in return. "He said nothing."

When Jordan leaned back, her scowl had grown deeper, firmer. "What did you say to him? Did you tell him he's the world's smallest man and you hoped global warming would eventually thaw out his glacial heart? Would be the only good thing to come from it."

Jordan with the better zingers than Lia, despite the months of practice and mental composing she'd done.

Lia just shook her head, no heart for it. "I didn't say anything. I wasn't expecting to see him yet."

"I was going to tell you. I arranged it so he couldn't get too far away if he wanted to sleep at all while he's here."

"That's his cabin?"

Jordan nodded, but one glance over her shoulder to the door showed her hesitation. "Maybe I shouldn't have done that. Or maybe I shouldn't have even told you he was here."

The worry in Jordan's voice and eyes helped her get some clarity.

"Nonsense. I want to be here. It's cold, but I'll get used to it. I just need to think of what to say before—"

"You have some time."

Ten days. Something she'd reminded herself at least ten thousand times on the trip down. "I was just about to drop my bags off and go to the clinic, as directed."

"And he was just standing there?" Jordan took the bags and the keys, and opened the door to lead Lia into what she would've called a closet under any other circumstances. A small closet. With a small bed.

"With the expression of someone who'd be packing as soon as possible and taking the first transport out."

Something she could appreciate as she mentally inventoried the tiny room. Two windows wrapping around the corner, as the cabin sat at the end of the pod. Twin bed. Bedside table. And a built-in wardrobe that might have actually been a cupboard. Half a meter area to walk from door to window and everything else to the right against the wall.

Cozy.

That's what she decided right then to call it. Yep. Cozy. A small space that would be easier to keep warm. There, some optimism.

"He looks at me like that every day," Jordan confirmed, placing the suitcases by the bed and gesturing Lia back out. "Well, not exactly like that, but we'll talk more about what a louse he is later. I'm not just the welcome wagon, I'm supposed to show you to your physical."

A physical she didn't need but understood the reason for. As they walked back the way she'd come, Jordan filled up the empty space where Lia still had no words, chattering on about the station and the job. And Zeke. Jordan's trip to the southernmost continent had led her to meet and fall in love with someone she may have never met otherwise. Lia would just be happy to meet the true Lia, not some version she'd learned to present, depending upon her audience.

"You won't go into the schedule until tomorrow," Jordan continued, walking Lia back the way she'd come. "I was going to ask if you wanted to have dinner tonight, but as tired as you look, I'm thinking you might just want to sleep."

That wasn't all she wanted, but it would probably facilitate her being able to think well enough to do the other thing: grab West by the beard and shake some answers out of him. Not that she had the energy for that, either.

"Play it by ear?"

"You got it. After I introduce you to Zeke…"

* * *

Every muscle in West's body ached by the time he made it to the clinic. How he'd gotten there, he couldn't say. One second, he was watching his second biggest regret catch up with him, the next he stood in the lobby of the medical center with his head buzzing and no idea why he'd even come.

What the hell was she doing there? He should've turned around and left Fletcher the moment he'd arrived and found Jordan Flynn stationed there. With her, it assured Lia would learn of his location. If he'd had any idea she'd come all that way, he wouldn't have stayed. When it came to Lia Monterrosa, he was weak. The only way he could see to giving her a better life, not ruining it as he'd ruined Charlie's, was to leave. Leaving had been the only way for them to both survive; he couldn't go through that kind of loss again.

Without him there, she could move on and find someone more deserving than a man who couldn't even hear her name without remembering the day, months earlier, when he'd had to claim the body of his little brother. Someone who would still be alive if it weren't for West's ultimatum. Not that it took hearing her name, or thinking of her, to be sucked right back there. It could barely be called a memory; it remained so present in his head it was like one long, unending day since.

He'd assumed once Jordan delivered the news, they'd both curse him and do whatever women did when thousands of miles separated them but there was an ugly breakup to contend with.

She hadn't been going to his cabin. She'd carried luggage, and worn the standard-issue red snowsuit given to every crew member.

She'd been moving into the empty cabin beside his. And he'd just stood outside his door because…

He rubbed between his brows, trying to will some clarity to his thoughts.

It wasn't morning. He'd…gone to the shop for supplies, then the post office to collect books he'd ordered a month ago, and…that was why he'd even been there. Dropping off his packages. After lunch. Which meant he was in the clinic because he had physicals to perform for the six new arrivals who the department head had put on the schedule a week ago: four scientists, a computer programmer and the doctor hired to overwinter.

Lia was there for the winter. The woman who lived for sunshine had signed up for six months of Antarctic night?

Whatever.

He wasn't staying on. He just had to hold on for the next ten days without groveling and begging her to forgive him. Even through the horror darkening the edges of his vision, his whole body sparked, and he breathed too fast. He needed to slow that down before someone came in.

Regardless of the constant state of chill in the station's open facilities, he felt sweat running down his spine, and did the only thing he could—ripped his jacket off and hung it on the wall hooks.

Damn it. The clinic was the last place he should be. Walking away from her just now had only hit the pause button on whatever she'd come to say. He just needed a minute to think.

Focus.

He walked to the counter at the wall where hard backups of patients' files were kept, and braced his hands on the counter for stability, then closed his eyes and took a deep, slow breath.

Get it together. With his current state of mental function, almost nothing permeated the towering brick wall cutting across his brain. He'd be useless like this if there was an emergency.

He never let himself picture what it would be like to see her again, but if he had, it wouldn't have been gut-churning. Leaving wiped the slate, let him have a start fresh. Always. And once he'd gotten past that big first hump, the pain of loss dulled. Sometimes slower than others.

The thought of her projected her sorrow-filled expression on that towering wall in his head. Sad. Heartbroken, even. But not angry. She'd obviously come to see him, but hadn't come out swinging. Something wasn't right.

"West." His name spoken jerked his attention back to earth and he turned to see the medical director, Dr. Tony Bradshaw, approaching, folders in hand. "The new arrivals—"

"I know," West cut in, shaking his head, "you told us days ago."

The man was getting so forgetful, West should be so lucky. And too thin, but he didn't comment on that. They'd had that conversation twice before, and there was only so much West could do to make the man accommodate the increased metabolic needs Antarctica triggered.

He took another slow breath, fighting his own body, depriving himself of the increased demands for oxygen through sheer force of will.

"Right," Tony said slowly, as if he truly didn't remember, and handed over the folders. "Jordan is coming in to help you. She went to round some of them up."

Went to round up Lia.

She'd just stopped outside his door, with eye contact that pulled at him like gravity, and dragged memories into the front of his mind. The way she smelled fresh from the shower. Or better, first thing in the morning when she had his scent all over her, and it all mingled together. His cabin didn't smell like home still.

The sudden heat returned, and he noticed the inconsistency of it—the whole front of him on fire, and his spine like an ice core down his back, a frozen ice dagger digging into the base of his skull. Twisting. Tangling the nerves there, spaghetti-style.

"I've got a meeting, so you and Jordan sort them out," Tony called from the door as West bent to gather up the paper he'd dropped.

"Right."

He sighed hard enough to waft paper off the top of the pile.

Just get through the next couple of hours. That was the only thing to do.

Then she could go back home now and management would have time to get another doctor in there, someone suited to the winter, and he wouldn't have to spend the next eight months thinking about her and wondering if the woman who lived in the sunshine was all right with the unending dark of Antarctic night. He needed a fresh start. Another fresh start.

"You all right?" Tony's voice came from behind him, still there. Not gone.

And still no answer to give. At least, that he wanted

to give. Far from all right. He hadn't been all right for months, why should today be better?

"Not sleeping great," he said. It was the only thing he could think of that wasn't a lie.

"Are you taking the sleep aids?"

"Aye." He stood. If they were going to talk about his health, he'd say something again about Tony's. The man was going to overwinter to head some project for NASA, and his weight loss would become more of an issue soon. "You still tryin' to increase calories? You're too thin."

Tony dropping inches was more of an issue than West's sleep troubles.

Tony redirected, ignoring his question. "Get Jordan to do a thyroid check on you when you're done with the newbies."

"Checked last week, man." West reminded him about that, too, refusing the redirect. "You do the same. Forgetfulness is a T3 symptom."

"Fine, fine."

Which meant *no*.

"Threw me straight out of the bunk." Jordan's voice came from the door providing the interruption Tony needed to slip out. He heard Lia's voice in reply and had to force himself not to look at her until his thundering heart slowed.

That was one thing he had going for him with this— no matter how riled up, Lia was a quiet talker. If she insisted on having it out with him, he could get her into a treatment bay, close the door, and whatever she had to say to him wouldn't carry through the walls. So long as he kept *his* voice down. The walls between the cabins were paper-thin, but not in the medical center.

But that would entail giving Lia a physical… The thought shouldn't make that heat burrowing into his chest grow, dip lower, grow hotter. The very last thing he should do was touch her in any capacity. It would snowball. It always snowballed. He had no restraint around her. Even wanting to avoid the conversation he knew was coming, he still wanted to look at her. He still wanted to touch her.

He picked up the stack of folders and turned to find both Jordan and Lia watching him. Waiting for him to say something. Too bad.

A quick sort of the folders, and he handed three to the other doctor, making sure Lia's was on top.

"Tony wants everyone done ASAP."

Jordan shared a look with Lia, but took the folders.

"If you're planning to ignore me the rest of your time at the station, get ready to be annoyed." Lia finally spoke, soft voice, pointed words.

It was still the three of them, waiting on the arrival of the rest of the new crew. He could risk saying something short. He just didn't know what to say, other than a direct response or ignoring her.

"I'm already annoyed."

He finally let himself look at her again, holding her gaze for a second before the curious presence of pink on her head had him looking up, and then down over her, cataloging differences between the woman before him and the one he'd known in London.

Tired. Tanned. Pink hat. She hated pink. Wispy brunette curls poked out from beneath the folded brim, longer than the short, edgy pixie she was known for. The effect was the same, drawing all focus to her soft, feminine features.

"Welcome to my life," she said, words still softly spoken in her usual custom, but with steel he'd never been able to resist. Strength he'd long admired. Strength he'd once upon a time pictured in her as the mother to his children. The kind of mother like he'd never experienced, and which might not even exist. A mother who would fight and die to protect her children.

Another life. Another future he'd failed to build.

"You seriously want to do this here?"

She didn't answer him. A couple of seconds passed, and she just turned to Jordan. "Can you do mine first? I'm the only one here, and I'm really tired from the trip. It's amazing I'm upright."

Shutting him out was fine. Shutting him out was perfect.

Showdown at least momentarily averted, he headed off to the side of the room where he could spread the files on the countertop for review. It gave him something to do. He'd take anything that dulled the knife at his neck, and helped him ignore the pull she exuded. It was all he could do.

CHAPTER TWO

ONCE WEST HAD made a decision he did his best to move on it. Over the hours between Lia's arrival and the dragged-out end of his shift, he'd decided the only way to handle things was to tackle his Lia problem head-on, as brutally as his conscience would allow.

The circumstances of his shift only served to wrench up his irritation—two of his three assigned physicals had showed up, but the third, a recalcitrant astrophysicist, had ignored multiple calls to the telescope. Then, five minutes before the end of his shift, an emergency bone-setting had dragged his shift out an extra hour.

By the time he made it to her cabin door, some of his gut-swirling panic had settled into annoyance, and he let it. Was glad for it. Annoyance helped keep fond memories at bay. He didn't need anything making him want to go to her, talk to her, make her smile. Kiss her. Even if he could drum up anger for her, he doubted he'd still want to be outside of her presence. Ever.

The only way to handle this was to make sure she didn't want him, make sure she hadn't come all the way to Antarctica to try and reconcile. Make sure she understood they were done.

Remove temptation.

He had to, harsh and quick, like a battlefield surgeon removing a gangrenous limb so the person would live. Only he was also the limb.

He took a deep breath to wrest control back from the willful, stubborn and half-wild, survival-focused part of his personality, and knocked.

Get the words out, move on. If she didn't want him, he wouldn't have to fight his own impulses for the next ten days. Not the best plan, but the only one he had.

He listened for signs of movement within. If she was there, he'd hear her.

Seconds ticked on, but no sound came from inside the tiny room. He knocked again, louder.

Then he heard the sound of bedclothes rustling, and when the door opened, her sleepy, confused face appeared in the frame. Four hours of frustration, but when he looked at her, memories of their mornings together and that old affection wrapped around him, making him want to wrap around her. Pretend now was then, and at any second, the sleepy confusion would warm to one of those soft-eyed smiles he'd so adored. The glimpses she'd reserved for him, past her strength, competency or expectations, to see the woman within.

But when her confusion cleared, there was nothing soft in her eyes for him.

Good. He did his best to ignore the exhaustion in her eyes, in her whole body.

"I'll make it quick," he said, gesturing inside with a nod.

"Tomorrow."

He finally noticed in the dim light that she was wearing pink from head to toe. Some fluffy pink thing.

Pajamas, maybe. It had a hood and feet built in. His annoyance had already started to fade.

Why was she wearing pink everywhere? She hated pink. Lord, he wanted to ask. But that would be showing an interest, the opposite of what he was trying to do. So would touching her, even though the urge to feel her skin against his boomed through him like a foghorn.

"Now or never, Lia." He curled his fingers to his palms with the control it took not to push the door in, haul her to him. Just looking at her hurt.

Hell.

"Speak now, or forever hold your peace?" She spoke softly, like the effort to utter every word shaved a year off her life.

The ceremonial words sailed straight and true, and hit harder than a sledgehammer. Despite his determination to be a stone, he couldn't hide the shock rippling through him, but grit his teeth, nodded once, and she stepped back to let him in.

This was why he didn't stick around to watch the destruction after whatever life catastrophe had triggered. He couldn't stand there, inside the bubble of pain he could almost see around her, warping reality. As if this cabin were some awful place that existed between two universes, the one where he'd gotten everything he'd ever wanted, and this one, where the last gift he could give her was walking away.

He closed the door behind him and leaned there, while she tracked the measly few feet that made up the whole of the walking space, getting as far from one another as was possible in the tiny space.

In his mind, all afternoon, when he'd pictured himself coming, acting it out, he'd dialed his performance to eleven. Shouted. Said ugly, awful things. Lied. Everything he could think of to make her angry, to make her hate him. But there with her, breathing the same air, feeling the pain written all over her, from the tilt of her eyebrows to the way she shifted from foot to foot, fidgeting, her hands hidden in her cuffs, he couldn't do it.

He couldn't do it, more proof that he had to make her want to stay away.

He forced himself to look her in the eye, but kept his voice quiet, and more sympathetic than he wanted. "I don't know what you're wantin', lass, but you're wastin' your time comin'. It's done between us. Over. Say what you want to say, and let's have done with it."

He heard his accent thicker than it had been in years, not just the shifting pronunciation, but the words, the cadence. Further proof this was scrambling his eggs.

"I didn't come to *say* anything. I wanted to see with my own eyes that you were alive and well." Her voice wobbled, like it had to pass through bubbles of emotion in her throat. This would be easier if she would just shout.

"And now you see."

"Alive. And I need to understand why the man who said he loved me, the only—" She stopped midthought, and closed her eyes, hands slipping from her sleeves enough to fidget before her as she struggled for composure. "Why would you just leave without word, three days before our wedding? I deserve to know what I did wrong."

There it was, her taking the blame for it. An example of exactly what she would do if he told her the whole damned story, try to take his guilt away or at least share the load. She'd probably say his brother had committed suicide because she'd taken too much of West's time, or that it was her fault because she was the subject of West's ultimatum. He couldn't have an addict around his new family, and he'd picked Lia over Charlie. And Charlie had picked drugs over rehab and family. A choice Charlie obviously wasn't ready to make, and he should've seen that. If he'd listened…

He lifted one hand to mash against his forehead, trying to rub away the tension headache already starting to drill in.

Don't think about Charlie.

He didn't need to explain. He wasn't *going* to explain. But if he wanted her to believe him, not take the blame, he had to give some excuse. Pinning some action on her would be an even greater sin than the lie he was about to tell. He couldn't make her take the blame. He'd take it. He deserved it.

"You didn't do anything wrong." The muscles all seemed to have tightened, and making his mouth form words was harder than running in water. "Something happened, and I needed to go. So I left."

"What happened?"

"I don't want to talk about that. I don't want to talk about any of this, and you know that."

Her shoulders bobbed quickly under the fluffy pink onesie she'd zipped herself into. In any other circumstances, the ridiculousness of her outfit would delight him—with the hood and the footsies attached—but he hadn't smiled in a long time.

"I don't care about your aversion to talking about the past. It's not that far in the past, and I need to understand."

"Aye, I see that. But you don't need to know everything. You're not part of my life now, Lia. We're not friends. We're not lovers. We're not engaged."

"If you had to leave, I would've gone with you."

"No," he said swiftly, searching for any route that would get through to her. "When I proposed, I thought it was love. I thought I loved you. Turns out, I didn't."

The color drained from her face.

"But when I left…" she started, but then just stopped. Like she didn't even have an avenue to try and argue it. Like it was almost expected.

Which it probably was. He had left her days before their wedding.

That was something he should apologize for; he could do that without explanations. But softening his position now would be a bad idea. Inside, he was already as soft as peat; it wouldn't take much for him to sink into the dreck. He'd apologize another day, after she'd accepted things.

"Is there anything else you want to discuss?"

Speak now, or forever hold your peace… She didn't even have to say the words this time.

"I guess I don't have anything else to say," she said, the words hanging there, sucking the air out of the room as she extended her left arm a bit, eyes fixed on the hand she'd let slide out from the cuff she'd tucked it into for warmth. "Just…"

He followed her gaze down to her hand. And the glittering diamond ring still perched on her finger. Where he'd slid it almost a year before.

The ice he'd felt cramming into the back of his neck earlier returned, a single, hard throb in his head stopping him from saying anything else. Why would she still be wearing that?

"I came to give this back." Her voice wobbled, then cracked, the sound as sudden and startling as a gunshot. "This beautiful ring we designed together, and the lie that it represents…"

Lia had other things she wished she had the strength to say, but as soon as she got feeling back in her face, she might be able to be proud of herself for still breathing after having him say the worst thing he could have to her. But all she could think of was to return the ring.

She flexed her hand, noted the way it trembled, the way her body could respond while mentally she still scrambled for anything to say. Her heart rabbited away. She heard her breath as if through a stethoscope, but it was as if every part of her brain was focused on keeping her upright and breathing. All emotion. No reason.

West stared at the ring, his jaw bunched and his brow beetled, but he didn't say anything.

Take it off. She was supposed to take it off now.

Forcing her arms to move, she latched on to the exquisite trigold engraved band and pulled.

In the first days, when she hadn't been able to locate him, the ring had been a comfort to her. When she discovered his empty flat, she'd clung to the promise she'd still trusted in and wanted to protect.

Her hands were cold enough that the knuckle, which always snagged it, had contracted, and it took nearly no effort for the ring to pop free. But everything still wobbled. Her hands. Her voice, when she finally found some words, the last she hoped she'd ever have to say to him. "I can't carry it anymore, or the weight of your broken promises."

The last word was whispered, no strength left to fake, all swept away with the sudden, sickly warmth washing over her face and down. Lightly stinging in her eyes and cheeks, then like a fever in her throat where muscles tensed, opened, hollowed so that when she breathed in it sounded strangled, choking…

Oh, no…

She was going to cry. As if she needed one more ounce of humiliation. The cascade of physical processes had already begun, the ones she could feel and which let her know it was too late to stop.

She thrust her hand out to him, the ring on her quaking palm.

He started to say something, but stopped dead a split second before her chin began the quiver and tears spilled.

Focusing on the process of it was the only thing she could think to do.

Useless Science Fact Number One: tears from grief and pain were chemically different from those summoned by dirt or onion fumes.

Useless Science Question Number One: How would these tears have dried on a microscope slide? Spiky or like a web of fractals, like that strange theory she'd once read which hypothesized that different tears produced different crystalline salt structures.

She looked away from his eyes, not wanting to see him through the wavering watery line, or the horror there. But that coping mechanism fritzed and she had to reach for any other information to sedate her emotions.

"Lia?"

What else?

Something…

Prolactin.

Useless Science Fact Number Two: prolactin was somehow present in tears—a hormone initially believed only to govern lactation and the reason babies instinctively suckled. There was no way to stop it.

"Lia?" He said her name again, confusion present in his voice. As if she shouldn't experience grief. Like she wasn't a human who'd gone through loss in the past, who wasn't having her third round of grief in a handful of months, just because he'd wanted to share those old pains with her, or know her. Never wanted to let her close enough to love her, just close enough to fool her into thinking she'd finally found someone who would.

Lia never cried.

Ophelia had, but only when she was alone. She needed to be alone now.

He said her name again, but she could only shake her head, her eyes fixed on the little closet at his shoulder.

Why was he still standing there? Didn't he have any decency? Couldn't he see that she…

The ring. He hadn't taken it; she still felt it weighing her palm down.

When she gave it to him, he would go…

She thrust it forward, finally looking again at his face, his horrified face.

Enough. He had to go.

She opened her mouth to tell him, but a short, choked hiccup came out instead, and in her own horror, she slammed her free hand over her mouth to hold it.

"Lia?"

He had to stop saying her name like he could make her stop feeling by him being horrified by it.

One step forward came with his word this time, so her knuckles touched his chest.

The brush of his hand on her well-padded arm got through the grief fogging her brain.

He thought he could be horrible and cruel and then just…what? Comfort her? Maybe tell her to stop being dramatic?

No.

She peeled her own hand from her mouth and slapped his hand away hard. Then again, because it wasn't far enough. She'd come all this way, and now all she wanted was distance.

Distance and getting rid of the ring, which he still hadn't taken. A quick survey of his attire provided an array of pockets where she could stick the cursed thing. She found one, and as soon as she'd stuffed the diamond band inside, she shoved at his chest.

"Lia, you have to take a breath. Calm down."

"Stop saying my name." She panted the words, because she was only half functioning on intention.

"Okay, but you have—"

"Get out!"

West lifted both hands, palms forward, to stay her, and backed warily out the door.

As soon as he stepped through, she took two big steps, made sure it was as closed as possible, then flipped the locks.

She crawled back into bed and pressed her face into the pillow to muffle the sounds she couldn't stop.

It was done. It was over. She'd wanted to know what she'd meant to him, and now she knew. But she'd always known that, in the back of her mind. She'd just let herself pretend otherwise.

CHAPTER THREE

WEST PUSHED INTO the clinic early the next morning, before anyone else had arrived, and flipped on the lights before heading straight for the supply room.

He'd endured many sleepless nights when he'd first arrived at Fletcher Station, but with the absence of dark, there was a healthy insomniac population for him to blend into.

Last night, he'd been unable to will away the image of her with tears on her cheeks, the complete breakdown of the steel-framed woman he'd known. In the moment, he thought he'd heard everything she'd said to him; he'd tried to listen, but it wasn't there in his head. All the times he'd concentrated, pressed the mental replay, all he got was the vision of her shaking and crying, and the understanding that it would take a long time to scab over.

Worse, he couldn't shake the notion that he'd ruined her as badly as he'd ruined Charlie. Yet more proof that he shouldn't be trusted with the psychological well-being of anyone.

The only good thing a sleepless night afforded him was early breakfast and getting to lock himself away before she arrived for her first shift. If he was lucky, he could busy himself counting everything, a task that would minimize contact with other people, while staying mostly out of sight. For her.

Instinct said *give her time*. Trust Jordan to be there for her to lean on as he was sure she had done at the start. But it also said *keep an eye on her*. Because he just wasn't sure how bad this could get. He prayed not as bad as it had with his brother, but then Lia wasn't an addict. She had Jordan looking out for her. Maybe he should quietly ask her to keep a closer eye…

He opened the digital inventory and sent it to the office printer. Working on paper would be easier on his fried brain, and anything he could do to make today easier, he would. Including throwing himself into monotony, testing the status of everyday machines used for testing and upkeep. Centrifuge, autoclave and irradiator for sterilizing equipment that would be reused—something he'd never encountered in any other hospital but was in Antarctica. Everything brought onto the continent had to be shipped out again, including all forms of garbage.

He left in nine days.

"Are we having fun yet?" Jordan asked after throwing away the last bits of a stitch kit Lia had used on a butter-fingered galley cook, her second patient of the day.

As part of her first day on the job, Lia shadowed Jordan to learn her way around and get a crash course in station medicine, which was like some cross between a small hospital and field medicine. "Oh, sure, nothing like stitching up a hearty thumb slice to get the party started."

"Or an asthma attack."

"That was the first party of the day," Lia corrected her thumb party joke, finishing up the file entry for the thumb.

She'd expected to struggle to find the old Lia, the version of her that Jordan knew, but a few minutes with her almost maid of honor had her stepping into London Lia's shoes once more, the ones she hadn't been strong enough to cram onto her metaphorical feet with West last night.

Not that she had to try too hard in that regard. Of all the people in her life, Jordan, who'd known her since medical school, was the most likely to be accepting of changes to the Lia she knew. But it was just one more thing on an already overwrought mind and Lia didn't have it in her yet to try and sort out who she was supposed to be while trying to sort out everything else. While still hollow and cold from last night's official breakup. Breakdown. Whatever. From feeling him very close by, but knowing she wouldn't be welcome if she spoke to him, that she shouldn't even want to speak to him, that he'd never smile for her again or cuddle under a warm woolly blanket with her to watch some silly movie with more special effects than story.

If being London Lia made it even a tiny bit easier, she'd stick to it for now. But that didn't mean she couldn't tell Jordan the truth about her situation, it just meant she had to be strong about it. No matter how helpless and heartbroken she might be on the inside.

"But I guess this is just my life now."

"While you're here, you mean?" Jordan asked, her tone saying she'd picked up on the undercurrent of dismay. "It can get more exciting here. Fieldwork can be pretty dangerous—not that you'll be doing any of that over the winter. Are you nervous about staying?"

"For the winter?" Lia popped her head out of the treatment room to make certain no other patients had come in while they stood there chatting. "Not really. I've decided it's adventurous and as my life is no longer going to be neurosurgery exciting, and even if my cabin is freezing compared to the rest of the station, it's adventure time and I should enjoy the memory-making."

"I'm going to come back to that whole life-without-adventure thing, but right now...your cabin was really that cold last night?" Jordan asked. "Inside the station never seems much colder than being at home."

She had a point. Lia didn't feel colder in the clinic, but no, her cabin had been colder. "Maybe I was just really tired. But honestly, I was always a little bit cold when I worked in London, and that was before I spent time in Portugal. Maybe the warm temperate climate had made me go soft."

Jordan snorted her disbelief, a testament to how well Lia had played the self-assigned role of all things unsinkable. "You'll do more than waste away in a little village. Maybe you can work part-time in Porto."

All Lia could think to do was nod. "Maybe."

But even if the authorities were still unsure if her father would return and take over the vineyard, she wasn't confused about it. Once he lost interest in something, that was it. Her mother. His second and third wives. Her—not that she could remember him ever having interest in her. Just the opposite. Disappointment that she wasn't male, and all the assurances that she'd never inherit. A point that had left her further confused when the lawyers had said, with him gone, she was the one indicated in his paperwork to manage Monterrosa Wine.

But that strange surprise had faded when they'd informed her that as soon as she married it would be her husband who actually inherited the vineyard. At that time, she'd thought that would be West. Now she might never feel comfortable enough to marry, not if she could be as wrong about West as she had been. A man who wanted her to believe he loved her? She'd probably fall for it without a drop of sense.

"But considering the village is called Monterrosa, I feel my first responsibility is to them, the people who have been loyal to Monterrosa Wine since the time of titles."

"Who was assigned Nigel Gates yesterday?" The question came from the lobby area, immediately shifting both of their attention from the spiky conversation.

"Tony?" Lia mouthed the question to Jordan, not yet able to identify people by voice.

Jordan nodded, then mouthed back, "West had him."

They both eased off the counter where they'd been leaning and drifted out to the lobby in time to see West coming out of the room where the autoclave and irradiators lived.

"I had him, but he never showed. It's in the file," West said, glancing toward the two of them, but focusing again on the medical director. "I was here with a broken arm an hour after end of shift, and he never made an appearance. Called up to the BAT twice before that, no answer."

Nigel was being uncooperative. Figured.

"BAT?" she whispered to Jordan, staying out of the

conversation between Tony and West, despite staying to listen in.

"Big-ass telescope," Jordan filled in. "There are a lot of goofy acronyms around here."

Lia nodded, but as it now all made sense, she had to join in the conversation. She could be an adult about this. She had to learn how to coexist with West at the station for several more days, couldn't spend the whole time avoiding him.

"Nigel is in a big hurry to get the telescope calibrated before the night sky appears. I guess it takes a lot of time and effort," she said, because she had picked up that much from the man's single-minded but strangely nonconversational conversation. "He's not going to take time away from that telescope without being forced."

"Why do you say that?" West asked, his voice growing quiet and sober enough that she had to look at him.

"We spent two days traveling with each other, talking and getting to know one another." Even if it was more like she was just there, listening to him talking to himself about his plans, she'd heard enough. "He's got a fire in his belly."

She immediately heard how it sounded—like she and Nigel had developed more of a connection than they had, and while seeming less pathetic, like someone who was still able to connect to another man appealed, West only had to meet Nigel to know how inaccurate that assumption would be.

"What's the goal? A study of some kind?" Tony asked from the doorway of his office where he continued to loiter.

She could only shake her head. "I couldn't tell you. He told me. In detail. But it was more like me listening to him thinking out loud than conversation. I mostly understood his drive. He said he'll never get this kind of unrestricted access to a large telescope again, and his future plans ride on proving some theory. He's not coming out of there without pressure. And it'll probably get worse once the night sky arrives."

West moved on. "I'll call up there again, and if he doesn't answer, I'll take equipment and go."

The way he turned his body away from her made it clear her part of this conversation was over, and she turned to Jordan, and tried to pretend she didn't see worry in her friend's eyes.

West got on the radio, and after a moment, he was speaking into the mic, calling Nigel by name, but no response came but static and silence.

"He can hear it broadcasting over the whole building?"

"It's basically a big dome with a room built on for entry. If he's with the telescope, he should be able to hear the radio."

And why would he answer West today when he hadn't yesterday?

She stepped away from Jordan and, although the last thing she should do was get close to West, stopped a couple feet down from where he stood with the radio. "Let me try. He might answer me."

A few moments after she made the call and announced who it was, Nigel answered.

"Lia, busy right now." He mumbled something else, something about cycling and whatever that was, but it was an opening.

"It's really important that I get your baseline and type your blood, just in case there is some kind of emergency this winter and we're all cut off from evacs. Maybe you can make up the time later."

"Time is fixed, it cannot be made up."

"Okay, but it can be saved. If I get dinner delivered to you later, you won't have to come down to the galley and take time away, just keep working."

He was silent a moment, and then agreed, "Fine. But be quick."

Right. She rang off and then looked back to Jordan. "Want to come with me?"

Jordan nodded, but West interrupted, stepping over to take the radio from her hand. "He's my patient. I'm going. You don't need to go. Just send the dinner later."

"If he's going to be a problem child for the winter," Tony interjected, "Lia needs to reinforce her relationship with him and learn where to find him when he refuses to come down."

West's answering grunt had all eyes on him, but he *stared* at Lia for several long seconds before he nodded. "Lia can come with me if she wants to."

She definitely didn't want to, but she also didn't want to let him keep affecting all her decisions, making her less than she had the potential to be, as she'd been since she'd found him missing.

One look around provided a befuddled-looking Tony Bradshaw, who clearly did not understand the angsty undercurrent flowing between them all, but didn't ask for clarification. He just gave final directions about blood typing and equipment, then returned to his office.

"Get your boots on and your outdoor suit," West directed, then pivoted to grab a bag from the wall and headed for the inventory room again, where he'd been all day. "Meet me here in fifteen."

Right. Great.

She looked over to find Jordan hurrying to her side. "Are you sure you're okay with this? It probably shouldn't be all three of us, but if you don't want to make the trek alone with him, you can bow out and I'll take you up there tomorrow. So you know where it is."

The question alone would've alarmed Lia back home, but here it just confirmed that she wasn't pulling off her quiet strength act as well as she'd used to, no matter how easy it was to talk to Jordan again.

"It's okay. I said I was after adventure, right?"

"Yes, but I'm not sure spending time with *him* means adventure, just…suffering." Jordan kept her words quiet, and the gentle assertion of support had that tingling returning to Lia's eyes. She shook her head and gestured to the door, eager to escape before that awful leaking came back. "I need to get my suit. It'll be fine. I'm not going to let him make me dread any part of my adventure. I'm here to revel. R.E.V.E.L. And climbing a frozen, snowy, almost-mountain is the kind of adventure I can't have in Portugal. Don't worry."

She silently repeated the words to herself. Don't worry. Don't worry because he couldn't say anything worse than he already had. And that stare of his hadn't said he wanted to talk to her about anything, just like him hiding out in the storage room all day said he didn't want to be in her presence any more than she wanted to be in his.

"I'm going to worry, anyway," Jordan muttered, still looking uneasy with the concept, but apparently with enough confidence in Lia still to say, "Call me for dinner when you get back. Zeke and I will meet you in the galley."

"Okay. Don't worry," she repeated. "We're just going to work. Said everything we needed to last night."

"You did?" If possible, Jordan looked more alarmed.

Suddenly, Lia didn't want to uphold any masks with her. She could shrug it off, she would've before, but she probably couldn't pull off the unaffected face. Not when she knew that her eyes were still a little red, which might become a chronic condition.

"I don't think I can talk about it yet," she said after a hard pause that made a little line appear between Jordan's brows.

Jordan squeezed her hand once and nodded, accepting. "When you're ready."

She had to swallow down another rise of emotion, but glanced toward the door. "If I'm late, he won't wait for me."

God knew West found it too easy to leave her behind.

CHAPTER FOUR

WEST STOOD AT the door of his cabin, a rigged heater in his arms, ready to take it next door to Lia.

She didn't know he was coming. Probably wouldn't want to see him at her door for the second night in a row, but he had to do something.

No matter how sound his reasoning, West knew he'd abandoned her. And he knew how bad that felt. How it wormed down into places you didn't even realize were there, and came out when you least wanted. Over the years he'd seen it from every angle—from the slow-motion abandonment of his mother, to Charlie's withdrawal into substance abuse, and even from the other side and the many times he'd walked away from friendships or half-formed relationships to outrun Charlie's problems.

Until Lia.

Until West had met Lia and was no longer willing to start over anywhere she wasn't. And in his fear of losing her, he'd hidden his biggest weakness from her—his addict brother. She knew he had a little brother, but he'd hidden the bad parts. To keep her from asking to meet Charlie, West had concocted a story about an adventure in the States, working his way across the continent, like some romanticized vagabond.

That was the first in a string of unforgivable sins that led him here.

If he'd told her the truth back then, he might have never felt the need to make Charlie choose. Or maybe he would've done it gentler, and actually listened to the words his brother said. West had heard *"Have a nice life"* as another passive-aggressive jab of guilt. It wasn't until much later that he'd understood it to have been a more final goodbye.

He needed to pay attention to Lia right now. Make sure she didn't have a Charlie reaction to his choices. She was still his responsibility, and if anything happened to her…

Not that he thought Lia suicidal, but he'd once thought her made of iron, stronger than anyone else he'd ever known. Strong or not, she'd still cried herself to sleep last night, and he'd heard every sniff and hiccup through the paper-thin cabin walls. He'd seen the evidence of it all day in her still-puffy eyes, and it ate at him.

He stepped out of his cabin, closed the door and took the two steps separating them to lightly knock on hers. Unlike last night, she didn't take long to respond.

With the door held half-open in front of her like a shield of protection, she met his gaze and some of the burning in his chest eased when she didn't flinch or look away. Of course, that meant he could see fresh redness in her eyebrows that contradicted the flash of strength. And still wearing the pink pajamas, but she hadn't been sleeping, at least not yet.

No greeting, no deep longing looks and no hope in

her voice, she glanced at what he carried and back up. "Flower pots?"

"Heater," he said softly, tapping the terra-cotta pots with one finger. If the promise of heat didn't buy him admittance, he had no words to ask. No words for anything. There was a time when he'd always had something to say to her. Waited, saving up thoughts throughout the day to tell her at night. Stupid things to make her smile, or things to spark debate. Teasing. Challenging. Playful. But now, every word he uttered could give him away. He couldn't afford to overshare.

"How?"

"I'll show you. It'll warm the cabin, those at the end of the pods are exposed to more outside walls than those stacked side by side. They don't retain the heat as well."

She considered the pots for another several seconds, door still in place, then simply let go of the door and moved back inside.

He closed the door behind him, then wordlessly stepped to the bedside table to clear it off while she burrowed back into a mountain of blankets on the bed.

Explaining how the pots functioned as a heater while he assembled it was easy at least. He lit four tea-light candles for the bottom layer and stepped back to mention safety; even if she didn't need to hear not to touch hot things, it was easier.

"But I guess you don't need to be warned about the danger of fire."

"Not really," she muttered. "Things I need to be warned about never come with a warning. Or I'm just really bad at picking up on hints."

So was he. Charlie had proven that.

And she didn't need to know that. "Hints?"

"Do you really want to know?" she asked, pushing down the blankets to her lap so she could sit up straighter, but stayed tucked into the bed.

He was suddenly sure he didn't want to know, but he said, anyway, "Tell me."

One purposeful nod, and she asked, "When did you know you didn't love me? Because I've had months of wondering what happened while I was gone. The last thing you said to me at the airport that day was 'I love you.' Did I miss something? Did you know then?"

Hell.

No more circling the problem. This was more like the Lia he knew than the sad-eyed woman he'd seen every time he'd looked at her since she'd arrived.

And he didn't have an answer. He never considered that he'd need to have more of an answer.

"I figured it out after," he said. "Probably good you didn't want me to come to Portugal with you."

"What does that mean?"

"You didn't want me to go."

Her eyes narrowed. "Why would I invite you to Portugal when you had no idea what you were going to be walking into? Because what is going on there? It's a mess, above what you've probably realized."

"Mess how?" he asked. "What's going on at Monterrosa now? Are you avoiding going there?"

"That seems to be your MO, not mine. I don't run away from pain—apparently I run toward it." She nodded once to him, then pointed to the door. "I think we're done. I understand exactly where you're coming from. You didn't love me, you figured it out as soon as I was out of sight because something mysterious happened. I'm guessing she had red hair."

"Lia."

"I don't suppose I need more details." She waved a hand toward the door.

He didn't move. He was finally starting to feel a little hopeful that she would get over him, that he wouldn't ruin her, too. "Are you finally getting angry?"

"Is that good, too?"

"Yes," he immediately answered, maybe a little too loudly.

"Why?"

He lowered his voice a little and shook his head. "Because I hate seeing you with red eyes."

"Sorry I'm disappointing you by being human."

"The Lia Monterrosa I know wouldn't let—"

"Maybe that's the problem, then." She cut him off. "You *don't* know me. And I'm tired of cleaning up messes of the men who should've loved me, but didn't. You left me to call off the wedding, after I figured out you weren't coming back, and I waited up until the last minute. Nine days after my father burned down half of the estate and dropped off the face of the earth so I've had to clean it up for the hundreds of people who rely on the vineyard for their livelihoods. Then I had to cancel my wedding because my fiancé disappeared, too. It was a great week."

He hadn't thought about the timing back then, but now seemed a good time to ask, since all information about her emotional state was of value. "Did you get it repaired?"

"Does it matter?" she asked, then stretched out in the bed, rolling to face the wall. "Thanks for the heater. You're still a *babaca*."

Final words if he'd ever heard them; even if he didn't

understand the actual last one, he could read between the lines. Jerk. Ass. Something like that. And a little bit angrier, thank God. Anger was fire, and fire meant the will to fight. That was better than just curling up and taking whatever life had thrown at her.

But staying out of her way as much as possible until it was time to go was the right call. He definitely should go on that day trip into the field tomorrow. Even one day of distance had to help.

"What're you doin'?"

The familiar cadence of West's nearly tamed brogue stopped Lia midstick.

She lifted her gaze from the butterfly needle she'd been fishing for a vein with at the crook of her elbow to see him in the doorway, leaning, rough from a prolonged field mission, still wearing the thick red thermal suit, large duffel bag hanging on his shoulder.

It had been three days since she'd last seen him. Three days since their really awesome and definitely not soul-crushing *discussion*. Of course he'd be the one to find her performing a sneaky blood draw on herself.

"Trying and failing to get some blood."

He dropped the bag outside the door and meandered into the small exam room. "Maybe because you're right-handed and trying with your left."

"I have tiny veins, they're hard to hit, and the best one is on the right elbow crook." She halfway withdrew the tiny butterfly needle again, tilted it slightly and pushed forward again, gritting her teeth. Somehow it hurt more having to watch the needle, and when she was doing the steering, she definitely had to watch.

He headed for the sink, washed his hands and stepped to her side. "Stop."

He didn't swat her hand, but she heard the reprimand coming as he pinched the butterfly above where she'd held it, and she let go.

"You just had panels run six days ago." Dr. Obvious held the needle still and used his free hand to lightly palpate the vein above, considering his next move.

"I know. I was there."

"You could've had Tony do this for you, or anyone else in the department."

"I know that, too."

He didn't try to press the needle into the vein again, just took it out and watched as absolutely nothing happened. No blood. No extra firmness when he prodded the vein, which would indicate she'd at least perforated it and would have an unholy bruise. Nothing.

"You didn't even hit it."

"I'm good with my left hand, but it kept rolling."

West cleaned the site and applied pressure, anyway, holding her elbow in one hand to keep her still.

Besides the single fingertip used to search for the vein, it was the first time he'd touched her directly, without fabric separating them, and seemingly subconsciously his fingertips all seemed to flex and move, caressing, massaging, stroking her skin far more than holding her still.

Even with all the crap between them, her heart rate kicked up and her gut gave a squeezing roll—somewhere between excited butterflies and nausea, enough to remind her how she *should* feel about him touching her. How she still didn't feel about him touching her, even after everything. Even after knowing it had only been love on her part.

And that, for some reason, when he realized he hadn't loved her, he no longer even wanted to try. He didn't want to keep going, see if his feelings developed. That was something else she didn't understand, how she went from being worth the effort and time all relationships required, to not.

"I don't need a massage," she whispered, shifting her gaze to her elbow so that he'd look that way, too, and it worked. He stopped, then frowned, let go and took one step back.

Then for good measure, he ran his hand, open-palmed, down the front of his suit, wiping the feel of her off, as if she were covered in goo.

"So why didn't you ask Tony?" he asked, like he had done nothing bizarre or insulting. "You're usually a play-by-the-rules type."

She couldn't help staring a little longer at the imaginary goo trail on his suit, but managed to answer, "I'm not a type."

In the time he'd been gone, she'd managed to build a little callus over the strips of flesh she felt carved off, but it was eggshell-thin. Almost an illusion. Maybe completely an illusion.

It was a lot of work to keep her emotions at bay with him there. The whole time he'd been gone, she'd been outside of the expectations of anyone who knew her—Jordan and Zeke were in the field, too—and she hadn't known how to react to anything, except that one core feeling of loss and grief. She didn't even know whether to be irritated by the emails with her consultants, or patient with them repeatedly questioning her decisions.

But in that moment with him, it was perfectly clear. What she wanted to do was shout at him. To lash out, make him feel as bad as that one little motion made her feel. But she didn't want to give him the satisfaction.

"I didn't ask because I didn't want help. Also, I only decided after my last patient that I needed to do it."

He stood back a little, his eyes sharpening. "Are we on winter hours now?" He nodded through the door to the dark lobby.

"People have already started going home, and there were a number of medical staff out in the field."

"And you didn't want to wait until tomorrow," he filled in.

"Somehow I wasn't enthused with the idea of having one more thing on my mind all night."

A single nod was the answer and he asked, "Want me to do it?"

"If you can stand touching me."

The careful quiet way he'd been looking at her sharpened, then with one hand he cupped her cheek and leaned forward, urging her to meet him.

Her heart squeezed, but the thundering settled into a gentler gallop when he tilted his head and pressed a warm, slow kiss to her temple, where he lingered and softly spoke, "Don't do that. That's not what that was."

Another painful squeeze to her chest, and the gallop accelerated, but she lost track of her pulse in the tingling that radiated from wherever he touched her, and it came again, that stinging in her eyes she hated. A simple touch to remind her of what she'd lost.

When he let go and stepped back, his expression was softer, but his lips twitched before he made a comically exaggerated show of wiping his mouth on his sleeve, and then wiping his hand on her trousers, right down the thigh.

A little laugh puffed from her and she swatted his hand away, smiling over the dewiness in her eyes.

"Tell me what this is for." He nodded to the pale green stoppered vacuum tube, as if he needed to ask. He knew what panels were run on that particular tube, the preservatives at the end that varied by tube color— and, given their location, which test was most likely the one she was going for. He might lead in with the charm she'd thought frozen dead when he'd come to Fletcher, but he was still going to make her say it.

"I had a patient with Polar T3 symptoms, and decided that I might need another check on my thyroid, too."

He made some sound of affirmation, then began lightly prodding her one good vein, and still seeing no signs that she'd so much as grazed the sucker with her errant needle driving, he opened another needle, found the vein again, swabbed and then slipped it right in.

A minute later, it was over and she had a cotton ball bandage to stop the bleeding as he left for the lab room to get it started.

"I can take it from here." She followed him out, crooking her arm to apply pressure to the site.

"You're not treating yourself."

"It's not treatment, it's just a test," she argued. "And I'll be doing it for myself when everyone is gone."

"And if you already have dropping levels?"

She sighed, checked her stick location to make sure it wasn't oozing and then let her arm relax. "Cross that bridge when I get to it. You just got back from a long trip, you're tired."

"I'm fine to run this."

"Damn it, West, I don't want your help. I could've gone to my legs or something to get the blood—it was just easier to let you do it. Running the equipment isn't going to be affected by it being my own blood. I can do it just like I'd do for anyone else."

"Don't care," he grunted. "Better start thinking of the reasons you're going to give me as to why you felt the need to do another thyroid check six days after you had one."

"*I* know the reasons. That's enough."

He logged the samples while the machine got to work, turned to look at her. "Are you having trouble sleepin'?"

"No," she said swiftly, then shrugged. "A little."

"Mood swings?"

That was the one that got her, her absolute lack of emotional control the past several days. One minute she'd been glad West was gone, the next she was worried about him in the field. Not worried about Jordan, who wouldn't be back until the day before the big *boa viagem*. But West she'd worried about, and kind of hated him for that.

"I'm taking silence for *yes*."

"Yes." She echoed the word just so he'd stop looking at her like she couldn't take care of herself—she'd basically been looking after herself since she'd been released from her luxurious Portuguese penitentiary to the strange freedom of an exclusive girls' school in the States at sixteen. Not to mention her years at medical school, where she'd met Jordan, and then when they'd moved to London to work in the same hospital, where Lia had met West. "Mood issues are probably to be expected after all of *this*, don't you think?"

"Aye," he said softly, not rising to her bait.

"Still, I'd rather find out if it's physical or emotional as early as possible. And in case I'm just being paranoid, I didn't want to tell Tony. He's overwintering, too, will be the only other doctor here with me, and I don't want him to think I'm unstable or a hypochondriac, or that he should in any way doubt my abilities."

"Why would he doubt your abilities?" He unzipped the top of his snowsuit, proof that he'd just arrived back from their trip, and pulled it down to pool at his waist, baring his double layers of thermals. Because he'd basically been camping in subzero temperatures for several days.

"Why wouldn't he? Seems to be coming from several directions in my life right now. Personal fronts. Professional fronts. All my local foremen don't think it's right that a woman should *have* to run Monterrosa Wine. My father spent my whole life telling me I wouldn't inherit, but apparently changed his mind right before he left for parts unknown."

"Unknown? He's still gone?"

She nodded once, then checked to make sure the tiny puncture was no longer oozing, then slapped some tape over the cotton ball and rolled down her sleeve.

Change the subject.

"Did you sleep at all when you were out there?"

He nodded, but didn't answer out loud. He also didn't budge from the spot in front of the buzzing machine.

"And the cold?"

"There's a two-room building at the site—they go back to it every year. Has a stove and emergency supplies." He answered that probably because it was easier than all this emotional garbage. "No beds. Not meant for overnight stays. We'd have been back same day but for a storm that sprang up. Ended up glad for the emergency sleeping bags, even while we all slept on counters or the floor."

And he'd slept in those conditions. Amazing after him not having slept at all the night before he'd left, after their Awesome Talk. She'd barely slept, and he'd somehow managed to pace in a room with about two square meters of walkable space. The only proof she really had that he was still upset to see her, or upset in general. Might be about the mysterious something that sent him running to Antarctica, for all she knew.

Part of why she'd been glad to find his goodbye note hanging on her doorknob the next morning, if one could call a bag full of tiny candles that, or the scrap of paper that said, *For the heater while I'm gone.*

And he'd be truly gone soon. No matter how raw she still felt, she didn't want to spend the next few days bickering with him, or giving him an itemized list of all the wrongs he'd contributed to, leaving the way he did. He knew it had been the cruelest way to leave her; nothing she could say would make it as real for him as it was for her. She was the one…who shouldn't be in love anymore, but was having a hard time turning that off.

"Thanks for the blood draw," she said, because just telling him that she wasn't going to feel her feelings in a loud, outside-the-brain way anymore with him seemed weird. "If the levels are off, would you…slip the results under my door or something?"

"I'll come tell you," he said, and just as she'd nodded and turned to go, he said, "I don't doubt your ability or your worth. I'm sorry about your da'."

"Thanks," she said again, the only word she could think to say, and then hurried out. Food. Sleep. Maybe tonight was the night she'd crack open one of the two bottles of the family's finest vintages she'd swiped from the cellar before leaving. Seemed like a good night to force herself to sleep.

CHAPTER FIVE

LAST NIGHT HE'D made Lia Monterrosa smile at him, and every time he'd seen her today that had been all he'd been able to think about. Those brief seconds when her hazel eyes had warmed and his chest had filled with honey, thick and sweet, had been there all the time. Even in the smallest measurements, when they were midquarrel.

West stepped out of the line with his dinner tray, and seeing as the only tables with available seating held Lia—who was distracted and bent over her mobile phone—and Gates—who had the charisma of a dead rodent—he invited himself to sit with her.

Not that he should be so stupid, but that voice of pragmatism and self-preservation was getting quieter daily, and fading into the echo of how peaceful it had been to love her.

But even when his day trip had turned into three days and hundreds of miles had separated them she'd been on his mind.

"Do you mind?" he asked, placing his tray across the long narrow table from her.

Lia lifted her grumpy face—a look he recognized—but shook her head. "They say every twelve hours it passes over, and I thought that meant seven and nine-teen, but here it is, ten minutes after and no signal."

Satellite. One of the difficulties with Antarctica was moving there as a modern, urban human who'd grown used to easy access to the internet, Wi-Fi, mobile services…getting used to the change was hard. They only really got emails twice a day, unless the sender and receiver were both quick and focused enough to send and receive multiple emails within the forty-five or so minutes they had on each pass of the uplink.

"Waiting for an email?"

"Several. Manager. Consultants. Investigator. My father…" She grimaced lightly at the last.

He hadn't asked last night more questions after she'd confirmed that the man was still in the wind, but with this opening… "He's answering emails?"

"No. I just keep sending them." She put her device down and reached for her fork. "I meant the private in-vestigators I've hired to try and track him down."

"They have news?"

She stopped eating, fork still in her mouth, the soft, pink slickness of her lower lip pressing to gently swell between the tines, her eyes wide and fixed on him.

"You don't have to talk about it. I was just mak-ing conversation." He shrugged, looked at her mouth again, dragged his gaze away, dropped to the table as other thoughts began swimming into his mind. Good thoughts. Wickedly good thoughts.

"You just never wanted to talk about that stuff."

True. Sort of. When it had been a danger that she'd start prodding around in things he didn't really want her knowing. "Did you sleep better knowing your T3 levels are fine?"

She watched him so closely that pragmatic voice turned a little paranoid, convinced she could see every prurient thought dancing across his mind just from the way he'd lamely fixated on her mouth.

After a weighty silence, she cautiously said, "I slept better than I would've had I been preoccupied with it." And then, "But I would've slept better still if there hadn't been a caged lion bunking next door, pacing."

West frowned at the idea they kept one another awake, then more deeply when he remembered the ways they'd once helped one another sleep. "I wasn't pacing."

And even if she'd just put off a vibe of not wanting to discuss things... "You were, but then you left the room and paced up and down the corridor for about a half an hour, where you probably growled and swiped at the air."

Demonstrably and adorably, she curled one hand like an ineffective claw and acted it out, swiping her paw while curling her upper lip into an exaggerated snarl.

He found himself smiling, that old chemistry still there. It had never needed too much prompting in the past. Affection he wanted to last, pretend that everything else wasn't there between them, no matter how stupid. Fall back into old habits before rings and tux fittings. "And you just laid there and listened?"

The phone momentarily forgotten, she still smiled, but as she watched him and considered her words, it began to diminish, growing smaller and then rueful.

"I laid there and worried actually." She waved one hand, as if to dismiss her own right to be worried. "Maybe you need to have *your* T3 checked."

The moment had passed, too hard for either of them to hold on to, and thrust them right back into spiky emotion territory, where neither knew what to do with any of it.

"I had it done the other day. This winter you should have Tony do yours. Keep up with it."

"I will. There was a grandparent with thyroid problems, I think. Of course, I could be misremembering. It's not as if my parents talked much with me about… well, you know."

"I know?" he repeated, and then shook his head. "Remind me."

"Anything besides studies and expectations? Then my mother died, and it was mostly about all the ways I disappointed by not having a penis."

It was the perfect opening for him to make a flirty joke, but he swallowed it down with his starchy meat stuff, which resembled what someone might think shepherd's pie was like, if they'd never eaten shepherd's pie, and only heard of it in stories.

The same way he knew about her parents, small scraps of information because he'd always wanted to look forward, to keep her looking forward. He didn't want to tell her about his mother, with her brassy, bottle-blond hair and too-red lips, or the last time he and Charlie had seen her. The neglect Lia seemed to have suffered was different, but still something they could've bonded over.

Just then, her phone pinged, then pinged again, over and over as emails began hitting her in-box. Her attention zeroed in there, reading and responding to emails, and not eating enough of her dinner. That he could legitimately comment on for her benefit.

"You need to eat more. People who overwinter tend to front-load the calories and try to put on some weight in the early part of the winter, because the last couple months are lean and it's better to have some cushion you can lose."

"I'll eat when I'm done," she said, but had clearly retreated from the conversation.

"Hey, you lot!" a man called from the double doors leading out of the galley. Lia and everyone else stopped talking, stopped eating, and heads swiveled in unison toward the man shouting for attention. "First aurora spotted on the horizon. Get your asses out there if you want to see them before you go home."

Aurora! The perfect timely reminder of the adventure she'd hoped to have. Or at least an experience she wouldn't have back in Portugal. The future stepping in when she was in danger of forgetting what they were now. Forgetting that it was never going back to the way things were with silly playfulness. Forgetting that, according to him, things had never been that way to begin with.

In danger of falling under the spell of old desires, the hope that things could turn around with them. Every time they shared a smile, it punched through her defenses, even punched through her exceedingly legitimate anger at him. Weakened her.

He obviously felt it, too, the wall she'd reconstructed, as he took a final bite and stood up before he'd even swallowed it. But before he went to return the tray, he stopped to say, "You should go see them, but come back and finish dinner after."

Still on about her eating after he'd done his best to wipe her appetite from existence.

As she stared at the tiny words on her screen, her desire to do the responsible thing wavered for once. She wanted to see the sky.

When she didn't respond to his nag to eat, West took his tray and left, grumbling beneath his breath as he went. Something else new about the bearded man, or just another fissure in the usually perfectly polished appearance and persona of the man she'd known. And she wouldn't let that feel like progress with him, even if she would have months ago when that had been her primary aim: get closer without driving the man who never spoke of his past away for badgering him about his past. Fat lot of good that had done.

If she just popped out for a minute, she could see the sky, and then come back inside, answer the most urgent emails before the satellite moved out of range and get the rest loaded to send the next temporary internet zone in twelve hours. She hadn't looked at the four emails that had popped up, but had looked long enough to confirm that none of them were from her father, then went about finishing the first one she'd started.

Hoping her father would answer her after all this time was probably another reason she was stupid. She'd been sending weekly emails to entreat him to contact her, reassure him things were fine, not putting any pressure to bear on him to explain himself, but still no word. It didn't really surprise her. She wished it did.

As she worked on the one email, a mass exodus of the galley happened. The people who'd been there all summer with daylight skies and no canvas for the aurora australis might not get another chance. They didn't start and stop with the flip of a switch, and the skies trended toward twilight now, with darkness far out into the wide, flat, fairly creepy distance—so different from her mountainous Douro River homeland.

As soon as she hit Send, she zipped into the light indoor jacket she wore all the time, returned her tray and hurried outside. Everyone's hurry to get out there had informed her decision not to go back to her cabin for warmer attire. She'd be fine for a quick pop out, and if she got too cold, she'd visit the saunas she'd only discovered yesterday.

When she finally made it outside, she found herself at the back of a crowd, all heads turned toward the flat horizon.

She stepped to one side and another, weaseling her way to a spot where she could best view the looming dark.

"You didn't miss it," West said from beside her, her first indication he was nearby.

"Did you make it out in time to see some?"

"I wasn't bent over my mobile phone." He smiled a little.

So there had been some, but he felt confident there would be more?

She tugged her ever-present hat down more firmly on her ears and shoved her hands into her pockets. "How do you know they'll recur?"

He turned back to the horizon. She actually felt him look away from her, because she'd determined not to watch him. She'd also determined not to interact much, and yet…here she was, interacting.

"I'm only staying a bit. It's too cold to watch nothing happening except the approaching dark, which is neat in a different way."

"It is," he agreed, then added, "Usually when aurora

happen, they happen for a little while. It's not a one-off. Comes in waves."

"You've seen them before?"

"Not here. In Scotland. Years ago."

Something else she hadn't known about him. His accent and name gave away his homeland, but she'd not known he'd been far enough north to view the aurora borealis.

"On holiday or at home?"

As privileged an upbringing as she'd had, with money and travel, Lia had never traveled north far enough to see the northern lights. When she skied, she went to the Alps. The rest of the time, she went to warmer places.

"Where I lived."

Where he'd lived…not at home?

"Where was that?" she asked, unable to stop herself.

"Hmm?" He glanced sideways at her, and she was watching him again, not the sky. "Inverness, mostly. Kinlochleven for a while."

"Where's that?"

"North." He looked back at the sky, then touched her insulated arm. "You want to haver on about nothin' important, or see the aurora?"

A murmur rose from the crowd just after his words, drawing her gaze back to the horizon, which now glowed a strange, unearthly green in a general, diffuse and…disappointing manner.

Not the light show she'd expected.

She'd watched videos in preparation for her trip, documentaries. She'd looked at photos and read blogs about viewing the aurora australis.

"Is that it?" she asked, truly beginning to feel the cold. Excitement had kept it a background buzzing before that, but a bit of green sky in the far distance?

"Might repeat like that. Dunno." He frowned as she pulled her hands from the thin pockets and began rubbing them together, then stuffed them back into the pockets in the vain hope of not contracting some dreaded Frozen Antarctic Finger syndrome. Or frostbite. That one was a real thing. "But if it is, you'll have plenty of time to see them again, catalog the colors and whatever, over the winter. If you're stayin'."

"I'm staying," she repeated. The man wasn't going to stop poking her to go. Until he went. When the lot of them were finally forever gone.

Ugh, she was wasting her time.

More important things to do than watch a whole lot of nothing spectacular happen. "I'm going in."

"Give it another minute," West said, and it should've sounded like an order, but the softness of his voice was all velvet suggestion, coaxing.

Two more days until the transport bus began driving people the short distance to the coast where boats waited to spirit them back to the world. Two days and then she wouldn't see him anymore. Maybe never again after.

It was more that thought than anything that had her pausing, looking back to the sky.

People kept shifting and blocking her view, so she edged into West's space to see the horizon.

The glow was there, rippling a bit or pulsing. She wasn't sure what to call it. Not something to fill her with wonder, as she'd hoped. But just when disappointment began to settle over her, the green grew brighter, and then rippled out, glowing fingers reaching from the dark horizon toward the twilight sky under which they stood.

It moved slowly at first, and then faster in undulating waves that almost looked alive.

She wasn't aware of having made any decisions, just the cold all around her, the dancing sky above her and one warmer hand. Because she'd grabbed his.

Not breathing. The murmuring that had taken hold of the crowd faded to reverent silence. All around them, the wind that continuously blew across the barren landscape whispered and whistled. Her own ragged breathing brought something low and deep into it, and the rapid beat of her heart. The music of a desolate, majestic landscape. Life and beauty where there should be none, deepened by the large, strong hand in her own.

The hand he wouldn't want to be holding.

Because this was something *she* felt. Not him. Not for her. Never for her.

It didn't take long for the truth of her situation to come swimming back to her mind, and with it, she found the strength and self-respect to unfold her fingers from his.

Under the glow of the green and yellow aurora, she felt his gaze on her instead of the sky, and balled her hands at her sides to keep from performing another round of self-destructive stupid.

One-two-three-four-five-six-seven-eight-nine-ten.

She counted heartbeats pounding so fast that she wouldn't have been able to breathe at all had she been saying the numbers aloud. Too fast. Too hard.

She closed her eyes.

Go in.

Go back in and take care of what was expected of her. Emails. Work. Sleep. Repeat.

She hadn't started moving—the thoughts had appeared in her mind, chiding her, shaming her into action—when she felt West's hand enfold her tight, cold fist again.

He didn't stop there, just gave a little tug until she was standing in front of him, and then repeated with her other hand, wrapping both in warmth.

"West?"

"You're cold," he said softly over her shoulder, holding her hands and keeping close, but somehow managing not to put his arms fully around her to do it.

She *was* cold. She should wish to be colder on the inside, to grow a callus around her still-smarting heart, to be as cold inside as she was outside. If it would help, she'd strip herself bare and pack her body in the snow like a kid packed himself in sand at the beach.

Coldhearted, less prone to emotion, more to reason. Then she could reason her way through how stupid it was to let him warm her hands when it also warmed her heart and a hollow she'd been babying for months.

The forking fingers of the green light show in the sky retreated, and even if the next round was guaranteed to be more spectacular than that, she'd still have gone inside. It was too confusing with West, and while she'd pretended she was only angry until she'd seen him, since then the wound had been ripped fresh open. It had never closed, never had the chance to scar. And if she knew anything about wounds and scarring, she knew the scar got thicker, grizzlier and harder to ignore the more times it was reopened.

A few words said, and she extracted her hands from his to put some distance between them, and hurried inside to her emails and responsibilities.

Two days couldn't come fast enough.

CHAPTER SIX

ALTHOUGH TONY BRADSHAW had taken them to winter hours only a couple days prior, after a day of nonstop injuries while maintenance crews worked to prepare the station to overwinter he had decided to keep the clinic and hospital open for a second shift. And, because he'd felt ill, had asked Lia to stay on and pull a double shift.

She'd said yes—not just because he was ill, but because it kept her busy and not obsessing over the final email that had arrived last night while she was holding hands with Weston MacIntyre under the aurora. The one that said her father had turned up at a Barcelona hospital. The one she hadn't seen or responded to until there was no signal, leaving her to only queue it up for the next moment her device could catch some bandwidth.

"All right, Mr. Hansen," she said to the man who'd most recently entered, wheeling the breathing machine into one treatment area and getting the liquid medicine dispensed into the breathing apparatus. "Have you done this before?"

He nodded, his breathing still labored. "More… and…more…frequently." He breathed shallow and fast, his speech broken as she started the vaporizer and held it over his mouth.

"In deep. If you can, try to tuck your tongue to the side or press to the roof of your mouth and breathe around it. This stuff is dreadfully bitter, but it works like magic on swollen airways."

He took over holding the mouthpiece, and she watched as, over no more than half a minute, his breathing became deeper, less labored.

Mr. Hansen wasn't a complicated patient, so she might even be able to pop out and get some dinner to bring back and eat here once he was hooked up.

The station had gone into some kind of carnival atmosphere, a party in the galley with nonstop food rolling, drinks and music. There were two bars at the station that had their own farewell parties going. The coffeehouse was full of folk music and desserts, or so she'd heard. Made sense. Buffet your way through dinner, then finish up in the coffeehouse with cake and pastries. Not her, she couldn't be gone that long, but the galley wasn't terribly far way.

And West would probably be there.

Okay, maybe she wouldn't go. Although, with twenty minutes before her emails might finally get a response, a trip might keep her from obsessing and worrying about the email that had arrived while she was outside, holding hands with West under the aurora.

Her father had turned up in a hospital in Barcelona. *Hospital.*

Now she couldn't stop herself running through possible scenarios to turn him up in a hospital. Accidents. Illnesses. Things just bad enough that a normal person would seek the comfort of family over... Then she felt guilty for almost hoping his hospital visit was serious enough to make him reach out, while still being recoverable.

Hansen didn't need her. The crews must also be on dinner break, or they were all injured and the work was no longer getting done, because her steady supply of distractions just dried up in the eleventh hour.

She went to tell him she was going to dash to the galley, when a man's alarmed voice sounded from the entry, and got her moving that direction.

Two men carried a woman who had a massive slice open down the side of her calf. They tried to hold a compress and stop the bleeding as they carried her, but it still dripped rapidly enough to switch off every other thought in her head.

"In here." Lia flipped on the lights in the trauma room, and they carried in her patient, placing her on the table while Lia washed her hands and shoved them into gloves. "Someone tell me what happened."

"Fan blade," one man said. "Came off. We were trying to fix one of the in-loaders."

In-loader? No clue. But fan-blade accident made sense. She grabbed several packets of gauze pads, ripped them open and wheeled them on a tray with other implements toward the woman. "What's your name?"

"Gossen," her patient said, pale around the mouth, her brows a deep, angry red that could've been from crying, or just the ferocity with which her brows crammed together. "Eileen Gossen."

"Okay, Eileen. I'm going to need to look at this." She took over holding the compress. "I want you to lie back and relax as much as you can. The harder your heart beats, the more blood pumps, the more comes out the wound, okay? Lie back."

She didn't take time to warn, just grabbed the fresh compresses, and got a quick peek at the wound as she switched them out. Not spurting. But deep. "Do you want me to tell you what I saw, or do you just want me to fix it?"

"Both," Eileen said, voice strained.

"All right. The blade hit veins, that's why you're bleeding so freely. It did not hit an artery—there was no spurting. That's good news." She pointed to the one man who'd continued lingering after the other who'd helped carry in Eileen had left. "I need some help. I want you to go to the galley and look for either Dr. Flynn or Dr. MacIntyre. MacIntyre will probably be easiest to find—he's the tall, broad-shouldered Scot with the black beard. Always wears a navy knit cap."

"You can't do it alone?" Eileen asked, sounding more worried that she needed backup.

"I'm a trained surgeon, Eileen. I can stitch this up so beautifully that, in a couple years, people will have a hard time believing you were ever injured. But I don't want to remove my hands from where I'm placing pressure in order to do the other things I want done to make sure you're as well taken care of as possible."

"What things?"

"Monitoring your blood pressure. Setting an IV and getting saline hung just in case you've lost more blood than I can see from this. I don't want you losing more while I try to make sure you didn't lose too much. Okay?"

Eileen nodded, and when Lia looked back to the man, he was already gone. She should've asked if he even knew Jordan or West. If worse came to worst, she could call for Tony. The medical director's cabin abutted the clinic, but with the way that man had shuffled around and slurred his speech, she didn't want to take a chance on him. It might even be better to go for it alone if Jordan or West failed to materialize. Was this how things would be over the winter? She might have to do a survey of all who remained behind and see if there was any medical training at all among them. CPR, firefighting, anything. Or make some learn. For emergency situations. Something about Tony's manner tonight unsettled her.

But she didn't have time for that. She needed to keep Eileen calm, so Lia kept talking. Asking questions. Where was she from? What was her job in the station? Was this her first tour in Antarctica?

It didn't take long for the man to fetch West, but her gentle, friendly, nonemergency questions helped Eileen relax. Her breathing leveled out. Her pulse, which Lia kept monitoring with one hand on the woman's ankle while she maintained pressure with the other, had slowed.

"What've we got?" West asked before his feet even crossed the threshold into the trauma room.

"This is Eileen. She has an overachieving slice on the right side of her right calf, and it's bleeding freely. Can you get a cuff on her and then a line in? We're also going to need anesthetic—that's the third thing."

"BP. IV. Anesthetic. Can do."

She kept pressure on until he'd given her a BP reading that let her know her blood loss wasn't yet to threatening levels, but that didn't mean she was going to change her mind on the IV.

"Do you want me to hang saline?" he asked, setting and flushing the line to make sure it was clear before taping it down.

"Yes." Lia and West never really worked together in a trauma situation. She'd assisted him in surgeries when her fellowship surgeries got light and he was in regular rotation as a general surgeon at their hospital, but they'd been more the usual surgeries than something dialed to emergency levels.

They fell into a kind of unspoken coordination. He monitored everything—blood pressure, pain management, the patient's emotional state—and she cleaned the wound and stitched, starting with the nicked vein, then moving on up. Eileen was lucky—the cut was remarkably clean. Fan blade sounded scary, but did less damage than she'd seen in some knife-wound repairs. Or, God help anyone, what bullets did once they entered the body and began weaponizing bone fragments.

In the middle of all that, she heard her phone go off, but had to ignore it. And not hurry just because she didn't want to miss the window, even though missing the window would mean she'd have another twenty-four hours to sweat out a response.

By the time it was over and she'd bandaged everything, Eileen had actually dozed off from the pain medication.

"We should move her into one of the patient beds," she said to West. "And let her sleep it off."

Her phone chirped again and she winced. "Actually, can you just put the railing up on her bed and let her sleep here for a few minutes while I go? I have to get this. I've been waiting for an email—kind of an emergency, too."

"Emergency at home?" West asked, doing as she asked and putting the rail up before following her out.

"Yeah…" she answered, then flipped on her phone. The three-word subject line hit like a truck.

Vitor Monterrosa located

"If you can, maybe peek in on Tony? He's… He's unwell. But only if Eileen is well and truly out. I'll hurry. I just… I…"

"Go."

She flew out of the clinic and off to a corner of a nearby lounge to pore over news from home.

West watched the doorway long after Lia had gone. It shouldn't have made him feel good that she'd sent for him when she'd needed help, and he hated that it did.

The tension in her forehead when she'd asked him to stay had done a lot to undo that good feeling. The news that Tony was sick enough to call off had burned through the rest of it. If his health was going the way it seemed the past few weeks, she'd effectively be locking herself into a dangerous winter prison for eight months without access to any other doctors. Not a fan. Not for her.

Her hands had twitched when her phone pinged, telling him everything he needed to know about how serious the emergency was. Twitching hands were a big deal for surgeons, and she was usually steady enough he'd trust her with the life of anyone—family, if he'd had any left. As steady and predictable as his inability to be there for the people who needed him.

He hovered in the door of the trauma room with

one eye trained on Eileen and the rest of his attention split between the short hallway to Tony's quarters, and the main lobby doors for Lia's return, or the arrival of more patients.

Eileen woke shortly and he had things to do, a legitimate, healthy way to clear his mind of the worry and guilt snapping at his heels, but not long enough. It took practically no time to transfer her to one of the four patient beds in the hospital ward, explain everything, ask a couple of questions and give a much longer-lasting shot for pain management.

When he was done, and Lia still hadn't returned, he broke off to seek out Tony.

He wanted to be flip about how *emergency* it could be, just to steady his own nerves. From all of Lia's descriptions, there was so much quaint and peaceful about the medieval walled village attached to her family's ancestral estate it was hard to even picture any real, modern emergencies there—whether it was *a mess*, as she'd recently stated, or not.

Fire and acts of God seemed like the extent of what could happen. But believing that would mean believing she was overreacting now, and that seemed less likely.

He knocked upon reaching Tony's door. Checking on the medical director was one thing he could quickly do to help Lia and occupy himself.

What he saw when the door opened did nothing to soothe his worry.

Sweat dripped off the man, as if he'd just run a marathon at the equator. His hair stuck up in all directions, except for the pieces around his face, which stuck to his forehead and overly defined cheekbones. Most disconcerting was how pale he was, even in that obviously sweaty, overheated condition.

"I was going to ask if you were all right, but I see you're not," West said, instead of greeting him. "I'll be right back. I need some tools."

"I just picked up a bug," Tony called behind him, words meant as a weak argument, but West didn't stop until he'd retrieved the nurse on a stick, a stethoscope, and pulled up his new patient's record on his device.

He didn't even bother knocking when he had returned, just let himself in as if it were a patient's room.

He'd actually been after Tony about increasing his caloric intake for about a month, but not doggedly enough. The man was a physician; he knew symptoms when they were plaguing him, one would think.

"If this is a bug, you have an immune system problem."

"I don't."

"You've had a few bugs lately, then?"

"Lia complaining?"

"No. Worried. She's like that." West wasn't there to fight; he was there to help, and would force his help on Tony whether he wanted it or not.

"You two knew each other before, right?"

"Yes. But that's not what we're talking about."

"I've noticed tension between the two of you. Everyone has."

West folded his arms. "If you're overwintering, you need to be checked now. Blood work, vitals. I respect you, I don't want to be a jerk, but I wouldn't be doing my job if I didn't force the issue when you clearly need help."

That earned him a wince. With the way Tony had been fighting all mentions of whatever was going on with him, West had a feeling he already knew something serious and was doing his best to ignore it. Not a great feeling to start an examination with.

"I understand not wanting to think about bad things, but sometimes you have to. Sometimes it's the best option. So, sit here and I'll get vitals and some blood. Start simple, do a CBC. If you've got an infection, it'll show. Then we can go from there."

When he turned to fetch the phlebotomy tray, Tony said quietly, "I have some swollen lymph nodes."

West looked back to see the man gesturing at his collarbone.

In his head, he went spinning through the symptoms he'd been mentally cataloging. Swollen lymph nodes alone could be anything, usually something that would resolve on its own, but when combined with the fatigue, weight loss and night sweats… Not a great string of symptoms.

"Anything else?" he asked.

Tony listed a couple more and increased West's alarm.

"I'll grab the ultrasound, too," West said, but asked first, "Are they sore?"

"No."

"Movable?"

"I don't know…" Tony said, but his tone said he did.

It was never comfortable for colleagues to examine one another, but when the possible diagnosis was such a dire one… West left the door open and went to check on the suspicious nodes indicated, but found two other smaller, unmovable nodes around Tony's clavicle.

Fixed. Hard. Not sore.

Damn.

"I'll get the cart."

"Tell me," Tony said, interrupting his flight.

West was a surgeon by specialty. He didn't usually diagnose cancer—he was the guy who cut it out once another doctor had these awful conversations.

"One of medium size and two smaller ones under the jaw." West explained what he'd felt. "Let me get the card."

Tony knew those symptoms; they could be benign, but when unmovable, hard lymph nodes got involved…

Once in the lobby, he paused long enough to check that Eileen was still asleep, then scribbled *Bradshaw* on a note for Lia, and headed back.

Still not back. And he didn't have time to think on it, or go find her.

A quick scan confirmed the solidity of the nodes, and added a fourth deeper one he hadn't felt before. The likelihood that this was benign plummeted.

"You think lymphoma?" Tony said the question with an astonishingly calm tone.

Stress made these things worse, and West didn't want to lay that extra weight on him. Didn't want to have this conversation, like so many bad conversations, especially when he couldn't say for certain without a biopsy. "I'm worried. It needs more than we can provide here."

Sweat continued rolling off Tony, but the calm persisted. "If it is, I won't be able to stay."

"Sorry, man. I'll run these labs now. You take some acetaminophen to try and lower the fever."

West returned to the lobby and found a red-eyed Lia leaving Eileen's room. The second time he'd ever seen her actively crying, and was starting to realize she could never hide it.

"What happened?" he asked immediately, wheeling

the ultrasound to the side of the room and grabbing the blood samples in one hand and Lia's hand in the other to pull her into the lab with him. "Something with the vineyard?"

"O pai," she answered in Portuguese, her voice thick and froggy—something he liked in bed, but not like this. "He was in the hospital in Barcelona. But he's not now. Why did you need the ultrasound?"

"Tony." He answered that first, but moved back to the subject of her father. A hospital visit didn't sound worthy of tears, unless the outcome had been bad. "Is your father all right?"

Her slender shoulders crept up. "I don't know. I guess. He's been gone so long. The only time we get a lead on him is when he pops up to withdraw money at a bank, right before he immediately leaves that city. They emailed to say that they thought he was in Spain, and then they needed family to contact them, and by the time the email came, it was too late."

Family emergency. Nothing to do with the anachronistic village that had no motor vehicles inside the wall.

One emergency at a time. He got the CBC started while she explained.

The idea that her father had stayed gone didn't make sense to him, especially knowing what a chauvinist the man was—not leaving the vineyard to her. It also made it seem a little more reasonable that as soon as she found out where one of them was, she'd gone. He didn't sigh, wouldn't sigh, or walk out on another important conversation with her. Sometimes you had to talk about bad things. When there were no other options.

"What was he admitted for?"

"Observation." She croaked the word, focusing on

him like he'd have an answer, or anything that could ease her worry. "But they wouldn't say more, except to tell me where he was staying. I rang the investigator, who's still in Barcelona, and sent him there, then waited for a response, but my father was already gone. Checked out this morning. Yesterday morning? Tomorrow? Time zones. Whatever. He was gone and…" She finished her statement with a helpless shrug.

"It doesn't sound like he wants to be found, love."

Her bitter, incredulous laughing shrug shamed him. She might as well have said, *How does this keep happening to me?*

"The whole point to finding him is to know he's all right, and to tell him not to worry about the vineyard. My tour here will be over two months before reconstruction is projected to finish. I'll be staying there forever. The welfare of the village or the people there who rely on Monterrosa Wine is no longer on him, and he truly never wanted it to be passed to him to start with. He doesn't have to keep running. Just let me know he's okay. But now? Under observation? That could be for anything. Injury. Illness. Am I supposed to just stop looking?"

All the things she said, when broken apart into singular elements, didn't add up to alarming. But with his own history of having an addict brother, it did. It definitely did.

"No," he said immediately, and then, "Lia, I know you don't want to hear this. I know I sound like a stuck recording, but you should go home. Having this time lag between sent and received communication isn't helping. Listen to me. I'll stay. I'll take the winter. Tony is leaving. He's…"

"What was the ultrasound for?"

"Looks like lymphoma. He has to go home for a biopsy at the least, and probably treatment. So they're going to have to get another doctor down here for that NASA project. You're going to be on your own for a while, maybe a couple of weeks until they get someone else. Say the word, and I'll take your spot. If your father is in trouble and you're here, you'll hate yourself if something worse happens. I know what I'm talking about."

She stilled, her damp eyes growing sharper beneath a pinched brow as she searched his face. "Did something happen to Charlie?"

Damn it. He really sucked at keeping secrets suddenly. She was in pain and he needed to help, so he just blurted things out.

"Yes," he answered quietly, because he couldn't see a way out of it. "Life is short, sometimes people need help holding on to it for a while longer. You don't get past that kind of failing."

"But you never said…"

"No reason to."

She stilled, her brows screwed to incredulity for several seconds, and he could see her doing the mental calculations. She knew. She might not know the details, but the sudden compassion on her face said she knew that Charlie's death was the thing that had happened while she was gone.

"West…" She breathed his name, and as soon as his hands were free of the computer interface to get the CBC started, she took his nearest hand in both of hers. "I'm so sorry. And I'm sorry I wasn't there. What happened?"

"I don't want to talk about it with you." The words came in a rush. She couldn't be the one offering comfort. His trauma was in the past, hers was here now, currently middeath spiral. He pulled his hand free.

The retreat did the trick, and she stepped fully back from him, but the sympathy and concern he saw written plainly on her face didn't budge, even when she nodded, and she softly said, "Okay. I'll…just… Thank you for your help with Eileen."

She was leaving. And he'd left their conversation on a note that would keep her from hearing what he'd said. After today, he wouldn't have any more chances to help her through this.

"Wait." He set the second vial of blood in the caddy of the next machine, and followed her. "Lia."

"I need to check on Eileen."

Not allowing her to dismiss him, he waited in the lobby for her return, letting her have a moment to catch her breath without him crowding the air. But the second she stepped back out of Eileen's room, he asked, "Your father…did he deliberately start the fire?"

He saw her shutters coming down as she looked at him for a long, heavy moment, trying to decide if she was going to answer. He'd just told her he didn't want to talk to her about Charlie, but here he was, digging into her own personal business.

She handled it with far more grace than he had. "I don't think he did it on purpose. My father didn't want me to inherit the vineyard, but he didn't want to run it, either. He had these great dreams about having a son to pass it on to, and didn't manage to pull that off before retirement age, even with three wives."

She watched him cautiously as she answered, telling

him more about her life at every turn now than when they'd been together. Even than when they'd been planning the wedding. He'd guarded information about his past, and done everything he could to keep her eyes on the horizon, and where they were going, not where they'd come from. And now that he wasn't trying to keep from having to repay her information with his own, he let her speak. He wanted her to speak.

"He wouldn't burn it down rather than give it to you?"

"I don't think he hates me…" she said, but it didn't sound like she was sure. He had to remind himself that this was the man whose disappearance still caused her tears. "If he'd done it on purpose, he wouldn't have run. Running from *failure* is more like my father than running from guilt."

"How do you set a whole lot of land and a castle on fire by accident if there are no other problems exacerbating the situation?"

"It's not a castle," she argued, then sighed. "But if he was drinking, that doesn't mean—"

"It doesn't mean he did it on purpose, it doesn't mean he's a drunk," West filled in. "But it might mean there is a bigger problem than simply 'my father doesn't want to run the vineyard anymore.'"

"He's not an alcoholic," she reiterated, one hand waving, her head about to shake off her shoulders. "You have a travel day tomorrow. Go. Get some sleep. Thank you for your help."

Still trying to dismiss him, and still upset.

He should go, just as she suggested, but he couldn't ever sleep through alarm bells. And there was Tony Bradshaw still to deal with, but he didn't want to leave it on that note. Especially when one of them would definitely be leaving for real in the morning.

"I could stay and let you get some rest—you're taking over the station tomorrow." Pathetic offer, which he knew she wouldn't accept any more than she was yet willing to accept his offer to winter in her place.

"I probably slept more last night than you did."

"Did I keep you awake?"

"You can't sniff without me hearing it."

But that would all end tomorrow, and the simple thought churned his stomach. "At least I didn't prowl the corridor like a lion."

She didn't even try to smile until he'd mimed her snarl and slow-witted claw swipe of the air, then she managed a little one.

"I'd best go sleep, then," he said, but his feet didn't move. He couldn't look away from her. Looked too long, too hard, too fraught…

"What?" She gave another little sad sniff that pushed him over the edge.

Without letting himself think it through, West grabbed her by the back of the neck and hauled her against his chest, wrapping his arms tight about her.

She didn't fight him an ounce, just buried her face in the crook of his neck and snaked her arms around his waist, then leaned.

He'd wanted to comfort her, but with her pressed to him, her breath fanning the side of his neck, the chaos of the station, of the world, seemed to fade away. It wasn't relief, though it was something like that. It wasn't lust, but that was always there, too, when he touched her, when he even looked at her. He just felt better, touching her. Like hope was a thing that could still exist.

He could feel her fists balling in the back of his shirts, a light tremble shaking her whole body. But she wasn't going to let him save her, even if she clung on to him for dear life. That steel spine he loved was still there even if it was occasionally washed by tears. Still fighting for people she loved. Even when they repeatedly let her down.

He squeezed a little tighter, dipped his head to breathe her in and suddenly realized the low-level headache he'd been nursing for months was gone, and it had left a strange kind of euphoria in its wake.

"If you change your mind, say the word. I'll stay." He whispered the words into her ear, and although it could've only been taken as a repeat of the offer he'd made to let her go home, that wasn't even what he'd meant. And that was exactly what he'd been afraid of: reaching that point where he would abandon his plans and principles to be with her. If she didn't keep pushing him away, the entire drive that had him telling her ugly lies.

She nodded; he already knew she wouldn't say the words. And he was lucky she wouldn't.

He'd be leaving tomorrow, and that would be the end of it. He'd go wherever the hell he was going to go, take the first connecting flight out of Dallas to parts unknown and be forced to email her daily to check in, make sure another doctor had arrived, that she was okay...

Not a clean break.

Maybe there never could be a clean break with her. She didn't know how to give up on people she loved. Even when they really didn't deserve her compassion.

He held her until she relaxed enough for the trembling to stop, and she was the one to pull away. He would've kept holding her, even standing there, in the middle of the clinic.

"Go to sleep," she croaked, but added sincerely and resignedly, "Thank you for all your help tonight. Safe travels. I hope you find what you're looking for."

Not just good night, but goodbye. This goodbye was a true goodbye, and he heard it for what it was this time. Not a Charlie goodbye—she wasn't going to push poison into her veins when he left—but a goodbye he still might never get over. She'd never track him down again, or maybe even email. Probably wouldn't have asked for his help at all tonight if she'd had other options.

He'd pushed, and she'd backed off, as soon as she understood. Or as soon as she'd accepted the lie he'd told her. She might have just shared one hell of an emotional load with him, but she didn't expect anything from him. This time was real, and he felt the difference in his marrow.

And in his empty, aching arms as he walked away.

CHAPTER SEVEN

"You're going to make it on time," Lia reassured the station's bus driver, pressing the mouthpiece of the nebulizer back to her mouth. "Panicking about delaying your departure schedule isn't helping. They can't leave without you. You're the driver."

"But…so…many…trips…today."

"I know." Lia parsed out the meaning of the broken speech, having grown more used to the breathless cadence of an asthma attack since she'd arrived. It was amazing how subzero air triggered them in people, even those who may have never had any signs of asthma in the past. She'd gone into the system this morning to order another crate of the vaporizing liquid to arrive before shipping stopped. Just to be prepared. Running out over the winter sounded like a deadly situation.

Another ten minutes and she'd go with Kasey, the driver, out to the bus to say goodbye to Jordan and Zeke, who were in the first departure slot this morning. She didn't know when West was scheduled, or Tony, whom she'd be glad to see go for the good of his health. She'd forced a couple nutrient-dense drinks on him this morning after having finished the labs West started last night. She just knew there was one trip scheduled every other hour today, and that by the time the trips resumed tomorrow, two-thirds of the station would already be gone.

"The deeper you breathe, the faster it vaporizes and the sooner you'll be on your way."

Luck was with her. When Kasey had finished her treatment and Lia had given her an injection of steroids and an emergency inhaler, they both bundled into their coats and hurried out of the station.

Almost as soon as she stepped outside, Lia regretted not having made time to say goodbye to Jordan earlier. It wasn't blowing hard, but snow fell heavily, and after how much she avoided the outdoors here, it was the first time she'd actually seen it coming down since she'd arrived. Big, fat, fluffy flakes drifted down from the heavens, painting the world ethereal shades of bluish white. The bus wasn't far, and was still somewhat visible. Would the heavy snowfall make driving more difficult here? Did it stop having all meaning when everything was covered by more than a mile-thick snow and pack ice? One more thing to worry about.

When they reached the boarding side, Lia made out three figures waiting.

Not just Jordan and Zeke—West stood to the side, a few feet away, making clear that he wasn't there with them. He was just among those waiting for her.

Kasey hurried onto the bus after a sharp word about dawdling, and Jordan and Zeke launched in immediately with farewells, promises to call, hugs, kisses on her cold cheeks and an oath to send more tea lights for her heater.

She barely heard any of it. The words may have made it to her brain, but they drifted away almost immediately, her attention so divided by the idea that West had waited to say goodbye this time. Even after he'd hugged her last night, she hadn't expected it. She also realized in that moment that she hadn't been letting herself think about him being gone, not for a couple of days. Especially not since last night, when she'd needed him.

She'd come to say goodbye, never thinking that she'd have to say it twice. That having it out with him and then spending more than a week around one another would allow the old familiarity to build back up. That she might even get to know him better after she'd given him back their engagement ring.

If she asked, he would take her place and stay the winter, he'd said.

If she asked, would he take Tony's? How much harder would it be to say goodbye for a third time once winter was over?

Jordan and Zeke pulled away and West met her gaze again. A cold couple of feet and a miles-wide canyon separated them. In the freeze, his naturally pale cheeks had turned pink, and bits of fluff clung to the navy knit cap he wore. Even looking so different as when he was temporarily hers, when she met his gaze her heart gave one sluggish thud and then began to rabbit away inside her chest.

It was quiet; the falling snow deafened the sound. She heard her own breathing but nothing else.

The bus ran at his back; she saw the exhaust fogging the air, Kasey no doubt going through the checks to get it going, but maybe also waiting for them to finish up. Not that they'd even started.

It was just heavy eye contact, and pensive frowns, no words. No actual goodbyes were uttered. It was like the slow-motion repeat of her first day in the station, but when he looked at her, she didn't see anger. Just sadness. Resignation. Worry. Because even if he didn't love her, had never loved her, he still cared enough to be worried. And last night she'd given him plenty to worry about. But then, he'd done the same for her. She knew he wasn't okay, the loss of his only family couldn't let him be okay, but he didn't want her involved. So it hung in the frosty air, both of them so much more aware now of the battles going on in the background, and letting the fight continue, unaided. He'd been right in not marrying her. Not in leaving the way he had, but that he couldn't marry her.

She still didn't know what to say.

He pulled his bare hands from his pockets and reached out to take her left hand. She hadn't had time to grab the big coat, or get on gloves. Her fingers, cold to the point of stiffness, still slid into his in a pattern that couldn't be familiar. He'd never been a handholder. Probably something else that should've alarmed her, back when they were trying to build their own forever. Probably something she shouldn't have shrugged off, or explained away.

Now, the heat of his hand thawed hers, his thumb stroking the well-worn rut that still existed where his ring once sat. The ring she'd spied on the chain around his neck, once and then not again.

Kasey gave the motor a rev—she heard that—and cracked the door to shout for West to get on if he was coming.

Still no words from him, or her. He just looked back at her again, a long, heavy look she might forever link with quietly falling snow and skies like twilight. The summer was gone, and autumn twilight would soon turn to winter night. It felt appropriate, like the end of everything.

Releasing her hand, he stepped forward, pushed the brim of her hat up to expose her forehead and leaned in to kiss her head. Warm whiskered tenderness.

She was going to miss him. Even if he wasn't hers anymore.

Before he got away, she flung her arms around his shoulders and hugged as hard as she could through the layers of insulated suits, and pressed her mouth to his ear to whisper the only words that came. Words for herself, an acknowledgment of what she'd lost, in her native tongue, and what it did to her. Safe words. Words she could only say because he'd never understand.

He looked confused as she stepped back, but she didn't stay to explain herself, just turned to hurry inside. She didn't need to watch them leave. Waving felt like an act of cheer, not bitter resignation.

Besides, she had a job to do. Even if people were being trucked away en masse from the station for the next couple of days, she still had a significant number of people to worry after right now. Now was all she could focus on.

Somewhere warmer.

Inside.

Away from the starkness of bluish-white.

The rest of Lia's day creaked by. Yesterday's onslaught of injuries had subsided, and she was left with a few small incidents and Eileen, who was now reconsidering her winter plans. She'd be on crutches for a couple weeks to minimize the stress to her leg, and that felt like being completely useless to someone whose job description included climbing into the ducts and other small spaces to fix things.

By the end of the day, the station felt like a ghost town, and Lia still carried with her the starkness of bluish-white.

Tomorrow, the numbers would shrink by another couple hundred, with all summer personnel gone aside from the extended janitorial staff who still had work to do, cleaning parts of the station that would go unused for the winter and be closed off to conserve power and the fuel needed to generate it. Another reason she was so thankful for the little tea-light heater West had given her. She could be warm without further depleting the fuel.

Tomorrow, after it had been cleaned, she'd move into Tony's cabin. She didn't want to move into someone else's space—it felt like moving into a stranger's home—but it came with the job. It wasn't unlike taking care of her village at home, only here it was the health of dozens, and at home it was the welfare of hundreds. Still, it felt kind of like practice. A case study in how to mingle living and working together.

Only at home, she wouldn't be expected to carry a radio with her at all times. Being on call twenty-four hours a day, and praying there were no genuine emergencies. She was a surgeon, and a good one—no one with mediocre surgical skills could get a neurosurgery fellowship—but since she'd returned home, she'd had to admit to herself that she was suited to a smaller GP practice, as well. Building a relationship with patients from cradle to grave appealed in some way that felt more meaningful than the prestige and excitement of neurosurgery. Something she could only admit to herself in hindsight, when the idea of performing emergency surgery by herself here, without any experienced medical personnel to assist, was enough to make her want to stow away on one of the boats back to civilization.

But that move would wait until tomorrow. She had the radio with her, the volume cranked up to levels she'd never have dared to use if there were other people sleeping nearby, and that would suffice for tonight.

Not ready to go sleep in another man's bed. May never be fully ready, even if she might one day make that decision—once she knew if her father's will was ironclad or not. She hadn't told West that he'd almost inherited a vineyard by marrying her—it only remained hers while she was unmarried. She hadn't known it until he was already gone. And even if she would've trusted him with the vineyard, she wasn't sure she could picture giving that power to anyone else. She didn't even want people finding out and it suddenly becoming a thing to try and woo her in order to inherit a vineyard. Pai should've thought of these things before that silly bit of legal tomfoolery.

This time away was supposed to be about adventure, but it might just be about mourning. Repairing herself.

West's cabin was empty, as was the rest of Pod C, which would be soon shuttered for the winter like other empty parts of the station. After ten days of thin walls and hearing every little thing, she was now the only one there, surrounded by empty rooms and the loudest silence.

She could sleep in his room tonight if she wanted to, maybe move to one of the warmer cabins. Or maybe just dart in and pinch his pillow to keep the essence of him around for a while.

Like she'd kept his ring on her finger last time.

The thought effectively killed her pathetic, sentimental urges. An instant ice bath to her dignity.

She set up the heater, lit the candles, lifted the blinds on her window, then wrestled her feet out of the boots she basically wore all the time now. Changed clothes. Put on the idiotic but warm pink onesie. Got into bed.

She'd no sooner climbed in than thought better of her decision, and turned to crawl to the foot of the bed to tuck in where she could watch through the windows to the sky, hoping the aurora would appear.

In the meanwhile, she grabbed a notebook and set about sorting out her life.

Lists.

Lists for work.

Lists for NASA, for those initial physicals she'd been saddled with in the interim while awaiting Tony's replacement.

Lists for the vineyard.

Lists. That was how you kept moving forward when life delivered another few gut punches.

CHAPTER EIGHT

"LIA?"

Hearing her name, complete with urgent electronic disembodiment, jerked hard on Lia's attention and her hands. She clumsily sprayed the air above the baby spinach she'd been tending in the station's greenhouse as her pulse instantly shot higher than the orbiting satellite she still planned her days around.

The radio she had been carrying like a dead weight every minute since the other doctors had left, even to the bathroom, and the shower, weighed at her hip. And until now, it hadn't so much as crackled.

She fumbled with the thing, wrestling it off her belt and looking at it for a full three seconds before remembering what she was supposed to do.

Push a button, talk, let go.

"Yes. This is Lia."

She'd no more than clicked off when her stomach did a little excited somersault and she recognized the voice.

West.

It took that long for her brain to catch up with the truth her body instantly had known.

"I need you," was all he said.

She didn't take the time to say anything else, just

took advantage of the adrenaline pulsing through her body and moved faster than she would've thought herself capable. Radio still in hand, she skittered sideways down the narrow greenhouse aisle, then ran for the corridor.

How was it even possible he was there? He left. Three days ago. He and Jordan and Zeke. Was Jordan back, too?

No. Jordan had emailed her pictures of sunny blue ocean from San Diego just this morning. Jordan was in California.

Lia hadn't stayed to watch the bus leave. Had he gotten off and just been laying low?

She didn't stop to take off the apron she wore there, just ran hard all the way to the clinic.

It wasn't far from the clinic, in the same part of the station, on the same corridor. In less than half a minute, she pushed through the swinging doors.

West stood just inside the main entry. Sort of.

He was on his feet, but both of his hands braced on the surface of the sign-in desk where a radio was located, leaning hard. Not a lazy lean. The lean of a man who didn't have the strength to stay upright without using all his limbs. Disheveled, eyes almost empty, like that second before anesthesia fully claimed consciousness.

A large, crumpled duffel bag sat on the floor a half meter away, along with the thick, regulation-issue coat he'd been wearing the last time she saw him, in the swirling snow and frosty air.

She reached him as he straightened, and immediately swayed hard to the right. He would've fallen if she hadn't grabbed him by the lapels and became a solid *something* for him to use to ground himself.

"Hey now, what's going on? West?"

One look at the blackness around his eyes and the network of red webs told her he wasn't calling because he *needed* her. He needed her. Something was wrong.

"I'm here to work," he said, then blinked hard, like his eyes had gone out of focus and squeezing them would make the world crystal again.

"You look like it," she murmured, then began steering him backward, turning as she did until he was perched on the edge of the desk and she could safely let go. "What's going on? Have you been out in the cold all this time?"

He said it again. "I'm here to work."

Definitely not okay, and the urgent need to fix it *now* had her mentally tumbling through scenarios and noting symptoms.

"Well, it's not your shift," she said, because that was the only thing she could think to say.

"No?"

She shook her head and tried again. "Where have you been? Did you come back?"

His hands again found her hips, like it was a natural armrest, and she could tell he was struggling to come up with answers. It was a kind of fun-house mirror to their last goodbye, when words had been hard to find only because the subject was hard; these should've been easy answers.

"Dallas," he finally said, and she didn't have to do any complicated math to realize that if he'd made it to Dallas and back in three days, he'd turned around and come back almost immediately.

This was exhaustion, dangerous exhaustion, and the pauses were more likely fleeting, frequent consciousness lapses.

He needed sleep. Emergency sleep…

"Okay, well, your cabin isn't prepared, so come with me." She took his hands and stepped back, urging him to his wobbly feet. He nearly tripped over the duffel, and that was the end of the chances she was willing to take he'd make it to one of the beds. Holding his hands, while comforting in a way that could shake her insides, wouldn't help get him there. She turned in, and slung one of his arms across her shoulders so she could get him around the waist and make him lean.

"Where are we going?"

Exhaustion could mimic drunkenness, she'd once read, but she'd never seen it before today.

"Bed."

"That's good."

She got him shuffled to the closest patient bed, then turned him to sit. She immediately launched in, unfastening his suit so she could get him out of it.

If his coordination had been something under his control, she would've been stripped naked by the time she got his coveralls pooled around his waist. As it was, he kept fumbling with the zipper pull on the lighter suit she wore inside, like it was some strange contraption he'd never seen and couldn't make his fingers effectively grip.

"You'll have to do it," he muttered, clearly thinking they were up to something besides her trying to get him undressed in case of emergency. She needed his arms bare for a line and vitals.

Playing along still seemed like the easiest thing.

"Okay. I'll do it later. You stand up for me? I want to get your coveralls down."

He nodded, grabbed the edge of the bed for support, and then the wall once he got upright, and she took everything down as quickly as she could, leaving him in just his boxers and the thermal shirt he'd worn beneath the coveralls.

Once more, he sat, and she stayed down there to get his boots off.

His skin always felt warm to her, but today he felt feverish. Did exhaustion cause fevers? She wasn't immediately sure. It made a kind of sense, any kind of trauma to the body could make it react with a fever, and extreme sleep deprivation was definitely a kind of trauma.

"Feet up," she said, standing and trying to swing his legs into the bed as she did, but his heels touched down on the mattress and she felt his arms around her the next second, the world tilting.

His coordination problems aside, his mouth found hers as if guided by a laser, and the mattress at her back confirmed what she really thought was about to happen. The man was probably only technically awake, but he still had enough energy to pick her off the floor and roll.

And kiss.

Sweet mercy, the man knew how to kiss. Months since she'd felt his mouth on hers, and it was the same, saturated with that drugging euphoria he'd always been able to create with the barest brush of his lips or the glide of his tongue.

She wanted to wrap her arms around his shoulders and just let the good feelings roll over her, but there was just enough functioning gray matter left to remind her: it wasn't right. He wasn't thinking clearly. Even if he'd started this, she'd be taking advantage to let it continue. Knowing that, it still took her several long, drugging kisses before she got control enough to press his shoulders back, giving a strong enough hint for him to understand.

He leaned back just a touch, so his nose brushed hers and his quick, warm breath fanned her cheeks.

"West?"

"Hmm?" He stayed up long enough to indicate he was listening, but then leaned right back in and kissed her again, trailing little nips and suckles along her jaw to the side of her neck.

The softness of his lips, the familiar and unfamiliar crisp brush of his beard, the way his tongue slipped out to stroke her skin, it all scrambled her thoughts almost as much as sleep deprivation had scrambled his.

He didn't seem to even remember they'd broken up. Twice, basically.

She gave a little tug to the hair on the back of his head, not enough to hurt but enough to urge him back again.

"What are you doing?" she asked softly, catching his gaze when he was up again.

He smiled, eyes half-closed, a dreamlike happiness flowing off him. "Snogging you senseless."

Had he ever looked at her that way? Unguarded and open and…it looked like love. God, she really didn't know how to tell what love looked like. He'd told her he didn't love her. He'd made it very clear.

Maybe they were both confused. Maybe he was mentally in those few days before Charlie had died…and he hadn't come to whatever realization had prompted him leaving.

Jerking him out of somewhere so happy felt awful, but she had to stop this.

She nodded to his simple, adorable answer, and when he leaned in to kiss her again, she turned her head.

Undeterred, he continued nuzzling and nibbling, and her foggy brain came to another realization. He wasn't trying to get her naked. This was cuddling. Kissing just to kiss? Not how they usually operated.

But she wished it had been. It was as sexy as it was sweet.

And she had to stop it. "Why?"

"Why am I kissing you?"

"Mmm-hmm..."

He pulled back again, still happy. Amused, even. "You suddenly don't like kissing me?"

God, she didn't want to do this. And she couldn't do it with the warm, solid weight of him pressing her into the bed, when every instinct said it was right. She got some traction in the mattress and slid up just a little, his gaze still tracking her, befuddled.

She couldn't just blurt out, *Remember how you don't love me and ran two hemispheres to get away?* It might be true, but it would be like kicking a puppy at this point.

"Where are we?" she asked instead.

Still confused, he looked up and at the room briefly before focusing on her again. "You don't want to kiss at work?"

Not about what she wanted. By the saints, she wanted to stay right there with him, kissing, cuddling, everything...

She tried again. "Where are we?"

"Medical ward?"

Good. This might work. Without unnecessary cruelty.

"Right. Where is that?"

He caught on that she was leading him somewhere, and his answers became slower and, for the moment, more confused. "Fletcher?"

"That's right." She puffed, watching him slowly starting to catch up. "Where is Fletcher?"

"Antarctica."

It was getting through. He leaned up just a little bit, clearly picking up that he was missing something, but not sure what yet.

"Why are we in Antarctica?" she asked finally.

She could see the second it clicked. His brow softened, then went slack. A look of undisguised grief bloomed in his eyes for an earth-stopping second, then he was moving, rolling off her.

"Lia... I'm sorry. I don't... I don't know..."

She slid off the bed and, once on her feet, turned to urge him back against the bed; doing things had a way of letting her feel in control. Or at least let her cover her lack of it. "It's okay. Why did you come back?"

"I had to," he said softly, his eyelids drooping.

"Why?"

Eyes closed, and mouth that had been working so beautiful started getting sluggish. "Didn'...have anywhere else...to go."

He'd be asleep in a moment. If she wanted answers, she needed to get them now. Even if it just sounded like he'd slammed her with the truth she knew he didn't realize he was saying. Like a drunken confession, but with a fever.

He wouldn't have been allowed to just come back on his own. He'd have to have arranged it, gotten permission. People didn't just get to visit Antarctic research stations without a job waiting for them or maybe special permission. There wasn't any other way to get there than through the actual official transport. He'd gotten permission, and came straight back.

"Are you taking over Tony's study?"

He opened his eyes, and nodded. "Yes. That's why I came back."

The official line. He probably didn't even realize he'd said something else a moment ago. Both reasons might be facts, but the first? That was *truth*. And that made her heart ache, too.

"Did you sleep at all while you were gone?"

"Couple hours in Dallas."

"Hotel?"

"Airport."

So, no rest really.

"Did you sleep on the plane at all?"

"Don' remember," he mumbled. She could almost see reality shrinking in his eyes.

"Boat? West?"

He shrugged, eyes closed again.

Basically, no sleep for three days on top of a few days with a couple of hours here and there, and thousands of miles of extensive, arduous travel. Amazing he'd made it at all.

Why would he do that? They would've let him recover a couple of days in Dallas before getting on another plane. There was time, at least a couple of weeks left before travel would become all but impossible.

She couldn't keep him awake any longer. "Let me get that shirt off you, and then you can sleep. I'm going to get your vitals, okay?"

He leaned up and she helped him out of the long-sleeved shirt, and when he laid back again, he said nothing else, breathing slow, regular and deep.

He hadn't answered, but he also hadn't said no. She'd be failing to take proper care of a patient if she didn't check him out.

She grabbed the nurse on a stick and went to work.

Temperature, elevated.

Pulse oxygen levels, great.

Blood pressure, also elevated.

Through it all, he didn't so much as flinch, sleeping hard enough to add to her concern.

Fever could be an illness, sign of either a bacterial or viral infection. Or it could be unrelated, and all about his lack of sleep.

A blood panel would make her feel better about letting him sleep it off…

Five minutes later, she'd drawn several vials of blood, which he'd also slept through, and she went to run it for results, one thought circling her brain: *he came back*.

If he hadn't been so clear about not loving her, she'd have taken it for a chance to not be *done*. But it was far more likely that she was the excuse that allowed him to come back, when the truth was more about his rootless existence. She may not want to live in Portugal full-time due to the expectations placed on her there, but she always could go there when she needed to. She was always welcome, even if that was also where she'd be reminded she was a disappointment. She had a fail-safe, break-in-case-of-emergency home to return to. It didn't seem like he did.

More worrying still, for a man who lived in the future and delighted in his future plans, him not having future plans to go to said something else was very wrong.

How had Charlie died?

CHAPTER NINE

BATHROOM.

The driving need for a bathroom dragged West from sleep.

Before opening his eyes, he swiveled and rolled, lifting the blankets as he went, but half turned, felt a tug at his arm and a little pinch of pain.

He froze, opened his sluggish eyes, and a hospital room came into focus.

Patient room. Fletcher.

He laid back again, surveying his body as he did.

IV in left arm, lightly stinging.

Hospital gown.

Need for a bathroom…

He lifted the blanket and peered beneath. A catheter line laid across his thigh.

Damn it.

He didn't need a bathroom. It just *felt* like he needed a bathroom.

Lia.

Her face swam up in his mind, pillows behind her head, cheeks pink. Lips pink…

Hell. He'd kissed her. In this bed. More than kissed, but less than he'd wanted to do. Still wanted to do, but was now in control enough to remember that he had no right to touch her. Not like that. Not anymore. Not after what he'd done.

How had he forgotten what they were now?

Always.

He groaned and flopped his head back against the pillow as the word came swimming back to him.

He'd been out of his mind, and plowed under by that one word rolling through his brain on repeat over thousands of miles. *Sempre.* Always.

In the next instant, he heard running and Lia appeared in the doorway, eyes wide, assessing.

"Catheter? Really?" he asked, then mentally kicked himself. Should've said something else. All the time gone, he'd only thought about that one word. *Sempre. Always.*

He'd abandoned her again, lied ugly, and she'd said *always* to him.

"You've been asleep…unwakeable—" she stopped to check her watch "—for almost twenty-one hours."

"Twenty-one hours?" he repeated, the words not seeming possible. "Since I got back? Twenty-one hours?"

She nodded, and he looked a little closer as she neared the bed. There was a hint of darkness under her eyes, made more noticeable by how peely-wally she looked. Tired. Exhausted. But *relieved*.

She moved around his bed to check his IV, the drip rate, the amount of saline left on the pole. "You had a fever, and you fell asleep while I was checking your vitals."

"And?"

"Elevated blood pressure. I did a blood panel, which

you also slept through, and ran it. Dehydration, elevated white count, and I was worried about dehydration, so I ran a line. A few hours later, when you still refused to wake up, I decided to set the Foley."

He didn't need to do anything but look into her eyes to see how worried she'd been. Still was. And he wasn't sure how to explain it to her. How he even explained it to himself.

Leaving had felt like dying. Like a mistake. Like another abandonment. If he left her here and something happened to her—he'd heard stories about how dangerous things could get in the winter. There were self-contained, survival pods dubbed lifeboats all over the station for a reason.

If something happened to her and he wasn't there... that would be the end of him. No matter where he was, that would be the end. Words he couldn't just blurt out to her.

Stay on point. The catheter. Just thinking the one word, he felt it again, and couldn't help wincing. "It's my first. I have new sympathy for patients who've complained about them in the past."

She grinned a touch, nodding. "I know."

"What else?"

"I did another panel a couple of hours ago. White cells decreased. I think you're on the mend."

His body bounced back faster than his mind.

"Let's check vitals again," she said. She wheeled the mobile tool caddy to his bedside, and he let her get on with it. "If your pressure looks good, and you feel like it, I'll bring a kit for you to deflate the Foley's balloon and remove it. I just didn't want to leave it when you were so far gone and I was pumping you full of fluids."

"Thanks," he said as she took the thermometer back and made a note of all the readings.

It was a matter of dignity, letting him handle it. She certainly had done a myriad of far more pleasurable things with his penis, but this was different.

And that intimacy had been before, when they were together, and they weren't now. Something he'd had to admit had to change. A faulty plan, at least once he'd seen her again. She was harder to walk away from in the flesh...with those big pretty eyes full of dashed hopes.

"I'll get the kit," she said, taking the mobile vitals trolley with her to the door. "But wait for me to get back before you get up."

"I was pretty bad, eh?"

"I'm not sure how we got you into the bed." She stopped at the door to look at him again, not mentioning his obvious mental break when he'd been a horny zombie at his return. "Are you feeling okay?"

Not really.

"I'm fine," he lied. Physically, he felt fine, but the rest? Conflicted about the deal he'd made with himself that allowed him to return, to even try to put things back together with her. "Just never slept so long before. Kind of hungover. And trying to think of what I can even say to you."

She nodded, the worry in her eyes spiking for a moment, then settling again into that same tired concern. She'd heard him, and didn't want to acknowledge the spiky topic. She focused on his health. "Headache?"

"No. Just sluggish, or something. And both amazed and dismayed to have needed such tending."

"You don't need to say anything. You'd have looked after me, too."

Either purposefully taking his words to be about gratitude rather than confession, or unaware it could be anything else.

"I abandoned you, Lia."

The word made her breath hitch, then her mouth actually turned down at the corners. The soft plushness he couldn't get enough of compressed with the ghost of worry and exhaustion. And again, she dodged it. "I'll get the kit and go to the galley to bring back lunch."

Before he said another word, she buzzed off to tick off her tasks, leaving what he needed to rid himself of the Foley, and disappearing.

He set to work with the syringe at the port to draw the saline out of it, and then took a deep breath, and pulled.

It came out, and with it, a relieved breath.

Always stayed there, in his mouth, ready to come out every time he spoke, but that seemed like something he should work up to, as well. He couldn't expect her to just take him back because he'd returned. All sins required penance.

The rest of the words—words he didn't understand or remember—seemed to be as hope-filled to him. But the foreign sounds hadn't stayed with him long enough to be translated. He'd drained the battery on his phone trying to string together what he remembered of the sounds to create faux Portuguese words for a translation app to work with, and got nothing. Tried to reverse engineer with guesses in English, but none of that had looked right, either.

Not the direct, traditional words of a love confession. He knew how to say *I love you* in Portuguese: *amo-te*.

But he'd heard the emotion in her voice, seen it in

her eyes. Nothing else fit with whispered goodbyes and teary cheek-kisses.

He wanted the IV gone, to be as right as he could be, before she got back, and he didn't need it now. On the opposite wall to his bed sat a cabinet where he found those supplies, then returned to the bed.

When he'd left London, it had hurt both of them, but it had felt surgical. Curative. Better for her in the long run.

This time, he'd hated himself before he'd even set foot on the transport bus. Known too well what he was putting her through—the torment of yet another abandonment, because that's what it was. That's what it had been both times. And he knew more about that particular pain than he'd wish for anyone.

But he'd still done it.

She came back with a tray of food and a tall glass of lemonade, placed both on a rolling bedside table and scooted to him. "Eat and then walk?"

He nodded, leaning back, unable to keep himself from looking at her—watching her look at his arm, the supplies where he'd removed the line and the cotton ball he'd already taped it down with.

"Or did you already get up?"

One more pointed look at the cabinet and back.

"Two steps is barely walking," he said, still holding her gaze and the unspoken questions he saw there.

"Wobbly?"

"Not too bad. I'm not a falls risk."

"No bed alarm needed?" She half smiled, trying to joke, set things on a more even keel with them, but he couldn't go along with it. Not now.

"Too many other kinds of alarms."

His words made her freeze, just a few seconds, and then she resumed gathering up the remains of the medical supplies he'd used to remove the uncomfortable implements, and looked at him. "Did you return to make me leave, or to fill Tony's position? Why are you back, West?"

"Always," he answered, paying no attention to the food she'd placed before him. Finding out what she'd said was more important than hunger. "That's the only word you said outside the bus that I understood. *Sempre.* Always."

Her breathing picked up. She looked away, removing the trash, then maintaining the distance from him, like she needed some air between them to take whatever he was going to say. Or to give her the courage to answer. "They were the only words that came."

"What were they?"

She licked her lips, obviously wary of answering. Then slowly, with pauses between each word, lacking her customary rapid manner of speaking her native tongue, said, *"Eu...sempre...terei...saudades...de ti."*

Despite the slowness, there was no nervous quality to the admission, just a heavy-eyed sense of vulnerability that said she knew she was exposing a lot. That he had asked a lot of her repeating it.

"Terry...sawdadesh..." He repeated the sounds back, trying on the feel of them and no doubt bungling them up. Making her answer his as-yet-unasked question.

"There is no direct translation. The closest is...'I'll miss you.'"

"Always?"

She flushed then, but nodded. "That word has a direct translation."

"Where does the other fall short?"

"Saudades." She said the word again. "It's like homesickness. In the soul. Usually for a place."

She waited to see if that explanation was enough.

It wasn't. If there was more, he needed to hear it. He waited.

"Terei saudades." She said the word again, shaking her head, voice falling back to her usual softness. "I have…missing feelings…that…can never be healed… by anything else. And I am broken by it."

Her voice rasped over the end, and when she leaned off the wall to make her exit, he saw tears in her eyes again.

His own eyes burned, his chest on fire.

"Lia…"

She stopped in the doorway, her gaze falling to the floor, not to him again. Waiting…

"I'm not worthy of those feelings."

"You don't get to decide that," she cut in, shaking her head, a little sniff preceding her swiping her cheeks. "You practically killed yourself getting back here when there was time for you to rest. Did they refuse to let you have a day of rest before getting onto another plane?"

"No. But you were the only doctor here. You saw how many people have gotten hurt this week while they've been shuttering parts of the station for the first time."

She didn't exactly roll her eyes at him, but the exaggerated slow blink had the same damned effect, and she folded her arms. Didn't believe him. "Are we done?"

Done with this conversation, or *done*?

He didn't ask, just felt the wave of nausea as his empty stomach churned, and he lifted one hand on instinct to touch his throat, searching and not finding the necklace and her ring.

In the silence, she came back to the bedside, hand dipping into one pocket. When she pulled it free, the chain and ring dangled from her fingers.

"Didn't want you choking yourself in your sleep, the way you usually move around. But then you didn't move at all."

"Twenty-one hours?" he repeated, the number still shocking, but took the offered ring.

"Twenty-one hours," she confirmed, then walked away again. "Welcome back, Dr. MacIntyre. Eat. You need to get your strength back."

Always, she'd said, and he'd still bungled it up.

At no other time in his life had anyone cared…had anyone loved him enough to track him down once he'd gone. Even his brother. But she'd gone halfway around the world for him, and even if she was rightfully wary of him now, she still loved him.

He had to say something now. It was one of those times he couldn't play it cool and wait, plan what to say.

"I'm not worthy of your feelings," he repeated, and she stopped again in the doorway, her back to him, "but I want them. You. And I'm selfish enough to admit it."

"Why?" she asked, not turning back.

"Charlie overdosed. I wasn't there," he said softly. It was easier to talk to her back. He could say words he'd never had the heart to utter aloud before, without having to look in her eyes and see her opinion of him sink. Just enough to try to explain.

"In the States?" she asked, half turning back toward him, her face a perfect combination of horror and compassion.

"I lied to you about where he was. I couldn't get him clean, and I was ashamed of my addict little brother. So. Not the States. Near Glasgow."

If she took him back, he'd probably have to tell her the whole story someday. Before they got to the rings and vows again. Somehow. But giving details meant picturing it, and he did everything he could not to picture it.

"Were you angry with me for not being there? I would've come back. I would've gone with you…"

"I know you would've. It's not that. Not your fault," he said, his accent thicker when he spoke while searching for the words than when he was fully in control of himself. "I'm still tryin' to work out how to deal with it. So, just to be fair to you, I'm goin' to say that I don' know if I can be what you need. I know I lied to you, I failed you, and that you probably shouldn' trust me. I'm far too good at breaking things."

CHAPTER TEN

HE WANTED HER BACK.

Before West had revealed how he felt and *didn't* feel about her, Lia had harbored quiet fantasies of getting back together. But since then, even knowing that she'd only days ago questioned why he hadn't wanted to keep seeing her and see if love developed, standing on the other side of it felt different. Scary.

Saying *yes* would mean entering an unequal relationship, where she loved him, but he didn't, and may never love her back. How long was she supposed to even give that kind of a trial?

She didn't want to be that stupid again, and had already proven she couldn't even correctly identify love. She confused it with general happiness, and probably lust. Would she ever be able to believe him if he said the words to her again?

"I don't want to sound cruel, and I don't want to have a fight in the clinic, but I won't lead you on, either. I don't know why you want me back when you've been very clear that you never loved me. I didn't realize it before, I didn't think anyone would propose without love, so I believed it. But the truth is I don't have any idea what that feels like."

"What *what* feels like?"

"Being loved. You say you want me, and I believe you do because want doesn't require more than physical connection—something we're very good at." Or had been before. They'd been too wounded and cagey since she'd returned to do more than feel things, and then stuff them away. "But you *don't* love me, so I don't know. I need to think about it, about whether we can have something healthy and happy." She licked her lips and shook her head. "I'm glad you're here. I don't really believe that you came back for me, but I am glad you're here."

"When I said—"

"No," she cut him off. "I don't want to talk about this more right now. You need to eat and get a walk in before I'm willing to discharge you." She opened her mouth to say more, but a loud, frantic cry for help from the lobby took precedence, and sent her sluggish heart back into instant overdrive.

Without another word, she turned and ran toward the voice.

"What happened?" West heard Lia say through the opened door.

"He's not breathing. I found him like this..." a man said.

West took two big bites of the noodles she'd brought him, then shoved the table aside and got up to fetch a second gown from the cabinet to use as a robe and conceal his backside. He hadn't gotten around to asking where his clothes were, and he was going to go help, with or without them.

"Air was really thin in there," the man said as West

made it out, breathing labored, and had obviously carried the patient in. He stood to the side, hands gripped together, worriedly watching.

"Where was it?" West asked. They'd gotten the man on the table and Lia was climbing up to straddle him, fingers linked to begin chest compressions.

"Mechanical room."

Another injury from Mechanical?

"Thin air," she puffed between compressions, but he heard her flinging open drawers to get a mouth guard out to breathe for him when she stopped.

He took and delivered two quick breaths before she resumed. "I know."

Suffocation could do that, if the room was pressure sealed, but why would Mechanical be pressure sealed?

"Oxygen?" he prompted, and she nodded, but didn't speak again, focused on applying the proper amount of pressure, and keeping count. Chest compressions were a workout and carried on for a long time. It was common to need to switch out with someone fresh, so the cadence wouldn't be affected. Exhaustion could set in quickly when someone was fully rested, let alone whatever state Lia was in.

He kept an eye on her, and breathed for the man when he was supposed to, mentally ticking through what else it could be. Carbon monoxide was a silent killer, odorless, and breathing didn't feel affected up until it was too late. So it was unlikely to be noticed as thin air, but did sound like something that could actually happen in Mechanical with the machines and exhaust.

Regardless, the treatment was the same. Pure oxygen would help, if anything was going to.

He dug out a laryngoscope, bag valve ventilator, and

connected it straight into the oxygen in seconds, readying himself to dive in and intubate the man the next time she stopped.

"He's still warm," she said, which was something at least. And as soon as she counted her last compression, she helped tilt his head back to lengthen the throat, and West slid in the blade and tubing, then began pumping straight oxygen into the man's lungs.

Three puffs, an extra to help, and she resumed.

After the fourth set of full oxygen breaths, the mechanical aeration of the man's blood worked. His head jerked once, and she stopped to feel the pulse in his throat, her hands shaking, and following up, he could see her arms shaking, too. Not nerves, but weakness that came from overexertion, because if anyone was going to have one of those TV doctor moments of having to be dragged away from a patient who was too far gone, it would be Lia. She'd keep going until he made her stop. Or until they got lucky.

She didn't climb down yet, instead grabbing the man's wrists to pin beneath her knees, in case he should wake and do what most people did when they woke up intubated—try to pull it out. He needed the oxygen. If this was carbon monoxide poisoning, he'd need hours of pure, undiluted oxygen.

They waited and watched for a full minute, but when he didn't fully rouse, she climbed down and they got his manual pump respirator switched to the machine and began attaching leads to monitor his heart.

"Thinking someone needs to get a detector down there." She breathed hard. "And we need to get him stable and out of here. His sternum cracked, and he'll need a lot of care for a while."

"If he wakes," West said softly. They both knew his chances weren't great.

"While the weather allows travel, we need to relocate him. Is there anywhere in South America with a hyperbaric chamber? Or maybe a navy boat?"

"I don't know." He didn't, but he would find out. "I've read that they help filter the blood, but there's no evidence that it helps."

"There's no evidence that it doesn't," she grumbled, breathing starting to even out, but she still shook as if by an internal earthquake.

The man they'd been ignoring made himself known again. "Does it always make you die? If you've got carbon monoxide poisoning?"

West glanced sideways at Lia, and despite still being in a hospital gown, he said to the man, "You went in after him?"

A nod was his answer, and he shared a look with Lia to let her know he was handling it.

"Let's check you out. You might benefit from some oxygen, too."

Still focused on their main patient, she didn't interfere, but did call after him, "Get blood."

"Get my clothes when you're done," he called back, ushering the man into an exam room. "How are you feeling? Anything off? And what's your name? I can't pull up your file—I don't have a device—but I can check this right now."

"Mario Correa," he answered first. "I haven't been feeling right since the day I moved into Pod A."

"Not about Mechanical?" West asked, and when the man shrugged, he continued. "Symptoms?"

"I don't know. Tired and off," Mario said, then

looked at West seriously. "Doctor, are you sure you're well enough for this? Maybe the lady doctor should see me."

"I'm okay," West assured him. "I've been discharged, just haven't gotten changed yet. So, after sleeping in Pod A you felt poorly?"

"It was before bed," he said. "I worked in the shop all day that day. Actually, it was the day after we'd shut down Pod B, where I had been, and some other parts of the station. I went to Mechanical to make a part for the ventilation system so we could change it."

"Repair?"

"Not broken, but the engineers came up with some way to save energy, and that meant closing down different parts than they'd originally planned. So we're reworking ventilation and electrical, those kinds of things."

Right. None of that meant much to him.

"We'll get some blood. That'll tell us if you've got a carbon monoxide concentration. But I'm going to get you on oxygen now, just in case."

"How does that help?"

"Pushes the carbon monoxide out of the blood. It takes a few hours to clean it out, but we can do that. You just have to wear a mask and breathe only the oxygen that comes through it," he explained, getting the man set up and turning the oxygen flow on. "It smells kind of weird, but it'll help. If you can, lie down on the table and nap after I get your blood. If it's clear, I'll let you go. If it's not, you stay until it is."

"I need to call my boss…"

"I'll get it," West said, getting that information from the man to make the call. It sounded to him like something weird was going on with ventilation, but it was a new station and this was the first time being overwintered. It was bound to have kinks that needed working out as things were used and bugs discovered.

He'd find Lia after. Get some clothes. Finish their conversation before sending her to bed. He'd slept twenty-one hours; he could stay awake for another eight so she could sleep.

It was fine. They had time. They weren't *done*. Even if he'd made this exponentially harder with his lie about having never loved her. A lie he still couldn't believe she'd bought, no more than he could believe her assertion that she'd never been loved, that she didn't know what it felt like.

Jordan loved her. Her friends. Certainly her family and the people in her village. Unless that was the big mess she'd wanted to keep him away from.

It was funny the things that occurred to Lia in the middle of an emergency. How it was possible to save a life with CPR eleven percent of the time if you performed the right steps, the right way, in the right amount of time after the last natural respiration.

Maybe in eleven percent of alternate universes, he said those words to her and it saved their relationship. And maybe the reason she'd been gritting her teeth all afternoon was how badly she wanted to take him back, and how bad an idea she knew that to be. But it would feel good in the moment.

All is forgiven.

Pretend nothing happened.

Pretend she didn't remember the *other* words he'd said.

What she couldn't work out was why he'd said them. And why hadn't *she*?

She could've lied, or just told him she didn't want to translate the words she'd said outside the bus, when she hadn't expected to ever have to own up to them. And couldn't bring herself to lie about them. Which could be something she did need to learn.

Instead, she'd spent hours trying to convince herself that this new pragmatism was a sign of growth. That she was just uncovering the real Lia.

She'd kept busy after resuscitation, arranging transport to get her resus patient back to civilization and the care he'd need. And where his family could go to him, where they wouldn't have to worry if he was all right.

West had gotten changed and dumped his belongings off at his new cabin in Pod A, no longer next door for her to worry about, then returned after dinner.

"I'm going to take the night shift so you can get some sleep," he said from the door to the office. She'd expected to have the rest of the evening to herself, to gather her wits, but there he was.

She fisted her hands in her lap, trying to hide her white-knuckling it through the conversation, a twisting grip on her jacket better than the grip she had on her willpower. Shoving him out of the office and yelling at him would probably be a bad thing, especially as he was now there to work. And she didn't even know if Kasey was running the transport bus now to escape.

"You don't have to. I'll set alarms, keep a radio with me and go check on him every hour..."

"Why?"

"It's my job. I don't want you thinking you have to

take care of me. Or that it will change things. We both probably need to stay in our lanes for a few days."

He made some sound of understanding, then moseyed in to lean against her desk. "So, by our lanes, you mean no hugging, no relationship talk, no random love declarations or trying to give you the ring back?"

"For instance," she said, but felt herself bristling when he said "love declarations." Her nails digging into her palms made her pull them from her lap and reach for an ink pen on her desk instead. Something to fidget with that wouldn't hurt.

He played it too cool, but when she looked up at him, she saw worry in his brow. Another thing she couldn't count on reading correctly. Instinct wanted to believe that you couldn't worry about someone you didn't love, but that wasn't true. She was worried about her resus patient, someone she'd just met while unconscious.

"For instance?"

"It would be counterproductive to comment further, and definitely strays outside of what my lane should be right now when I'm trying to picture what this is going to be like, working together in close quarters for eight months," she grumbled, giving voice to what was in her head, because why not? "Besides, it would be a lie, wouldn't it?"

"What would be a lie?"

"Love declarations," she repeated, then looked up at him, not ready to back down on that one. "It feels manipulative when you say things like that, given what I know. You never loved me. So, if you didn't love me before, when I was actively trying to be what you wanted, you certainly don't love me now."

"I did love you," he argued, then, "You were trying to be what I wanted?"

"I always try to be what I think people I love want me to be. Everyone does it. Some better than others." Her energy flagged, because it had been an exhausting couple of days, and that was before the morning CPR. "And you didn't. You told me you didn't. You practically said it again when you told me to not cry because you dislike me having red eyes."

"That's not why I said that." He looked kind of bewildered, and that just made her want to cry again. "I lied. I lied about Charlie, I lied about loving you. And you know what? There's more. I don't… There's…"

He stopped and pinched the bridge of his nose, eyes closing. "It seemed like the kindest thing to do at the time. I did love you. I *do* love you, as well as I'm able."

"Even if I wanted to believe that, I know it's not true. How can you really love me when you don't even know me?"

"Of course I know you."

"You don't know me. *I* don't even know me." She threw her hands up, her voice rising with them, but through her evident exhaustion, she remembered where they were and lowered her voice again. "We went over this. It's just rehashing at this point. If you loved anything, it was on the surface, or what you thought we would become sometime in the future. When plans worked out. Living the dream. But I can't do that anymore. I'm making changes, which no one seems to notice, anyway, so why are we even having this discussion?"

"By changes, you mean being grumpy?"

"Growing my hair out. Wearing pink things. Not

forcing myself to project optimism that I don't feel, though I guess that's the same as grumpy." She stood up to mostly close the door, leaving it open enough to hear if anyone called for help.

"Of course I noticed the changes, but what does a haircut or pink pajamas have to do with who you are as a person?"

"We all have reasons for the things we do. Even if they're stupid reasons, we all have reasons. My father is on the run because he doesn't want to deal with the vineyard anymore, or the mess. And maybe so he doesn't have to see me succeed with it, because I will. Reasons are important for the things we do."

"There's a deeper reason behind growing your hair out than you simply want to change your hair?"

"Yes," she said, then went to check the radios on their charging stations, to see if they were getting a full charge. "And the reason I'm calling this conversation to a close right now is that I'm tired. And disillusioned. And wishing I had a superpower right now."

He chuckled. "What superpower would that be?"

She nodded toward the door. "Heal him."

"Ah, see, that's why you're a better doctor than I am," he said, and when she turned to look at him, he reached out to take her hand. "Do you want to know what superpower I want to have?"

"No," she said instantly, the way he looked into her eyes and stroked her hand giving her a silly little turn in the conversation gravity. "What?"

"Time-travel," he said softly. "But I can't fix the past. All I can try to do is do better. We have eight months to work this out, don't we? I'm not a patient man, so don't expect me to just give up and wait, but

I can do something for you tonight, and take the night shift, keep an eye on our patient so you can get eight hours. I think after twenty-one hours of straight sleep I can manage that."

She opened her mouth to argue, but suddenly couldn't think of why. Instead, she nodded her agreement, and when he tugged her over to wrap his arms around her, she leaned in. But she couldn't bring herself to put her arms around him in return. Her hands and cheek rested against his chest, and he propped his bearded chin atop her pink knitted hat, and there they stood, swaying together for far too long.

Up close, she could see the shape of her ring under the thermal shirt he wore, and felt that pit open back up in her stomach.

Hugging was definitely to be avoided. And she'd tell him that, too. Tomorrow.

CHAPTER ELEVEN

WEST WAITED UNTIL THEN, when it was likely that Lia would wake up on her own and be ticked at him, before he elbow-knocked on her door.

From the cacophony that preceded her opening the door, he could only assume that the new layout of the cabin was throwing her.

"G'mornin'…" He gave his best smile, then stretched out the hand holding her gadgets. "Brought these back."

"Brought back?" she repeated, then picked them up as if they were foreign gizmos she'd never seen before. "Did I leave them out?"

He shook his head, then held out the mug of tea he'd brought in offering. "I came in and stole them last night so you could get a little extra sleep. Have tea, and get woken up a little. I've had a whole night of thinking, and you know I'm an impatient man."

She took both offerings, pausing to toss the phone and radio behind her onto the bed, but kept the steaming mug in her hands. "You came and took them?"

"Aye," he said, then nodded. "And I'm on duty still. It's only ten, so I need to make this quick. May I come in?"

Last evening, he'd seen her run the emotional gamut

from sad, to incredulous, to seriously annoyed, to far too quiet. It was the last one that had stayed with him. The one that had informed this morning's decision.

"Why?" she asked, still not awake. Still adorably squinty-faced and now missing a hat, he could see how much her hair had grown out. Something he needed to ask her about. Those reasons she'd so passionately referenced.

"Because I have to say something…"

Last night, he hadn't been able to properly appreciate how much roomier these quarters were, or the view. The room might end up colder than the ones at the end of the pods, as one wall had an immense, outwardly bending bubble of a window. Could've been on a submarine, or one of those retro midcentury designs for what they expected the future to look like: all modern lines and bubble windows. Would be hard to cover in the summer. Which might account for some of Tony's insomnia. But that wasn't why he was here.

He closed the door behind her and waited for her to take a perch on the corner of the bed with her cup, then just launched into it. He was rubbish at talking about bad things, and doing it like ripping off a bandage seemed the cleanest way. Put it on the table, then go back to work.

Confessing during your morning break, it was also kind of safer. No long drawn-out discussions could happen in such a short time period.

"I thought about this all night, and as far as I could come up with, I have only two options on how to handle this," he said. "I can repeat myself until you punch me in the junk, which is neither productive nor fun. For me. Might be fun for you, depending on how angry you are."

"Pretty angry."

He nodded. "Or I can explain why I do...stupid things."

That didn't get a verbal response. She just looked instantly worried, and as alert as someone who'd been up for hours, and smartly stretched across the bed to put her tea down on the bedside table.

When she resumed a normal seated position before him, he instantly regretted not having tried to script it out, be eloquent.

"The reason I always look forward is because my rear view is... Pompeii, Sumatra and San Francisco, you know?"

"Volcanos?"

"Catastrophes. Earth-moving catastrophes," he explained, already off to a banging start. "Only most of the catastrophes I see when I look back have been my own doin'. So, I don't like to look back. I don't like to talk about it, any of it. Or think about it. Or answer questions. Because of that, I've given you the impression I don't want to know you. I still want to believe that none of that in the past matters, only what people can build together, but that hasn't worked out so well."

She shook her head, still saying nothing, and still worried, though he could see a spark of hope growing in her eyes.

"I shut down subjects I think might lead back to those things I don't want to talk about. I know it's a coping mechanism, but it's helped me get over a lot of bad since I was a boy—focusing on the next good thing to replace the current *bad* thing."

He paused to make sure she was still with him, but before she could say anything, he held up one finger to let her know there was more coming.

"When your city is buried under tons of ash, all you can do—the easiest thing, the *cleanest* thing you can do—is move on and start over." God, he hoped she didn't start asking for details on those bad things.

"How many times?" she asked, taking advantage of the pause he had to make to take a breath and get ready to say the big thing, the thing he prayed she'd hear and believe.

It only took him a couple seconds' consideration to know he couldn't possibly put a number to it. "I don't know the answer to that. But that's not the point, love."

She frowned, but nodded in a way that said she was going to let him continue for now, but she wasn't done with the number-of-moves thing.

He stepped closer, then squatted down so he was on eye level with her sitting on the corner of her bed. "I never look back at what's been buried. When I said I never loved you, I thought you needed to hear that so that you could move on, too. But it was a lie. And I really need you to hear this…"

She nodded slowly, and waited, but the completely undisguised fear he saw in her eyes almost made him turn back. Illuminated another instance where he understood how much he'd hurt her.

"Besides the death of my brother," he said, his throat thickening, and he could feel the water coming to his eyes, "*You* are the only disaster I've ever wanted to dig out from and rebuild." He licked his lips, nodding, as much to himself as for her to see. "I do want that."

"West…" She said his name, but he could see it wasn't going to be followed up with other words. It was shock, and joy, and sorrow rolled into one syllable, and a year's worth of feeling in her eyes.

"I know I referred to you as a disaster, and maybe that's not the best romantic thing to say, but it was over in my mind, and there was no going back. So, not artful, but—"

She shot forward, arms shooting out to wrap around his shoulders. He would've fallen, but even in these more spacious quarters, he still only had a few inches behind him of space before the wall caught them both, then it was only a matter of straightening his legs to slide his back up the door, and pull them both to their feet. It was either that, or lie down with her in the floor, and if he did that, more would follow. And no one would be minding the clinic.

"You don't have to say anything. I know it's…kind of a lot to put on you first thing when you wake, but if you decide you want to give it another go—today, two months from now or the day we leave to go back to the world—I will say yes and count myself lucky."

She nodded, and as much as he didn't want to move from where they stood, arms locked around one another, he said, "No one's mindin' the store. I should get back out there."

Although her arms loosened, she didn't let go, actually cupping his shoulders to hold on to him. "Wait. I need to know…about the moves."

"That matters?"

"Yes. I don't understand—how can you not know how many times you've made big moves?"

The number wasn't important, but the reason it was so high… Yeah, she was right about the reasons. "I'll think about it, see if I can make a list. But give me a time frame. Does that just mean as an adult? Or as a child, too?"

"Is it more than five times?"

He nodded. "Let me work on that number, right? You get ready for work, have your lunch, then you can come on duty. I'll hold the fort until. Maybe later I'll have a figure for you."

He wouldn't have a figure later, but he would make generalizations which might give her an even bigger shock. Later. He'd worry about it later.

A hug wasn't a promise. He couldn't just take the ring off the chain at his neck and slide it back onto her finger, but it was something.

Lia had said her goodbye to West outside of Kasey's bus less than a week ago, but it could've been months. Or even a different lifetime, and different people.

She hadn't even gone on duty today until around noon, and now, at the end of the day and having seen him exactly once in the hours in between, it could've been a week. Like a child counting down to Christmas, she'd counted half-hour increments until she'd be off official duty, and could talk to him alone again. Because she'd had some thoughts, once her brain kicked back in. And they were good thoughts. They might not sound like some kind of Highland poetry as his words had done, but no one could compete with that.

So, at half past six, she'd called for him over the radio, doing her utmost to sound terribly official, asking him to come speak with her. So probably everyone now knew it was anything but official, but when *everyone* was fifty-six other people, it didn't much matter.

A knock came within minutes to her private cabin door and she peeked out quickly, noticed him there looking curious and like he'd fallen for the officiality.

She also took note there was no one in the clinic to see them, grabbed his sleeve and pulled him inside.

She had taken off her insulated suit, the thin one she even tended to wear inside, and set up the heater he'd brought her to get the room warm. Because it was time for dinner, and she wanted to be alone with him, she'd laid out a little picnic on the bed, with grub from the galley. Stuff that wouldn't wreck her bedclothes if a dish tilted. Mostly hearty sandwiches and sides light on sauces.

He took all this in silently, then gave a cautious smile before asking, "So, are we picking up right where we left off? Before it all went badly wrong?"

"Not exactly," she said, then felt the need to add, "Because we are changing things, right?"

"We are." He punctuated his quiet words with a single nod, but then followed up. "Is it going to throw a wrench in the works if I steal a kiss before we get started changing things? You wouldn't…mind terribly, would you?"

And when he said it that way, with a quirk to his mouth and his head tilted so his blue eyes were full of meaningful sidelong flirting, she couldn't say no.

She leaned in to meet him halfway, intending a quick kiss of greeting, but he steered her backward until her back was against the door, and cupped both of her cheeks to press the sweetest, slowest kiss to her lips.

West's kisses always made statements. Usually, that statement was *I want you. Right now.* Sometimes the statement was *I want you and I'm cranky that I have to wait because of Reasons.*

But at that moment, the statement could not have more clearly been anything but *I missed you.*

Tenho saudades...tambem.

There may have been shades of *I love you* in that kiss. She couldn't be sure if it was there, or if she just really wanted it to be there.

Like with all their kisses when alone, soon even a sweet, lingering, loving kiss heated up. Deepened. Got them both a little stupid.

Just when she got breathless and grabby, he curled his fingers into the back of her hair, which was now long enough to pull, and gave a tiny tug. He leaned back enough that his nose touched hers. "What's the reason?"

"For?" She didn't follow.

"Your hair." He tugged lightly again at the three-plus centimeters of length that had been previously razored to her neck for as long as he'd known her—practically a military cut in the back.

She could've laughed, just to hear they were on the same page. His question led right into the things she'd been thinking about, things they'd have to talk about if they were going to be able to have a relationship. And sudden, unexpected kisses almost as soon as they were alone.

"Short pixie is too edgy for village life. They expect a *lady* hairstyle." She didn't actually make air quotes around the word, her hands were too busy holding on to him, but she eye rolled some implied air quotes to him. "Ironic since they prefer to follow a man, but if it's got to be a woman, she shouldn't have a manly cut. I was advised."

Again she made use of the eye punctuation.

"So if you don't grow your hair, they want you to sell the vineyard?"

"No one said that, but the way things are, the way

I'm expected to be there? Exactly opposite to how you know me." She was still pinned to the door, and it was hard to do serious talking like that, and it could get out of hand quickly. She stopped grabbing and patted his shoulders instead. "I'll explain more, but I need to say something else first because I totally forgot I was going to say it before you kissed me. I had a plan, see?"

He grinned and leaned back, then stepped cleanly away, so they were no longer touching, and things wouldn't get out of hand. "Of course you did. So what was your plan?"

"Eat these ham sandwiches, then turn off the lights and watch the aurora through the big window."

"Is 'watch the aurora' a euphemism?" he asked, cheeky smile back.

She smiled, but pretended she didn't want to grin at him. "That was the other bit. The avoiding euphemism and innuendo-related activities. For now."

"No sex?"

"For a bit?" she requested, then crawled onto the bed to sit against the wall, and tucked her feet in atop the blankets, careful of the food. "I had a plan when I came to Antarctica, for after the people who know me to be a certain way—you and Jordan—left. And it's the reason I never invited you home with me. Why I don't feel like I know myself. I want to know who I am, and I want you to know who I am before we start tearing one another's clothes off again. Because once we start that… Like a first date. Sort of."

"Right." West stayed standing for a time, a little of his natural broodiness returning to the furrow of his brow. "Tell me the boundaries. You invited me to this wee room, and I'm supposed to sit on your bed? First date? I wouldn't, well, I mean I would've done far more than sit on your bed on our first date. But generally... boundaries?"

She shook her head in a bit of a tsk. "It's the only furniture here. You can sit on the bed." There was a pause to discuss how taking his boots and suit off would be the only civilized thing to do, lest he mess up the bedding. And that it didn't mean sex was happening.

Once he was in his thermals and sitting opposite her on the bed, he waved a hand, but looked far more relaxed. "Continue."

"It's a very long story, but the short version is I was raised to be a certain way—demure, proper, sweet, ladylike, et cetera. When I went away to school in a different country, I'd already become exceptionally frustrated and I went as far the other way as was in me to go, not thinking about what I wanted so much as what boundaries I could push that I could've never pushed in Monterrosa. I decided that was the new me, made some friends and that was established. Me and Opposite Me. Hair was one thing I could easily change while I was away. Or continue changing. I began growing it out at home. But if I keep it up, I can return home with longer hair."

"Is that what you want?" West asked, looking skeptical of her plan in a way that made her want to throw her sandwich at him.

"I have no idea what I want. But hair affects how people see you, doesn't it? If it's a bold cut, it projects strength. Long bouncy waves project femininity and grace. It's two very different images. So what I'm trying to figure out, my plan for myself, was stop making decisions according to the expectations of others."

"I see." He said one more word before taking a bite of his sandwich. "Pink, too?"

"Ophelia wore lots of pink."

West almost choked when Lia referred to herself as Ophelia. And in the third person. In five words, he understood exactly what she'd been trying to tell him about not knowing herself. And how much it dismayed her.

"What happened if you didn't do as was expected?" he asked, and then realized he might be making her think of the kind of things he didn't like to think about, and changed his question. "Or now. How does it affect things now with the vineyard? Do they call you Ophelia?"

"They call me Dona Monterrosa," she said, her eyes getting a little buggy.

"Not following."

"Lady Monterrosa," she said in English. "It's over a century since the time of titles, but if you want to understand how traditional the people are, they still call the heads of *my* family Don and Dona. And before you ask, I don't know how it makes me feel to have them call me that. Besides being responsible for their welfare."

Drastically different from his childhood. And he wanted to hide it again, the exact same feeling that had led to him hiding Charlie on a fake adventure in the US. All he wanted to do was change the subject. Turn off the lights. Watch the aurora, which might not even happen tonight. Or distract her by proving how much he had missed her…despite her rules.

"You're quiet," she said, then ate the last bite of her sandwich, her eyes still full of concern but tangled with a fair amount of wariness. "You think it's shameful to not correct them when they call me Dona?"

"No," he said, having gathered that she had trouble getting them to listen to her enough as it was, so she probably needed the built-in respect of a fake title to give her words a little more weight. "I guess I was trying to figure out how I can help you with this quest to know yourself."

Not really what he was thinking, but if he told her the truth, this would all get very personal, very fast. Her problems, while definite problems, weren't bitter and twisted. She had the kind of childhood problems that weren't so ugly they couldn't be discussed. Her problem had been parents that gave her what she wanted, but only if it came with a price tag, not support. Not time. Not love…

And that's probably where this all came from, he realized. Definitely a problem, but not as ugly as a mother who'd abandoned him at nine, expecting him to take care of his little brother, age four, and the progressively worse foster homes they'd been shuffled between because of his behavior and scheming.

"You're supposed to tell me if the things I change make me unlovable," she said softly. "And, I hope, tell me your sad secrets, too."

"I don't…" He started to say *no*, but watched her mouth thin and twist to the side. That had been her complaint, hadn't it? And he'd said he wanted to dig out the ashes around them. "My sad secrets are…bad, love."

"I know." She cleared everything else off the bed and crawled down to sit beside him, leaning to turn off the light as she did. "Know how I know?"

"Because I likened them to famous catastrophes?"

She lifted his arm and tucked in at his left side, and just the act of touching helped him push some of the bile back down that always rose in his throat when he got too close to those thoughts. He contracted his arm to pull her closer, but she didn't settle until she'd taken his right hand in hers, and weaved her fingers in between. "It was pretty indicative."

"I don't know where to begin," he whispered, because saying the words out loud felt wrong in the small dark room. "Or what might be too much. We all change as we age, and things I did…"

"If the things you did are no longer secrets, they don't hold as much power to hurt you anymore." She lowered her voice, too, and he was grateful. Painful words shouldn't ever have the strength of a full throat. Painful words whispered could still bruise, but words shouted or given force could tear out big holes.

"It's not that simple."

"It is."

He shook his head.

"You don't look in the rearview mirror because something bad happened, and you want to leave it behind. Something you said was your fault?"

"Yes."

"And you're afraid of me knowing?"

He didn't immediately answer; the more she prodded at it, the faster he felt his heart rate going. It didn't take long before she felt it, too, or heard it, with her ear against his chest.

"That's why you need to tell me. And we need to take the physical stuff slow, *o namorado*."

The endearment made him smile a little. There weren't many Portuguese words he knew; most of them were endearments that sounded beautiful from her soft lips, and comforted him somehow.

He had taught her less Gaelic, but the one she preferred came out on its own on reflex. *"Leannán sídhe."*

She released his hand and turned his chin, gentle but insistent, until he was gazing down at her in the low light. "You think I'm not going to love you? I think you don't really love me. You say that's not true and want me to believe you, right?"

"You still don't believe me?"

"I'm…" She struggled for words, then said, "Faith is a choice. It's your job to prove my faith. And it's my job to prove yours. If you tell me the bad things now, and I don't go anywhere, you don't have to be afraid of them anymore. You can trust me. And if I change something, a few things—if I cry when things hurt me and don't feel like I have to hide it from the world and be strong all the time—and you don't go anywhere, I don't have to be afraid of that anymore, either."

He closed his eyes, suddenly very tired. "It sounds so easy when you say it that way."

The last word uttered, he opened his eyes to look at her again, and found her face lit in soft blue light, and both of them turned to look out the wide bubble glass at the blue whispers across the starry black sky, pale and ghostly waves that stretched to brilliant, almost neon blue.

She clutched at his hand, anchoring herself to him in that way they'd never really done outside of these aurora sightings. In that moment, such peace settled over him that the heart, which had been threatening to pound out of his chest, slowed, and then slowed some more. He almost wanted to tell her everything, to empty himself out to see if that would make room for more of this peace.

"Where do I begin? I don't know how many moves yet," he whispered.

She pulled her gaze from the dancing sky to look up at him again. "Then tell me your saddest memory. I'm not going anywhere. Watch the skies with me and we'll let it go."

His saddest memory. He didn't have to think to know what that was, and he could tell her that. He didn't have it in him to say those words yet. To tell her it was his fault Charlie was gone. But he could tell her about that night. Even without his guilt, it would've been his saddest memory. The faster he got it out, the more time he'd have to win her back, if he did accidentally say more again than he meant to, and she found out how disgusting he could be.

Pulling her closer, in as few words as he could, while they both watched the serene seas swirling above them, he told her about a six-hour train ride north to a Scottish morgue to identify and claim his baby brother's emaciated body.

CHAPTER TWELVE

WHEN LIA HAD invited West to view the aurora in her cabin, she hadn't really intended on him sleeping there. Sleeping beside him made it harder to avoid sex. Although she knew that boundary wouldn't last long with them, she wanted to lead back into that physical intimacy more naturally, as an emotional progression, not just because it was difficult to keep their hands and mouths from taking over when they were alone. Those kinds of distractions would allow them to duck the other things they needed to do. The important emotional excavating they were doing.

He'd told her one story about his brother, just one, and it had already changed things. When he looked at her now, that confidence she always saw was just a little dimmed. Whatever he was hiding scared the devil out of him, and he hadn't told her all of it. The only way she knew how to prove to him that she wasn't going to walk away was to dig down to the bottom of whatever was eating at him, and just accept it. Whatever it was. Whatever he felt such guilt and contrition over that he'd run from her. Because that's what he'd done. Charlie had died, and West had fled to one of the world's harshest climates, and away from the bright, sunny future they'd planned.

She'd worked out before his trip to Dallas that Charlie had been the trigger, but at that time, she'd thought his decision had been about wasting time with someone you didn't really love. A life is short epiphany. But if she accepted that he loved her, and that he'd lied to her as a way of putting distance between them for a reason, his unannounced flight took on more meaning.

He'd thought he was protecting her. He'd still thought that when he left with Jordan and Zeke. Saying *sempre* to him couldn't have changed that much, could it? She hadn't made that connection yet, or figured out whatever he'd decided meant he could come back. And that was okay. Like he said, they had some time. It was enough that they were talking.

But tonight they weren't going to do any of that. No sex. No emotional excavation, at least not for him. Her own digging was obviously less painful than his, and could be done in some fun ways. She wasn't racked with guilt, she was just living a life of faux confidence to hide from the world. To protect old hurts, but not the same kind of hurts. Hers came from people telling her she wasn't good enough, and her believing them.

"Why are we dancing in the lifeboat again?" West asked, closing the secure, water- and weather-tight door behind them as Lia went about setting up speakers and her phone to play the music she'd set to download this morning.

"Because I don't know if I like to dance," she answered. "Well, I know I say I don't like to dance, and I know that I'm a terrible dancer, but I don't actually know if I like it. It's possible to like things that you're just terrible at, right?"

"I suppose." He shrugged, but he'd taken part in scheduling their deep dives, as well, and he knew this was a no-torture zone. He wouldn't have to bare any parts of his soul tonight, unless there was some part of the soul that showed whether you could or couldn't dance.

"Help me move the furniture back." It mostly consisted of oversize ottomans pushed together in clumps to act like elevated platforms. Easy to move out of the way in all directions to make a dance floor. Even a dance floor for terrible dancers.

"Tomorrow are we going to practice kickboxing to see if you like it? Gates didn't seem to think much of it." West made a goofy face at her.

She felt her face wrinkle in dismay, remembering the strange fight between Nigel and a very angry guy called Wilson in the dining hall earlier. "I can already tell you I don't want to be punched in the face. We should probably have stuck around to ask what was going on with those two."

"It's not a medical problem until security refers them for violent behavior," he said, urging her out of the way and taking over sliding the big weird ottomans.

She wasn't sure. "I can't see Nigel being violent. Just mostly inspiring it."

"There's that." West offered her a hand in his most debonair pose once the floor had been cleared.

There were several lifeboats littering Fletcher, which weren't exactly boats, but were designed to protect those inside in the case of catastrophe. Fire being the big worry, it could grow wildly out of control in moments on the Earth's driest continent. The lifeboats had separate ventilation systems, separate power, separate heat and water and meager food supplies. Basically, large capsules that could hold and keep alive a few dozen souls until evacuations could ensue.

So maybe they were useless in the winter; Lia wasn't sure. What she did know was how very unlikely they were to be interrupted by anyone, especially two people squabbling about whatever and throwing punches, or even just throwing shade. Only West would have to suffer through her attempts to dance, and probable further attempts to *enjoy* the terrible dancing.

Once that was done, he nosed into the bag she'd also brought and pulled out a bottle of vintage Monterrosa Port proudly dated 1985. "Am I holding a small fortune here?"

"Aye, lad." She tried to Scottish at him, and then amended, "Laddie? What *do* you call a big handsome fellow?"

"You call him West—or I believe you have other special names for him." He gestured to ask if he could open it, and she gestured in return to the bag.

"I decided Monterrosa Port had probably never made it to Antarctica before, and if I was going to bring it, then I should bring one of the best vintages. Spirited it from the family cellar while packing."

"Spirited, eh? Have you already been into your cups or does dancing inspire terrible puns in ya?"

"We haven't danced yet." But they were going to. "I brought lots of different styles of music, so we can go about this in a thorough and scientific manner. This is a research station, after all."

He poured them each a small glass of the fragrant

dessert wine and took a sip. "Ye gods, why have we not drunk this before? Did you keep it back in London?"

"Not this particular vintage, but I always had a small amount."

"I might have to forgive them for making you be Ophelia if they keep making this stuff." He looked at the screen on her phone where it was mounted with the little speakers, and hit Play.

It was a good thing they'd eaten before coming, as West tackled the exercise with all the glee of a drunken Scotsman. For no less than four hours, well past a sensible hour for sleeping, they danced, or tried to. Pop. Hip-hop, where she almost blacked his eye. Waltz. Salsa. She tried to *chula*, and it looked like she was stomping on ants.

By the time they caught glimpses of strangely pink aurora through the long bank of windows along one side of the lifeboat, he'd even made a comical *forbidden dance* come-on, which was all eyebrows and swirling hips that had them both tumbling onto the nearest ottoman laughing.

But as the laughter faded, and they rested from all the graceless flailing about, she still couldn't catch her breath.

"Is it stuffy in here?" she panted, words she hadn't uttered since she'd arrived. "I need some air, and I want to see the pink aurora outside without glass in the way."

"Ophelia's aurora?" he teased, and they both went giggling like idiots again to the exit.

"I think I got to the bottom of that one question."

"Do you like pink?"

"I do."

"Me, too. Especially when it's got a bit of a warm brown tone to it."

She almost laughed again; the fool was making nipple jokes. "I heard that about you."

He grabbed the handle for the door, gave it a twist and a jerk, and nothing happened. He tried again, then bent to examine the handle. Instantly, the laughter stopped.

"It's locked?"

He felt around with his fingertips, and then gave it another twist, then pulled up on it as hard as he could. "Don't see a lock on it."

"Panel," she said as soon as she noticed the very small electronic screen on the far side of the frame. She tapped it, but it didn't come on. Then employing West's method of fixing the broken door, she slapped around at it a few times, then looked for other buttons.

"Not working, either?" he asked, and she realized it wasn't just her. He was breathing as fast as she was. He stepped up behind her to eye it over her shoulder. "No buttons."

"Nope. Looks like a dead smartphone, but no side button to reboot."

"You brought your radio?" he asked, and they both turned to look at the counter where the phone sat with speakers broadcasting country music, because they hadn't gotten to the line-dancing portion of her experiment. Beside the port and the phone sat her radio.

"I'll call someone…" She glanced at her watch, frowned and hurried over to make the call. "Maintenance is on call all the time, too, right? Like for emergencies?"

"Far as I know. Someone should have a radio, even if it's after midnight now."

* * *

About ten minutes later, now fully aware the reason the door didn't open and the panel was not powered up, they stood on the other side of it, listening to men working on the outside, trying to fix the electronics.

"This is kind of a bad design, if it locks people in and suffocates them. How many ventilation issues could they have?" Air issue. And it was getting colder, probably because they'd stopped their hours-long thrashing about in the most rhythmic manner Lia could muster.

"I don't know. They said that things got switched around from the original plan when they changed up the parts open and closed for the winter," Lia said, and he could see that she was back to trying to be stoic, but the only light in the room came through the bank of windows, casting everything pink. "Let's just go sit and watch the aurora through the window. They'll get this open, but we're using more air standing around than if we went to sit."

With all their things stashed in the bag she'd carried in, and no more country music or death metal, they took a seat on the ottoman that had landed below the windows, and he kept one of her hands in his while she gripped her radio with the other.

Another twenty minutes in, West became fully aware of how little oxygen he was getting when his vision started to darken at the edges. He looked over to see Lia with her chin to her chest, and the radio now only resting in her lax hand.

"No! Lia, open your eyes," he barked at her, then shook her shoulders until she did as commanded. "We're going to get out, okay? Right now."

"The door?"

"No, baby, we're going out these windows." It took far too much effort to pick himself up from the ottoman where they'd been lounging, but he managed to move one down so when the window shattered, it wouldn't get on her. All he needed was a weapon.

He looked around in the low light and saw nothing he could swing. No stools. There was a table. Could he break a leg off?

Keep on going became his mantra in those minutes, especially when he looked at Lia and found her unconscious again.

He flipped the table over, examined the construction, then cursed it. No-breaking molded steel. What else? What else?

The bottle.

He took a big swig for luck, then smashed the bottom against the table, knocking it off and making a nice, jagged weapon out of it.

The crash made her open her eyes again, but they were so bleary he wasn't even sure she'd really awakened.

"You wanted to know how many times I've moved? Right? Wake up. I'll tell you." He climbed into the tall windowsill above her and began using the broken end of her port bottle to dig at the seal wrapping around the Plexiglas windowpane. "As a kid I moved three or four times per year between foster homes."

"Foster homes?" she repeated, her voice small, and she looked really out of it, like her eyes wouldn't focus and she was trying hard to keep them open.

"Yes. And they sucked."

"All of them?"

"Yes. I didn't want Charlie in them, or they didn't

want us." He looked over, breathing heavily, to see her head drooping forward. "Lia!"

Nothing. He got hold of the long strip of seal and pulled, opening up a tiny gap around the window frame. Cold air pushed right into the space. He got two breaths, then shouted, "Ophelia Monterrosa!"

He jumped down to pick her up and hold her face by the air gap. In about thirty seconds, she'd regained consciousness.

"Stay there," he said, climbing back into the frame to dig out another strip of the rubbery sealant, and rip that down the seam. It didn't tear evenly. Sometimes it just started stretching, then tore, but when it did, he'd use his broken bottle to dig out another handhold. "My rubbish childhood is going to get us out of here, though. Using the skills learned there."

"You learned to break into places?"

"No, though I could've done if I felt it necessary." He got out one entire side, and then jumped down to do the bottom edge. "I discovered that if I broke things, they moved us. We're getting out because I was a bad kid who could figure out how to break anything. And if I break two seams on this window, to the corner, we'll be able to pull it out of the frame."

"Why did you break things?" she asked, still not keeping up, still not functioning on all cylinders.

"Because the next place could be better. For me. For Charlie."

He'd never admitted that before, denied it through all the times that he was rightly accused of it.

"We're going to need the men to come around and push it in for us. Call them on the radio."

She had to move away from the fresh air crack to get

to the radio, and with her oxygen levels so depleted, she began to droop and slur her words much quicker than she previously had.

He dragged her back to the corner, which he'd freed, and they both sat, faces to the crack, watching flashlights bobbing their direction through the dark. Soon, four men stood outside the glass, and through a series of gestures and West pulling Lia the hell out of the way, the glass soon bent inward, and the sound of the rest of the remaining rubber sealant ripping almost drowned out the hissing of exceptionally cold wind entering the lifeboat.

"You know that door saying?" she asked, coherency returning. "About God shutting doors?"

"He opens a window?" he asked, and when he looked over, he found her smiling at him and pointing.

"Pretty sure that was me. And those lads with the torches."

They took a moment and just breathed, leaning into one another, and when she looked steady enough and like she was getting too cold, West grabbed her bag, slung it over his shoulder and helped her climb through the window to their rescuers.

Half walking, half stumbling through the snow, they reached an entry port, and made their way inside to warm air, then the clinic, and finally the hospital, and sat together, each with cannula of oxygen running across their noses.

"I'm feeling a little better," Lia mumbled when she saw how intently he watched her. "But I know we said no sleeping in the same room...for a while..."

"I'm sleeping in your cabin tonight. Don't even try to send me to mine." He meant it to sound kind of like a joke, but it didn't come out that way, too many what-ifs in his head.

What if she'd died just when he was getting her back?

What if he hadn't come back when he had?

"We need to tell the captain to have the other lifeboats tested. Pretty sure this one is out of commission until summer when they can replace the window."

"They can put the glass back in and do another seal if they get on it tomorrow. Otherwise, it might fill with snow."

"Hey," she said, sharply enough to draw his immediate attention, and she pointed at his hands, which were still fisted and white across the knuckles in his lap. "What are you thinking of?"

"Nothing good."

"Tell me."

"I was thinking that if I had stayed gone, no one would've gone to the lifeboat to dance tonight and gotten trapped."

"Regretting coming back?"

"No. But the problem might not have been discovered until it was critical if you hadn't wanted to go dance terribly there." He tried to explain. "If people had gone there in an actual emergency, that boat could've become a tomb. People who are in this part of the station, near the clinic. You."

"It's good you came back. Why is that making you want to punch something?"

"I don't. Just…having a hard time shaking it off. I'm tense all over." He leaned down to the nurse on the stick, grabbed the pulse oximeter and slipped it onto her finger. When they'd arrived, her blood oxygen was very low, but with a few minutes of the good stuff, it was once again in the high nineties. Soon to be better.

"Would a hug help?" she asked, voice sweet and arms open.

He didn't wait for her to ask again, and didn't wait for her to come to him. He slid off the trauma table and stepped between her legs to pull her against him. She wrapped her arms around his shoulders, and looped her legs around his thighs, then laid her cheek on his shoulder.

Warm, soft and alive in his arms... He felt the tension begin to ebb away, enough for him to admit, "I'm wondering how many people have been hurt by me leaving to have another fresh start."

He knew of one, but he wasn't ready to tell her he'd caused Charlie's in every way but by his own hands. Not yet, but even he could see that was where this was all leading. Like a bomb that ticked without a countdown clock. He knew it was going to go off, he just didn't know when.

"He's not answering," Lia called from inside her office, listening to the phone at the BAT on at least the twentieth ring.

"I thought you two were travel pals." He poked his head in, and though the teasing was there, neither of them really had the energy to mirror last night's playful idiocy before they almost died in the lifeboat. Never mind the day was made longer still by security ordering they give the dining hall brawlers a blood test to make sure tempers hadn't risen due to hormonal fluctuations.

She'd asked West to go to Nigel, since Angry Guy

was probably in his cabin and that didn't involve going outside to reach him.

They should've been off the clock at this hour, settling in to sky-watch from her cabin, where there was plenty of oxygen and the big bubble window.

Her email chirped just as West came into the office, and she shook her head, hanging it up. "Two minutes of ringing…he's not going to answer. Probably has his nose stuck in some galaxy or other. Told you he was going to be difficult once nighttime rolled around."

"That you did," he said. "Give it five and call again, then I just go up."

She nodded, then looked at her phone, and the speculation about Gates's problematic behavior immediately turned serious.

"What is it?"

"Email from that hospital my father was admitted to. They released his records. We only had to get an attorney involved and email a ton of documents, but…"

He moved to stand behind her and she felt his hand on her shoulder as she opened the document.

"In Spanish?"

"Well, yes."

"Can you read it?"

"It's close enough…"

He couldn't read it, though he might recognize a few words here and there. She babbled through different vitals and doctor's notes.

"You're going to have to translate before my curiosity kills us both."

"I feel like I'm looking at test results from someone who's here. Angry Guy, or Nigel," she said, then pointed to one word. "He's hypothyroid…" She scrolled back. "Damn it, Pai."

"More, Lia. What else?"

"Immature red blood cells. White cells skewing low."

"Platelets?"

"Low." She sighed again, and West's question about the fire suddenly came back to her. "How did you know?"

"That he's alcoholic?"

She nodded.

"I didn't. But your family owns a vineyard—it's not much of a stretch. With Charlie…" He stopped, sighing as if it was an act of will to say anything about his brother, or just exhausted him. But he was doing it, either to live up to his end of the bargain, or because he wanted to help. "The more he used, the more trouble he got into. After the fire, even though I know you said it was an accident—"

"It was carelessness," she cut in, dropping her phone onto the desktop. "He was on the veranda during the dry season, smoking, and tossed a used, still-burning cigarette into the garden behind."

"I thought it started in the fields?"

"No, it mostly *destroyed* fields. The people in the village, the firefighters, the farm workers, everyone helped save the manor first. The buildings. The winery. The fire ate the other direction, through the oldest Monterrosa vines. They're now mostly gone. Some were saved, but I don't know how long it'll take for them to propagate back. Even with lots of help. Which is why things are precarious. The Monterrosa grapes make the port. If we don't have them, we don't have Monterrosa port. We just have port. Douro River port, and sure that's great, but all the stores we currently have will probably become immensely valuable if we can never make any the same."

"That's the problem with the vineyard? I thought it was just reconstruction and the old guys not wanting to listen to you…"

"The cellars where it's aging are fine. We didn't lose any product, so we have several years of sales ahead of us. But then we have a looming dry season that will span however long it takes us to replant."

"Aw, hell, love."

"Making more sense why I have to live there and run the vineyard now?"

"If you've all those people counting on you," West said. Normally, he'd have been put out that her personal family calamity might be changing the future from what they'd planned and dreamed up, but at that moment, he didn't want to consider what would come after they'd left Fletcher. Eight months was a long time.

To smooth that over, he said, "If it makes you feel better, that might not have been a drunken mistake. Judging by the tests, carelessness and inattention are probable symptoms. Mental impairment comes with low thyroid."

"I guess," she whispered, slumping a little in her seat. "He was admitted for that. Thrown out of a bar for fighting. Can you imagine? A sixty-three-year-old man, in a bar fight, and belligerent with police? They brought him to the hospital once they found out who he was."

"Not arrested?" Wealth had privileges.

She shook her head. "This behavior might be a little

more exaggerated than usual, but it's still *him*. It doesn't surprise me. But this thyroid business does."

"You didn't know about the alcoholism, either," he reminded her.

"No." She sighed. "Maybe it's just shock. I wasn't expecting this. I was expecting something injury related, not...pathology."

He made a mental note to keep a sharp eye on her thyroid levels as another thought occurred to him. "You said you might have a grandparent with thyroid issues."

And now he wasn't just her jerkish father who messed things up and dropped off the face of the planet. He was her jerkish father who did all those things maybe because he was sick. And she was a doctor, and she hadn't paid enough attention to him to notice.

"No other word about where he is?"

"No. His mental capacity is strong enough to keep ahead of us, the way he's making withdrawals just before he leaves somewhere."

"What have you tried?"

"Investigators, contacting friends, family, acquaintances, staking out favorite places, sending frequent emails, sending regular paper mail to his flat in Lisbon, sending people by, paying off the doorman. You know, the usual. Everything I can legally do."

She was dancing all around it, and he'd heard twice now that her father withdrew money from the bank before he left somewhere. She might be able to freeze that account, providing it was a family account, but she was smart; she'd have thought of that.

He gestured for her to come to him, and opened his arms. It took one second for her to catch on, and she stood and leaned against him, arms circling his waist as he brought his around her.

Freezing the account would find him, but it came with risk. The same kind of risk he took when he drew the final line in the sand for Charlie. Tough love…

He squeezed her tighter and tilted his head to nose her pink knit cap.

"Anything we're missing?" she asked, turning her nose to his neck, and anything he might have thought to say would've been gone, anyway.

"Sounds like you're doing what you can."

"It helps, just talking about it." She squeezed. "Feels better."

It didn't solve anything, talking…but he said what he was supposed to say. "Good."

"Want to help some more?"

"Sure?"

"Stay with me tonight? I want to talk to you about something else with the vineyard. Something I've been mulling over."

"Yeah…" He let go, kissed her cheek and stepped back. "Then I'd better go drag Gates out of the BAT for blood work."

"I'll get Angry Guy."

"Does Angry Guy have a name?"

"Wilson, I think," she answered, then picked up the supplies she'd already prepared to go do it. "Call when you get there."

"Why? It's not a drive across country."

"So I don't worry you've been lost in the snow."

"Take security when you see Angry Guy, so I don't worry about you being alone with someone prone to violence."

* * *

Lia's trip to see Wilson was much quicker than West's haul up the steep snowy hillside, so she got back to the clinic about five minutes before he called, one word: her name through the radio.

"You made it, I see," she answered. "Are your bits frozen off?"

"I need assistance," his voice said, all playful teasing vanishing. "Gates has been stabbed. I need a stretcher, saline, emergency triage supplies and security."

"Who stabbed him?" He'd just gotten into a fight with Angry Guy, how many enemies had he made?

"Don't know," came the quick answer, then, "Send security. Don't you come, it's not safe."

Lia snorted, and immediately disregarded that order. She did get the supplies, and two from security to accompany her, but she wasn't sitting out of this for any reason.

Twenty minutes later, with two helpers loaded with two separate emergency surgery bags, they made the mad scrambling climb to the telescope.

All the while, her mind wouldn't stop spinning. What if the one who stabbed Nigel was still there? With West? Logically, she knew that Antarctica was a dangerous place, especially in the winter, but she didn't expect to be worried about their survival on a day-to-day basis.

Her lungs on fire, she let the security go in first, with guns to make sure it was safe, but only seconds before she went running, calling for West with what was left of her lungs.

"Over here!" His answer came immediately, from the other side of the telescope rotunda, and as soon as she got close enough, he said, "I told you—"

"You knew it wouldn't work," she said, taking in the setup. Nigel had been helped onto a long table to lie on his back, but it was all but impossible to see any details of his wound until she broke out a flashlight.

"How is he?"

"In pain," Nigel answered, breathless and struggling to keep from crying out.

"And awake," she added. "Hi. We're going to look after you. Just worry about breathing." She smiled down at him, on the off chance that it might give a tiny bit of comfort, then asked West, "Angry Guy?"

"Yes. Wilson, he said. Because he was snoring every night, keeping him awake."

Mark another one down for Polar T3. "I was just about to run those labs."

"So they know where he's at?"

"In his cabin, last I heard."

While they worked, cutting away minimal clothing so his wound could be visualized, one security officer relegated to holding the light for them while the other called down to the station and within minutes announced, "Wilson's in custody."

She didn't say anything else, just got Nigel's arm wrapped in a tourniquet so she could get a line in and hang saline. The blood flow didn't seem to be too much, but saline would help keep the volume up.

"Did you bring coagulants?"

"Yes." She shifted the contents of the bag she'd brought to drag out needed supplies, along with additional gauze for packing the wound. "Pack it as hard as you must to slow bleeding so we can get him down the hill."

"Did you bring a sled?" Nigel asked, making her

smile this time. Joking. He never did that before. Maybe something to worry about, considering how uptight he had been about spending time in the telescope for his research.

"I always bring a sled with me, everywhere I go now."

In about ten minutes, they had him stabilized and strapped to the stretcher, then out of the BAT and on the stairs back down.

Although she was the physician on duty for these situations, Nigel was West's patient. They got him into Medical and she fell into step behind him, ready to assist as he had assisted her with Eileen's fan-blade accident.

Unlike that night, they needed blood tonight. "I'll get the files and get his match in."

"Sedate first. It'll slow his heart."

"Slow my heart?"

"That's good, Nigel," Lia explained while digging the appropriate medication out of the cabinet and getting it loaded up to dispense into his IV. "It means you're not pumping as much blood, and less of it is leaking out. You have any allergies I need to know about?"

"No…"

"Don't worry, we're going to take good care of you. Okay?"

He nodded, and she slipped the needle of the syringe into the port on the IV to put him to sleep. "See you in a minute, Space Man."

Or a few hours, but sedation would make it only seem like a moment once he woke.

West cut off Nigel's jacket and shirts, but got the rest of it off without destroying anything. Lia checked his

file for blood information, the notes she'd made about
who he cross-referenced with, and called two of the
crew for impromptu donations.

"How bad is it?" she asked, rejoining him after making the calls and getting ready to help.

"Not enough blood on the outside, considering his
pressure. It's going somewhere."

"We should get a CBC before getting started, if he's
more or less stable, and we're waiting for his donors,"
she suggested. West went with it, getting the blood kit
he'd taken with him to the telescope to do a draw as she
ducked back out to set up the donors with chairs and
needles as soon as they arrived.

They alternated watching over the patient while the
intervening tests were done and two donated pints of
blood collected.

Once West was certain he wouldn't immediately
bleed out, they prepped him for surgery.

Both of them scrubbed in, and once they were certain his anesthesia had fully taken hold, West opened
the wound further to see what damage had been done
and repair it.

"Spleen?" she asked, once he'd stopped cutting.

"Nicked it. I need more light."

She tilted a ring light to the wound, then got a wand
to suction out the blood pooling in the abdominal cavity.

"I think it's stopped bleeding… Very small nick."

Again he was struck by what could've happened with
her there alone, without another doctor there. Over snoring.

"We need to do weekly thyroid checks, and maybe
start a log where everyone marks down how much

they're sleeping per night. Before any of this gets further out of hand," she grumbled, handing him whatever he needed before he needed it.

"You know, it's not endemic. It's this one fight that's been repeating."

"I heard tales of overwinter syndrome when I got here. I just thought it was exaggerated."

Spacey was what he'd been seeing, but the mood swings? Part of him wanted to grab her and run to the nearest boat home—it was bad enough that the station was trying to kill them, now there were people getting in on the action.

His only comfort was that this time when the urge came to run, at least it was to run *with* someone, not away from them.

CHAPTER THIRTEEN

IN THE WEEK that passed since Nigel had been stabbed, Lia had learned to treasure short moments where she and West could steal a kiss, or the half an hour window after someone had checked on their one inpatient, the stabbed astrophysicist. In those brief periods, they would sneak into her cabin and sit on the bed to watch the night sky for streaks of color, whatever shades they may be, and talk.

That was their time, between the chaos of two doctors monitoring one patient around the clock. Moments between when he left her bed, where he'd slept alone, and she crawled into the sheets that still smelled of him later.

But today Nigel had been discharged to sleep in his own cabin, and his now-contrite and formerly stabby neighbor, now on thyroid therapy, had been moved to a bunk in the security office until they could figure out what to do with him. Barring emergency, it was Lia and West's first night together since the one where they'd nearly died in the lifeboat.

They'd had dinner, talked about work, then retired to her cabin to change into sleep clothes and curl up on the bed together, her back to his chest and his arms around her, bearded chin on her shoulder, watching the sky. It took a clear sky to see the aurora, and it was a little overcast, which led to other thoughts brewing.

It wasn't long before West's low voice rumbled in her ear. "We haven' talked about whether we're still in the 'no good touching' zone."

She knew that timbre in his voice. Teasing, playful, definitely hoping to stir something up.

And she couldn't resist him in this mood. She twisted to meet his gaze, adopting her best fake scowl. "Are you saying my touches have been bad?"

"Oh, no," he denied quickly, pressing a quick little kiss to her mouth. "Your touches are always good. I imagine. I almost remember them."

"We might need to check your thyroid levels," she tsked, because she was nowhere near as good at the playful shenanigans as he was. "Because of forgetfulness. You got that, right? The forgetfulness part of low thyroid?"

When he laughed, she laughed with him.

"If you have to explain the joke…"

"Yeah, yeah," she groaned, but shrugged. She had to play along. There was no choice to be had. It made her smile too much, even if it was quite literally the only dance she was good at—what came next, not this clumsy verbal tango he exceeded in. "I've got nothing."

"Got me."

Just hearing those two words made every cell in her body smile, but going gushy wasn't how the game was played.

She lifted an eyebrow at him.

He lifted one in return.

Then both brows.

Then wiggled them and graced her with such a cheeky grin she had to laugh at the fool.

With her off her game, he turned her to face him just as he rolled to meet her. The bed wasn't big, and rolling involved a bit of scooting and adjusting, but soon, he had one leg between her furry pink legs and his arms around her, their noses nearly touching as he stared down, looking happy, relaxed, charming as the devil.

Just looking, up close and personal, in a way that demanded attention and fully gave his own. He stole a little kiss, and then another. Almost chaste, were it not for the full-body contact happening.

"You could charm the starched white panties off a nun, you know that?"

"Never tried." He shifted to one elbow so he could pull her hat off, then did his. "I think I like the new hair. It's out of control. Feels right for Antarctica. Have you decided if you like it?"

"Oh, I hate it," she admitted, then shrugged. "But I think I might like it in the future. When it's a little longer and I don't feel like I'm going to be accused of time-traveling from the 1980s. I've been fantasizing about having a ponytail on hot days, and not having to fix it every day."

"It's *haircuts* you're fantasizing about?" He sounded so outraged she laughed again.

"In my defense, when you get a supershort pixie, you think it won't need work to make it look right, but it's tons. You have to blow it dry every single day."

"Or wear a hat."

"Or wear a hat!" she echoed with a grin she felt in her bones, then she slid her hands up his back, just to feel him, up and down the flexed muscles along his spine. "Which you removed."

"I could help you out of those terribly sexy, fuzzy pajamas, too. I mean, if you wanted."

She made like she was considering it, then shook her head. It only took a little pressure from her hands sliding to his chest for him to ease onto his back.

"You undressing me would not provide any surprises. Instead, you've been in Antarctica on the insane metabolism diet for months, grown this manly beard. I'm curious to see if you've sprouted impressive fur elsewhere. In the name of science, I must do research!"

This time it was him laughing. He splayed his hands, palms forward, to show them off. "You should probably look here for hair. I heard that sometimes it's a problem when a lady puts her man in the 'no good touching' zone and he must 'good touch' himself."

She laughed again. "Well, if you pass inspection, the ban might be lifted. But I'm going to have to get this shirt off you. And the pants. Everything must go. My medical integrity is on the line."

"Can't have that, can we?"

The way he watched her was some heady mix of desire, amusement and contentment, and made it impossible for her to go as slowly as she wanted.

She rid him of his top, and then froze as she saw her ring on the chain around his neck. He looked at her for a moment, and the chance this evening could turn upside down suddenly sat between them.

Not what she wanted. It wasn't time to talk about the ring. And she could see the clasp. Gingerly, she pinched the little claw and removed the chain from his neck, placed it onto the bedside table and turned her attention to his drawers with the same kind of popping eyebrow wiggle he'd given her.

Just like that, the tension passed. She was free to go as slowly as she wanted, draw out the moments that somehow felt new. He helped wrestle his thermal layers off, then unzipped her ridiculous onesie to find three layers of thermals beneath.

"You're like one of those Russian dolls." He didn't stop to count layers, just burrowed his fingers beneath all the waistbands he could find and, once he hit skin, pulled them off, knocking her socks off in the process.

"I'm built for a more temperate climate. You're going to have to keep me warm."

Stretching out beneath the blankets, he pulled her again half under him, and made his intentions clear with the kind of kiss that could turn her inside out. One kiss, and then another, all thought of playing doctor gone in the moment. Kissing until breathless, just to stop again so he could look at her, at her hair, her face, into her eyes.

His arm supported her head, fingers twined with her hand curled there, and just looked. Nose to nose, his warm breath fanned her cheeks, eyes just locked to hers for long, intimate stretches of time. She couldn't even say how long, just long enough that she had to know what was going on in his head. She wanted complete connection, not just hands, eyes and skin molding together.

"Are you telling yourself a story for the future?" she asked, because that's what he did. He dreamed of the future, built castles in the air, and had invited her into them.

"No," he said softly, his eyes crinkling at the corners

as he smiled. "I'm right here. With you. Right now. One hundred percent."

She had to swallow a sudden thickness in her throat, his answer cutting through the need to name what she felt, to know if he felt it, too. He did.

It was different this time. They were different. All the times they'd touched and loved had been different. Had been less, somehow, even if she hadn't known it in those moments.

Passionate, desperate, hungry, playful, flirty, but this...connection. And he wasn't even inside her yet.

Hand free, she slid it down his chest, ruffling at the crisp male hair dusting his chest and belly, all pretext of a fur inspection gone as soon as she reached the hard length of him pressed at her belly, and she stroked her fingers over the wet head, making his breath stop, then stutter. One little touch and he let go of her hand so he could free his arm and slide over, center himself above her.

She pointed to the bedside table where she'd already made a small tear in the condom packet she'd placed there.

No words passed; he simply covered himself, gripped his erection to ease through her slick folds, then slowly slid inside her. Several months had passed since they'd last been together, but it had never been like this. They'd never had this searing connection that made him go so achingly slow, eyes still locked to hers. Still there, with her, one hundred percent.

They'd been that couple who would annoy everyone with sneaky kisses and flirting, and the lighthearted, playful, energetic coupling of the first months of their relationship had barely deepened. Until life had torpedoed them. And she'd made sure it had been devastating.

And it all could've been avoided, if she'd been unafraid to tell him the truth about what was going on in her head, why going home was so hard for her. Why she didn't want him to witness it, or how weak she knew she'd appear to him there. If she'd asked him to come with her, for support, she'd have been there when he needed her, too.

Would he have accepted her then? Without months and a painful separation? Without life breaking down their barriers? Maybe. Maybe not. But he'd deserved the truth.

"I'm sorry." She whispered the words, feeling her eyes dampen, and he stilled, the love in his eyes so completely undisguised even she could see it.

"Why are you sorry?"

"I'm sorry I didn't trust you and explain that last day in London." She sniffed and stilled as he kissed away the tears trickling from the corner of one eye. "I'm sorry I didn't trust you would still love me."

"You did," he reminded her softly, still holding himself perfectly still and hard within her. "You came all the way to Antarctica for a reason, love."

"Yeah…"

"Maybe we're just slow learners." He smiled then, a tender, soft curl of his lips, then leaned in and kissed her. Long, slow and deep, a kiss that bordered on worshipful. When he began to move again, she couldn't stop the stuttering, gasping sounds he wrung out of her.

Under the glorious thickness of him, the friction and depths built slowly, until she felt it scratching down her spine, and spiking the arches of her feet. He held her there until she couldn't take one more second, then picked up the pace. Faster. Deeper. Until the world went white and that desperate, clawing pleasure sang through her. But more, it wasn't just pleasure he gave in that moment, staring into his eyes, feeling him quaking inside her; it was more than that future they'd planned and promised. It was them, truly who they were, without armor, sharing the pieces of their hearts that had been hidden and protected for so long. The parts of their souls that had never been allowed to join before.

After, when he'd rolled with her in the narrow bed to anchor her to his side, his chest rapidly rising and falling beneath her cheek, she knew he'd felt it, too. It was in his long, trembling fingers continually petting her hair back from her forehead, and the other hand that twined with hers.

And the silence. No quips, no teasing, no joking boasts about his exceptional performance, just holding, touching, until hearts slowed. Until she lifted her face to look at him again, and noticed the pink cast of the room, the pink light.

He lifted his chin purposefully toward the bubble window, and she tilted her head back down to look out.

The dazzling light show could've just started, or it could've been going on as long as they had. Pink and blue in alternating waves, purple where they overlapped.

Beauty, peace and contentment. She watched until his hand stilled, and his breathing turned slow and deep, then turned to watch him instead, the soft light playing over his handsome features, relaxed in sleep, until she followed him.

West woke sometime later, the two of them curled together in the small bed, nose at the back of her neck, and the unruly brown hair she currently hated, but which made him smile, tickling his face.

She shifted and he tightened his arms around her and murmured in her ear, "Don't go squirmin' unless you're lookin' to wake the beast."

Her soft laugh and purposeful bum wiggle was sexy and adorable in one go.

"Unless that's your wish, then I'm sure I can oblige."

"Well, I would absolutely—" she paused, looking over her shoulder at him "—but after, can we talk about the vineyard first? I meant to do that earlier."

Talk about the vineyard? He tried not to groan, he really did, but his throat did what it did.

"It's not a bad thing. I just want your opinion on something. I woke up a while ago, and I've been thinking to the dancing sky and the music of soft snores in my ear."

He grinned, even if she couldn't see it, and gave her a good squeeze. "Right, then, talk fast. Get it done before I let the lad have his way."

She squirmed and made to roll over, so he loosened his arms to accommodate her, and soon had one shapely leg wrapped over his hips, and a tangle of arms together.

"Traditional village, right?" she said.

"*Sim*, Dona Monterrosa."

His meager Portuguese earned him a grin, but she kept on with her deep thinking. "Things are not that much different than they were a century ago. They didn't get electricity until the 1960s, so it's been very slow adapting to modern ways," she murmured, with a touch of dismay clinging to her tone. "I want to bring them more into the twenty-first century…"

"How? Broadband?"

"Don't laugh. I actually got that done when I first went back."

"For real?"

She nodded. "Wasn't dial-up before, but it did run over phone lines and was hideously slow. Also pulled some strings and got a new cell tower installed closer for more reliable service."

"Impressive."

"The cell tower was an easy decision. What I'm considering isn't so clear-cut."

She sounded uncertain, and he was starting to see that anything to do with the vineyard and the village was where she was most uncertain in her life. That and her father, but he wasn't really in the picture now. She might not think she knew herself, but it seemed to him that it was more that she didn't know how to fit into what they wanted her to be.

The way she lay there, with the lights returned to the skies, the pink hue colored her dusty pink nipples, which stood from the chill in the air.

The urge to interrupt her with his mouth nearly overwhelmed all sense, but she touched his arm and helped him refocus.

"What do you want to do?"

"I've been thinking about giving forty-nine percent of Monterrosa Wine to the villagers. Profit-sharing. Giving them more of a voice in the company and bringing the families in more economically as they all work hard to help us recover."

He blinked, scrambling mentally to pay a lot more attention to what she was saying. "You want to give away almost half of your company?"

"Well—" she nodded, but it was still an uncertain

kind of rolling head jiggle "—I'd keep controlling interest, which would allow me to overrule any bad decisions they might not fully understand the ramifications of. Keep the company on steady ground while they get to know more of the business. Selling wine is different from making wine. Or growing grapes…"

"That's…" West didn't know what it was. Brave? Generous? Foolish? *A risk to her future security.* "Are you allowed, legally, to do that?"

"Pai only had to be gone for ninety days with proof that he was alive but neglecting duties. Then it became mine. One hundred percent. Abdication of duty clause."

"I see." Her voice said she was already certain it was what she wanted to do, but there again, maybe looking for permission? And that was something he couldn't help her decide. All he could do was try and gather more information. "Are you doing it to get away from the business and back to medicine?"

She tilted her head, brows bunching up. "I haven't left medicine. I plan on practicing part-time in the village. But I have to do something for them. They're too much in the past, and while that can be good in some ways, in others it's bad. The population is aging and the younger people move away, to one of the cities, to find opportunity. If the families have a financial stake, there is incentive to stay."

"I see…"

"You see?" she repeated, and then sat up to turn on the bedside light, a deep frown creasing the corners of her mouth. "You don't think I should do it?"

It wasn't exactly an accusation, but there was some measure of alarm in her voice.

"I don't know." He waved a hand, trying to make

sure she didn't read too much into his commentary. "It's yours, your…you know, ancestral inheritance, or whatever you want to call it."

And he didn't want to muck that up. She had to know that.

"But you can have an opinion."

He sat up, too; the sexy feeling that had been wafting over him dissipated too fast to even picture trying to recover. "You don't need my opinion. You have people to consult with."

"No, I don't. Not about this." The pleading in her voice made his shoulders stiffen, alarm bells starting to sound. "I'm flying half-blind on this part of my life, and I can't exactly ask the people if they think I should do this. They would say *yes* regardless. And I value your opinion. Is that something that you would've wanted? Something that would've helped your family when you were little?"

The conversation turned, and so did his stomach. "No, but other families probably."

"But…before foster care?"

"Before foster care, it was just me, Mum and Charlie. And she didn't work in a factory or anything like that."

Her voice lost some of the shrill notes. "What happened there? Did she die?"

"She's still alive, love. She just was a bad mum, and the government came in, took us. And she never cared to try and get us back. For about six months, when she would sometimes visit, she'd tell us that was the plan, and what she was working on, but then she gave up custody. She wasn't one of those parents who struggle to give their children better lives."

When he looked back at her, she looked stricken, and almost frozen there. "I don't know what to say."

"About?"

"You don't like sympathy."

"Not so much," he admitted, then stood up, needing to move, muscles across his shoulders starting to stiffen again. "And I don't like giving my opinion on this, something this big and important to your future."

She didn't stand, too, but she did look up at him, confused, arguing in the dark. "Just tell me your first thought?"

"My first thought is, this is *your* future. I can't make decisions about *your* future."

"My future?" she said, and a little edge of frustration crept into her voice, dampening the worry.

"Your future."

"Do you still see us trying to have a family, vows, rings?" She reached over to pick up the ring on the chain from the bedside table and held it up to him, her sweet face stuck somewhere between scowling and those seconds before someone cried, when the domino was about to fall.

They hadn't spoken about a new engagement, hadn't had enough time to talk about much of anything this week. He took the chain and slung it over his head. "Let's just take a breath. I'm not saying no future together. That's nothing to do with this."

"Of course it is. The vineyard is your future, too, if we're together."

"And you'll still be running it." He looked around for his thermals, and pulled the pants on. "The men will get used to having a woman for a boss, and start listening without so much effort. Isn't that the whole point of modernizing it?"

"No," she said, and was full-on scowling now. "I'm not talking about the vineyard anymore. I'm talking about how you keep doing this. You give diagnoses on my father, but no opinions about how to deal with him. You don't give them about the vineyard, either. You have opinions—I see them running all over your face—but you won't share them with me. I love that we're talking about our lives and we're both trying to be open and grow together. Lean on each other. And when we were together…it was different. It was more. We're *more* than we were. Why don't you want to take part in that future? Do you not want it?"

"If you want to do it, you should do it," he said again, but he was already half-dressed, ready to make his escape. But first give her a minute to calm down.

"I can be strong. I can be the strongest person in the world, but I don't want to have to be that person all the time. We're great partners, we work together so well, and we can play and have fun and have…tonight. We—" She stopped, words obviously failing her when she tried to describe what had happened tonight. Which had definitely been more. A kind of more he didn't have words for, either, and which suddenly seemed fragile and transitory when earlier it had felt like peace. "But I want us to be partners in everything. I value your opinion. Just tell me what you're thinking."

She scampered in between him and the door, still fully naked. And cold. Her eyes locked to his, and her hands flattened against the door, like her palms touching the wood would add just enough weight to make it immovable.

Just tell her?

"Okay, fine. When I came back, I made a deal with myself that I would only be able to be with you if I was putting your safety ahead of my own. Your life is more valuable. That was my deal with myself. Physical safety. I can't make decisions about your future, or about your family, for you. My job is to keep you from harm."

"Why?"

"I don't even know if we'll make it once we get past the winter. Maybe we'll both go screaming the other direction once we set foot back on soil instead of snow."

"What happened?" she asked, then grabbed his cheeks to keep him looking her in the eye. "I know this is about Charlie. I know that he died. You told me you never loved me to keep me away from you, didn't you? And you said that the catastrophes in your rear view are your fault. Is that what this is about? What happened to him?"

"He overdosed."

"Did you shoot him up?"

"No. But I might as well have. Okay?" The question was like battery acid in his mouth, and his reaction was just that, words said by reflex, at least at first. "He didn't overdose by accident. And he did it right after I went to tell him that he couldn't be a part of our family unless he got help. Because I couldn't risk you, or our future family, exposing them to an addict who was erratic enough to be dangerous. Get clean or get out. And he…"

He stopped there, the back of his neck aching enough he felt the need to rub it away.

"You told him to get clean, or he wasn't welcome with us, and he took too much on his own?"

He nodded.

"That's not your fault."

Those words brought that ice dagger back to the base of his skull, the sharp, frigid pain he'd felt that first day he saw her.

"See? I *knew* you would say that. But it *is* my fault. I was so busy and so focused on how I wanted that conversation to go that I didn't hear what he actually said. I didn't hear him at all. I heard excuses. When he said, 'I hope you have a good life,' I heard a passive-aggressive jab. Later, when I replayed the conversation—what I could even remember of it—I realized he was saying goodbye. He even told me he loved me, and I didn't hear him. Tell me that's not my fault."

She opened her mouth, but nothing came out, just a kind of confused and near frantic waffle of her breath.

"If you still want me after this, I will stay with you forever." He crammed his feet into his boots, fully ready now to go. "There's probably very few lows I wouldn't stoop to, to keep you safe. But I make bad decisions when it comes to the emotional health of people I love. You can't ask that of me if this is going to work."

"West…"

"You want another example? You want to know what I want you to do with the vineyard?"

She looked less certain then, her eyes once more full of worry and fear, but she nodded.

"I want you to keep it. I want you to keep the whole damned thing because money means security. Sure, you're doing fine with your job, but money means security. You don't know what will happen in the future, and I don't give a damn about those sweet little cartoon people who live in the nineteenth century and probably all sing while they work, in four-part harmony, and everyone knows the words. I care about *you*. That's it."

"That's not true," she said, but it was just a processing sound. She wasn't agreeing, she was trying to figure out how to argue with him. "You care about your patients."

"For a while," he agreed, but then asked, "Your father? You want to know my opinion there?"

Again she nodded, but a touch slower. Wary.

Good.

"Cut off his access to bank funds. No company funds. He disappeared after burning down the vineyard. Press charges. He'll be found when governments get involved in tracking his passport. You want to find him? Play his game, play dirty. That's how you find him. You like my ideas?"

"I appreciate them, and—"

"Don't do that." He cut her off with one silencing jerk of his hand. "These are not decisions you would make and I cannot make them for you. I make bad decisions for other people, and they suffer for it. And then I suffer, too. See? It's not just me feeling protective. I have to protect you because if something happens to you that I should've seen coming, I won't survive it. I'll have ruined you. Taken this beautiful person and…and… maybe you end up like Charlie."

When he noticed tears starting to leak from her eyes, he dialed it back a little, and asked, "Have you changed your mind?"

"No," she squeaked. "Have you?"

It took him a second, but he nodded. "This isn't going to work. If you need someone to count on so you don't have to be so strong, or because you don't know what you want, I can't make those decisions for you. I picked you because you're strong. You wanted to know if I'd still love you if you changed? Maybe the answer is *no*. Or maybe the answer is *I love you*, but we can't make this work."

"I've already been counting on you," she whispered. "No amount of me telling you it wasn't your fault is going to help, is it?"

"A less selfish man would've heard him. That's on me. I drove him to this with a threat to take away the last person in his family. And that's on me, too."

Since she wasn't moving from in front of the door, he gently as he could took her by the shoulders and moved her out of the way.

"You can stay here. This is just a…it's a bump," she said behind him, and shifted when he gestured for her to move her nude body out of where people walking by could see in when he opened the door. "We can sort it out."

"I'm going to my cabin."

She reached a hand for him, eyes pleading. "I'm sorry you had to go through that. I'm sorry, too, that you keep trying to run from it. You can't outrun painful memories. Punishing yourself for something beyond your control isn't—"

"It's not punishing me." He was dressed; there was nothing left to do but to go, and that's exactly what he did. "It's saving you and *your* children."

CHAPTER FOURTEEN

ACID SWIRLED THROUGH West's middle, burning everything it touched, like it could eat through the very core of who he was.

He couldn't outrun it.

Now that she knew about Charlie, about how that was one long string of everything that could've gone wrong for that kid, initiated or exacerbated by West's decisions, she couldn't think he'd be okay to help with her own family problems. She had to be realizing that right now.

He closed the door on his cold, empty, tiny cabin, and dropped like lead onto the side of the bed.

The last tenant had left the shade pulled down over the wee window he had in this one, to block out the constant summer sunshine and make sleep easier. But at that moment, it made the room smaller.

Was the aurora still there? He hadn't even looked at her window before going. If he watched the aurora maybe he'd feel that peace again. Maybe he would be distracted enough not to dwell on what he'd almost had, and what he never could.

Leaning over, he rolled up the shade. The dark sky

obliged his need, and he watched quietly as pink tendrils grew bolder, more intense, coming in waves from the side, like the tide washing across his window.

Pink. Which she'd realized she loved, even if it had belonged to Ophelia. But he didn't feel the peace he needed.

He'd just broken up with her, and they would be trapped at Fletcher together, in the same department, forced to work together, for the next seven and a half months. God help him, this was a mistake. Dallas would've been fine. He could've stayed in Dallas.

The pink waves broke red here and there, like warning bursts that made the back of his neck tighten and itch, and then the colors turned and wave after wave of bloody wave slithered across the night sky.

What washed over him wasn't a joyful, comforting peace; it was closer to an itch for physicality, also not the kind he preferred. He felt like prowling the corridors to keep from punching a wall.

West yanked the shade back down over his window to hide it, and flopped back onto his cold, barren bed. He unfastened the chain on his neck to slide the ring off. Something to fidget with. Something to look at other than the alarm-increasing red skies.

He slid the ring onto the middle section of his ring finger with effort, then flipped on the bedside lamp and swiveled his hand toward it to look at the thing.

Vines and flowers in three different metals, because she loved rose gold, but he liked white gold, so they added the regular gold to provide balance to the two. They braided together in a vaguely Celtic style, because the vines were her history, and the knot was his.

Flowers with tiny diamond centers dotted the vines, because grapes represent the harvest, but flowers represent the *future* harvest, what they were cultivating toward.

Everything snaked around to support the chunky perfect diamond in the center, bracketed at four corners with tiny grape leaves.

How long had it taken them to get the design to this point to submit to a jeweler? Two months? Two and a half? A long process. Back and forth. Ideas, requests, offers, counteroffers. If it had been left to him, she would've still loved it, because that's the kind of person she was. But what had she called the ring? The physical representation of their promises for the future. Only they never could get that future going, it seemed. And he didn't even know if that was a blessing or a curse. If he should've walked out, or should've stayed. He didn't even know what was better for her anymore.

Always had brought him back, but he didn't know if he could stay, not without the confidence he would make her life better by doing so.

When he'd left Charlie, he'd been thinking of himself. Maybe he was learning. But maybe it was too late for that.

Lia slept fitfully after West's wild-eyed departure, with dreams mostly filled with meaninglessness.

Her standing in a white room, surrounded by fast-moving grapes that bounced like tiny superballs.

Her wearing a pair of shoes that judged everyone else's footwear, loudly, and for all to hear.

And the one good one, the one that felt like prophecy and instead of leaving her with a sense of frenetic, uncontrollable chaos in and around her, flowed over her like a warm, soaking bubble bath. She and West were painting a mural on the nursery wall at the manor, pink aurora on a field of purple. She didn't know how she knew it had been a nursery, but it had.

That comfort carried her through a long day without chasing him down and making him talk to her. She'd had West sightings, but zero interactions. He was grim-looking, but still functioning.

With nothing to do, she had time to think, to inventory the clinic's supply room, and think some more. Try to sort out her West-shaped riddle.

Things could be fixed; they had to be fixable. She just wasn't sure how to go about it. She didn't even know if it was for her to fix. Seemed like the kind of thing that should be a joint effort, if they were ever going to make things work.

And she had to find a way to put them on equal footing. He'd shared the kind of information that would make anyone feel vulnerable over, but most especially someone who blamed himself for the loss of someone he'd spent most of his life protecting.

He thought he'd given her a weapon to use against him. She had to do the same for him. Get them on equal footing, show him she was still there and let him work out the rest.

She'd taken one detour to visit Eileen Gossen, who had managed to stay at the station and was healing, and enlisted her help obtaining a small part from the shop.

Now, at just after six, she stood outside the door of West's cabin, and tapped one fingernail on the wood, but with the way her hands shook, it might sound like scratching to him.

He opened the door, saw her standing there, then gestured her inside.

"I'm not sure what there is to talk about," he said, sitting on the edge of his bed, making the most of the little cabin room so it could hold two people without too much pain.

She fiddled with the small gasket Eileen had dug up for her, worrying it between her shaking fingers as she spoke.

"You don't have to talk, just listen. I'm not staying long. I just want to tell you something."

"What thing?"

"A thing I've been hiding, because I'm not going to try and pretend that we're without some issues, or that we're perfect together. I'm still sure I'll never find someone who loves me like you do. I know I won't find anyone else I love as much as you. And there's no one I trust as much as you."

"You weren't listening," he said softly, sighing as he braced his elbows on his knees.

In the cramped little room, she took one step, turned and sat on the edge of the bed beside him. "I heard every word you said, and I understand what it cost you to say it. So I'm here to do the same. And I'm here to say your words back to you. If you still want me, I'll stay with you forever. Trust you, as I trust you now. My father left me the vineyard, and it is mine right now, in a sort of temporary ownership until I marry. Then it belongs to my husband. And he had it written up that way without specifying a name, or having someone in mind. He had it written before I met you, and I just didn't find out until I was at home and he was gone."

"What?"

"When I signed the papers, that was part of it. I don't know how it would hold up in the courts, but what I do know is that it will hold up if I don't ever challenge it. And that if you were my husband, I wouldn't need to. Our children would still inherit, and it would still bear the Monterrosa name, because we'd hold to that fine Portuguese tradition of stacking names on names on names. Itamarati da Monterrosa MacIntyre. And I know you'll do whatever you can to protect me, and them."

"Love," he said, and it sounded like it took all his strength to say the word, but he'd still picked an endearment, which told her everything she needed to know. "I don't know what you want."

"I want you. And I want you to prove to yourself that you can do more than break things and hurt people you love. You broke your streak of running from people who love you when things get hard. You broke the window and got us out of the lifeboat. Now break this pattern, and trust me like I trust you."

"What do you want me to do?"

"I want you to look for a way to break my father's silence. In a way that won't hurt me, so in a way that won't really hurt him."

He looked at her strangely, but for a moment, he didn't look lost. "I don't know your father."

"But you know me," she said, then reached into her pocket to pull out a piece of paper rolled up like a scroll, with an electric blue silicone gasket wrapped around it to hold it closed. "That's his email address. He's been ignoring me."

He took it, rolled the slim blue band off the paper, and when he went to throw it in the trash, she grabbed his hand. "Eileen looked hard for that for me. Keep it safe."

"Rubber washer?"

"Gasket, a small version of what you dug out of the window for us, and I think just about the perfect size for a makeshift wedding ring. You know, if you do decide you want me still." She leaned up and pressed a quick kiss to his stunned cheek, then stood up to make her exit. "We still have about seven months to make this work. But I'm not a patient woman, so don't expect me to give up on you already."

Still using words he'd said to her, and praying they both remembered them correctly—the conversion of short- to long-term memory was harder when a brain was saturated with cortisol or oxytocin.

The next morning, knocking at her cabin door yanked Lia from sleep, her heart instantly pounding as she scrambled out of bed.

The last she remembered looking at the clock, it had been about three, hours after she'd left West, and the amount of time it had taken for her to work through the nerves knotting in her stomach. A glance at it now confirmed she'd gotten just about three hours of sleep. Her radio hadn't gone off. Not an emergency.

She staggered to the door, wearing her favorite pink pajamas, and wrenched it open.

West stood there, laptop tucked under one arm, looking tired, as she'd grown used to seeing him.

He gestured to the room, brows up and questioning. "I have an idea."

He had an idea. The stressed awakening had popped

her heart rate up, but those four little words turned it from a possibly scary situation, to one of hope.

She stepped back, pulling the door open wider so he could enter, peeked past him to be sure that the clinic was still dark, then closed the door.

Quietly, he sat on the corner of her bed, propped the laptop on his lap and opened it. "About your father... is he as proud of the vineyard and village, all that, as you are?"

"I seem prideful about it?" she asked, not following at all, but unable not to frame it that way with the rest of her chaotic thoughts about the vineyard.

"It's something you *should* be proud of. Is he? Does he love it? Is that why he's been running, do you think?"

"Oh." She squeezed her eyes shut and then knuckled the sleep out of them before she answered his question. "Yes. He loves the vineyard and the history of it. He always enjoyed the pomp—when we receive orders every year for the same ceremonies and celebrations. He just doesn't like the work bits. Not good at them."

Though her eyes were still gritty with sleep, she sat beside him and waited to see if her answer aligned with his idea.

"I know you don't approve of cutting off his access to funds or having him arrested for arson," he began. "Too risky. If he's not thinking straight, depriving him of money might send him off the rails. And requests haven't been working."

"Right," she said slowly, working to keep any alarm or dismay from her face or voice.

"With the caveat that I only know a few things about him, that he's a jerk to his daughter and that makes me want to punch him in the face, that he probably wouldn't

mind that much since he was almost arrested for brawl-
ing in Barcelona, and that he loves his vineyard and almost burned it down, so…guilt."

She tried to keep following along, but her brain was
still fritzing. "Still not following."

"I think the best chance of getting a response from
him is to pick a fight about the vineyard. If it were me,
I'd respond faster to a fight than a request," he said,
then added, "I did actually respond to a fight when you
showed up here."

She'd emailed West so many times, requesting,
pleading, for him to answer, and he hadn't. She hadn't
even thought to ask if he'd read her messages, or maybe
had seen and deleted them, maybe blocked them. So…
he had seen them, maybe even read them.

"Don't do that," he said suddenly, breaking into her
thoughts. "You can yell at me later—the satellite will
be here soon. Stay with me a little longer."

"I don't know his other weak points." And the idea
of exploiting weak points made her uneasy, but at the
same time… West was helping. Or trying. "Did you
sleep last night?"

"Red aurora kept me up." He gave her a lopsided
and still-half-guarded grin. "I think we know enough
weaknesses to pick a fight. I think if we pick a fight
with him, if *I* pick a fight with him about the vineyard,
he'll answer me."

"What do you mean? What kind of fight?"

"A dirty fight." He turned the laptop around to
show her an opened, unsent email. Where his fingers
bent around the edge of the screen, she saw her ring
crammed down as far as it would go on his ring finger,
just past that first knuckle, and on that same finger sat

the blue silicone gasket. He was wearing their rings, not just on a chain around his neck, hidden away.

She squeezed her eyes shut again, trying to find some focus.

"Just read it."

A deep breath, and she did as he asked.

He didn't call him names. Didn't point fingers. The email was written like a very professional letter between businessmen, stating that she had agreed with him to give up making wine. And begin making whiskey, since proper Scotch couldn't be made in Portugal. Too many of the Monterrosa grape vines had been destroyed, so they were going to plant barley, which would enable brewing to resume in one growing season instead of the years it would take for the vineyards to get back to what was needed.

It took her all the way to the bottom page where he'd included a fake logo to realize that this was just bait, not an actual proposal from him to switch production to whiskey. West had lied. Claimed a quiet elopement days ago, and that as the sole owner of the vineyard now they could make this decision without involving him. But, man-to-man, he felt he owed him a chance to convince him otherwise. And attached a deadline.

Two days, followed by the logo MacIntyre Whiskey. Not even Monterrosa Whiskey. He was going for the jugular, right in the pride centers.

"Where did you get the logo?"

"I doodled the barley with the stylus that came with the laptop, then put it on an oval, then stacked up some bigger ovals in black and white to make a frame. Picked from the fonts on the computer. It took a lot longer to make the logo than to write the inflammatory email."

"Oh." She blinked a bit at the email, then read it again, her brain still soggy with sleep. "You think he'll answer to stop us from pretend-doing this? It *is* pretend, right?"

"Of course it's pretend. I'm feeling a bit bitter that I had to smash your bottle of port to pry out the lifeboat windows. I definitely want to drink that in the future."

The future. She couldn't think about the future. Couldn't ask about it, either. It didn't mean anything that he'd done this until he said it meant something.

"Are you going to send it?"

"Not without your approval," he said, then added, "That's how we designed the ring. Do you remember?"

"We had to agree?"

"Veto power." He reached up to brush her hair back from her face, then tuck a lock behind her ear.

She nodded, somehow managed to resist tilting her head into his hand and focused on the idea still rolling around in her head. If it didn't work, did it cause any harm? Her father couldn't be angrier with her for trying anything to get him to surface.

"It's about ten minutes before the satellite passes over," he added. "Which was why I knocked to wake you up early."

What time was it in Portugal when the satellite passed over? Seven in the morning would be ten in the morning. Still morning. He'd have time to respond, and maybe even fire off an angry response immediately.

She moved the mouse to hover over the address bar, considered the email address she'd given him, then scraped her memory to come up with two more. That done, she hovered over the Send button and nodded to him to do it. "Those are all the ones I know of. But I don't know if he's checking them."

West nodded, then picked up the laptop, clicked Send to queue it up for the instant the Wi-Fi established. "I'll let you know when he responds. If he responds."

"What if he doesn't?"

He stood up, tucked the computer under his arm again, then mashed down a spot on her crazy hair to kiss her messy crown of curls.

"Cross that bridge when it gets here. I'm ready to work, so I'll just be out there getting my schedule in order for the day, and I won't leave the department until after the sat passes out of our orbit again."

She nodded, and though he caught her looking at the ring, neither of them said a word about it, and he went out as he'd said, to get started with his day.

Reading something into either instance would make her stupid. Maybe his chain broke. Maybe he just wanted to help her so that they could work together with a little less stress for the months and months remaining of winter.

She couldn't read anything into it. He still hadn't sanctioned her plan to give part ownership of the vineyard to the village, which she was going to do. But she could wait. They had seven months, and she wasn't giving up.

The rest of the day passed at an achingly slow pace. When the satellite had passed out of range, West had made sure she saw him packing the laptop back up and carrying it out with him as he went about chasing down his physicals.

If his plan worked, she might get her father back,

sort of. Or at least get to tell him he didn't have to run anymore. If it worked, it might change West's mind about whether he could do anything but damage to the lives of those he loved and not view them as one more catastrophe waiting to happen.

If it worked, she might get her fiancé back.

If it didn't? She'd be stuck waiting on Pai to come forward, or slip up so her investigators could find him. West would definitely not get over thinking he couldn't be trusted with important, life-changing decisions.

The evening satellite had come and gone, and West stopped by her cabin long enough to let her know there had been no response, looking as glum as she felt. And no longer wearing the ring.

That night, she'd visited a bar to get a couple shots of whiskey in her, in honor of their lie, like an offering to the universe for a little help. It also helped her sleep.

The last thing she remembered doing was watching an aurora-free starry sky out of her window, thinking about how someone could fall in love with the sky, and the next she knew, someone was knocking at her door.

Like yesterday, she staggered out of bed and opened it to find West standing there. This time, he didn't ask, just scooted right past her, opening the door wider and turning sideways to get into her cabin. "You overslept."

"I did?" She closed the door, then swiveled to see the clock. Five minutes past seven a.m.

Her breath caught and she turned back to West, who was grinning and opening the laptop.

"He emailed?"

He actually laughed as he spun the laptop to show her. "He's really mad."

"Did he say where he was?"

At the last second, as she almost took the computer, he pulled back. "Keep in mind, that email was designed to make him angry enough to get in my grille about this plan."

"I know." She said the words before really considering what he meant by that warning. "He's mad at me?"

"A bit." That was underplaying it; the set of his mouth gave it away as he considered more fully how it might affect her. "Are you okay with that? You can choose not to read this, and I can give you highlights—well, the bits I can understand. His English isn't as good as yours and he resorts to Portuguese in several places."

"I've been waiting for months, I'm ready. I know we set him up to be mad." She licked her lips, rubbed her eyes again to make sure the letters would be clear and held out her hands for the laptop.

Certain phrases stuck out, and mostly they were the ones in their native tongue, the one he could most effectively jab at her in. The email was written decidedly to her, but in the form of Tell my worthless daughter...

A few familiar jabs about her being a disappointment, and how much better his life would've been if she'd been a boy. Everyone's life. Et cetera. Things designed to make her feel as badly as possible, but which had stopped having much power over her as she'd heard them so many times.

Suddenly, he took hold of the computer and pulled it right out of her hands to sit on the table. "Enough. I think you've seen enough. I'll email back…"

Suddenly, him having sent those things to West was what tipped her over the edge from mildly dismayed to actually angry.

"Oh, no," she said, snapping her fingers for him

to hand it back. "I'll write to him. Because you know what? He's done way more damage to the family name than I ever could. I'm cleaning up his mess, like I always do. And you know what? I *am* going to have his bank access shut down. See how well he does without someone else's work supporting him."

At some point, she'd stood up, and now paced in the short space around the bed, West's brows practically gone beneath the brim of his usual navy cap.

"Well, you know, maybe." He waved a hand, then stood up. "Let's just take a breath. Sit down. You don't have to respond this minute."

"Yes, I do. I have to send that email to my investigator so he can do whatever computer magic he does to trace it. Then go find him, and…and…"

"And what?"

"I don't know!" She grunted and then flung her arms toward the ceiling before flopping her bum back onto the bed.

West didn't sit beside her. He also didn't let her reach for the laptop again, snagging her hands as she leaned and pulling them in front of himself as he squatted down to be more on eye level with her again.

"We made him angry, and now he's lashing out. We made him angry so he'd talk, right?"

"It's one thing to say those things to me. It's another to say those things to you, and the implication that you were lowering yourself."

"That must have been one of the Portuguese bits."

"Yep," she confirmed, then decided against translating anything else. "He didn't have to say those things to you."

"No, he didn't. And you're right to be angry, but if

you respond to him angrily, there is no way to salvage this." His voice was gentle, and when she looked at his hands again, her ring was back on his finger, where it had been yesterday when he wasn't on duty. "An angry email is worse than no email at all. Send it to your investigator, and let it sit until you don't want to break his heart in return."

She wiggled one of her hands free so she could trace it around the ring. It worked; she'd asked him to break her father's silence, and he'd done it.

"Forward it to me, and I'll forward to my investigator. Though I don't really know what I want him to do. Aside from go there and slap some sense into him."

A couple of minutes later that had been sorted, but she still wanted to send him an email in all caps.

"Before this morning, what was it you wanted to happen with him? You said you wanted him to know everything was okay, and have his health checked, right? Did you see him having any part of the business in the future?"

"Yes, just not the work."

"The pomp and ceremonies?" he asked.

She nodded.

"You can still have that. You're not converting to a distillery. There is no MacIntyre Whiskey. Right?"

Again, she nodded. This time, he lifted her hands as he straightened from his squat, pulling her to her feet and directly into a tight hug.

"Remember, he isn't himself. He might have been drunk when he emailed. He might be affected by his hypothyroidism. And he knows right where to hit you to make it hurt the most."

His words were nice, but the fact that he'd done anything at all was nicer. And nicest of all was the warm arms around her, and the heart thudding beneath her cheek. "This is what I need, you know?"

To make sure he didn't misunderstand, she squeezed him tight.

"Me, too," came the soft reply, and a nuzzle in her hair.

"I want my ring back."

He laughed at her grumpy demand, and although she was admittedly sulking and probably pouting, and definitely mentally picturing all the ways she wanted to scream at her father, West took the grumpy demand, let go of her and sunk right down to one knee.

She pushed the hood down on her fuzzy pink one-sie, and splayed the fingers of her right hand expectantly, a smile starting to come back to her face as he twisted and tugged on the ring. "Are you going to say new words this time?"

"I might need to ask you to go get some of the ultrasound jelly…"

"It's stuck?"

He licked his finger, gave another twisting yank and the intricate band finally slipped past his knuckle. "Sorry, it's a little slobbered on."

She wiggled her finger, anyway, laughing. "And many years from now, when our children ask to hear the story of how Pai proposed, we'll sigh wistfully and say, 'Sorry, it's a little slobbered on.'"

"No, we've got time to come up with a better story than that." He slipped it onto her finger, and it settled into the well-worn rut that had not yet filled back in. Comfortably back where it was supposed to have been. "Maybe something like this beautiful ring that we designed together represents the wonderful life and family we will build together."

Words she'd painfully lobbed at him when she'd first arrived, but twisted to add new promises where promises had been broken.

She couldn't think of anything to add, just shook her hands at him urgently until he stood up, and she launched herself at him, her arms flinging around his shoulders as she kissed the side of his neck and said one word, "Bed."

"I thought you were supposed to say *yes*. Last time you said *yes*." He chuckled at her, back to teasing as his arms wrapped eagerly around her.

"Yes," she said, then, *"Sim."* And, while backing toward the bed, "Bed—*cama.*"

He didn't let go, the biggest smile on his face as they waddle-swayed back toward the thing. "We only have—" he paused to check the clock "—fifteen minutes before shift starts."

"We can do a lot in fifteen minutes." She let go of him just long enough to yank down the zipper on her onesie while his lips found her and he fumbled for his trousers.

EPILOGUE

One week later...

WEST STOOD WITH Lia and all nonessential personnel in the lounge, lights off, before a long bank of windows showing a midnight-dark late-afternoon sky.

"I've got another ten minutes before my window closes, have a call at seven I need to prepare for," the captain said, casting a dubious eye toward the windows and the sky utterly devoid of aurora.

"If they don't come, we'll do it tomorrow," West said, standing behind her, his arms wrapped around her heavily insulated body. Her wedding outfit was standard-issue red, and they were planning to make a mad dash out into the howling wind to say, "I do," and kiss, just as soon as the first shock of color arrived.

She shook her head, and argued, "They'll come. I have a good feeling."

Everything else had come together, from the captain agreeing to the odd wedding, to the galley cooks baking a cake, to Eileen lending her metalsmithing skills to smelt and polish some tinfoil from a ripped out, unused section of ventilation to make West a proper, non-silicone-gasket ring.

The only thing that was missing was an internet connection, so Jordan and Zeke could witness from their sunny, Southern California beach. But she was recording it to upload once the satellite passed over.

Just after the captain had given the five-minute warning, the sky began to glow ever so faintly blue.

Someone shouted it out, and a stampede of red suits made for the nearest exit, funneling through. The sky was clear—it had to be to see them—but wind was an issue today. A blast smashed her into West as she turned to face him, and with them both grinning and gripping cold, gloveless hands, the captain began talking. Not that they could hear anything. They got their cues by him slapping one of them on the arm and making gestures and mouthing, "Do you?" at each in turn, and pausing for a nod. Finally, he jabbed a gloved finger at their hands, and they hurriedly crammed rings onto stiff unruly fingers as the sky finally lit up. A wave of blue undulating to purple and pink rippled past them, and while she still had her eyes toward the heavens, West grabbed her by the cheeks and got his kiss.

Three minutes flat, probably the fastest wedding in Antarctic history, and they all ran back inside, teeth chattering but big smiles. On their way to the cake, which was probably why everyone showed up, the guests formed lines from the door to the lounge, inside, and tossed homemade construction paper confetti at them—because no one was willing to waste dry-goods staples at the start of winter, but everyone wanted cake.

Much later, after they'd adjourned to the sauna to thaw out a little, and did their best to steam up the bubble window on the cabin they now shared, Lia lay with her cheek on his chest, her favorite position, and they watched the window, which had now gone dark and starry again.

"Aurora." She said the first name that came to her mind of all the things she wanted to plan for.

"Where?"

"If we have a daughter her name should be Aurora."

"And if it's a boy?"

She squeezed his waist with the arm she always draped over it, then whispered, "Charlie."

His chest dipped in sudden and quick, bouncing her head slightly as he felt for her hand, and squeezed. He didn't say anything—he didn't need to. She slid up to him, and hugged his head, pressing her cheek to his for as long as he needed it, and that was progress.

Just as she was giving up to comfort and exhaustion, she heard him whisper, *"Amo-te."*

And she whispered back, "Always."

* * * * *

COMING SOON!

We really hope you enjoyed reading this book. If you're looking for more romance, be sure to head to the shops when new books are available on

Thursday 31st October

To see which titles are coming soon, please visit

millsandboon.co.uk/nextmonth

MILLS & BOON

Coming next month

HIGHLAND DOC'S CHRISTMAS RESCUE
Susan Carlisle

Cass picked up her other shoes and placed them in the box while Lyle held it. She met his gaze. "By the way, what's your favorite color?"

"Green." His eyes didn't waver. "I'm particularly fond of the shade of green of your eyes."

Her breath caught. "Are you flirting with me?"

"What if I am?" He took the box and set it on the bench. "I've been thinking about that kiss."

A tingle ran through her. "You shouldn't."

"What? Think about it or think about doing it again?"

"Both," she squeaked.

"Why?" His voice turned gravelly, went soft. Lyle stepped toward her.

Because she was damaged. Because she was scared. Because she couldn't handle caring about anything or anyone again. "Because I'm leaving soon."

"Cass, we can share an interest in each other without it becoming a lifelong commitment. I'd like to get to know you better. Couldn't we be friends? Enjoy each other's company while you're here?"

Put that way, it sounded reasonable. Lyle moved so close that his heat warmed her. Why was it so hard to breathe? She simmered with anticipation. His hands came to rest at her waist as his mouth lowered to hers.

She didn't want his kiss. That wasn't true. Until that

moment she'd had no idea how desperately she did want Lyle's lips on hers. Her breath caught as his mouth made a light brush over hers. He pulled away. Cass ran her tongue over her bottom lip, tasting him.

Lyle groaned and pulled her tight against his chest. His lips firmly settled over hers. Cass grabbed his shoulders to steady herself. Slowly she went up on her toes, her desire drawing her nearer to him. Sweet heat curled and twisted through her center and seeped into her every cell. She'd found her cozy fire in a winter storm.

The sound of the door opening brought both their heads up. Their gazes locked with each other's.

Continue reading
HIGHLAND DOC'S CHRISTMAS RESCUE
Susan Carlisle

Available next month
www.millsandboon.co.uk

MILLS & BOON

THE HEART OF ROMANCE

A ROMANCE FOR EVERY KIND OF READER

MODERN

Prepare to be swept off your feet by sophisticated, sexy and seductive heroes, in some of the world's most glamourous and romantic locations, where power and passion collide.
8 stories per month.

HISTORICAL

Escape with historical heroes from time gone by. Whether your passion is for wicked Regency Rakes, muscled Vikings or rugged Highlanders, awaken the romance of the past.
6 stories per month.

MEDICAL

Set your pulse racing with dedicated, delectable doctors in the high-pressure world of medicine, where emotions run high and passion, comfort and love are the best medicine.
6 stories per month.

True Love

Celebrate true love with tender stories of heartfelt romance, from the rush of falling in love to the joy a new baby can bring, and a focus on the emotional heart of a relationship.
8 stories per month.

Desire

Indulge in secrets and scandal, intense drama and plenty of sizzling hot action with powerful and passionate heroes who have it all: wealth, status, good looks…everything but the right woman.
6 stories per month.

HEROES

Experience all the excitement of a gripping thriller, with an intense romance at its heart. Resourceful, true-to-life women and strong, fearless men face danger and desire - a killer combination!
8 stories per month.

DARE

Sensual love stories featuring smart, sassy heroines you'd want as a best friend, and compelling intense heroes who are worthy of them.
4 stories per month.

To see which titles are coming soon, please visit

millsandboon.co.uk/nextmonth

MILLS & BOON
True Love
Romance from the Heart

Celebrate true love with tender stories of heartfelt romance, from the rush of falling in love to the joy a new baby can bring, and a focus on the emotional heart of a relationship.